ANY GIVEN CHRISTMAS

Also by Candis Terry

Second Chance at the Sugar Shack

ANY
GIVEN
CHRISTMAS

CANDIS TERRY

AVONIMPULSE

ANY GIVEN CHRISTMAS. Copyright © 2011 by Candis Terry. All rights reserved under International and Pan-American Copyright Conventions. By payment of the required fees, you have been granted the nonexclusive, nontransferable right to access and read the text of this e-book on-screen. No part of this text may be reproduced, transmitted, downloaded, decompiled, reverse engineered, or stored in or introduced into any information storage and retrieval system, in any form or by any means, whether electronic or mechanical, now known or hereinafter invented, without the express written permission of HarperCollins e-books.

Excerpt from *Second Chance at the Sugar Shack* copyright © 2011 by Candis Terry.

EPub Edition December 2011 ISBN: 9780062105233

Print Edition ISBN: 9780062133298

10 9 8 7 6 5 4

For Picklehead and Binks, my beautiful girls.
You both make my heart swell with love and happiness.
I'd be lost without your smiles and your silliness.
I love you both more than I can ever express.
Oh, and Picklehead? Here's the football player you've
always dreamed of. Don't say I never gave you anything.

ACKNOWLEDGMENTS

A simple thank-you never seems enough when people make such a difference in your life. I can only hope you all understand how deep my appreciation goes.

Thank you to Amanda Bergeron, my amazing editor, for believing in me enough to hold onto my manuscript until an opportunity arose. You made my twenty-two-year-long dream a reality. You are one of the nicest people I have ever known and I count my blessings daily.

Thank you to Jennifer Schober. How did I get so lucky? Not only are you an amazing agent but you are an energetic and wonderful soul. Not to mention someone I can trade crazy farm stories with. One word: WINNING!

Special thanks to Daryn Colledge, Green Bay Packers NFL Super Bowl champ, and his lovely wife Megan for graciously taking time from their busy schedules to answer my numerous questions. Daryn, it's been fun to watch you mature from a Boise State player to an NFL star. Congratulations and the very best to both of you.

Game time.

Nothing in NFL quarterback Dean Silverthorne's career of media blitzes, celebrity propaganda, and general mayhem had prepared him for the wedding-day brouhaha in which he found himself immersed.

His formula for a happy marriage?

Stay single.

Not that he didn't believe marriage worked. His parents proved it did with a thirty-six-year union.

He just didn't believe marriage would work for him.

Ever.

He'd been smart enough to figure out that mystery of life at the age of fourteen. While his seventeen-year-old cousin had stood inside the smallest chapel in Deer Lick, Montana, and pledged his life to a girl he'd knocked up but barely knew, Dean had been rolling in the hayloft of Old Man Wilson's barn. One hand firmly on third base beneath Cathy Carlisle's pretty pink tank top, the other sliding into home beneath her grass-stained 501s.

The misery Dean witnessed that day on his cousin's face had compelled him to make himself two promises. Never get suckered, lured, conned, or tricked into exchanging the dreaded I Do's. And never, ever let anything or anyone stand in the way of his dream to become a star NFL quarterback.

At thirty-four he could claim success to both.

For twenty years he'd played it smart *and* safe. Touchdown passes and reliable condoms. Victorious teams and supermodels more intent on landing magazine covers than putting a *Mrs.* before their names.

In his book, weddings and all the froufrou crap they entailed were more trouble than an intercepted pass on the final play of the game. For years he'd avoided such occasions. Yet here he was, smack-dab in the heart of matrimony central, stuffed into the monkey suit he only hauled out for awards banquets.

As he stood inside Deer Lick, Montana's local Grange he glanced around the spacious room and almost laughed. Someone with a very twisted sense of humor had transformed the plain white cinder block walls he'd known as a kid into some kind of girly circus tent with twinkling fairy lights. The long-deceased masters who'd built this farmers' fortress must have turned in their overalls.

Though an early December snowstorm blew a bitter cold wind outside the big metal doors, inside the corners were draped with autumn bouquets wrapped in gold ribbons that swirled toward the concrete floor. Dinged-up folding tables had been covered by white cloths and mirrored centerpieces reflected the glow of tapered white candles. The entire display was an outrageous departure from the usual sparseness of the women's Friday-night Bingo games or the annual Texas Hold 'em tournament that stunk up the place with stale beer and cheap cigars. Even Kate's big-pawed pup, who sat perfectly humiliated near the gift table, had been bedecked with a pink satin tux.

The redhead who'd bullied him into attending the event waltzed by on the arm of her new husband. The bride—a.k.a. his baby sister—had the balls to wink at his obvious discomfort.

"How's the shoulder, Dean?" Edna Price clamped an arthritic hand over his good shoulder and smiled. Her weathered face crinkled like an old dry chamois.

"Great." Thankful for ditching the arm sling that labeled him as weak, Dean rotated his shoulder slightly. A simple movement to prove he wasn't in agony for the pain pills that would temporarily numb the ache.

"Bull pucky." His mother's dearest friend shook her blue-haired coif. "The minute that Denver tackle drilled you into the turf, I told your daddy you was gonna be in a big hurt."

Dean's lips compressed so tightly the blood drained from them. *Big hurt* didn't begin to describe the pain that had sliced through him after that hit—the pain that had twisted in his shoulder like a dull-edged razor. The air had been sucked from his lungs and he'd barely managed to get up off that field. In a haze of agony he'd lifted his hand in a wave to his team and to the stadium of fans, before they carted him away to the locker room for a series of x-rays and MRIs.

He smiled now at Edna, and the blood flowed back into his lips. He refused to display an ounce of weakness. Whining was for pussies. "Just another day at the office, Mrs. Price."

The sympathy in the older woman's faded eyes told Dean he couldn't fool someone who'd had her own share of pain. "Well, we're real proud of you, son. And we're sure lookin' forward to the Stallions winnin' a spot in the Super Bowl this year."

"Yeah," Dean grumbled. "Me too." Only he wouldn't be there to participate. And didn't that just piss him off.

Last year he'd let his team down. The coveted Lombardi had been within their reach. But in the final forty seconds of the game he'd stayed too long in the pocket. The defense had been fast and his feet hadn't been quick enough to buy time for his receiver to get in position. He'd overcompensated. The pass flew over the receiver's head and into the gloves of the opposing team, who took the ball in for the winning touchdown. A rookie mistake. And he'd been no damn newcomer to the game.

The vicious sack he'd received during the Thanksgiving Day game last month had drilled his already-ravaged shoulder into the unforgiving turf. As a result, he'd been placed on the "injured" list for the remainder of the season—or longer, if he listened to the bullshit they tried to feed him in rehab.

His team had lost that day and now his guys had to rely on the backup QB to take them to the show. He'd failed them twice. No way in hell would he fail them again. No. Way.

A few of the boys had visited him after the surgery—his third within four seasons, on the same shoulder. They'd apologized for not having his back. And they'd sworn they didn't blame him for the loss that day. But anyone with eyes could see their disappointment. Hell, it burned in his gut.

While the guilt blazed, he returned his attention to the

present, determined to sail through the remainder of the matrimonial festivities and get back to the real world.

After a few quick anecdotes about life on the NFL Super-highway and a hug that smelled faintly of moth balls and Listerine, Edna Price moved on. Dean downed his crystal flute of champagne.

The doctors were wrong.

Damned wrong.

He'd prove it to them and everyone else of little faith.

"Well, well. The hometown hero returns."

Fawn Derick, the first girl in junior high he'd managed to educate on the finer points of "Show me yours and I'll show you mine" sauntered toward him in a little black dress and pearls.

Fawn no longer possessed the long, lithe body she'd once flaunted in tank tops, tight Wranglers, and strappy little sandals. Now she had an excess of curves. Some natural, some man-made. As she leaned in for an air kiss, she pressed herself close enough for him to decide which was which. Even more impressive than Fawn's after-market assets? The huge diamond on her finger she'd received from a rich Californian who played rancher.

"And you've just become more beautiful in my absence."

Obviously flattered, Fawn leaned in for a full-breasted embrace. "Are you staying long?" she whispered against his ear.

Though Fawn had once been tempting and it might be fun to reminisce, for him, married women were more forbidden than women who salivated over a possible future trip to the altar.

He gave a shrug that fired a spike of pain through his shoulder. "Once they break out the hokey-pokey or the chicken dance, I'm outta here."

Coffin-black cat claws drifted down the sleeve of his Hugo Boss. "I meant, are you staying long . . . in town."

Not if he could help it. He had a life to get back to—one where a good time did not come with rules and attachments. Besides, he'd only be good for a day or two in his hometown before he became bored out of his mind. Or a target for females with big ideas.

The women in Deer Lick, God bless them, subdivided into three categories: single, married, and single again. They came in all shapes and sizes but they all had the same ambition: a band of gold around their finger and a ring through their intended's nose. Being a wealthy NFL star quarterback made him a prime target.

Fawn wasn't the first tonight to let him know she might be open to a little action down at the Cottage Motel. As much as he hated to disappoint them, he didn't do groupies, strangers, or anyone who may have a jealous significant other. He didn't want to end up like the Ravens' former running back who'd taken up with a groupie and ended up gut-shot like an opening-day buck. So to preserve his unrivaled reputation among the townsfolk and not to come off as a total ass, Dean turned on his *aw-shucks* charm.

"Sorry, gorgeous, it would be great to get together like old times. Unfortunately I've got to get back to the team."

Her hopes disintegrated with her smile. "But I thought—"

"Hey, big brother, they're playing our song."

With an exaggerated look of apology, Dean turned away from Fawn and her thinly veiled invitation toward his baby sister, who gave him a smug smile that proclaimed she knew she'd just rescued his sorry ass. No doubt she intended to collect her reward later. So while Sinatra serenaded them, Dean swept his sister into his arms and out onto the dance floor. He'd deal with the painful repercussions later.

His heart gave a proud stammer when he looked down into her green eyes. Marriage may not be for him, but it already seemed to be sitting well with her. "Has anyone mentioned how breathtaking you are?"

"Just the man I married, you, and maybe a few dozen others. Who's counting?" She gave him a wide grin and smoothed her hand over his injured shoulder in a motherly gesture. "You don't look so bad yourself. A tux looks *so* much better on you than that stinky old football jersey."

He chuckled to cover his flinch at even her softest touch. "That stinky old jersey generates million-dollar contracts."

"Happiness is not always about money, you know."

"Is that how you convinced yourself to give up your glamorous Hollywood career?"

"*Au contraire*, big brother, I didn't have to *convince* myself of anything. My career appeased me, but it never brought me deep satisfaction. You know, the kind that makes you go, 'Oh yeah. *This is it.*' But that man right there . . ." She tilted her bridal veil toward her new husband as he waltzed by and twirled his seventy-year-old partner in her orthopedic shoes. "*He* definitely gave me my *aha* moment."

"Uh-huh." Dean let his gaze drift so he wouldn't insult

her with an eye roll. "You were surrounded by the Spielbergs, DeNiros, and Madonnas of the world. What could possibly make one small-town deputy stand out above the rest?"

"Oh, that's easy. Honesty. Heart. Compassion. Not to mention the toe-curling sex."

His gaze snapped back. "TMI, Kate."

Her laughter rang as light as Christmas bells. "Someday you'll find the right woman and fall in love. Then you'll know what I'm talking about."

"I don't fall in love." He grinned. "Lust . . . is another matter."

"Well, *Mr. Perfect*, I hate to be the bearer of bad news, but you *will* fall in love. And when that happens, you will be shocked down to your jock strap. Because nothing else in this world will be more important to you than every breath she takes."

The catered hors d'oeuvres in his stomach dive-bombed at his sister's use of the nickname he'd earned after his first flawless season at USC. *Mr. Perfect*. He couldn't claim to be perfect anymore. Far fucking from it. "I doubt it. There are still too many long-legged blondes out there."

"Silly me. By the tabloid covers I see at the Gas and Grub, I'd have thought you'd already sampled them all."

"Nope. Still a few left. When I'm done with them I'll move on to the brunettes."

"You can talk smack all you want, big brother. But I know the real you. And that party-all-the-time playboy image you portray isn't the real you."

"Says who?"

She laughed. "Says me. Because Dad would kick your ass if you were truly that disrespectful."

Dean smiled. Kate was right. He had a deep appreciation for women. He didn't expect to have any woman he wanted, but he didn't mind it. And he certainly never took advantage. But where baby sister was concerned, he had no intention of letting down his guard. Otherwise the next thing he knew she'd have him set up in some cozy little cottage with a white picket fence, a wife, and 2.5 kids. Family meant everything to him. But appreciation didn't mean he had to have one of his own.

While Sinatra sang about flying off to far Bombay, their sister Kelly, middle child and kick-ass prosecutor, twirled and wobbled by in the arms of the best man. James Harley's wild reputation spanned the Rockies. Not exactly Kelly's brand of testosterone. Kelly tilted her head back and giggled.

Giggled? Sister Serious? No way. "Our sister appears to be drunk," Dean said. "And flirting."

Kate glanced over her shoulder. "She's having fun. Leave her alone."

"You're not worried she might do something stupid?"

"She's a big girl," Kate said. "And she deserves to have a little fun. The case she's on is ugly and tragic. She's not eating and she's losing sleep. So if she lets her hair down for a night, who the hell cares?"

"Not me?"

"Correct. Not you. And not me."

After another quick check on their tipsy subject, he conceded. "I guess a little happiness never hurt anybody."

Concern wrinkled Kate's forehead. "I want you to be happy too, Dean. With something more than throwing a football."

"Careful, you're starting to sound like Mom."

"Really?" Her smile brightened. "Maybe that's not so bad."

"*This* from the daughter who believed our mother out-wickeded the Witch of the West?"

"Maybe I've changed my mind. We women are allowed to do that, you know." She gave his hand a squeeze. "And the first thing Mom would tell you would be to stop pushing yourself so hard."

The look she gave him was all-knowing. But Kate didn't know half of what she thought she knew. No one did. And no one would find out, either.

Everything in his life was trashed. And for a moment, the tremendous losses stole his breath. He glanced away at the festive decorations. They reminded him of what his mother would create. Only this time she hadn't. She hadn't even been there to see her last-born walk down the aisle.

Their mother had died suddenly a few short months ago. No warning. No goodbye. Just *bam!* She was gone.

His eyes stung and he blinked.

He missed her.

She'd been his biggest fan. And more times than not, his best friend. And it seemed as though Kate intended to pick up the baton now.

"If that new husband of yours ever gets out of line, you better come to your big brother," he said, steering the conversation away from himself.

"No way." Kate tilted her head back and laughed. "If he gets out of line, *I* get to use the handcuffs."

Go figure. Kate had found her paradise in a town with a population of six thousand. His paradise, however, was a thousand miles south in the Lone Star state on the deep green field of football dreams.

"Now, what's this about Mom?" he asked.

"Mom is . . ." Kate paused and looked over his shoulder. Then she gave him a faint smile.

Her odd comment snapped his attention back to the present and he found they'd waltzed toward the edge of the dance floor. "Mom *is?*"

"Never mind." Kate stopped in front of two women who appeared to be in the midst of an entertaining conversation. One of them happened to be the little blonde he'd escorted down the aisle just a few hours earlier. She turned toward them with laughter still playing at the corners of her mouth.

"Dean, this is my very good friend, Emma Hart." Kate slipped his hand from her waist. "Why don't you two dance and get to know each other better?"

Dean whispered against her ear, "Do *not* play match-maker, Kate."

As though she didn't hear, Kate embraced the blonde dressed in a strapless chocolate gown that hugged some pretty knockout curves. "If he's not nice, I give you permission to sack him."

A smile and a wink later, Kate glided away, leaving him alone with a too-short woman who looked too intellectual, seemed much older than the models he dated, and by the lack of gold on her finger, was most likely single and man-shopping. Still, his sister would never forgive him if he didn't display uber-politeness. He had no choice but to turn on the charm he usually reserved for the media after an opposing team had opened up a can of whoop-ass.

As Frank Sinatra faded away, the DJ put on a country ballad. What was it with all the hokey slow dances? Dean took his cue and extended his hand. "Well, Emma, very good friend of my sister Kate, would you care to dance?"

She looked up at him and sparks flashed deep in her unique Mediterranean-blue eyes. Lips that looked marshmallow-soft parted slightly and revealed the slightest space between her two front teeth. In an instant, studious turned to sexy and a deluge of testosterone flooded Dean's system that he couldn't have held back if he'd been the Hoover Dam.

She hesitated.

He held back a laugh.

Like she'd really turn him down?

She tilted her head and silky hair draped across her bare shoulder. He took that as a yes and reached for her hand.

"Thanks." She tucked her hand behind her back. "But no thanks."

Emma looked up at Deer Lick's golden boy and found bewilderment shading his green eyes.

He'd never been turned down before.

Poor baby.

In the space of a heartbeat he recovered as smoothly as the pro who commanded the football field, and he surprised her when his sensuous lips curled into a smile.

Too bad the gesture was wasted. She didn't plan to stick around and wait to be dazzled. She turned away from the man who was paid millions to repel gigantic ogres in gladiator garb, and who apparently possessed some kind of magic that caused women all over America to drop their panties like coins in a wishing well.

As a bridesmaid she had duties to attend to. Especially since it appeared the maid of honor seemed a bit too tipsy to handle the task.

Emma curled her fingers into the dupioni silk of her dress and lifted it so she wouldn't fall on her face as she walked toward the bar in her borrowed high heels. As much as she hated to admit it, even to herself, coming face-to-face with Dean Silverthorne had rattled her composure. When he'd walked her down the aisle at the wedding, she hadn't looked up and he hadn't looked down. Their eyes had never met. When she'd stood on the altar, she'd focused solely on the beautiful vows being exchanged between the loving couple. But now, standing an arm's length away with his penetrating gaze focused on her? That had been an entirely different matter.

"Champagne, please," she told the rent-a-bartender, who promptly popped the cork on a fresh bottle. While Emma waited for her drink, Carrie Underwood's passionate vocals filled the room. The sweet rhythm of the music poured through Emma's bones and she started to hum along. As she accepted the fluted glass from the bartender, she became aware of a large tuxedoed presence taking up space to her left. He leaned an elbow on the rented bar, and the luxurious scent of pricey aftershave and warm male settled over her like a seductive web.

"So, you come here often?" The deep timbre of his voice was tinged with humor.

Emma smiled into her glass of champagne and sipped. The bubbles tickled her nose. She looked up, a smirk still on her lips. "Actually, I do. On Wednesday nights I meet here with the ladies' auxiliary and once a month we hold a Mommy and Me crafting class."

Her own attempt at humor was met with the imaginary sound of crickets.

"Oh." She gasped dramatically. "I'm sorry. Was that a pick-up line?"

His smile slipped and his dark brows pulled together.

"And that works for you?"

"No." A burst of amusement rumbled in his broad chest. "But I try at least once a day to put my foot in my mouth. How'd I do?"

"I'd give you an A+."

"Perfect." He leaned toward the bartender and ordered a glass for himself. Champagne in hand, he turned his back to the bar and lifted his glass as if to toast her.

Hmmmm. She thought she'd made herself clear. *Not interested.* So why didn't he go away?

Intent on discouraging further conversation, she turned her attention to the dinner tables across the room to see if the disposable cameras were in use. One of her bridesmaid duties was to make sure everyone had a good time, and Emma always took her responsibilities to heart. The man beside her, however, appeared not to be deterred.

She looked up. "Is there a problem?"

"No problem." He shrugged his non-injured shoulder. "Just curious."

"About?"

"Why you didn't want to dance." His head tilted. "Don't you know how?"

"Of course I know how." Was he kidding? She knew how to bust a move. Poorly. Alone in her living room with only her cat watching. "I simply choose not to."

His *Sexiest Man of the Year* smile widened to a grin as if he'd been challenged. Emma looked away. She took a sip of her champagne and scanned the room again, searching for any excuse to politely escape his overwhelming presence. He was a gorgeous man who, in his tux, would put a red carpet George Clooney to shame. She could clearly understand how women would fall prey to his kind of drug. But she'd sworn to never put herself in that position again. Once had been enough.

His dark brows lifted. "You don't like me, do you?"

"Don't be silly." She kept her attention across the room and wiggled her fingers in a wave to Dean's father, who was doing his best to avoid the attention of man-eater Gretchen Wilkes. Poor man. "I barely know you."

"You know . . ." He took a long sip of his champagne. "I believe I like this kind of dance much better."

She looked up. The lingering grin on his face clearly said he was quite entertained for some odd reason. "I'm afraid I don't know what you mean."

"This banter." He waved his hand between the two of them. "You know, verbal dodge ball."

"Really? Well now *I'm* curious," she admitted.

"About?"

"Why you're wasting your time talking to me. I'm not a supermodel or a movie star. I don't even mud wrestle."

"Well, that works out great." Charm oozed from every virile pore in his body. "Because I much prefer Jell-O wrestling."

She shook her head. "Why is it that men are always drawn to women who don't mind humiliating themselves?"

"Guess I've never regarded a friendly little Jell-O tussle as humiliating."

"Well, of course not. Because men like you always see the end game."

"Which is?"

"Meaningless sex. A one-nighter, nooner, or whatever time of day you manage to find a willing body."

"So, from your point of view," he responded, pointing a long, masculine finger at her, "that's all *men like me* are looking for? A quickie?"

"Isn't it?"

"Absolutely not."

"Right." *And sunflowers grow on Mars.* "You don't remember me, do you?" she blurted out in a choked laugh.

He looked down at her, studied her face. Then his mouth slid into a cautious smile. "Don't take it personal."

Emma held his gaze. Men like Dean Silverthorne gobbled up women like her. Men who used women, ruined their reputations, then moved on without a sprinkle of apology.

Love 'em and leave 'em.

Been there. Done that.

Didn't need to make a return trip.

"I wouldn't dream of taking it personal." Emma set her half-empty glass on the bar. "If you'll excuse me." As she scooted around him, his big hand touched her arm.

"Wait a minute." Concern tightened his brow. "*Should* I remember you?"

"I have to go. Your sister is about to throw the bouquet." She shot him an exaggerated look of regret. "But don't worry. Men like you never remember women like me." She tapped her chest. "We're completely forgettable."

CHAPTER TWO

Dusk fell across the Houston skyline as Dean cracked his eyes open. He turned onto his back and blocked the invasive sunshine with his forearm. The movement shot fire through his shoulder and into his chest.

"Damn."

Beside him the sheets rustled. A cool hand and long fingernails pressed against his arm. "You okay, baby?"

"Yeah." He threw back the covers and strode naked to the bathroom. While he washed his face and hands, he prayed the woman in his bed would get up and leave so the hot shower calling his name could massage the kinked-up muscles in his shoulder. The knock on the bathroom door confirmed she had other ideas.

"I need to go, too," she said in a squeaky voice that might have sounded good after a couple shots of Patrón, but failed miserably without the drone of eighty-proof buzzing through his brain.

"Help yourself to the one down the hall." He stared at his reflection in the mirror, unwilling to admit that between his physical therapist's pessimism and his subsequent agonizing workout to prove his PT wrong, he'd been desperate for a distraction and broken his own rule. He didn't do strangers, groupies, anyone with a jealous significant other, or women with marriage on the mind. Yet with little effort he managed to pick up the attractive blonde—a complete unknown—in the physical therapy reception area. He knew nothing about her. Not even her name. "I'll give you a call tomorrow."

"But you don't have my number."

"Leave it on the dresser," he said, knowing he'd never make that call. He set the controls on his hydrotherapy shower and dialed in the temperature to just this side of scorching. While he waited, he grabbed the prescription bottle from the cabinet and downed two pills to kill the pain that raged through his shoulder.

"Oh. Okay then." The female voice pouted.

God, when had he turned into such a selfish dick?

Guilt burned a hole in his chest. He snapped off the shower, opened the door, and went down the hall to give his guest a proper goodbye. She'd been sweet and accommodating and she didn't deserve to be treated like trash. He didn't use women. Ever.

Once *Dana*, as he'd discovered her name to be, got on the elevator, he went back into the bathroom, opened the shower door, and stepped inside. Steaming water pounded into his aches and sluiced across his shoulder and back. The pain pills started to take effect and his muscles began to uncoil.

Men like you are cowards. You only see the end game. Meaningless sex. A one-nighter, nooner, or whatever time of day you manage to find a willing body.

Shit.

The disembodied voice charged at him from inside his head, but no way was it his own thought. And it wasn't the first time he'd heard it. Since he'd flown out of his hometown, his sister's crazy bridesmaid had haunted him. Not her. Her words. She didn't know what she was talking about. She didn't know him. At all.

So why had he just picked up a woman he didn't know—before two in the afternoon—and brought her home purely for the purpose of sex?

"Fuck!" He smacked his palm against the cool blue tiles, and water splashed him back in the face. He knew even less about Emma the Tormentor. Small, smart, and sassy. That's all he knew.

Yet somehow, from a thousand miles away, she managed to make him feel a slap of shame.

He didn't do shame well.

Hell, he'd never conned a woman into his bed. Never made false promises. He'd always been respectful and appreciative. But he'd also been one hundred percent honest that the only long-term commitment he had time for was his career.

Little had changed except at the moment he was a bit banged up. Come time for training camp he'd be good as new, no matter the BS the surgeon and physical therapists tried to feed him. He knew his body, knew his mind, knew what he was capable of.

For twelve years they'd called him Mr. Perfect. To hell with what some nut-job doctor told him. To hell with what everyone in the organization thought.

It was better to burn out than fade away.

Hours later Dean parked his Mercedes SL in the stadium players' parking area and stepped out into the cool December night. The aroma of burgers, brats, and BBQ drifted above the parking lot from the swarms of tailgaters geared up for the big game. After he stopped to autograph a few t-shirts and foam fingers, he pushed open the locker room doors and stepped into a world of familiarity. The energy. The focus. The smells of athletic tape, tape spray, and fresh washed jerseys.

God, he missed this.

Jim Craddick, the equipment manager, gave him a grin and a fist bump. Further into the room he became enveloped by the familiar. *Bring Me to Life* by Evanescence rocked the sound system while NFL greats in various stages of dress and undress blocked the view to their open lockers. Some were laying out their uniforms; others were getting stretched and reading playbooks.

This was where he belonged—strapping on his armor instead of strolling around in a polo shirt and slacks. Though the Stallions logo emblazoned his ball cap and jacket, the symbols weren't half as significant as slipping his arms through the sleeves of his blue and red number-eleven jersey.

"Where you been hidin', QB?" Frankie Martin, nickelback extraordinaire, shook his hand. Gently. A not-so-subtle reminder that he was one of the walking wounded. Not always the inspiration the team looked for in their pre-game mode. The rest of the boys gave him a round of nods and a few good-humored jabs aimed at his slacking off; then they returned to psyching themselves up for the physicality of the imminent battle.

"Had to go back home for my kid sister's wedding," he said.

"You? At a wedding?" Frankie's over-bleached teeth flashed. "Hope someone got visual documentation."

Dean laughed. It felt good to be back with the guys. He didn't need to wear his jersey to fit in. He was one of them. One of the chosen few who showed up every week to leave their blood and sweat on the field. And in his case, some torn tissue and muscle.

He walked past his empty locker and barely gave it a glance.

He'd give anything to be in their athletic shoes.

Anything.

After a few handshakes, he moved through the room and headed toward the guy in the jersey at the end of the row of lockers.

Number seven.

His replacement.

Scratch that. His *temporary* replacement.

The kid glanced over his shoulder then turned his back. Dean smiled at the arrogance. Overconfidence would only get the rookie so far. But then he had to put up or shut up.

Dean swallowed down the Texas-sized lump in his chest. This was *his* team. And no matter how much it hurt that he would not be running out onto that field with them, he knew he had to make sure he left them in good hands until he made his return.

"How's it going, youngster?" Dean leaned his good shoulder against the backup QB's locker.

Jared Jacoby lifted his pretty-boy face and grinned. "Good, old man."

Dean chuckled. He enjoyed sparring. Verbal. Physical. Didn't matter. He just loved the way his blood pumped thorough his veins at a good confrontation.

"So what's your tactic?" he asked. "The Ravens' offense is explosive. Defense is like a concrete wall."

"Smashmouth." Jacoby shrugged. "No turnovers."

"Just don't try to get too showy with that arm of yours. Keep your head. Don't let them read your eyes."

Jacoby grinned. Snapped his gum. "I got coaches, Silverthorne. You aren't one of them."

Dean propped his Ecco Terrano loafer on the bench. "How many times have you gone up against Baltimore?"

Jacoby looked away and shrugged.

"Yeah. A big zero," Dean reminded him. "I've been there, done that. Many times. Just trying to lend you a little advice."

"Don't need it, old man. Don't want it."

"Too bad your dick isn't as big as that ego," Dean shot back with a hope that between now and the time the kid took the field, he'd find at least one humble bone in his body and realize the game was about more than just making a name for himself. "You take care of the team. You're their captain now."

Jacoby gave Dean a defiant lift of his chin.

"Try not to fuck it up," Dean said as the coach called the players together for the last-minute strategy and inspirational *go kick their purple pansy-asses* speech.

Dean stood among his men and let the blood rush through his veins, just as if he'd be stepping out onto the field with them. But he wasn't. This time he was strictly an observer. A cheerleader. And that didn't settle well in his soul.

Didn't settle well at all.

At the end of the fourth quarter the Stallions squeaked a W by a field goal. It had been a hard-fought battle but his team had moved forward. Without him. They'd embraced Jacoby as their leader as if he'd been their QB for a decade, and Dean congratulated the cocky little bastard.

Suddenly Dean needed to be away from the celebration. Away from the reminders of his weakness. His failures.

He walked through the corridor, his lone footsteps echoing against the concrete floor. He pushed the release arm on the steel door and stepped out into the parking lot where the cold air slapped him in the face. He'd taken two steps toward his Mercedes when a local reporter appeared from nowhere and thrust a video camera and microphone in his face. The lights that had once annoyed Dean were now like an old friend.

"How's the shoulder?"

Dean flipped the switch on his on-camera charm and flashed the smile that had brought him millions in endorsements. "Doing great."

"Looks like Jacoby's ready to take the team to the playoffs."

"He's capable. As long as he doesn't let his nerves or ego get the best of him."

"If the Stallions go to the Super Bowl without you, do you plan to retire?"

Irritation snapped up his spine. With any luck the gnashing of his teeth wouldn't be heard through the microphone. "Oh, don't go rolling the carpet up on me just yet."

Dean gave the reporter a polite nod and a goodnight and headed toward his car. He slipped inside to the comfort of the leather interior, started the engine and let it rumble. The muscles in his neck and jaw knotted. Man. He was tired of the naysayers. Tired of the loaded questions. Tired, period. Maybe he needed a break. Away from the spotlight. Away from those who'd lost their faith.

It was two weeks away from Christmas. Might just be a good time to take a few weeks of R & R and head home to Deer Lick. He threw the gearshift into drive, stepped on the accelerator, and roared away from the glare of disappointment.

_____

CHAPTER THREE

Snow.

Everywhere Dean looked there were hills and mounds and piles of white stuff. The current downpour wasn't doing much for visibility. What the hell had he been thinking, leaving the comfort of Texas for this?

On top of the weather conditions, he'd had to leave his Mercedes behind, and now he was stuck driving his mother's beat-to-hell beast of a Buick. Why his father had refused to get rid of the old bomber after his mother died was a wonder. The old man never drove it. The rusted chassis sat in the driveway, took up space, and reduced property values. A shabby reminder of the lively woman who'd driven it for over two decades.

Dean tested the brakes as he maneuvered the car through a wintry obstacle course toward his newlywed sister's house for dinner. Kate had been so excited when he'd come home, she'd started to interfere with his plans. His sleep-in mornings. Tranquil afternoons. Peaceful evenings. He'd agreed to one dinner and Christmas Day festivities. After that, he'd head back to Texas to ready himself for training camp. An athlete could never start the conditioning process too early. Especially if his doctors and physical therapists were Nancy boys who had no faith he'd be back out on the field throwing perfectly tight spirals into the gloves of his receivers.

He drove down Main Street where a banner stretched across the road and wished everyone happy holidays. Where tinsel wreaths with twinkle lights hung from every lamppost. Where neon green posters announced the upcoming Christmas parade. He drove past Purdy's Pawn Shop and Old Man Crosby's used bookstore, toward the Sugar Shack, the family's bakery. Dean originally intended to drive right on by. Instead he pulled over and parked out front.

The doors were locked. Lights were out. But he could still picture his mother in her overalls and apron flitting about the shop, sliding cookies off bake sheets and into the hands of eager customers.

During his teen years, when he hadn't been honing his football skills, he'd helped out after school and on Saturdays, baking chocolate pecan cookies, loaves of honey wheat bread, and washing pots and pans. He'd hated every sugar-filled second. He'd seen the results of all that work at the end of the day. While he and his sisters sat at the kitchen table doing homework, his father would massage lotion into his mother's dry, chapped hands. Or he'd see his father soak his tired feet in a tub of Epsom salts. But Dean also remembered the affectionate looks that would pass between his parents. The laughter. Even amidst their sighs of utter exhaustion he recognized the love.

Those times—the sights, the smells, and the devotion—

would be forever embedded in his brain. He loved his parents. They'd been good to him. They'd always believed in him. His mother had always been his biggest fan. She'd always worn her replica Deer Lick Destroyers number-eleven jersey on game day.

Sorrow squeezed his heart and he absently rubbed at his chest.

This would be their first Christmas without her.

At that moment, the little setback with his shoulder paled in comparison to the breathtaking loss of the woman who'd given him life. Who'd wiped his nose, taught him his ABCs, donated hundred of pastries for football fundraisers, and who'd sat on splintery bleachers in rain or snow to watch him play the game he loved. He smiled and shook his head. She'd been the best.

God, he missed her.

Several memory-filled moments later, he gave the Sugar Shack another glance, twisted the key in the ignition, and eased the car away from the curb. Nightfall had descended and he didn't need to be late to Kate and Matt's, or he'd never hear the end of it. Fresh off their Hawaiian honeymoon, Kate was eager to show off their photos and her newfound culinary skills. Dean hoped she'd do better than the tofu, bean sprouts, and slimy vegetable combo she'd tried to serve him the last time he'd visited her in LA.

The long stretch of road out to his sister's lake house was deserted. Those in town had long ago bundled up in their cozy homes—out of the cold, and into their nightly routines. If he were in his own home right now, he'd be headed out to meet the guys at Johnny Ray's for wings and a beer, or calling up a sexy blonde to join him for a dinner of slow-baked salmon at Reef, his favorite restaurant.

Everything about his childhood hometown screamed the opposite of the trendiness of his adopted hometown of Houston. Deer Lick was simple. Ancient. Boring. Even the oldies radio station he'd tolerated surrendered to static. He punched the buttons to search for a station that didn't reek of political commentary or Lawrence Welk.

"It's not unusual . . ."

Great.

Tom Jones.

His mother's favorite.

Dean moved his finger away from the radio. Another reminder of his loss. Seemed like his days were filled with them.

Beneath him, the Buick's wheels rolled across hard-packed snow while old Tom did his laughable best to sound sexy. The interior of the car grew crisp with icy air. Dean adjusted the heater fan to high, but even after a few minutes it hadn't helped. An odd glow brightened in the rearview mirror and Dean squinted against the glare. Damned cars following too close. And on a deserted road? What the hell was the matter with them?

Upon closer inspection through the side mirror, he realized the glow couldn't be coming from another car. There wasn't another car. Instead the light appeared to be in the back seat. He figured a flashlight—maybe on the floorboard—accidentally got turned on when he'd hit a bump in the road. He eased up on the accelerator so he could reach into the back to find it and turn it off.

He shifted in his seat, looked over his shoulder, and froze.

"Hello, Son."

Every hair on the back of his neck sprang up like porcupine quills when he realized the green eyes he stared into belonged to his mother.

His ... mother ... lifted her finger and pointed toward the windshield. "Oh. Honey. Watch out for that car."

Dean swung back around in his seat just in time to realize he was headed in the direct path of oncoming headlights.

With gloved hands, Emma gripped the wheel of her Subaru and braced for impact. The Christmas tree tied to the top of her old Forester shifted as she swerved at the last second to avoid a head-on collision—something no experienced driver ever attempted on an icy road. But better to spin out than end up a scrambled egg.

The jerky motion sent her car skating toward the culvert on the side of the road. With a splash of white powder over the hood of the car, everything came to a bone-jarring stop. Her headlights cut across vacant land and shone into the branches of the perfect little ponderosa pine she'd just cut down in the woods behind the now-vacant Clear River Lodge.

She swallowed the lump of petrified terror stuck in her throat and glanced out the window to find the other car had come to a stop across the road. All four wheels were on the ground.

Somehow they'd missed disaster by mere inches.

Relief poured through her. She dropped her forehead to the wheel with thanks to whichever of her busy guardian angels had been on duty. Then she inhaled a steadying breath.

Exhaled. And scrunched her face to keep from crying. As her heart rate declined, her temper accelerated.

What kind of jerk drove like that in such treacherous conditions? Someone probably too busy texting to keep their eyes on the road.

She shoved the car into park, unhooked her seatbelt, and swung open her door.

"Are you crazy?" Her gloves slapped against her antiquated parka as she shouted at the other driver. "Where the heck did you get your driver's license? A gumball machine? Why don't you—"

The door to the old brown sedan creaked open and way over six feet of muscular male slid out from the front seat.

The blood drained from Emma's head. Her ears buzzed. Inside her knitted gloves her fingers went numb and her heartbeat kicked back up into overdrive.

While she wished she could Houdini herself to somewhere else on the planet, Dean Silverthorne stood across the icy road and stared at her as if she were a Keebler elf on crack. The soles of a worn pair of cowboy boots dug into the snow at his feet. Relaxed jeans hugged his slim hips and encased his long, long legs. The buttons of a dark-colored henley peeked out from behind the zipper of a hooded parka.

Damn. He really did look as good in real life as he did on all those magazine covers.

She'd thought she'd seen the last of him when she'd left him behind at Kate's wedding. She thought he'd gone back to his Lone Star play land of supermodels and super stardom where she'd never need to think of him again. Obviously she'd thought wrong.

If it hadn't been for the dazed look on his face, Emma would have continued to nail him to the floorboards about his less-than-acceptable driving skills. But since she didn't want any accusations or future lawsuits to come her way, she figured it might behoove her to check on his health and welfare. She could only imagine the level of attorneys he could afford. "Are you okay?"

His dark brows pulled together. "Are you?"

She folded her arms against her parka. "I asked you first."

"Yeah," he said. "I'm good. You?"

"No damage." She glanced at her car. "Not sure I can say the same for my Christmas tree, though." Turning back toward him she found he hadn't moved. Not an inch. And maybe only cartoon eyeballs spun in cartoon characters' heads, but Dean Silverthorne's jade-colored orbs gave the tilt-a-whirl thing a run for its money. "Are you sure you're okay? Do you want me to call 9–1–1?"

He looked down the road. When his gaze returned to her, he seemed to have gathered his wits. If he had any to begin with.

"No need."

"Okay. Good. Then . . . what the hell were you thinking? If you can't handle the icy roads, then don't drive. You could kill someone."

"I . . . ah . . ." He bent down and looked through the sedan's back window. "Yeah. Sorry about that. There was something . . ." He hitched a thumb toward his car. "In . . ." He righted himself again. Shook his head as if to clear it. "Yeah. Sorry."

Wow. Okay. Talk about taking too many hits to the noggin. Rumor was his football career was kaput because of the shoulder injury. Emma thought he just might not be playing with a full box of Wheaties.

"Where were you headed?" she asked. *And why are you still here?* "Do you need a ride? Because I'm not sure you should be driving. You do look a little shook up."

Apparently sanity along with his *muy* macho ego roared back. His head snapped up and he started across the road toward her. A puff of warm breath hung in front of his face that made him look like a fire-breathing dragon about to tackle her on the fifty-yard line. She pulled a gulp of icy air into her lungs and took a step back.

"Let me help you get this back on your car." He marched right past her, toward her once-perfect little tree, which now teetered on the edge of the culvert.

Bum shoulder. Bad idea. She marched behind him. "That's okay. I can get it myself."

He turned and her nose came within inches of smashing into the front of his Kodiak parka. The scent of warm male and expensive aftershave rose up to tickle her senses, and she had to remind herself that he played poker with the devil.

"What are you saying?" His large hands came up to steady her. "That I'm not man enough to pick up a little Christmas tree?"

She looked up past the dimple in his clean-shaven chin. Did her best to ignore the heat of his hands clasped onto her sleeves. "I didn't—"

"You know, that's not the first time you've questioned my manhood."

"I'm not question—"

"Good." In one smooth motion, his lips tilted upward.

"But just in case you do have any doubts, I'd be happy to prove to you that I am 100 percent."

"Sorry. Not interested."

"Because that's all *men like me* think about. Right?"

The conversation they'd had at Kate's reception rolled back. Wow. Had she wounded his overblown ego? Why would he even remember what she'd said? "Ummm. Sure."

"You know," he said, "maybe you should get to know someone better before you toss out accusations."

"And maybe *you* should have more than your shoulder examined." She shrugged off the hands he had clasped around her arms and strode toward the poor little pine tree, hoping the branches were all intact. She needed to get home. To her mug of hot chocolate. Her CD of Christmas classics. The purr of her cat. And the cherished ornaments she intended to put on her once-perfect little tree.

Dean came up behind her, reached down—noticeably not with his throwing arm—and lifted the heavy end of the trunk. "What's that supposed to mean?"

She grabbed the smaller end at the top of the tree. Needles poked through the woven loops of her gloves. And a familiar stab jabbed her in the heart. Every time she saw Dean Silverthorne, all he managed to do was dig up old and rotten memories. "It means nothing. Just help me with this so I can go home. Oscar's waiting for me."

They walked the tree to her car and with little effort Dean tossed it up onto the roof. She reached for the end of the bungee cord that had done a poor job of holding the tree in place prior to *Mr. Perfect* hogging the road. He pulled the cord from her hand and somehow she found herself pressed against the car, trapped by his big body and long arms. He leaned against her to connect the end hooks together and gave a whole new meaning to the term *up close and personal.* Her chest got tight and she tried to fight the warm tingles she had noooo business feeling. Before she could escape beneath his arm, he backed away. His green eyes were now focused and penetrating.

"You going far?" he asked.

She shook her head. "I just live over on Spotted Fawn."

He stepped backward. Gave her a nod and said, "You drive careful."

Hello. Pot calling kettle. "Yeah. Sure. Than—" *Thanks?* She was about to *thank him* when all this was his fault in the first place? Man, she needed a long vacation in a nice warm place. Somewhere she could think about the sand between her toes and the umbrella drink in her hand and not this smooth-talking charmer.

Dean Silverthorne was *not* a prince.

Dean slid onto the front seat of his mother's car. He waited until the taillights of his sister's crazy bridesmaid's car disappeared before he turned the key in the ignition and cupped his hand over the ache in his injured shoulder. He dropped his chin to his chest and exhaled.

He hated weakness.

Hated the lack of control.

Hated that nobody had faith.

Hated that he'd lost his edge.

He lifted his head and stared out into the darkness cloaking the road before him. When he would catch a break?

Sure, it had been just a few weeks since he'd been pile-driven into the turf at Mile High Stadium, but he expected more of himself. And he certainly didn't need anyone like his sister's loony friend looking at him like he was weak as a kitten. Or that he was a marauder of innocent women. All he needed was to get back to his team. Back to his life. Then no one would question his ability—on the field or elsewhere.

As he reached for the gearshift an arc of golden light flashed across his hand. He glanced up into the rearview mirror to find the hazy glow once again hovering in the center of the backseat.

He turned and there she was. In her standard attire of worn overalls and a red plaid overshirt. A chill washed over him.

He shifted back around to face the front of the car and stared through the windshield to where the moon fought to break through clouds heavy with snow.

"Breathe, Son. Before you pass out."

A whoosh of air pushed from his lungs. "I don't believe in ghosts," he said to no one in particular. "Or demons or psychics or luck. And I already have my hands full with rehab from the surgery so I don't need to work a psychiatrist into my schedule, too. I just didn't get a chance to say goodbye. That's all. No closure plus the pain pills equals hallucinations."

The music of a feminine chuckle rippled down his back. "Oh, honey, you've always been too rational for your own good. Come on, open your mind to the possibilities. It's a helluva lot more exciting than knowing what's around every curve."

Dean blinked. Took another breath and turned again in his seat. Yep. There she was. "Mom?"

She gave him the same broad smile she'd flash when he'd brought home a good report card. Or when he'd thrown a touchdown pass. Or when her fingers straightened the bow tie of his rented prom tux.

"I'd say it was me in the flesh," she said, "but that's not exactly right, is it?"

"Mom?"

"Oh, honey," she let out a hoot of laughter. "You sound just like Katherine when I popped in on her the first time."

"Kate knows about you?"

Another laugh leaped from her pale lips. "Does she ever. And believe me, the first time, she was not a happy camper." She leaned forward. "How's the shoulder?"

Dean leaned away. "It's . . . fine?"

"Oh, we both know that's a lie, don't we? Why don't you shift around in the seat there, so you don't strain it?"

"I'm good," he said. Albeit crazy as hell.

"Okay then. Let's go with that." She reached a ghostly hand up to push at the messy gray bun at the top of her head. "I'm so glad you came home. Your daddy has been feeling a little lonesome since your sister moved out."

"I'm not here for long. Have to get back for physical therapy."

"Can't Mark Johnson over at the clinic help you with that?"

"I don't know him, but I'm pretty sure he doesn't know much about sports med. Mom?"

"Yes, sweetheart?"

"What the hell is going on?"

"You mean, why am I still hanging around?"

"Something like that."

"Aren't you glad to see me?"

Bulldozed might be a better word. "Of course I'm glad to see you. I'm just . . . not supposed to be *seeing* you."

"Well, like I told Kate, you don't just wake up one day and say, 'Gee, I'm going to leave all this unfinished business behind.'"

Okay, so not only was he talking to his mother's ghost, she wasn't making any sense. "And that means?"

She held up one translucent finger. "Katherine." Another finger went up. "You." A third finger. "Kelly. All unfinished business. Well, I guess I can scratch Kate from the list. Boy, I had to work hard on that one. That girl is stubborn."

He smiled. Like mother, like daughter. "So you're taking credit for Kate staying in Deer Lick and getting married?"

"Credit?" She tapped a finger against her cheek. "No. But we did manage to patch up our relationship, and that opened up a whole lot of doors for her."

"Well, I'm glad you made amends. It was a long time coming."

"Yeah. One that almost didn't happen." She shook her head and her glow kind of jiggled. "But that's what I'm talking about, Son. Unfinished business."

"You didn't need to come back for me, Mom. As happy as I am to see you, I'm okay."

She reached out as if to touch his cheek then withdrew her hand. "Oh, my precious boy, you are so handsome. So strong. And so smart."

The compliment warmed his heart. "Thanks, Mom."

"And so clueless."

Chapter Four

"Did you ever think about giving up?"

The next afternoon, Dean sat with his new brother-in-law and Deputy James Harley at one of the bistro sets Kate had installed when she'd transported the Sugar Shack from the faded era of disco into the new millennium with shades of Neapolitan ice cream.

He took the last bite of his ham and Swiss on wheat and leaned back against the iron chair. For the first time since he entered high school he felt truly lazy. No place to go. Nothing to do. No skeptical doctors or pessimistic therapists messing with his chi. He was on his own. Enjoying some peace and quiet and a little hometown hospitality.

"Giving up?" Matt raised his dark brows. "You mean did I give up thinking your sister would ever come back home?"

"No. That she'd ever come back to *you*."

Matt nodded. "About a month after her tennis shoes hit the highway."

"That's a long time."

"Ten years and worth every second."

They both glanced across the busy bakery to the red-headed subject of the conversation as she packed up a box full of red and green sprinkle-topped cupcakes.

"Ten years you could have been together," James added.

A frown tugged at Dean's brows. The last time he'd seen the man had been when he'd danced with his sister Kelly at Kate's wedding. Kelly had been two sheets to the wind and full of giggles. Dean just hoped Harley hadn't taken advantage of her. He'd hate to have to kill him.

"I don't think of it that way." Matt brushed the paper napkin across his mouth and wiped away the crumbs from his tuna sub. "If she'd stayed and we'd gotten married so young, it probably wouldn't have lasted. Too much growing up to do."

"Yeah, and you weren't any angel all that time, either," James said with a grin.

Matt frowned. "Could you not mention that in front of someone who could kick my ass sideways?"

"Busted wing." Dean pointed to his shoulder. "You're safe this time."

"Yeah, like we don't know all about your escapades, Silverthorne," James added. "Doesn't it piss you off when all those pictures of you and your supermodel of the week end up on the cover of *People* magazine or the *National Enquirer?*"

"Really, Harley?" Dean cocked his head. "You think I'm going to complain about being seen with a supermodel or two?"

The sandwich in James's hand halted midair. "What the hell? I'm a jerk for even thinking that."

"Might have to take your man card away." Dean loved women. He loved the way they thought completely differently, and most of the time more rationally than he did. He loved the way they smelled, the way they felt against him, the way they laughed, the way they moaned his name when he was buried deep inside them. There wasn't one detail he didn't love about women. Well, most women. He didn't love a woman who nailed him with a critical glare and then lumped him in with every other jack-off on the planet.

"All right, Mr. Perfect."

Dean looked up as Kate walked toward him with a white pastry box perched on her palm.

"Schmoozing-with-the-locals time is over." She set the box on the table in front of him. "I need you to make a delivery for me." She leaned down and gave her new husband a kiss on the cheek.

"I don't believe cupcake deliveries are in my contract, Commissioner," Dean said. He'd known it wouldn't take long before she'd wrangle him into her bakery deeds.

"Remember all those times I caught you sneaking through your bedroom window?"

"I'm too old for you to blackmail me now, baby sister."

"Oh really?" She pulled her cell phone from her apron pocket. "Then how about I give Fawn Derick a call and let her know you're back in town for an extended stay. I think her husband just left for a golf tourney in Hilton Head."

Dean crumpled his sandwich wrapper into a ball and stood. No way in hell did he need a married woman with wandering hands to complicate his life. "Excuse me, gentlemen," he said to his lunch partners, "It appears I have a delivery to make."

Dean rolled his mother's beast of a car into the Deer Lick Elementary parking lot. The designated parking-space lines were obscured by four inches of fresh snow, so he chose a spot near the playground to keep from bumping the Buick into the SUVs and minivans already parked.

The old brick building was exactly as he remembered it— only now it seemed much smaller. The steel letters on the front were topped by a skiff of white and the big glass doors looked smeared with kid prints and germs. He grabbed the pastry box and headed toward the doors, reminding himself to use his elbow to push his way through. He didn't need a nasty cold or flu to add to his misery.

A sign posted said he needed a pass to enter, so he wiped his wet boots on the floor mat, then walked into the office.

"Oh my heavens, if it isn't Dean Silverthorne. I haven't seen you since you played for the Deer Lick Destroyers." Mrs. Mayberry and her rhinestone glasses had worked behind that counter since he could remember. She was old as dirt but she'd always been one of the nicest people he'd ever known.

He clapped a hand to his heart. "And here I thought you'd watched all the touchdown passes I'd made since."

"Well of course I have. My husband Ned never misses a game." She came around the counter to give him a hug. "I'm so sorry about your mama. Letty was such a wonderful woman. I could always count on her to bring in gobs of donations for the women's auxiliary fundraiser."

Dean smiled at the warmth the memory brought him. His mother had always considered herself an advocate for any charity that came across her plate. She'd probably raised hundreds of thousands of dollars to help others. He'd tried to follow in her footsteps. Maybe he hadn't put in the actual sweat equity, but he'd delivered ample funds to his favorite organizations. Mostly those that involved children.

He loved the outright honesty of little kids. And when he did have the opportunity, he helped. He'd gotten to know a few of the little guys who often came to the Stallions games via the Houston charities. Even when the kids hadn't been feeling a hundred percent, they still lit up at the opportunity to be able to go into the locker room and meet the players or walk through the stadium tunnel and out onto the field. In those times, Dean realized if the sick children could put themselves out there for him, he'd be selfish not to return the favor. All the children left with souvenirs, autographs, photos, whatever they wanted. Their charities went home with sizable donations. The only regret he'd ever had was that he hadn't been able to wave a magic wand and heal them.

"So what brings you here today?" Mrs. Mayberry asked.

He lifted the pastry box. "Kate sent me here on a delivery. Guess the kindergarten class is having a holiday party."

"Around here we still call them Christmas parties." Mrs. Mayberry grinned. "Room eight. Down the hall, fourth door on the left."

Dean left the office with a promise to send her husband an autographed ball cap. The soles of his boots echoed on the tile floor as he made his way past pint-sized lockers and posters that announced various school activities.

Quietly, so as not to disturb the class in progress, he opened the door to room eight and stepped inside. At least twenty-four little kids in bright sweatshirts and fresh-faced innocence looked up at his sudden appearance. All of them looked, with the exception of one little boy in the back who appeared intent on stacking colorful blocks on the top of a long table. Paper snowflakes and candy canes decorated the walls. The room smelled like dry erase marker, sweaty little boys, and bubble-gum Chapstick.

Dean glanced toward the front of the class and the teacher who stood with her back to him while she wrote on a large white board nailed to the wall. She wore sensible black pumps, a classic straight skirt, and a fitted white blouse. Not the most eye-catching ensemble, but the curves beneath those plain clothes were in all the right places.

Her hair had been pulled back into a sleek blond ponytail that gently swayed as she wrote the word *umbrella* with a blue marker on the board. When several of the children giggled, she never broke her concentration but said in a smooth, patient voice, "Okay, let's calm down and focus."

When the giggles continued, the teacher slowly turned her head in his direction.

Recognition dawned.

Her pillowy pink lips dropped open on a gasp and a slight hint of the tiny space between her front teeth emerged.

Dean's instantaneous physical reaction forced him to lower the pastry box and hide what was most definitely not general audience rated.

No doubt about it, he would have to strangle his matchmaking sister.

Why was Dean Silverthorne standing in her classroom?

And why did he look like he was about to drop the white box clutched in his highly insured hands?

Emma slipped the cap back onto the marker and set it on the metal tray beneath the white board—a stalling tactic to give her heart time to settle back into a normal tempo. "Can I help you?"

He looked behind himself as though she were talking to someone else. Then those green eyes focused right in on her.

"Kate told me to deliver these cupcakes for a holiday party in room eight."

"We don't have a party scheduled. Are you sure she didn't mean the middle school? Or the high school?"

"Pretty sure she said this one." He smiled, knowing he'd been had by his own sister. "I'd hate to see these cupcakes go to waste." He turned to address her class. "Any of you kids want me to take these cupcakes back to the Sugar Shack?"

"No!" The students shouted.

He turned back to Emma. "How about it, teacher? You up for a little impromptu celebration of the season?"

Like she was going to tell him no? And suffer a mutiny in the kindergarten classroom from pint-sized mischief makers? No thanks. "I'm always up for a party." She walked toward him and the closer she came, the taller he got. The thickness of his parka only added size to the exquisitely cut muscles on his lean-hipped frame. The midnight blue sweater he wore would make a lesser man look pale, but Dean Silverthorne, of course, looked like a sun-kissed god.

She took a step closer. His aftershave drifted beneath her

nose. She inhaled and fought the urge to close her eyes and let go a hum of appreciation. Why did this man always have to smell so darned good? With a forced calm she extended her hands to take the pastry box, while her crazy side wished she could curl them into the front of that blue sweater and drag him closer for another whiff.

Beneath the cardboard box their fingers touched and a sizzle of warmth tickled her spine. She looked up to find his eyes smiling.

"How about I stay and help?" he asked in a low, deep tone that made the warmth in her spine race around to her belly and head south.

"Well . . . I'm not sure that's such a good idea."

"I could pass out the cupcakes while you finish your lesson."

"I don't have napkins," she answered with what she thought was a logical response.

He shrugged his good shoulder. "Icing tastes better when it's licked off anyway."

Oh, dear. "I'm sure paper towels will do." She took the box from his hands. "But I do thank you for the inventive offer."

With a careful motion his coat slid down his arms and he tossed it on the table near the door. For a man with an injured shoulder his movements were smooth and almost elegant.

"What are you doing?" she whispered, in an attempt to keep their conversation private from curious little ears.

"Helping."

"But I didn't say you could stay."

"You didn't say I couldn't. You just said you didn't think it would be a good idea. I think it's a great idea." He took the box from her, flipped open the lid, and turned to the class. "Who wants a cupcake?"

Twenty-four hands shot into the air and the words *me, me, me* echoed until it sounded as though hungry seagulls circled overhead.

Taken aback, Emma stood by her desk as one of the world's highest-paid athletes strolled desk to desk and placed a cupcake in each child's hand. He chatted with them, laughed with them, and soon her class fell under his spell like he was one of their playground buddies. When he came to the table in back, Emma held her breath. Dean set the box on the table and hunkered beside Brenden Jones. While the rest of the class chattered like squirrels and licked at the icing on their cupcakes, Brenden had his head down, focused on the task of stacking blocks.

"That's a pretty nice row of blocks you made there," Dean said.

No response from Brenden. Not that Emma had expected one.

"What's your name?" Dean asked.

Again. No response. Emma expected Dean to rise and walk away. Instead he lightly tapped the desk beneath Brenden's gaze. The boy's head came up but he did not make eye contact.

"What's your name?" Dean asked again in that same, even tone he used the time before. Not an ounce of the typical frustration an adult usually displayed when being ignored by a child showed on his face or in his body language. Emma found herself oddly fascinated.

"Brenden."

Dean smiled. "Do you like red cupcakes, Brenden?"

The boy's gaze darted around the room. Once again he offered no response.

"How about green cupcakes? Do you like green cupcakes, Brenden?"

"Yes," the child answered. "Green."

"Great. Here you go. One green cupcake for my friend, Brenden." Dean lifted a cupcake from the box and set it in front of the boy. Then he slowly stood and walked toward the front of the class.

"You should have asked him to say thank you," Emma said. "He—"

"Has autism," Dean said, setting the near-empty pastry box on her desk.

Surprise tilted her heart a little. "How did you know?"

"I do a lot with children's charities. Bo Miller, the Stallions' defensive tackle, has a son with autism." He leaned his super-fine butt against her desk and crossed one worn cowboy boot over the other. He snagged the second to the last cupcake from the box, peeled back the paper, and took a bite. "Kids are all different. You just have to find a way to communicate with them."

Emma couldn't stop staring at the fascinating way his mouth moved as he spoke, while white icing and red sprinkles clung to his beautifully curved top lip.

"It's like plays called in the huddle," he said. "Most people who watch the game have no idea what all those numbers and grunts mean." He leaned a little closer. "But the running back? Now he might have heard his number called out in the mix. Kids like Brenden benefit from straightforward questions and responses."

"That's a very astute realization," she commented, completely shocked that a man with his over-the-top lifestyle would have that level of insight on children with autism.

He glanced across the classroom. "I imagine kids like him are a challenge for you."

"Yes," she admitted. "In a good way." She watched Brenden meticulously pick the sprinkles off his cupcake and eat them one at a time. "I like to think of kids like Brenden as gifts. I think they teach me far more about myself than I can ever teach them."

"Then that should tell you one thing," Dean said.

"What's that?"

"That you're in the right place doing the right thing at the right time."

Their gazes met and for once Emma didn't feel like she needed to jump on the defensive. His green eyes were warm. His smile friendly. His posture relaxed and unassuming.

"Thank you," she said. "I'm not sure *this* is the right place for Brenden, but I plan to do everything I can for him while he's here."

Dean stuck the last bite of his cupcake in his mouth, scrunched up the paper cup, and scored a perfect basket in the trash can. "Then he's a lucky little kid."

Something inside Emma began to melt like ice cream covered with hot fudge and before she knew it he was walking toward the door. As he grabbed up his coat he gave her a wink, waved to the kids, and like a tropical storm blew through the place, leaving a whole lot of *what the heck just happened* in his wake.

On Saturday morning, Emma found herself in the heart of chaos at Cindi Rella's Attic, helping teen girls from Deer Lick and nearby towns try on and choose formals for their high school Christmas dances. Her friend Kate had been a genius when she'd convinced some of her previous celebrity clients to donate the red-carpet gowns they'd worn once or twice. The end result made dreams come true for young girls who'd longed to play Cinderella for a night. All for a nominal charge of ten dollars plus a dry cleaning fee.

Though the shop had never intended to make a profit, it did create a bright spot in the town. Today it buzzed with giggling girls and a few grateful moms. Emma herself had even borrowed a dress for her one and only date with Matt Ryan. But even a fool could have seen, once Kate came back home, that she and Matt were meant for each other. It was hard to be jealous of true love. And besides, Emma had gained a lifelong friend in the process.

"Are you sure you don't mind helping me out this morning?" Kate asked, while she slid a gold chiffon Taylor Swift baby-doll dress back on the hanger. "I know you've got finals for your online class and your kindergartners have a float in the parade this afternoon."

And Emma had yet to find time to decorate her tree, hang her stocking, and make her frosted sugar cookies. "Are you serious?" She laughed as she placed a rhinestone tiara on top of Chelsea Winkle's all-American-girl ponytail. "This is like playing dress up. What girl gets too old for that?"

"Not me," Chelsea said with a grin that brought out some very deep dimples.

"One of these nights, when my sister comes home," Kate said, "we are *all* going to play dress up until we can't possibly stand to look at another rhinestone. I've been dying to try on the Elie Saab that Katy Perry wore to a movie premiere last month."

"What do you think of this dress, Kate?" Chelsea spun in a slow circle to display the red chiffon A-Line V-neck Selena Gomez had worn to the Oscars.

"It's perfect on you. But dump the tiara and wear that gorgeous natural blond hair in a loose updo," Kate instructed. "And I have a sweet little pair of black satin heels in the back. What size are you?"

"Six and a half." Chelsea handed the tiara back to Emma.

"Close enough. They're sevens. We'll stuff cotton balls in the toes."

Emma had a hard time keeping up with the energy that zipped through the shop. As a more or less *safe* dresser, she'd had just a taste of dress-up, and found she rather liked slipping into something sexy. Which was only one reason she'd just spent half of her *fun* money on thongs, boy-short undies, and push-up bras from Victoria's Secret. And she hoped one day soon she'd find someone to actually wear them for. "Who are you going to the dance with, Chelsea?" she asked, keeping her mind out of the flustered zone.

"Bobby Davenport." The teen sighed. "But I really, really, really want to go with Alex Harley."

"Whoa, honey," Kate said, "I know James is trying hard to be a good big brother and steer Alex in the right direction, but that boy is all kinds of bad attitude."

Chelsea wrinkled her nose. "I think he's just misunderstood."

Kate laughed. "That's like saying Colin Farrell is misunderstood."

"I know, but Alex is soooo cute," Chelsea said with stars in her blue eyes.

Emma wanted to warn the girl about falling hard for cute boys with egomaniacal attitudes. She'd been in that same situation and look what had happened to her. "Cute is overrated," she said. "And Bobby Davenport is not the kind of boy who will break your heart."

Chelsea's smile drooped along with her shoulders. "I know." She turned to Kate. "Can I go get the shoes now?"

Kate laughed and tapped her on the nose. "You bet."

As soon as the teen skipped out of earshot, Emma felt the heat of Kate's eyes. She looked up. "What's wrong?"

"Sounds like you have some personal knowledge of bad boys and broken hearts," Kate said.

Emma exhaled. "You can say that."

"Anyone I know?"

Not anyone Kate would remember. "No. Just a jerk I met a long time ago. I consider him a lesson well-learned."

"And now you stay away from bad boys?"

"I want to be married some day," Emma told her and added a laugh. "With any luck while I'm still young enough to enjoy it. Bad boys don't make very good husbands or fathers. I'm sure you saw plenty of that when you were in Hollywood."

"Seriously. You know what's really sad is that there are some men who deep-down inside want to be good husbands and fathers. But they get so caught up in the BS of celebrity they end up not knowing who they are anymore. First the media treats them like a god, then it convinces them that there's somebody better just around the corner. As in, there's a better actor or there's a better fashion designer or record producer or there's a better endorsement or, heaven forbid, the next A-Rod or Joe Montana."

"Are we still talking about Hollywood?" Emma asked, as her friend tensed up. "You sound pretty passionate."

Kate shrugged. "I'm just glad to be home and away from that. You know? I never thought I could be this happy." Kate hugged her. "I want you to be this happy, too."

Amen, sister. "Hopefully I will someday."

"Hopefully sooner rather than later." Kate gave her another little squeeze. "So . . . I hear my dopey brother delivered a box of cupcakes to your class by mistake."

In a drizzle of snow, the Deer Lick Christmas parade began to line up at Reindeer and Main. The first float belonged to the Boy Scouts and included several artificial trees with a teddy-bear-driven snowmobile atop a bed of real snow.

Dean had never known another parade to go up the street, then turn around and come back. But that's exactly how parades in Deer Lick went down. Otherwise they'd be over before anyone had a chance to buy a cup of hot chocolate from the 4-H kids or a bag of cotton candy from the Destroyer's pep squad. The folks in his hometown had become professionals at putting the hokey into the holidays. And as he stood there watching a little girl no more than ten years old and dressed as a candy cane wrangle a wreath of bells around the neck of a St. Bernard, Dean realized he kind of admired hokey.

In search of his sister, he walked past the "D" street dancers all bundled up in their parkas and leotards. The Deer Lick Rodeo queen looked warm on her white horse in her white hat, white coat, and white leather chaps. But he didn't think the horse had much of an appreciation of the gold pipe-cleaner halo dangling over his ears. Or the gold fabric cuffs on his legs. And probably not the huge white and gold floral arrangement perched on top of his butt.

The parade committee members were making their way down the line of entries when they stopped to ask him to be a secret judge.

"I don't think I'd be much help," he told Mayor Remington, "unless I could put them all in first place."

"Don't tell me you've turned PC on us," Edna Price quipped, with a poke of her moosehead cane.

"Keeps me out of trouble." Dean shrugged. "Have you seen Kate?"

"Oh yeah, she's back there in the non-judging area with Matt. He's drivin' Old Man Carter's John Deere. Gotta get a handle on that upcoming sheriff election, so he's throwing out salt water taffy to the kids."

Dean laughed. "If you can't get to the voters' hearts, get to the voters' kids stomachs?"

"Exactly. Now get on back there and give your sister a hand. She's tryin' to make sure that husband of hers gets elected but I don't think puttin' tinsel on his gun belt is going to make it happen."

"Thanks, Mrs. Price."

"Nice to see you around, young man."

That was one thing Dean loved about being home: people were genuinely happy to see him. Unlike those he'd left in Texas. Once he'd been slam-dunked at the forty-seven-yard line, many treated him like a nasty cold they didn't want to catch. A lot of players were superstitious and believed going near an injured teammate would open some kind of bad luck voodoo portal, and they'd be injured as well. And the media? With them you were either Alice in Wonderland or the pathetic Dormouse.

As if in accordance with his thoughts, the ache in his shoulder cranked up a notch as though he'd been skewered like a shish kebab. He rotated it slightly.

Just the cold getting to him. No need to worry.

Since he'd traded in his cowboy boots for a more logical pair of insulated hunt boots, he continued down the line of entries. He dodged a sheep-drawn Radio Flyer and wondered how those tiny wheels would make it through all the snow on the street, let alone how those sheep would be smart enough to know to walk forward and not go look for some hay. In the distance he saw his brother-in-law up on top of a big green tractor. Dean gave him a nod and made his way through the crowd. At the end of the judging area was a flatbed trailer being pulled by a Chevy half-ton with a Christmas wreath on the front grill and a blow-up Santa on the hood. Even better than the truck itself were the participants who sat on that flatbed trailer.

Emma Hart's kindergarten class was on-board, garbed in red sweaters, red foam noses, and reindeer antlers cut from brown construction paper. Brenden Jones sat at the end, fascinated by the gold garland looped around the trailer. The rest of the kids rehearsed *Rudolph the Red-Nosed Reindeer* while their teacher handed out kazoos and jingle bells. The fact that she also wore brown construction paper antlers did not surprise him. The big brown fuzzy reindeer suit . . . now that was another matter. And almost sexy.

He stood back a moment and watched her in action while she continued to hand out the musical gadgets. She straightened crooked antlers, cupped her furry reindeer paws on little faces with cold cheeks, and offered smiles to anyone who looked her way. Anybody within a mile could see that Emma Hart was a kindergarten teacher kids would remember all their lives.

"Come here, Bobby," she called to a little boy who looked like he'd only used up half his quota of energy for the day. "You've got a serious waterfall going on." The boy bounced over to her with an eye roll while she pulled a tissue from her sleeve and wiped his runny nose.

"Tough day?" Dean came up behind her and her fluffy reindeer tail.

She jumped as though she'd been stuck in the butt with a pin. "What are you doing here?"

"Seeing if Olive could come out and play."

"Olive?"

"The other reindeer?" Her eyes grinned but her mouth didn't follow. Damn, and he'd looked forward to that killer smile tilting those soft, plump lips.

"I can't believe I fell for that."

"Nice to know I haven't lost my touch. Hey, kids," he said to the squirming, wiggling bunch of five-year-olds.

"Hi, Mr. Cupcake Man."

"Thath not hith name," a chubby little redhead said. "My mommy thaid hith name ith Mither Purfeck."

Ah, a football fan. "Who's her mommy?" he asked Emma.

"Fawn Derick. Know her?"

Up close and personal. "Nope. Can't say I do."

While the kids tooted away on their kazoos, Emma slid her gloved hands down to her knees, bent at the waist, and whispered, "That's odd. She's been bragging about you for years."

"She has?"

"Of course she also said . . . hmmm, how do I put this?" She finally flashed him that killer smile and the blood in his veins started to hum. "Actually, Fawn mentioned that you had a bit of a *quick release.*"

"I was in junior high."

She straightened. "Then maybe you've improved."

That brought a grin to his face. "I'd be happy to show you."

"Mmmmm." The tip of her cold pink nose wrinkled as though she was actually giving the offer some thought. "No thanks."

Dean shook his head. Small, smart, and sassy. He'd never met anyone like Emma Hart before. And he couldn't quite figure her out.

He slid his gaze past her luscious mouth and down her fuzzy reindeer suit. He leaned in and was pleased when she leaned forward as well. He breathed in a lungful of her sweet scent. "Nice tail."

Arms filled with kazoos, Emma watched Dean's long stride take him to the back of the trailer, where Brenden Jones kept busy organizing individual strands of shiny gold tinsel. Brenden's mother stood close by, immersed in a deep discussion with a group of other moms. All conversation stopped and heads snapped up when the *football god* stepped within their little circle. The moms were young and pretty and one had even succumbed to doing a hair flip.

Nothing like a hot body and gorgeous face to put a little silly in a girl's step.

Surrounded by adoring women, Dean Silverthorne was totally in his element. Ah, if only they knew. Then again, it wasn't her job to educate them—just their children. Emma shook her head and returned to wrangling her little deer, who all seemed to be operating on a candy cane overload. She handed out the last kazoo to Jeffy Barnett, Maggie and Oliver's youngest.

"Miss Hart?" Jeffy whispered, grabbing himself in the crotch and doing the little shuffle that was all too familiar. "I gotta whiz!"

"Oh." Darn, she couldn't just walk off and leave her other kids unattended. She glanced over to the gaggle of women who surrounded Dean Silverthorne like he was the Pied Piper of Pedicures. "Ummm, Maggie?" Emma called out, but her friend was too engrossed in whatever it was the hunk in their midst was saying. He, however, turned and caught her eye.

Emma pointed down to the little boy now performing a frantic pee-pee dance. Dean tapped Maggie on the shoulder and let her know her son was in dire need.

"Oh!" Maggie giggled and swept her son off the back of the trailer bed. "I'm sorry, Em. I was just . . . umm . . ."

"No problem. I just couldn't leave the other kids."

Maggie gave her a wave while she hauled her son in the direction of the nearest potty room.

Yeah, Emma knew exactly what Maggie meant. Men like Dean had a hypnotizing way that could send all kinds of crazy sexy images through a woman's brain. Lucky for her, she was beyond that kind of cranial interference. She was as solid as an oak.

She repositioned her reindeer nose and glanced across the back of the trailer bed. He may have been elbow-deep in discussion, but those sharp green eyes tracked her every move like she was a wide receiver in the red zone. When the corners of his mouth kicked upward, all the lessons she'd learned about love-'em-and-leave-'em bad boys were replaced by the urge to flip her hair.

Yeah, she was an oak all right.

That night boredom grabbed Dean by the throat and threatened to take him down to the mat. Cabin fever didn't begin to describe the nervous energy that zipped through his veins. For a week he'd reveled in the mundane. He'd cooked dinner, done dishes, helped his sister with her overflow of holiday bakery orders. He'd tossed out salt water taffy along the parade route in support of Matt's sheriff campaign. He'd woken up in the same bed he'd slept in from the time he'd been four years old until the day he'd left for college. These days his feet and arms hung over the edges, and every time he turned over to get comfortable the wooden slats beneath the box springs groaned in protest. He missed the super-soft California king mattress he slept on at his high-rise. He missed his condo. The custom billiards table. His massage therapy shower.

He leaned back on the sofa and tucked one of his mother's hand-crocheted pillows onto his lap. On the positive side, his shoulder seemed to be on the mend. He now only needed a pain pill to sleep. But the motion and strength were nowhere near normal. And since he'd now been visited multiple times by his deceased mother, he could probably say *he* wasn't quite normal either.

Impatient for faster signs of improvement, he'd called the Stallions' PT, who'd given him a few light motion exercises, but so far Dean had seen little return on his efforts. *Failure* whispered in his ear as each day he attempted to push the healing envelope just a tiny bit further without re-injury.

"I don't like this show as much as *Man v. Food*." His father pushed his recliner back into the lounge position. "Never could understand why someone would purposely choose to eat sticks and bugs when there's a good burger joint on almost every corner."

The show his father referenced was a new episode of *Man vs. Wild*. Before he'd landed back in Deer Lick, Dean hadn't even known any man-vs.-whatever shows existed. His sixty-five-inch big screen at home remained locked on a sports channel. Whether home alone or playing Texas Hold 'em with the guys, he kept it on as background noise.

He wasn't one who usually stayed in the same place for long periods of time. Even in the off-season he'd grab a plane to Cabo or to a celebrity golf tournament. Or when in town, he'd visit players and their families or hang out with his closest friends. He smiled. Or he'd be sweet-talking a supermodel out of her skinny jeans.

Men like you are cowards. You only see the end game. Meaningless sex. A one-nighter, nooner, or whatever time of day you manage to find a willing body.

Shit.

He sat up.

How had crazy reindeer-suit-wearing Emma popped into his conscience?

"Nothing to do?" Kate asked him as he watched her hang a glittery snowman ornament on the tree in the corner of the living room.

"Thinking of making a bag of microwave popcorn."

"Maybe you could help me decorate?"

"Apparently you've forgotten the time I broke the heirloom tree topper."

"Right." She reached for a shiny glass candy cane. "Tell me again how it is that you can throw a perfect spiral into a pair of gloved hands yet you can't manage to hang an ornament without breaking it?"

"Leather. Glass."

"Ah." She nodded and her red hair brushed across the back of her blue Stallions sweatshirt. "Got it."

He sighed. How did people around here manage not to go crazy in the winter months? How had he lasted eighteen years in a town that barely registered on a map?

"I saw Emma Hart at the Gas and Grub earlier," Kate mentioned. "Why don't you call her up and ask her out?"

Because he'd like to keep all his limbs intact?

He could swing a bat in any direction and still hit on the fact that Emma Hart didn't like him. Why? Who knew. He never had issues with other women. Emma was just odd. Cute. But odd.

Besides, he dated women with long, long legs. Women with names like Desiree and Layla. Hell, one time he'd even dated a woman named Delight. And she had been. He didn't date short women with attitudes who had old-fashioned names like *Emma*. She might as well have been called Gertrude or Harriet. He didn't do groupies, married women, or women looking to put a ring on their finger. And he didn't do old-fashioned. Period.

At his no-response response, Kate tugged the sparkly green and red garland into place. "So you're not going to call her?"

He exhaled. "Your matchmaking efforts are getting old, Kate."

"That Emma is a real sweet girl, Son," his father added. "You'd be smart to act before some other guy grabs her attention."

Two words that didn't belong in the same sentence. Emma and sweet.

"Suit yourself," Kate said with a shrug. "Doesn't matter, really. I saw Jesse Hamilton heading in her direction. I think he's got a thing for her."

Jesse? So who was Oscar? Emma had mentioned the name the night he'd almost mowed her down on his way out to Kate's. If she'd had someone waiting for her at home, why would Jesse Hamilton set himself up for rejection?

"I'm pretty sure Jesse was about to ask her out, anyway," Kate continued. "Probably just as well. I don't think she likes you very much."

No. Shit.

Everyone liked him. Everyone except *her*. What was wrong with that woman?

Two hours and two episodes of *Cupcake Wars* later, Dean thought he would lose his mind. He needed to get up off the sofa and get out of the house. Maybe he'd hit up the Naughty Irish bar and see what his old friend Oliver and his wife Maggie were up to. Too bad he couldn't play a game of pool. That would eat up a few hours. Or he could cruise by Wholly Bowlers and grab a beer. Unfortunately, watching bowling rather than actually engaging in the sport was as exciting as watching fungus grow. Or maybe . . . he'd just drop in at Emma Hart's house and find out why she didn't seem to like him very much.

Yeah. No question about it. He was bored.

CHAPTER FIVE

The bright red door to the small craftsman-style bungalow opened wide. Emma Hart stood there in a pair of Scooby Doo pajama bottoms and a pink tank top. No bra. Hair piled up on top of her head in a messy bun.

Perfect. He'd caught her off guard. And hopefully alone.

"Hi there."

Her flawlessly arched brows pulled together. "What . . . are you doing here?"

Good question.

He planted his palm on the door frame above her head. "I know it's been a couple of days since I basically forced you off the road, but I thought I'd make sure you got that tree into your house okay."

An icy breeze pushed at his back and snuck past him. Emma folded her arms across her chest. Too bad. She might be crazy but that didn't mean he couldn't enjoy the view.

"Oh." Her pillowy lips compressed. "Yes. Thank you." She turned and looked behind her. "I was just putting on the ornaments."

"Same thing is going on at my house. Kate came by. She didn't think Dad would put a tree up this year."

Sympathy darkened her blue eyes. "I imagine this Christmas will be very difficult for all of you."

"Yeah." Understatement of the millennium. The breeze hit his back again and though he wasn't all that cold he gave an exaggerated shudder. "It's pretty cold out here. Do you mind if I come in?"

"Why would you want to?"

"Why wouldn't I?"

She gave a humorless laugh. "In case you haven't noticed, I don't think we like each other very much."

"Oh that."

"Yes. That."

He shrugged. "I can call a truce if you will."

She shifted her weight to one smooth hip. "Is this how you disarm your opponents?"

"Is what how?"

"This . . ." Her hand flitted in the air. "This *aw-shucks* country boy charm shtick you do."

"Ah, so you're not buying into it."

"Not for a minute."

"Too bad." He flashed her the same smile he'd perfected for the Stetson cologne ad last year. "Because I'm usually pretty damned good at it."

She lowered her head and chuckled. Unfortunately he missed the firepower of her killer smile.

What was it about her that made him want to grab her with both hands and capture that mouth with his own? To slick his tongue along the seam of those ultra-soft lips until she opened for him? He'd never been turned on by a woman's mouth before. Unless it happened to be doing erotic things to his body. He'd always been a breast or leg man. Sometimes change was good. "So, can I come in or are you going to ruin my reputation and make me beg on your doorstep."

"As long as you don't ruin mine."

He gave her his Boy Scout best. "Promise."

"Then I guess you can come in." She unfolded her arms and stepped back.

"'Scuse me, ma'am," he said as he edged by her. Too bad he didn't have a hat to take off, because the interesting parts of Emma Hart hidden beneath that thin little tank top were definitely giving him a salute.

While Bing Crosby crooned on the stereo, Dean stepped inside and froze in place. *Holy shit.* Every inch of space was bursting at the joints with lights and Santas and snowmen and . . . was that a cat wearing an elf suit?

"That's Oscar," Emma said from behind him as if she'd read his mind.

The snow-white seriously overweight feline garbed in a green-and-red-striped sweater and pointy hat rose from his perch on the back of the sofa and arched his back.

Great. A cat. He hated cats.

The cat yowled and hissed.

Apparently the feeling was mutual.

"He's not very sociable with men." Emma walked past and picked up the furry elf to cuddle. "I think he gets jealous."

The cat pressed his front paws into the soft mounds of her

breasts and kneaded. His subsequent purr spoke volumes, and Dean completely understood. "I've never been much of a cat person."

"Most men aren't."

Dean eased his arms from his parka and tossed it onto a nearby chair. "We're not going to launch into another *men-like-me* conversation again, are we?"

She stroked the cat between the ears. "I'll do my best to refrain."

Golden flames licked at the pine logs in the corner wood-stove. Dean glanced around and tried to see past the garland, twinkling lights, and poinsettias to find the true character of the room. Antiques, white furniture, an iron bird cage filled with glittery holiday foliage.

Definitely chickville.

It smelled good, too. Like a girl. All soft and powdery fresh with a hint of sugar cookie. As Emma moved a shoebox full of ornaments off the sofa to make a spot for him to sit, he wondered if she tasted as good as she smelled.

"Would you care for something to drink?" If the rigidness of her shoulders was any indication, he made her very tense. She set Oscar down on the floor. The cat flicked its tail and the bells dangling from his sweater jingled.

"Scotch?"

"Sorry. The strongest I have is a bottle of cooking wine. All I have is some hot chocolate, herbal tea, or water." She brushed her hands down the very nice curves of her waist and hips. His eyes tracked every move.

"I'm good." He ignored the look she gave him that clearly

said she doubted him and was wondering why he didn't just go ahead and leave.

And why didn't he?

"I didn't mean to interrupt you," he said. "Go ahead with what you were doing."

"Are you sure?"

He nodded. A long sigh lifted her breasts against that pink tank top and Dean was glad, for the moment, he was sitting down. He watched as she removed a shiny red choo-choo train from the shoebox and threaded a wire hanger through the ribbon on top. She hung it toward the middle of the tree then reached for a shiny white ballerina slipper.

"Those ornaments look like family treasures," he said, while the growling cat at his feet stared up at him as if he were a giant mouse.

"They are. Most of them are from when I was a little girl. My Memaw—"

"Your who?"

"My grandmother. She bought a new ornament for me each year."

"My mom did the same for all of us."

"Oh, that's nice. Do you put them on your tree?"

Hell, he never bothered to get a tree because he was rarely home during the holidays. In December the race for the Super Bowl heated up and the Stallions rarely had a home game. "No. They're still at my parent's house, stuck in a box somewhere."

"Hmmm." She turned her attention back to the tree and hooked the slipper onto a lower branch. Then she reached into the box again.

Hmmm? What was *that* supposed to mean?

"This is my favorite." She lifted a glass star and laid it across her palm as if it were precious and fragile. "Memaw had a glassblower friend who made amazing globes and vases. She made this topper the year I was born. It's been on my tree ever since."

"Can I see it?"

She eased her hand toward him. He studied the delicate piece, then looked up at her. "You've mentioned your grandmother, but not your mother. Has she passed?"

She shook her head and scooted a footstool closer to the tree. "I don't know. She took off right after I was born. I've never actually met her. I don't know if she's dead or alive. And I really don't care either way."

The tight quality to her voice said she cared a lot. Dean thought it was too bad that her mother hadn't stuck around. She'd probably be pretty proud of her daughter.

Before Emma could climb up onto the stool, Dean stood. "Let me help you with that." His fingers brushed against the soft skin of her hand as he took the ornament and carefully slipped it onto the very top of the tree. That small contact did something odd to his stomach. Or maybe he'd just indulged in too many slices of his father's spiced pumpkin bread.

She stood back, tilted her head, and gave a nod. "Perfect."

"Yeah, I get that from all the girls."

Her eyes met his, wide with disbelief.

"Kidding." God, that was lame. What was it about this girl that reduced him to say such dopey things?

Her jingle-bell cat jumped up onto the sofa, stretched, and scratched at Dean's Levi's.

"Right," she said with a laugh. "Even Oscar knows you're full of it."

"As long as he knows to keep his distance, we'll be fine."

The cat arched his back and hissed again. Dean had an urge to sweep the nasty animal off the sofa, but even one touch would send him into an allergic fit of sneezing and watery eyes.

Dean draped a dangly ornament made of shiny buttons on a high branch. "You know, before I came over here, Kate was trying to get me to help her decorate our tree. You're not going to rat me out, are you?"

Emma ducked beneath his arm to get to the other side of the tree. "If I did, would it be painful?"

"Only if I don't mind having my skin fried in donut oil."

She chuckled. "I don't suppose that would help get you back on the field any faster."

"No, I suppose it wouldn't."

"I'm sure everyone associated with your team is worried about you."

Dean stuck a fuzzy red cardinal between branches. "Not sure they're worried about *me*. Now, the shoulder . . ."

Emma stopped in the midst of hanging a beaded gold heart. "What would make you say that?"

He shrugged his good shoulder. "Because it's true."

"I'm sure you're imagining things."

"Nope. Every call starts with 'How's the shoulder? How's the arm? What's the doc say about that shoulder?' Sometimes it feels like they've forgotten there's a person attached." And why was he telling her all this? Before he got in too deep, maybe it was time he headed home.

"I'm sure you're exaggerating," she said.

Was he?

"They wouldn't pay a gazillion dollars just for your arm." She tossed the empty shoebox on the table, picked up a new one and lifted the lid. "There's more to quarterbacking than throwing a ball."

"Are you telling me you're into football?"

"Isn't everybody?"

Not the women he dated.

"So you're not one of those girls who thinks the game is sweaty and violent?"

"Yes." She laughed. "But I still like to watch."

Dean watched her bend over to reach inside the new shoebox and smiled. "If that offer for hot chocolate is still open, I wouldn't mind a cup."

She straightened and one of her brows lifted. "Um. Sure. Mini marshmallows?"

"Absolutely."

She placed a satin angel on the tree, then went to the kitchen. Dean watched in appreciation as the Scooby Doos gracing the sweet curve of her backside lifted and settled with each step she took.

An hour later, with the tree done and the cat curled up on his parka, shedding and drooling onto the sleeve, Dean couldn't find another excuse to stay. Oddly enough, he found he wanted to do just that. They'd found some common ground. They'd discussed his family, her newfound friendship with Kate, and how she helped out his sister at her charity prom gown shop. They talked about her class—Brenden Jones in particular, when Dean asked how she managed to teach the class while giving a child with unique needs some special attention. She became completely animated when she'd told him of the classes she was currently taking to obtain her master's degree in special education. And while she talked, Dean found himself mesmerized by the energy she put into her thoughts and dreams. She wanted to help kids. How cool was that?

Time had whizzed by and he hadn't talked about himself, his career, or his shoulder. And while he'd enjoyed the way Emma's tiny tank top moved and cupped her breasts, he hadn't felt the need to talk his way into those Scooby Doo pajama bottoms. He'd simply enjoyed the conversation. Kind of a nice change.

"Well, guess I'd best get going." He slid his drooled-on parka sleeve out from under the evil elf paws and received a hiss for his troubles.

Emma stood back and looked at him as though he held the answer to the million-dollar question. "There's something I need before you go," she said.

He looked at that soft mouth and those blue-on-blue eyes, and his heart pumped up into overdrive. "I'm an open book. Fire away."

"While this little visit has been nice and everything, I thought it was pretty apparent that we didn't like each other much and—"

"And why is that?" Not that he really wanted to know.

A little crinkle formed between her brows. "Straight up or sugar-coated?"

He smiled. "How about with a sprinkle of sugar?"

"No offense, but I try not to associate with people I know I could never trust."

"Ah, so you have trust issues."

"No, I have jerk issues."

"Ouch. I think you forgot the sugar on that one." So Emma had been burned, and now all the men who followed would have to pay the price. Too bad. "So you're judging me on what? My behavior at my sister's wedding?"

She laughed. "Hardly. How about ten plus years of scandalous tabloid headlines and breaking news reports of sensational partying."

"Oh. That." Damn, he couldn't control what the press put out there any more than he could control the universe. He could tell this woman that half of what she saw was absolute bullshit. But then he'd have to own up to the other half. During his first year in the NFL he'd been schooled by some of the most well-known players in the league. All of them had preached to him the importance of making a name both on the field and off. So he'd created his persona. Unfortunately now it appeared Bad Boy Dean's lifestyle was about to bite him in the ass.

"So back to my question." She folded her arms, erecting a *don't look and don't even think about touching* barricade. "Exactly why did you come over here tonight?"

His boots thunked against the wood floor as he walked to the front door, opened it wide, and stepped onto the small front porch. "Just curious."

The roads were icy as Dean made his way home and snow flurries fell onto the windshield of his mother's beast of a car.

Beneath him the tires bumped along as though they were water balloons. The traction was deplorable and he couldn't understand why his father had allowed his mother to drive such a death wagon.

But that wasn't what was really on his mind.

As many years as he'd played football he'd been judged—by his pass completions, interceptions, strength of schedule, the command of his players on the field. He'd been compared to Joe Montana, Ken Stabler, and other noteworthy quarterbacks. He didn't mind any of that. But when it came down to a woman judging him based on inaccurate information? That bothered him. Then again, he had no one to blame but himself.

He couldn't wait to get back home to Texas. To slip behind the wheel of his Mercedes for a smooth ride out to the stadium and the state-of-the-art workout facility. He planned to make good use of that facility upon his return. The harder he worked, the faster he'd heal and the quicker he'd be back on the line of scrimmage. Back to where he didn't have to prove himself anymore. Back to the life he'd created—right, wrong, or indifferent.

He punched the buttons on the radio and was met with static until he turned the corner of Spotted Fawn and Reindeer Avenue, and Tom Jones began to sing *It's Not Unusual.*

"Nice visit?"

Dean's gaze jerked up to the rearview mirror. Sure enough, a golden glow hovered over the backseat. Shit. Since he'd learned his lesson last time, he pulled the car to the curb and twisted around in his seat.

In her red plaid shirt and overalls, his mother leaned against the rear cushion as though she were merely along for a Sunday drive.

"I'm hallucinating. Right?"

Letty Silverthorne laughed. "Not quite, sugarplum. But I'll give you an A for effort."

"Mom?"

"Hooo-boy." She rolled her eyes. "Are we going to go through this again?"

"There's an explanation for everything," he said. "The play of light bouncing off the snow. Or shadows. Or any number of reasons I think I'm seeing my dead mother."

"Only got one reason, Son. You need my help."

"I need your help?"

"Thank you! I thought you'd never ask."

Dean closed his eyes against the headache sandblasting the front of his skull. When he opened his eyes, his mother had disappeared.

Emma parked her car near the front entrance of the Sunny Bridge Nursing Home and gathered the stack of tabloids on the passenger seat. Judging by the colorful covers, John Travolta had encountered aliens while flying his private jet to Bermuda and Whoopi Goldberg had been abducted by aliens on a recent trip to Paris. Obviously it hadn't been a good week to be in the air without a tinfoil hat.

She stood at the glass entry doors and pushed the intercom button. Moments later an attendant buzzed her in. The facility took care of many dementia patients and often they'd wander right out the door. The locked facility was just one of the safety precautions that had impressed Emma when she'd been searching for just the right place for her Memaw.

With a wave to the attendants at the nurses' station, Emma headed down the Calla Lily Court corridor to the last door on the right. She gave a gentle knock, then opened the door to find her grandmother sitting in her wheelchair looking out the window. Emma's heart stuttered. The woman who'd raised her looked lost and fragile. Her white hair was curled from a tight perm. The muumuu she wore was purple with big red and yellow hibiscus. Emma came up beside her wheelchair. With faded blue eyes, her grandmother looked up and Emma waited for recognition to set in.

"Oh. Hello, dear." Her Memaw reached out a knobby hand. "I was just thinking about you."

Emma took her hand and kissed her paper-thin cheek. "I brought you your favorite papers." She set the tabloids on the bed, then pulled up a seat next to her grandmother's wheelchair. "How are you feeling today?"

Slim shoulders lifted beneath the loud muumuu. "Can't complain."

Emma brushed a curl from her grandmother's forehead. "You look good."

"I do?"

"Mmm-hmmm. I thought maybe you might feel good enough to come home for Christmas morning." The thought of having her grandmother home for even a few hours sounded wonderful. The house felt empty since Emma had had to put her in a full-time facility. She'd hated to put her there, but the incidents with her dementia had become more frequent and more dangerous. When her grandmother had fallen and broken her hip, Emma knew it was time. She missed having her grandmother to talk to. To hug every day. She missed seeing her crooked smile each night when she'd come in the door after work. Her Memaw was the one person to whom she had a real connection, and she missed having her there in her everyday life.

"Oh, I don't know," her Memaw said. "I don't like to leave. What would they do without me here? I've got to keep things running smooth. There's no one else who knows how to restock the embroidery thread. And that wall of yarn is just a mess."

Emma gave her grandmother's hand a gentle squeeze. "Memaw, you sold the knitting shop five years ago."

Her grandmother looked up. "I did?"

Emma nodded. "But you sure took good care of that place. I remember the time you had a sale on fuzzy yarn and everyone in town started showing up with so many winter scarves you had to put a place in the store for them to sell on consignment."

"Oh, that was a good idea."

Emma chuckled. "Yes, it was. You had a lot of good ideas."

There had been a time when her grandmother had put knitting and crocheting back in fashion. She'd bought fuzzy yarn and baby yarn and all kinds of odd varieties. Then she'd made samples of items and hung them in the front window to entice patrons not only to buy the yarn but to take lessons, too.

"I miss you, Meems." Emma wrapped her arms around the woman who'd held her through her nightmares and cheered her through her victories.

Her grandmother's fragile hand came up to pat her arm. Then she leaned her head back and looked up into Emma's eyes.

"I'm sorry. Who did you say you were?"

As it did on every visit, Emma's heart shattered for the loss of the wonderful, witty spirit that used to be Sadie Hart.

Sportsman's Locker was a closet-sized version of the sporting goods warehouse Dean frequented in Houston. It had the basics—some free weights, a few choices in treadmills, and a pathetic selection of athletic wear and shoes. Dean looked through a small rack of exercise shorts, then back up to James Harley, whom he'd come across at the Gas and Grub. They'd got to talking, and since James had the day off he'd offered his help to carry whatever Dean purchased.

"The red ones are definitely you," James said with a smirk.

Dean held up the shorts—or what there was of them—and frowned. "I think I saw Richard Simmons wearing these when we were both on *Houston Live* right after I signed with the Stallions."

"Yeah, I thought short shorts went out with disco and roller skates."

Dean laughed. "Apparently not."

"So what's with the big purchase of all the weights and stuff? I thought you were headed back to Texas ASAFP."

"I promised my dad and Kate I'd stay through Christmas."

James leaned his forearms on a rack of jerseys. "That's just a few days away."

"I put a call in to the team PT. If he says to get the shoulder moving more, I need to be ready. So as long as I'm here I need some tools to get the job done. I figure I can donate them to the high school when I head back home."

"That hit you took? Pretty devastating to even watch," James said.

"No shit," Dean admitted. "First time in my life I actually saw stars."

"You feel pretty good about getting back to a hundred percent?"

Dean looked up and considered the question. And when he found genuine compassion and not doubt on James Harley's face, he answered, "I'm not ready to walk away from what I've worked for all my life. I love playing football. It's what I do. It's who I am." Without it he had nothing but an extravagant condo and a really nice car.

James flashed a grin that probably had women peeling off their panties as fast as they could. "Then let's get this pile of workout shit home so you can get back to kicking those Steelers' asses."

Dean laughed. "Not your team, huh?"

"Not a fan of that douche-bag QB."

You had to like a man who despised the opposition. But even as Dean watched the deputy set the dumbbells on the checkout counter, he still wondered about the man's disappearing act with his sister Kelly at the wedding reception.

He might like James Harley, but if the man messed with his sister, he'd have to die.

Chapter Six

On Friday afternoon, Emma slipped out the doors of the school and hurried to her car before anyone could stop her and ask what she planned to bring to the teachers' association potluck at the Grange.

School was out for two full weeks. No kindergarten. No online classes. No classes at the university. And best of all, no homework.

She had exactly fourteen days of stay-up-late, sleep-till-noon freedom. The last thing she wanted to do was sit among the people she worked with, talking shop and eating mac and cheese casseroles and platters of cold cuts.

She had fun on her mind, and it came in the form of a girls' night out with Kate, her sister Kelly—who'd just flown in for Christmas from Chicago—and Maggie, the good friend and owner-slash-cocktail-waitress of the bar they'd chosen to invade for the occasion.

Emma needed a distraction. One that would take her mind off the fact that she was thirty-two years old and spending yet another Christmas alone. Her last *real* date had, oddly enough, been with Kate's now-husband. Matt Ryan had been the nicest man Emma had gone out with in a long time. They'd gotten along well. But she couldn't begrudge him for ending up with Kate. That destiny had started way back in high school. Matt might have tried to forget the woman he'd loved since forever ago, but once Kate had come back to town, he'd been toast. Just the way those two looked into each other's eyes made it clear who they belonged to and with.

Emma wanted that.

She wanted love from a man who couldn't live without her. A man who would look at her every day like she was the most important person in his world. She wanted a man she could trust with her heart and never fear he would stomp it into dust.

She wanted the dream.

She wanted forever.

On the way home she stopped at the Gas and Grub to fill her tank and grab a bottle of wine, just in case the party flowed over to her house. She topped off at the pump, then ran through the snow and inside the store. Down the potato chip and beer-nut aisle she chose a bottle of zinfandel, then grabbed a large bag of the kettle corn Mrs. Patterson cooked up daily to supply to local businesses. Further down the aisle, packages of Hershey's and mini Reese's stopped her in her tracks. The G & G's glass doors swung open and icy air whooshed down the aisle. Deep in her chocolate selections, she shivered when the atmosphere behind her shifted and a tingle slinked down her spine.

"Party planning?"

Emma's head jerked up. She turned to find six feet-plus of

trouble behind her. So close she could smell the snow on his parka. His warmth. His aftershave. And a good dose of virile male. "Maybe."

He flashed his Mr. Perfect smile. "Am I invited?"

"I don't think so." She swung her attention back to her choice between peanut butter cups and chocolate kisses, with a hope and a prayer he'd just go away. She should have known better.

"Aw, come on. I thought we were friends," he said.

She looked up. "Seriously?"

"I helped you trim your tree."

"And I thanked you for that."

"You could thank me again by inviting me to your party."

"I don't think you'd be interested."

"Are you kidding? I was looking for something to do. I came in here for—"

"Dirty magazines?"

He laughed with three deep *huh-huh-huh*s. "No, but that's not a bad idea. So where's the party?"

Smart enough to know he'd never leave unless she gave him some kind of response, Emma relented. "I'm meeting a few friends for a girls' night out. I just needed a few supplies in case they all come over after we close down the bars. There. Are you satisfied?"

"I could be if you tell me your *girls' night* includes a sleepover in see-through nighties."

"Your sisters are coming."

"Oh. Damn." He whacked himself in the forehead. "I'll have to burn that image out of my head."

She laughed. She couldn't help it.

He reached past her and the bags of Hershey's, grabbed a bag of Reese's and tossed it on her pile. "No kisses unless I'm included." He snatched a pack of beef jerky from the shelf, then turned. His cowboy boots thudded on the tile floor as he strolled away. Emma watched until his wide shoulders and lean Levi's butt disappeared around the end cap before she took a deep breath.

Much as she hated to admit it, Dean Silverthorne was one fine-looking man.

The trouble was he knew it.

"Shut up! You did not!" Maggie squealed.

Emma laughed at Kate's flabbergasted expression.

The Naughty Irish was hip-to-hip deep with holiday revelers and those who'd come in to catch the cover band from Missoula currently tearing it up with a tasty version of Skynyrd's *Freebird*. The place was loud and rowdy and Emma immersed herself in the fun.

"I did," Kelly, a lawyer and in general a quite subdued person, admitted. "At least I think I did."

"Lester Crabtree might be old but he does hold a certain outdoorsy appeal." Kate wrinkled her nose at her sister over the rim of her glass. "Guess that's one of those times you can thank God for the alcohol."

"I'm sure Mr. Crabtree enjoyed your flirtatiousness." Emma patted Kelly on the hand. "Although Edna Price put in her two cents' worth as well. I noticed a lot of flirting at that reception."

"Yeah. When you weren't dodging our brother's not-so-subtle passes," Kate chimed in.

Emma flinched. Many things had happened that night. But Dean Silverthorne making passes at her? Not one of them.

"I noticed Kelly didn't leave the reception alone." Unaware that she'd just rescued Emma, Maggie leaned further into the scratched-up table. "So give us the down and dirty details on the hunky James Harley."

Kelly's big eyes widened. "I . . . ummm."

Emma's ears perked up. Was it vulgar to live vicariously? And when had been the last time *she'd* had sex? Hmmm. When one couldn't remember the last time, then no, it wasn't vulgar. Pathetic? Without a doubt.

"Was he as good as he looks?" Maggie asked eagerly. When all eyes turned on her, she threw her hands up and said, "Hey, three kids, married ten years, too tired to have sex. I get to ask. So was he?"

Kelly took the Fifth. The rest of the women at the table took her silence as verification, with a big red check next to *hell yeah.*

"Well then, ladies." Maggie raised her glass. "To good sex."

They all raised their glasses.

"No. How about . . . to *great* sex," Kate amended, and the glasses clinked.

At that moment Deputy Matt Ryan and Deputy-in-question James Harley strolled toward their table. It could have been coincidence. But in a town the size of a peanut shell, happenstance did not exist.

"Speaking of great sex." Kate's inebriated cheeks flushed with pleasure at the sight of her new husband.

Kelly's gaze darted around the bar for a place to hide. But men in uniforms who carried guns were much quicker on their feet. Much to Kelly's dismay. Kate's sister suddenly became very interested in the red straw dipped into her rum and coke.

"You ladies having a good time?" James asked.

"It depends on whether my husband lets me use the handcuffs later," Kate said.

Matt leaned down and said against her ear, "Uh-uh. My turn tonight, beautiful."

"Even better." Kate raised her hand to cup Matt's cheek and he kissed her fingers.

Emma smiled at the familiarity in the couple's touch, the effortlessness in which they could tease. Someday, she hoped, she would know that, too.

"Good evening, counselor," James leaned his handsome face down over Kelly's shoulder. "You need a personal escort home tonight?" *Preferably to my house.*

Okay, so maybe James hadn't said those words, but Emma heard them all the same.

Kelly looked up, and though a blush brushed her cheeks, desire darkened her green eyes. "No. Thanks. I'm good."

James gave her a smile that said he agreed.

Good Lord. Emma felt like a complete voyeur. The air thickened with sexual tension till she thought she'd explode. She wanted to grab Kelly and tell her to take that man with the gorgeous brown eyes home and give him what he practically begged for. Then again, it looked like maybe she already had and he'd come back for a second taste.

"Let me know if you change your mind." James rose to his full height and told Matt, "I'll take a look around. Meet you outside."

Emma didn't want to be envious. She really didn't. It didn't mean there weren't still a few decent-looking single guys left in Deer Lick. There were. Looks didn't mean a lot in the full spectrum of life. But she'd yet to find one that looked at her in that adoring way Matt looked at Kate. Or even the hungry way James had looked at Kelly. Did she need to move to a bigger town just to find a man?

Great. Now she sounded envious *and* desperate.

"You ladies about ready for your DD to give you a ride home?" Matt asked.

"Oh, is it that time already?" Kate whined.

Matt shrugged. "I can come back later. But I'll only be able to transport two of you at a time."

"Oh, sweetie, you don't need to go through all that trouble," Kate said. "Ollie has Mags covered and Emma is going home with—"

"Me."

Emma looked up and about lost her socks when she found Mr. Perfect looking right back.

Dean had stood in the pool room while Boyd Palmer and Jason Ward battled it out on the green felt. His hands had twitched to grab a stick and join them. But in the scheme of things, a perfect spiral into the end zone held more importance than knocking the number-six ball into the corner pocket.

Good thing he hadn't played anyway. His attention had been completely distracted by the table-for-four across the bar.

Emma and company—drinking and giggling and discussing god-knew-what that had made feminine eyebrows lift and dip. Dean had been raised with two sisters who gossiped, sparred, and cried on each other's shoulders. He should be used to girl chatter. But that had been as a boy. As a man, he saw them in a whole different light.

As girls they'd been careful what they said in front of anyone, for fear of being judged. As women they weren't afraid. Others could feel free to judge if they snorted soda through their nose when they laughed, if their hair was out of place, or if they had to unbutton the top of their jeans (thank you, Maggie) when they'd consumed too much beer.

These women were beautiful and animated and having a great time. They were in their element. Dean felt as though he were watching a silent TV sitcom. More than once they'd made him laugh out loud. But it was the curvy blond in the tight jeans straddling the chair backward who had held him captive. It was the way her smile broke all the way across her face until it reached those amazing blue eyes. Or even the way she tilted her head and her straight hair tumbled like a ripple of water across the shoulder of her snug pink sweater. Before he could stop himself, he'd headed in her direction without a clue about what to say. His brilliant baby sister had offered up the perfect opportunity.

"Are you stalking me?" Emma looked up at him and asked.

"Just having a beer with the boys. Overheard my brother-in-law's dilemma." His gaze slipped down to those snug jeans. No muffin top for the schoolmarm. "Thought I'd help out."

"That's really nice of you, Dean," Maggie said. "See, girls, he's not the big arrogant ass you all thought."

"Mags!" Both Kate's and Kelly's eyes widened even as they giggled.

Dean laughed. He leaned down and bussed Maggie's chubby cheek with a kiss. "And it's thanks to down-to-earth people like you who keep me humble." The band launched into James Otto's slow and sexy *Just Got Started Lovin' You* and the appeal of holding Emma in his arms was too much to ignore. He held out his hand. "How about a dance first?"

She didn't need words to convey her displeasure at his suggestion or his out-of-the-blue offer for a ride home. Emma's eyes had a way of turning almost purple when she wasn't quite pleased. Which only made him wonder what color her eyes would turn when she *was* pleased.

She took a sip of her girly drink and set the empty glass down. "I don't think so."

"Aw, come on. You turned me down once. Do you really want to bruise my ego a second time?"

"Don't buy into that, Em," Kate said. "His ego is made of solid steel."

"Indestructible," Kelly added.

"But it does look good in a pair of jeans," Maggie tossed in and everyone laughed.

Emma looked up at him again. "Fine. This is my favorite song anyway."

"Excuse us," he said to the five pairs of eyes glued to them. He set his beer down on the table and took Emma by the hand, lifting her from her chair and pulling her out onto the crowded dance floor. He drew her against himself and had to find his footing in the rhythm of the song. She felt amazing in his arms. Soft and warm and . . . damn.

"You don't need to worry about taking me home. I can get a ride with my friends."

"Your friends are gone."

Her head whipped around toward the now-empty table. "Oh." A sigh lifted her shoulders as she looked back up and tried to put some space between them. He was smart enough not to let that happen and tucked her deeper into his arms. The sweet cushion of her breasts pressed against his chest. Her hand felt small in his. And the top of her head barely came to his chin. But he liked the way she fit. "How tall are you anyway?"

"Five-three. Why?"

"You're short."

"I am not. You're just used to those supermodels with all those legs and no brains."

"Now why would you want to go stereotyping like that? The last woman I dated had a BA."

"I'm guessing that's the same as T & A?"

"Great song, isn't it?" He sidestepped the remark and guided her through the dance. God, she was soft. In a very good way. No offense to the women he dated, but they were all hard-bodied. They worked out, ate little, and worked out some more. Not an ounce of their flesh would conform to the contour of his hand. Emma was soft and rounded. With her breasts pressed against his chest and his arms holding her close, she felt the way he always believed a woman should feel.

What they were doing on that dance floor could hardly be called dancing. Swaying in place was more like it. The two-stepping couples who shared the space had to dodge and maneuver around them.

"So, how long have you been here tonight?" she asked.

"Long enough to watch you make a face when you downed the Jell-O shooter."

"Uck." She shivered. "Why do people think those taste so good?"

"They don't. They just want a fast way to get trashed. Which usually translates into an excuse for Bohemian-like behavior they will regret the next day."

"Something you know from experience?" Her body moved against his and made it hard to think.

"There are a lot of college weekends I can't seem to remember." He chuckled. "In fact, I did a lot of crazy shit in college I'd be better off *not* remembering. How about you?"

"I was too busy hitting the books."

"Don't tell me you were one of those who missed all the keggers in exchange for good grades."

"I went to one. Didn't ever see a need to go back."

"No?"

She shook her head and her silky hair slid across the back of his hand.

"Think of all the fun you missed."

Something briefly clouded her eyes before she said, "Not really my kind of fun."

The song ended and she stepped away from his embrace. "I guess you can take me home now."

"You sure? I can buy you another drink."

"Nope. I'm done." She slipped her hand from his and while her tight blue jeans sauntered away from him, he couldn't help but wonder when the playful banter had turned to something . . . more.

With a shake of his head he followed her and helped her on with her seen-better-days parka. The same parka she'd worn the night he'd almost mowed her down on his way to Kate's house. Then he escorted her through the crowded bar and outside into the icy night air.

For the first time in days, the sky was a clear, velvety black. The Milky Way lit up the dark like a path across the heavens as he led her through the parked cars toward his mother's bomber.

"You know." Emma tucked her gloved hands into the pockets of her coat. "I really don't live that far. I can just walk."

"Oh, I see. You're embarrassed to ride in my mother's hot rod."

She slid a quick glance across the parking lot to the rusted beast. "No, I'm not. I just—"

"Good. Because my mother loved that car. And I know she'd be happy for it to see you safely home."

"I've seen the way you drive. My safe arrival home is doubtful."

He laughed. "Regardless. I couldn't live with myself if I let you walk and something happened to you."

"This is Deer Lick. What could happen?"

"You could get taken out by a four-point buck."

"Fine." She relented with a smile. "You can drive me home."

"It would be my pleasure."

While they drove through town, Emma silently stared out her window. The few times he tried to engage her in conversation had been met with an "Uh-huh" or "Hmmm." Which left Dean to wonder what might be going on in that obviously intelligent mind of hers.

As he pulled the car into her driveway she broke her silence and surprised him with her concern.

"How are you doing with your shoulder?"

He turned off the car and looked over at her. "Better."

"I imagine you'll be good as new in no time."

"Funny you should say that. Everyone else has doubts I'll ever be able to throw a long bomb into the end zone again."

She turned her head toward him and even through the darkness he could see the tiny furrows between her brows. "Well, that's stupid."

He fought a smile at her stubborn tone. "Why's that?"

"Because you won't let anything stop you from what you want. You're an NFL quarterback. It's what you've worked for your entire life. Doesn't matter what any doctor says, you won't back down from what you want."

She was defending him? A strange tickle fluttered through his chest. And then she smiled and his heart melted like a snow cone on a summer day. "That's the nicest thing you've ever said to me."

She gathered up her purse and reached for the door handle. "Yeah, well, don't let it go to your head."

"Wait there," he told her. "I'll get that." Oddly enough she stayed put. He went around and opened her door. She slid out of the car, furry snow boots first. While she stood in front of him, a long moment passed. He looked down into her eyes and his heart danced a funny step.

Her straight blond hair smelled of honeysuckle. Her skin was smooth and flawless. Her lips, full and pink. If he wanted to see eye to eye with her, he'd need to lift her by the front of her coat.

Emma Hart was the type of woman who took care of sick relatives or baked cookies for fundraisers. The type of woman who needed a ring on her finger. She wasn't *his* type. At all. Still, she intrigued him. Maybe because she made him laugh. Or because she wouldn't take any crap from him. Or maybe because even though she held some kind of grudge against him, she'd just shown him the one generosity few others had managed in recent days.

Faith.

"Thanks for the ride, superstar." She gave him a little pat on his chest and turned toward her front porch.

Dean caught her hand and spun her back toward him. She ended up against him with both palms planted on his chest. He cupped her face and looked down into the confusion that clouded her eyes. Then without further thought or argument he lowered his mouth to hers.

Her lips were cool but just as soft as he'd imagined. Softer. It was just a brief touch of their mouths as he held her face between his hands as if she were breakable. But even as his heart pounded and his body lusted, he'd never been a forceful man. He'd never taken what hadn't been offered, even when every law of nature had tribal drums beating through his blood.

Her small hands pushed against his chest and she drew her head back. Everything inside him stilled. The man inside him wanted more. Craved more. Needed more. His hands slipped to her small waist.

She looked up, brows pulled together, and studied his face. "I don't like you," she whispered.

"I know." His gaze dropped to her mouth. "But please kiss me anyway."

She searched his eyes for what seemed like forever. When he expected her to push him further away, she slid her hands up his chest and around his neck.

Then she did exactly as he asked.

The initial kiss was a mere press of her lips, and she was gone before he even got started. She leaned her head back, looked up at him again, then came back for more. This time the kiss was slow and eased through him like a drug, warming him and igniting his every nerve like a row of stadium lights popping on at dusk. Lust rolled over him in breath-stealing waves as she fed him a hot, wet, open-mouthed kiss that tasted like pineapples and maraschino cherries and desire. Their tongues touched, mated, and fought for dominance.

In that battle he didn't give a damn who won.

He slid his arm around her back and brought her up onto her toes, brought her body against him. Her fingers combed through his hair and she pressed herself even closer. The tingles in his scalp moved all the way down through his heart. Then she moaned a sound of frustration and excitement and want and need. He cupped her bottom and pushed his erection against her. The heat of her body made him forget they stood in the middle of her driveway. She made him forget he dated long-legged models and not short, sassy schoolteachers. She made him forget everything in his life that had been lost.

God, he wanted her. So bad.

He wanted to take her in that house, lay her down on a bed, and make love to her until she *did* like him. And then he'd make love to her some more. Just to be sure.

Too soon, she broke away. His heart pounded as she tilted her head back and swept her tongue across her bottom lip. Then without a word she slipped from his arms and headed toward her front door.

When she reached the top step, sanity roared back. "Hey," he said softly.

She turned slowly to look at him. The moisture of their kiss still glistened on her lips.

Damn.

"Why are you always running away from me, Emma? What are you afraid of?"

Her hesitation made his heart pound a little harder.

"I don't know what you think you want from me," she said. "But I don't play games. And I don't want any part of any of yours."

She disappeared into the house. After her front door shut him out, Dean stood in the middle of her driveway, his back pressed against his mother's car. Arms empty. Body aching. Heart hammering.

Who knew his little schoolteacher contained so much passion?

And who knew he'd be such a willing student?

He considered himself a man of the world, primed with experience and knowledge.

But that kiss?

That kiss had rocked him right off the axis of his perfectly planned universe.

At two in the afternoon the following day, Emma sat at a long table just inside the bookstore in Bozeman, surrounded by rolls of holiday gift wrap, bags of bows, and leftover crafting odds and ends that would put a personal spin on the packages she would wrap to benefit the Alzheimer's Association. The previous year she'd been able to collect enough tips and hand over five hundred dollars. She hoped to add at least another hundred to her jar by day's end. Anything that could add to the research coffers to find a cure for the disease that was slowly stealing her Memaw away would be great.

As she finished up wrapping an entire detective series a woman was gifting to her private investigator husband, an elderly couple strolled up to her table. The man had his hand placed at the woman's back. Though he looked to be about seventy years old and had a belt cinched in tight to hold up his high-water pants, he had that *This is my woman, isn't she beautiful?* look in his eye. They were so cute Emma immediately wanted to adopt them. At the same time a pang tangled around her heart. She wished her Memaw had found that kind of love again after her grandfather had died in a farming accident. Yet over and over her grandmother had insisted that there would only be one man for her. Emma wondered if she still remembered the fierceness of the love she'd had for Leroy Hart. Emma wondered if her Memaw remembered him at all.

"Can I help you?" she asked.

The woman set a pile of books down on the table, looked up, and grinned. "Can you wrap all these individually? I promise to tip good. Lost my sister to Alzheimer's three years ago. Count my blessings every day."

Emma felt a sting in her eyes. Before she turned into a blubbering fool she picked up the stack of books and smiled. "Wow. Somebody likes romance."

"Oh, you bet," the husband answered. "Bertie here joined a reader group that just devours these books."

Bertie chuckled. "Stanley won't admit it, but he's part of the group."

Intrigued, Emma asked, "Are you the only gentleman?"

"So far. But I don't expect that will last long, once the guys figure out where the women in our town disappear to every Thursday night. Plus, it just gives me more time to spend with Bertie."

Okay, how cute was that?

"Well good for you." Emma picked up the rolls of paper. "Do any of these gift wraps speak to you?"

"Hmmm." Bertie studied the rolls, tapping her chin. "How about you surprise me. I may be old but I don't mind getting caught off guard once in a while. Makes life more interesting, don't you think?"

"Absolutely," Emma agreed before she realized she'd somehow removed the element of surprise in her life and replaced it with safe and sane.

"Here's a list of names to put on the tags." Bertie held out a scrap of paper. "Doesn't matter which one goes to who. They'll get passed around anyway."

Emma took the list. "Can you give me about fifteen minutes to get these done?"

"You bet." Stanley looked at his wife and grinned. "I'm going to treat this gorgeous woman to a mocha over at the coffee spot."

Emma watched the couple walk away hand-in-hand, and she wondered how long they'd been together. With a little sigh, she looked down at the books in her hands. *Whoa, baby.* She raised the one on top for closer inspection. In the gritty cover image you couldn't see the top of the man's head—only his strong chin and sensuous mouth. But the half-naked body that came below that nearly stole her breath. Wide shoulders. Broad chest. An *eight*-pack perfectly shadowed by professional lighting. And a pair of loose exercise pants hanging super-low on lean hips. In his gloved hands? A football.

Her mind immediately dashed in the direction of another football player.

Surprise.

If you'd asked her a million times why Dean Silverthorne kept popping up on her radar, she'd have had a million different responses. Not one of them would ever have been that he'd wanted to kiss her. He'd caught her off guard last night. *Way* off guard.

Would Bertie consider that interesting?

Emma had.

When Dean's mouth had covered hers, everything inside her went off like a bottle rocket. And when he'd asked her to kiss him back, she'd jumped at the chance with springs on both feet. How had she let that happen? She didn't like the man.

Yes, he was gorgeous. Yes, he had an incredible body. Well, at least, through those tight pants he wore on the football field he looked incredible. And, yes, he was a confident man. But sometimes he made these goofy remarks that just made her scratch her head. Fortunately he seemed able to laugh at himself. In fact, he laughed a lot. Emma had to admit that the times she'd been around him, he did not act like the overpaid playboy superstar athlete she saw in entertainment news. In fact, there were times she even forgot he was the man who played a brutal game for a living, a man who could calmly step back while a thousand pounds of flesh charged toward him. She forgot he was the man who escorted Victoria's Secret models to galas and gorgeous actresses to movie premieres.

It had been a long time since she'd been held in a man's arms the way Dean had held her. Like he wanted to keep her there for a good, long time. Like he wanted to use those strong hands to possess her and to make her come undone in his arms. It had been a long time since a man had kissed her like he wanted to eat her up. It had been a long, long, time since she'd wanted to tear her clothes off, throw caution to the wind, and just let go.

Silly thought. Emma knew of the repercussions of letting go. There were lonesome nights filled with tears and regret and heartaches so deep they felt like they might never heal. She'd been a foolish girl the summer she was eighteen. She'd never been a part of the "in" crowd. She'd tried. But most mothers had morals. And her mother's reputation had prevented Emma from being allowed to associate with their daughters. But that summer, Dean Silverthorne had brought home a football buddy from college, and Emma immediately became smitten. Nick Harris had been cute, and smart, and strong. The times she'd seen him in town, he'd flirted with her. The night he'd invited her out to the bonfire party she'd broken her Memaw's rules. She'd snuck out and gone to meet her crush.

She'd learned her lesson that night about the love-'em-and-leave-'em type. But that was years ago. And she'd moved on.

For years she'd been too busy with getting her degree to get involved with anyone. After that, her time had been consumed with building her career and making her mark in the education process in her small town. After that, she'd had to take care of her grandmother.

Since then she'd only made a half-assed attempt at finding a man to love. She was thirty-two years old and not getting any younger. Maybe she should look into a dating service and get serious in her search. Time to let go of the stigma of her mother's shameful behavior and subsequent abandonment. It didn't take a thermonuclear physicist to know she was nothing like the woman who'd given her life. Nothing like the man who'd been the other half of that equation and whom she'd never met.

She deserved to be happy, didn't she? A relationship like that wouldn't just show up at her front door. She had to go out and explore the possibilities. She didn't want just a one-night stand. She wanted a man who would love her and cherish her. A man who would fill her days with laughter and her nights with passion.

The very last man on earth capable of that task?

Mr. Perfect.

"Oh, that's a good one."

Emma's head came up at the female voice coming from across the table and she realized she was still standing there with the romance book in her hand.

"I just finished reading it last night," the twenty-something woman sporting the boho look said. "The hero? Unbelievable. I never thought the heroine would wrangle him into her way of thinking, but she did."

"But this is only fiction," Emma protested nicely.

"All fiction is based on a certain amount of truth. At least that's what my mother always tells me." The twentysomething grinned as if she had some kind of personal knowledge. "So I'm going to believe that there's a hero out there for every woman. Someone perfect, just for her. And all she has to do is pay attention."

Emma watched the young woman walk away, then she grabbed a roll of dancing-Santa paper and began to wrap Bertie's books.

All she has to do is pay attention.

If only it were that easy.

Chapter Seven

On Christmas night, Dean reluctantly put on his dress pants and shirt and climbed into his mother's car. Kate and Matt had decided to draw out the holiday by inviting friends and family out to the lake house for a get-together. He'd thought the festivities were over that morning when the newlyweds had bombarded their father's house with their presence and presents. Kate had dragged him and Kelly out of bed to have an old-style family Christmas. But without their mother, Dean hadn't felt like celebrating.

Letty Silverthorne had always gone overboard with the holidays. Christmas had been her favorite. She'd over-decorated, over-cooked, over-bought gifts. She'd been the queen of indulgence. After the opening of the presents, her Christmas breakfasts had been twenty-course meals. Pancakes, waffles, eggs, bacon, sausage, fritters, muffins, biscuits and gravy, and homemade huckleberry syrup and jam for their family and friends and neighbors or anyone who wanted to join in. She'd always woken at the crack of dawn to make sure things were perfect. On this particular Christmas morning, without her buzzing through the kitchen or snatching up discarded wrapping paper or refilling coffee mugs, it just wasn't the same.

Dean wished he hadn't come home.

Anxious to give Kate a hand, his father had taken the truck and gone on ahead of him. So flying solo, Dean twisted the key in the ignition of the car that still smelled like vanilla. Still had a back seat piled with pastry cookbooks and knitting and quilting supplies. With a heavy heart he headed toward the lake.

Being Christmas night, the streets were deserted as he drove through town. When he passed Spotted Fawn he thought of a particular schoolteacher who'd managed to avoid him for days. Chances she'd be at Kate's tonight were good. Chances she'd give him the time of day? Not so good.

"It's been a marvelous day."

Dean almost ran up onto the sidewalk at the abrupt sound of his mother's voice. He pulled to the curb and turned around in his seat. Her glow was a brilliant rosy gold tonight and the smile she wore he'd been blessed to see a thousand wonderful times.

"Merry Christmas, Son."

"Merry Christmas, Mom."

She laughed. "What? No denial tonight? No 'I'm losing my mind and need to see a shrink' babble?"

"It's your favorite holiday. I don't care if I'm crazy," he said. "I'm just glad to see you."

She leaned forward. "And I'm so glad to be seen."

He smiled. "Who'd have thought it possible?"

"Not me." She planted her transparent hand against her

transparent chest. "Though I admit I am kind of used to it now. I seem to be in much better control of my landings. Still occasionally off on my timing though." She shook her head and grinned as if she had a specific moment in mind. "Are you headed out to Kate and Matt's?"

"Yes. Dad is already there."

"Oh, I know, honey. The pumpkin pie he made looked wonderful. Just wish I could have smelled it. And Kate has her house decorated so beautifully. Who knew she'd take after me?"

"*You* knew," Dean said with affection. "The only reason you and her argued so much was because you were just too damn much alike."

She nodded and a smug smile tilted her mouth. "She's so happy now. Not like before when she *thought* she had everything she wanted."

"She does seem to be over the moon."

"Ha! Understatement. And how are you doing, Son? How's the shoulder? And before you say anything, I want you to be truthful, not give me the same line of BS you feed everyone else. Don't forget, I gave birth to you. I know when you're lying."

"What about all those times I snuck out the bedroom window?"

"Among other atrocities. You think I didn't know about that stuff? Of course I did. But you had to learn. And you had to grow up. And the only way you could do that was the hard way. I think we just got lucky you dodged the bullet so many times."

"Does that mean my number is about to be up?"

She shrugged. "So how are you?"

"Fine."

"Cut the crap. How's your shoulder?"

"Hurts like hell."

"I'll bet it does. Do you remember when you were a freshman at USC and you were chomping at the bit to be the starting quarterback?"

"Of course."

"Do you remember all those phone conversations we had of deciphering exactly what your coach was really telling you?"

"Yes. And your point is?"

"The answer today is the same as it was then. Patience. Right now it's time to sit back in the pocket a little longer than you're used to and look out over the options."

"Hard to look at the options when the doctor won't even let me start working the shoulder out for another few weeks."

"What if it doesn't heal?" his mother asked.

"It'll heal."

"But what if it doesn't. What will you do?"

"You know me, Mom. I don't think in those terms. I don't accept defeat."

"I also taught you to be a reasonable man. Just because you want something or won't accept something doesn't make it any less a fact. Look at me. One minute I was putting on my apron, the next I was looking down at myself, wondering if maybe I should have invested in a little Botox over the years. You think if I had the choice I'd have let that heart attack take me out?"

"No."

"You're darn tootin' I wouldn't have. I wanted to be able to rock away the years on the back patio with your daddy, watching sunrises and sunsets. I wanted to be able to see all my children get married and have grandchildren I could love and spoil rotten. Life is about so much more than football, honey." She reached up and a whisper of cold air brushed his cheek. "*You* are about so much more than football. In the days to come, I want you to remember that."

"I don't want to let you down, Mom."

"The only way you would let me down, Son, is if you didn't stay true to yourself. Promise me that you will."

Dean sighed. "I promise."

"Good. Give your daddy a kiss for me," she said and was gone.

His mother had spent years teaching him about life, helping him run through plays, and he'd always accepted everything she said as good advice. But for once his mother was wrong.

Without football he was zilch.

"It's about time you got here." Kate shoved a bottle of Sam Adams at him.

"I had a small detour." Dean accepted the beer, handed her his coat, and gave her pup who'd also greeted him a pat on the head. Then he brought himself up and he scanned the crowded room. From the looks of it, his sister had invited anyone in town who didn't have a prior post-Christmas engagement. She'd also picked up his mother's talent for overdecorating. Funny. He knew another Deer Lick resident with the same issue. Must be something in the water.

"Meaning what?" Kate asked. "You had a flat tire? You hit a deer? You had a conversation with our dead mother? What?"

Dean whipped his head around. "What did you say?"

Kate flashed a smile. "I said you need to go mingle or at least stop Edna from holding mistletoe over everyone's heads. I don't even want to know what that crazy old woman will be like on New Year's Eve."

"That's not what you said."

His sister folded his coat over her arm. "So how is Mom tonight?"

He leaned in. "Are we supposed to admit we know about her?"

"Like we can ignore the facts? Come on, big brother, you don't want to ride that crazy train all alone, do you?"

"No. And thanks for giving me prior warning about the fact that she stills pops in even though she's been gone for four months. I about wrecked the car the first time."

"Guess I was lucky then. I was parked in front of the Shack."

"Does she ever *pop* into other places?"

Kate shrugged. "A few. Mostly her car is a sure thing. I think it gives her some kind of woo woo power." She gave him a little pat on the arm. "We can talk about the weirdness that is Mom later. Right now I want you to go mingle. Enjoy yourself. Especially since you're only here on borrowed time."

Dean shook his head as his sister walked away. What was weird was that his sister talked about their mother's ghost popping in and out and giving advice like it was just a normal everyday thing.

He took a pull from the bottle of beer, then stepped into the living room to be greeted by a round of handshakes and pats on the back. Dean found his father chatting with Woody Blake about the new hunting regulations. When his father reached out to shake his hand, Dean pulled him into a bear hug. Then he gave his father a kiss on the cheek.

His father chuckled. "What's that for?"

"Just passing on the love, Dad."

Moments later a hand snagged him by the arm and pulled him into a spirited exchange about his brother-in-law's chances in the upcoming election for Deer Lick Sheriff. Not that Dean would be around when it came time to cast a vote—and not that he wasn't behind Matt 100 percent—but Dean found the discussion a distraction from the conversation he really wanted to have. With a blonde who'd probably tell him what elevator he could take straight to hell.

True, he'd kissed her. But she'd blown the right to complain by kissing him back. As far as he could see, they were even. Then again, he always played his best game when he had to come from behind.

While the election debate heated up, Dean sipped his beer and nodded his head at the appropriate times, just waiting for the perfect moment to escape. When Edna Price barged in with a sprig of mistletoe, he found his break.

He wandered through the expansive room, stopping to chat, answer football-related questions, and maintain his good-old-boy status. He'd searched from corner to corner but found no sign of Emma. Maybe she hadn't come after all. Surely Kate had invited her.

He turned, and through the corner of his eye caught a

flash of white outside the double glass doors. On the deck Emma stood in a creamy wool coat, talking to a tall man with the shoulders of a linebacker. In her mitten-wrapped hand she held a half-empty glass of red wine. On her face was the smile that never failed to kick him in the gut.

Dean didn't like the idea that she shared that smile with someone other than him. And he didn't like the way the man smiled back. On his way out the door, Dean traded his empty beer for a new bottle. In football, timing the pass was imperative. In real life as well.

Just as the man leaned in to whisper in Emma's ear, Dean stepped out onto the deck. "Well, if it isn't Jesse Hamilton."

The man turned with a frown as though he'd been interrupted from something significant. Like a kiss? Dean congratulated himself on his skillful stoppage of play.

"I haven't seen you for what?" Dean extended his hand. "Ten? Twelve years?" Jesse reciprocated while Emma's arms folded across her pretty white coat.

"Heard you were back in town." Jesse pulled his hand away and settled it at the small of Emma's back. "Sorry, though, we were just about to go back inside. Emma's gotten a little cold."

If you aren't man enough to keep her warm, then back the fuck off. Dean leaned a hip against the rail and turned on the magic. "It's a beautiful night." He lifted his hand in an arc to draw attention to the way the moonlight glistened on the snow and made it glitter like diamonds. "Emma, maybe you'd like to trade that glass of cold wine for a nice hot buttered rum?"

"Would you like to stay out here?" Jesse asked Emma. "Well . . ."

"Then I'll be right back," Jesse said.

"You sure?" Dean interjected. "Because I'd be happy to go get one for her."

The flash in Jesse's eyes said he'd caught on to the game. "Nope. I'm good." He gave Emma's sleeve a little tug. "I'll be right back."

As soon as the door closed behind him, Emma turned to Dean. "Wow. That's a first."

"For what?"

"I've never been caught in the middle of a pissing match before."

"What?" He clapped a hand to his chest. "Honey, I just saved you from a boring conversation. Weren't you bored? I saw you out here and you looked bored. And I said, 'Now, Dean, there's a woman who looks like she could use rescuing.'"

She pursed those sexy lips. "Well, aren't you just a saint."

"Sorry. Wrong team. I'm a Stallion."

"Among other things." She looked away toward the lake.

"So what were you and old Jesse talking about that had you looking so vaguely interested?"

"In case you don't know, *old* Jesse owns the farm supply store," she said, like she was announcing the man owned the universe. "We were discussing brands of cat food."

"Wow. Cat food? Really?"

"Oscar needs to lose a little weight and I was asking Jesse's advice," Emma said in a defensive tone.

"Honey, that cat doesn't need to lose a *little* weight. He looks like he's been eating for three." Deane took a pull from his beer and licked a drop from his top lip.

"He's not that fat."

"He's *fat*. I'll bet he can barely squeeze into that elf suit."

She shook her head and glanced down at the snow-tipped toes of her boots. "What are you doing, Dean?"

"Just thought I'd come out and see how you were doing. New coat?" He touched her sleeve, thinking instead he'd like to run his hands up inside that coat and touch her warm skin. Touch her all over.

"It's a Christmas gift to myself. And why would you care how I'm doing? You don't like me."

"It looks good on you." He lifted the beer and took a drink. Smiling he lifted a finger off the bottle and pointed to her. "Want to bet?"

"Bet?"

"On whether I like you or not."

"I don't gamble."

"Oh, come on. It would be fun. And the prize could be . . . if I win, you go out with me. If you win, I go out with you."

"So, *you* would just win. No matter what."

"Can't blame a guy for trying to bend the odds in his favor."

She tried to fight back a smile.

He wished she wouldn't try so hard.

"Sorry," she said. "Not interested."

"You were interested the other night."

"I was drunk the other night."

"You didn't taste drunk. You didn't smell drunk. And you definitely didn't feel drunk."

"And I think all those pain pills you take have messed up your head."

"Well, that would be a good excuse if I were actually taking any pain pills. But I'm not."

"Then I'm really sorry for the damage that hit to the turf did to your brain."

He laughed. God, he loved her quick comebacks. He looked at her. Studied her shiny hair, her warm eyes, her straight nose, smooth skin, and those soft, full lips he'd now tasted and wanted to taste again. "Why have you been avoiding me?"

Her head came up. "I haven't been avoiding you. I've been busy. I have classes to plan and I'm trying to get caught up on the thesis for my degree."

"Your degree? If you're a teacher don't you already have one?"

I have a bachelor's degree. I'm working on my master's."

"Because?"

"I'd like to expand into special education. Working with kids like Brenden has inspired me to want to know more so I can help them more."

"You're an impressive woman, Emma Hart."

"I'm nothing of the kind. I just have goals."

"Meaning I don't?"

"Sure you do. It's just that your life and your goals are a thousand miles away. You're a temporary fixture. And just because you're the brother of one of my closest friends, I don't think I need to answer to you about where I've been or what I've been doing."

"You're right." He reached for her hand and when she didn't pull away he felt a shot of courage. "I just thought after the other night—"

"You thought what? That I'd melt in your arms like all those other women?"

He caressed the back of her hand with his thumb. "I could have sworn there was some melting going on."

"Nothing has changed from the night of Kate's reception, Dean. I'm still the same small-town woman. I'm still only five-foot-three. And in comparison to the arm candy you escort around, I'm still completely forgettable. So do us both a favor."

"What's that, honey?"

"*You* don't try to pretend like you're attracted to me and *I* won't try to pretend like I'm flattered that you might find me tolerable enough to help you pass the time while you're stuck here in Deer Lick."

She withdrew her hand from his. "And please stop calling me honey."

Dean watched her disappear into the house and instantly the temperature dropped twenty degrees.

She was wrong.

Nothing about her was forgettable.

Not one damn thing.

CHAPTER EIGHT

"What's got you so tangled up inside, Son?"

Dean looked across the living room—which hadn't been redecorated since Jimmy Carter sat in the Oval Office—to his father, who sat in a worn recliner enjoying a rare day off. Deep furrows creased his father's forehead and the corners of his eyes. What little hair remained on his head was gray and stuck up like weeds. The man looked exhausted. And lonely.

Even with his shoulder and career in shreds, Dean knew his own troubles were only half of what his dad had been through. Dean realized that he'd come back home to escape the pile of crap his life had become when he really should have come home for his dad. After all the years his father had been there for him, Dean knew it was his time to return the favor.

Dean moved aside a faded pillow his mother had crocheted years ago as he sat down on the sofa, folded his hands together and dropped them between his knees. "How about we drive over to that little Basque restaurant on the main highway? I know you love a good lamb stew."

"Don't sidestep the question, young man. Bad news?" his father asked.

"No worries. Everything's fine."

"Bull. You know you can talk to me. If not your dad, then who? So drop the crap and tell me what's up."

His dad had that relentless gleam in his eye, and Dean knew he'd be better off just spilling his guts so they could get down to how his dad was doing. "I talked to the doctor this morning. He's still not ready to release me for exercise."

"It's only been a few weeks since you had the surgery. What's the rush?"

How about the fear that everyone was right? That his career is over? That he'd let down his team again?

Dean knew if he could just get back in the weight room, or hell, even the bedroom he grew up in with those free weights he'd bought last week, he'd see some kind of improvement. He'd be making progress. He needed to make progress. Right now he was making squat.

"I need to be a hundred percent by spring," he said with a shrug. "Summer will be here before I know it, then training camp, and right behind that the season will start. They'll release the schedule in a few months, and when they look at those game dates I want them to know I'll be ready to throw."

"You're too hard on yourself," his dad said. "No one else has those expectations."

"No kidding." Dean gave a humorless laugh. "Everyone else thinks I'm done."

"Not everyone, Son. But you've had a pretty good ride. So what if it did end? Surely you have something else planned for your life beyond football?"

"Honestly, Dad, I haven't given a single thought past playing. I love this game. I love the life it offers me."

"You're spoiled."

"Yeah." Dean nodded. "I am."

"Your mom and I didn't raise you to be spoiled." The creases at the corners of his father's eyes deepened. "Maybe it's time you looked around and figured out where else you might fit in. Because, I hate to be the one to break it to you, Son, but life isn't always fair. Sometimes the things you love the most in life are ripped away and there's not a damn thing you can do about it."

Dean's chest tightened as tears filled his father's eyes. His father—a man's man by anyone's standards. A man who'd been the gentlest soul when he was with the woman he loved. A man who'd lost the love of his life and who must now find his way through the world alone.

A man who never cried. Until now.

What right did Dean have to sit and complain?

The pressure in his chest caved in. He stood and crossed the room, leaned down, and hugged his father tight. "I love you, Dad. And I promise I won't let you down."

His father hugged him back and Dean felt the warmth of his father's tears on his shoulder.

In that moment Dean knew if he even became half the man his father was, he'd consider himself fortunate.

Hours later, after sweet-talking his dad into the truck for a deliciously thick and meaty lamb stew at Anderazo's Diner, Dean piled into his mother's car to go for a drive and shake off the melancholy that had sunk its teeth into his soul. He passed Kate and Matt's house, thought about stopping for a quick hello, but continued the loop around the lake.

Time to take his father's advice.

Sometimes he got so busy with the Stallions schedule or the chaos that filled the rest of his days, he forgot to take a breath and look beyond what was right in his face. To see the beauty of life around him.

He'd been to over half of the contiguous states and nowhere on earth displayed more splendor than his home state of Montana. The place where he'd been raised had a healthy sense of family and community. Its four seasons taught you when to work your hardest and when it was okay to slow down. It was easy to lose sight of all that when you lived in one of the biggest cities in the nation.

Around the curve, the sledding hill at Upper Mill Creek had come alive with kids and parents in a rainbow of snowsuits. Even through the closed car windows Dean could hear shrieks of laughter. He smiled, remembering the days he'd played big brother and hauled Kelly and Kate up that hill, only to push their sled down and then lug them back up again. They'd spent hours and hours there, having fun, just being kids. He slowed the car near the parking area when he recognized a familiar face.

Brenden Jones sat on the tailgate of a white pickup, eating a sandwich while his mother poured him a steaming mug of hot chocolate. She handed the boy the drink and caressed his cheek. Her touch went unacknowledged. His mother's shoulders lifted and Dean could almost hear the disheartened sigh escape her lungs.

His stomach turned over as he thought of his teammate Bo Miller and his son. He thought of the fierce love the huge man had for that little boy who didn't have the capability of displaying affection. But that didn't stop Bo from trying to find ways to break through the wall that autism erected between him and his son. In the past year Bo's heavy heart had lightened when he'd discovered a place just outside of Houston that offered equine therapy for children with Asperger's and autism. He'd told Dean that the rhythmic motion of a horse helped the children learn to focus, and that their tactile senses were stimulated, which helped them develop communication.

Dean had checked out the organization. When he'd seen for himself the progress of the children who participated, he'd pulled out his checkbook and made a substantial donation. Only now did he realize that just writing a check was too easy, too empty. Compared to the volunteers who worked with those kids every day, writing a check was a big fat *no big deal*.

Easing his foot down on the accelerator, he continued down the road that looped around the lake where his father had taught him to fish and swim. The same lake where, as he'd gotten older and learned the fine art of persuasion, he'd convinced his female companions that skinny-dipping was good for the soul.

A few miles beyond Matt and Kate's house, a bright red and white *FOR SALE* sign stood out beyond a familiar row of pines on the side of the road. Dean was surprised to discover that after all these years the family who'd built the estate had decided to let it go. There'd always been talk of offers on the

Clear River Lodge but the Plummer family had never considered a single one. Dean wondered what now prompted the sale.

Curious, he pulled his mother's car into the driveway and removed a flyer from the plastic box attached to the sign. The advertisement showed color photos of the inside of the five thousand square-foot lakefront cedar and stone house. Massive windows revealed the property, which included a barn and indoor riding arena, stables, corrals, and three guest houses. The strongest selling point had to be the river that sliced through the property and the hot springs that pooled in a cove beneath old forest pines.

Dean looked at the price, glanced back down the road from where he'd just come, then looked at the price again. Without hesitation he reached into his jeans pocket, pulled out his cell phone, and punched in the number on the flyer.

A few hours later as the sun set behind those ancient pines he'd set a plan into motion and signed on the dotted line.

New Year's Eve was never like you saw in the movies.

There were never parties where women donned glittery gowns or men wore tuxedos or where Dom Pérignon was served in Waterford crystal. No one stood around, and, accompanied by an ebony grand piano, sang *Auld Lang Syne* in perfect pitch. And at the stroke of midnight gold and silver confetti did not mysteriously float from the ceiling. New Year's Eve had been designed as a torture device for single women. The holiday ranked right up there on the crap-o-meter with Valentine's Day.

Emma knew that from personal experience.

Tonight, as in past years, her oh-so-thrilling New Year's Eve plans included working on her thesis, a cuddle with her cat, and a romantic comedy via the DVD she'd rented. And if she really felt like tooting her horn, she might just throw in a bag of microwave popcorn and the bottle of champagne she'd bought on sale at the Gas and Grub. Not that she didn't love her cat, romantic comedies, or popcorn and cheap champagne, but at thirty-two a woman looked for something a little more . . . exhilarating.

Something a little less predictable.

Something that banged her drum and shot confetti from a cannon.

Everyone had something going on. Kate had rightfully bragged that she and Matt planned to spend the holiday in bed with champagne and nothing on but the radio. Kelly Silverthorne planned to spend a quiet night fixing her father his favorite meal before she had to fly back to Chicago. Maggie planned to spend it side-by-side with Ollie at the Naughty Irish. And though Jesse Hamilton had asked Emma out and she'd gotten her hopes up, he'd suddenly been called out of town. Which left her to either drag herself to the Grange to celebrate with the women's auxiliary and their spiked punch bowl . . . or spend it alone.

With her cat.

Yippee.

By the time ten o'clock rolled around, Emma lifted the deeply purring Oscar off her lap and turned off the TV. She didn't think she could go through the entire twenty-seven dresses that had inspired the title of the movie.

She was that girl.

Always the bridesmaid.

Never the bride.

The movie was just too depressing to watch. Oh sure, she knew Hollywood would wrap it up in a nice little bundle of happily-ever-after at the end because that's what Hollywood did. Even if she didn't have a friend who'd once lived that so-called glamorous life and who still had to move back to her miniscule hometown to find true love, Emma knew fairy-tale endings were just that. Pure fiction.

Gee, when had she become so cynical?

While she paced the hardwood floors of her small house, Oscar padded behind her on silent paws. Once he realized her destination did not include the can opener, he'd given up and plopped down in the doorway with a pathetic *feed me* scowl. She stepped over his pudgy body without an ounce of guilt.

First, she spent the better portion of the afternoon researching the effects of autism. The more she learned, the more she wanted to know. After her eyes had begun to cross from all the reading, she'd taken a break to take down her holiday decorations. After that she removed her spice jars from the cabinet and reorganized them alphabetically. Labels out, of course. When she found herself headed to the laundry room with an armload of whites, she stopped. She didn't care how bored she was, no way would she do laundry on New Year's Eve. That was just too pathetic.

Maybe tonight could be the night she'd treat herself.

She'd been patient.

She'd overpaid her dues.

She deserved a little *ahhhhhh* time. Didn't she?

She looked up at the Chanticleer wall clock over her stove. She still had time before midnight to take her bottle of bargain-basement bubbly out to the hot springs and hope for the fireworks display someone would inevitably shoot off over the frozen lake. Sure, maybe she'd only have one glass and toss the rest, but at the price she'd paid she didn't need to wrestle with guilt. And if she decided to drink more, the MADD members offered free rides home.

It was the perfect plan.

Without another thought, she slipped her arms through her old standby parka and grabbed her keys, cell phone, and supplies. With a *sorry you'll be spending New Years Eve alone* kiss to the top of Oscar's head, she headed out the door.

The lake road was deserted as Emma flipped on her turn signal and steered her Forester down the long driveway of the Clear River Lodge. The place had sat empty for over a year now, since Mr. Plummer had passed away and no one else in his family wanted to travel from their elegant home in California to some peashooter town in the Montana wilderness.

The thought made Emma sad. The grand cedar and stone home was a beautiful place that deserved to have someone to love it as much as the man who'd brought it to life.

At least from the outside it appeared beautiful. The closest she'd ever gotten to the inside had been to peek through the windows after the *FOR SALE* sign went up. The Plummer family had left the house fully furnished, which Emma recognized had been expensively implemented by the hand of a very talented decorator.

As usual the house sat in total darkness while she parked near the corrals, which were close to the hot springs. She opened her door, grabbed her champagne and towel from the back seat, then headed down the trail previously made by the footprints of people like her, who, on occasion, snuck out to enjoy a little piece of nature that didn't belong to them.

When she reached the steaming pool of water, she set down the bottle and paper cup she'd brought in the snow and proceeded to step out of her boots. She scanned the area. Completely alone she decided to be daring and go sans bikini. The air was cold so she quickly removed her clothes and hung them on the nearby corral fence. Then she twisted her hair up, secured it with a plastic claw, and eased into the hot water with a long appreciative sigh.

The pines towering above the hot springs filled her nose with a fresh bouquet. While the moon above played hide and seek behind large puffy clouds, Emma peeled the foil off the champagne bottle, untwisted the cage, and dislodged the cork with her thumbs. It exploded into the air with a loud *pop* and she laughed. Maybe that's all the fireworks she'd get for the night, but it was better than watching a movie that only reminded her of her own lackluster life.

She poured the drink into her paper cup and settled down into the water until it floated above her shoulders. She took a sip of champagne, wrinkled her nose at the bubbles, and let out another long sigh. She closed her eyes and allowed herself to relax.

"You're trespassing, short stuff."

Dean chuckled as Emma squeaked and splashed away from where he sat amid the shadows. Earlier when he'd slid into the relaxing pool he'd had no idea anyone would join him, let alone that he'd be offered up the vision of Emma stripping down to her shapely birthday suit and slipping into the water with him.

Happy New Year.

"Who's there?" she demanded.

He chuckled again.

"Oh, my God. Is that you, Dean?"

"You plan to share that bubbly, honey? Or keep it all to yourself?"

"I only brought one cup." Her tone suggested she might be a little miffed that her quiet spot was already occupied.

"Lucky for me I quit worrying about cooties in the third grade." He took the cup from her hand and drank. But not without making a bitter beer face. "Is this your regular brew?"

"It was on sale at the G & G."

"Ah. You ever had champagne that costs more than a gallon of gas?"

She settled onto the rock ledge a decent distance away and avoided his question. "What are you doing here?"

"I could ask you the same thing."

"It's obvious I needed to relax."

"No date?" he asked.

"He was called away."

Fool. Dean didn't know what stars had aligned so that *he* was the one sitting beside a very naked Emma Hart, but he wasn't about to complain.

Beneath the glow of the moon, the sweet curve of her full breasts bobbed at the waterline.

Nope.

Not going to complain.

At all.

She took the paper cup from his hand, turned the rim to the opposite side of where he'd drunk and sipped. Apparently she hadn't passed the cooties stage. As those soft lips pursed over the paper cup, his heart took off on a high-speed chase.

"No date?" she returned. "No supermodels named Britney Big Boobs to help you carve another notch on your goal post?"

He laughed. "That's a good one, schoolteacher."

"Thanks." She smiled.

Damn. That flare of her full, kissable mouth forced his high-speed pursuit to switch on the after-burners.

"So how'd you find out about this place?" she asked. "I thought I'd have it all to myself."

He leaned toward the other side of the pool, grabbed the champagne bottle, and refilled her cup. "I've been coming here since I was old enough to drive."

"So you're a repeat offender?"

"Guilty." When he sat back down—much closer this time—his thigh brushed against hers.

Her eyes widened. "Are you naked?"

"Well, I wouldn't want you to be embarrassed by being the only one in that state of undress."

"Did you watch me take off my clothes?"

"Yes." He grinned. "Do I need to pay you now?"

She lowered her head back to the rock ledge and groaned. Which tempted him to lean over and kiss that silky column of warm skin down to those succulent breasts.

"Honey. This is a skinny-dipping hot springs. Absolutely no clothing allowed. Didn't you read the sign?"

"There is no sign."

"Well, remind me to put one up."

"What do you mean, remind *you*?"

"It's my place. My responsibility to designate this as a *clothes-free* zone."

She lifted her head and stared at him. "What do you mean, *your* place?"

"You sure ask a lot of questions. I suppose that's instinctive for a teacher person."

"What do you mean, *your* place?" she repeated.

"I bought it. Signed. Sealed. Paid-for."

"You *what*?" She retreated to the other side of the pool but stopped there. Obviously too chicken to get out of the water and give him another peep show.

"Isn't that what spoiled athletes do?" he asked. "See something they want and pay cash to possess it?"

"I didn't say you were spoiled." She lifted the cup to her lips and slugged down a desperate amount. "Much."

"Well, at least you didn't say *men like me*. That's a step in the right direction."

She lowered the cup and looked at him over the rim. "Do you even know how much you *don't* make sense? For weeks you've been complaining about how you can't wait to get back to your team. Back to Houston. So why would you put out an ungodly amount of money for a home in this town?"

"Who says I've been complaining?"

"Kate. Matt. Your dad."

"Maybe those are the exact reasons I bought it. So I could be around them more."

She laughed. "Do you really expect me to believe that?"

"Maybe." He smiled—something he seemed to do a lot around her. "And maybe if you bring that champagne back over here, I'll tell you the other reasons I bought it."

"I don't trust you." She hugged the cup to her naked chest. "What have you got up your sleeve?"

"No sleeves." He held his arms up. "I'm naked. Remember?"

"Vividly."

If she was picturing him naked that was a very good sign.

"Come on, honey. I'm not going to bite."

"Fine." She slid back through the water but sat a safe distance away.

He snatched the cup from her hand, refilled it, and when her mouth dropped open to complain, he handed it back to her.

"Are you trying to get me drunk?" she asked.

"Me? No way."

Drunk? No. *Loosened up?* Absolutely.

He pulled a move he hadn't used since high school. He slid his arm along the rock ledge above her shoulders.

"Doesn't that hurt your shoulder?" she asked.

"It's the other side. But thanks for your concern."

"Only because I know you're dying to get back on the field."

"Right." At the moment, being back on the field was the last thing on his mind. In fact, his mind wasn't even in the conversation at the moment. Other parts of him? *Oh yeah.*

"So why did you buy the lodge?" She sank a little deeper into the water and the top curve of her breasts disappeared.

Bummer.

"I can't imagine spending so much money on a house you'll live in just a few weeks out of the year," she said.

"Brenden Jones."

"What?"

"You know, the little boy who sits in the back of your classroom."

She nudged him with her shoulder. "I know who he is. I just don't get the connection."

"I bought the lodge because of kids like Brenden Jones. See those guest cabins?" He motioned the direction with the paper cup in his hand. "That indoor arena? The corrals where you hung your clothes? And if I haven't thanked you for that, let me do so now."

She gave him a slightly inebriated giggle.

"Close your eyes."

"Why? What are you going to do?"

"Such distrust." He tsked. "Close them, honey. I promise I won't touch you."

"Okay."

"Unless you ask."

She sighed. "You are impossible."

He leaned toward her. "Are your eyes closed?"

"Yes."

"Then picture this place as a summer camp for kids with special needs." He told her of his buddy, Bo Miller, and his son, and the equine therapy they'd found so successful. He told her of his plans to form a camp for kids who could benefit from that same type of care. The more he talked, the more excited he became to put his plan into action. "This place can offer hope to parents and add a little fun to the therapy for the kids. Can you picture it in your head?"

"Oh yes."

The smile in her voice made his heart tumble. "As an added benefit," he told her, "I'll be able to offer employment to some of the people in the town I grew up in. And with a few well-planned events, bring some revenue into the area as well."

She remained completely silent and if he didn't know her eyes were now open, he'd think he'd put her to sleep. She was the first person to whom he'd revealed his plan. And for some reason her approval meant a great deal.

"What do you think?" he finally asked.

She leaned forward and studied his face for what felt like an eternity before she said, "I think you're a dangerous man."

Not exactly what he'd wanted to hear. But she looked so beautiful bathed in wet moonlight he could forgive her anything. "Dangerous good?" He tucked a strand of blond hair behind her ear. "Or bad?"

A smile curved her sexy mouth. "I haven't decided."

He tilted his head, studied that beautiful mouth, and thought he'd like a taste. "Meaning?"

"Either you are exactly the professional bullshitter I think you are, or . . . you are a man with an amazing heart."

He looked into the dark of her eyes and lifted her small hand to his chest. "Feel that, honey?" His brisk heartbeat thumped against her palm. "What does that tell you?"

"That you're a very dangerous man with a very strong heartbeat?"

He cupped her cheek in his hand, threaded his fingers

through her silky hair. For days she'd haunted his thoughts, his dreams. She intrigued the hell out of him and he didn't know why. But when he'd bought the house he found she'd been the first person with whom he'd wanted to share the news.

He'd only kissed her once. But it hadn't been enough. Not nearly enough. "I'm not dangerous at all. I'm just a guy who finds you unbelievably smart and attractive."

"Oh."

"I think about you, Emma." He slowly shook his head, trailed his fingers down the smooth column of her neck to her bare shoulder. "I think about you a lot. More than I should."

"You can't get in trouble just thinking."

A hum vibrated low in his throat. "I think about touching you." His fingertips brushed the water-slicked cleavage between her breasts. "Kissing you." He paused and saw the surprise in her eyes.

"I think about making love to you, Emma."

She swallowed.

"I think about making love to you all the time."

Unaware that she was doing so, she leaned closer. Beneath his fingers her heartbeat picked up speed. Everything about her called out to him. Made him want to pound his chest, toss her over his shoulder, and mark her as his own. But they didn't live in prehistoric times. And though he wanted her so much he ached, though he took the chance of her slipping from his grasp, he needed to be completely honest. He needed to give her the opportunity to make a choice.

"I *dream* about making love to you, Emma. Really hot, and wet, and dirty dreams."

His hands came up and cupped her face. His thumb brushed across her pillowy-soft bottom lip. He hadn't imagined her response when she'd kissed him in her driveway that night. And he wasn't imagining the look in her eyes right now. She was shocked that he thought about her, let alone dreamed about her.

Still, what happened from here was her call.

His voice lowered. "So before you drink anymore of that champagne, I want you to know that you were wrong about what you said at Kate's house Christmas night. I don't have to *pretend* to be attracted to you. I *am* attracted to you. And any man who would just use you to *pass the time* is a damn fool."

"I . . ."

He softly kissed her lips once. Twice. He tried to keep it gentle. To ease into it. But the third time her lips parted and he slipped his tongue inside. The kiss she gave him sucked away all thoughts of being gentle. The kiss she gave him made him hot, and hard, and achy.

He leaned back and looked deep into her heavy-lidded eyes. "I want to make love to you, honey. And if you don't say no right now, that's what will happen."

"But we don't like each other."

He kissed the corner of her mouth and felt her melt just a little. "I think we do." He kissed her lips. Her nose. Then settled in nicely just below her ear for a long, slow lick. "So what do you think?"

"Just like I said." She tossed the empty paper cup over her shoulder, climbed onto his lap, and wound her arms around his neck. "Dangerous."

Dean had never been more surprised. Or more grateful.

She straddled his lap, pressed her wet, naked breasts against his chest, and fed him a really hot grab-you-by-the-balls kind of kiss. He went from zero to rigid in less than a blink as their tongues touched, swirled, and caressed.

She seduced him like a woman who knew exactly what she wanted. And what she wanted was *him*.

Happy freaking New Year.

She kissed the side of his neck. Spread her hands across his chest and kissed the three puckered scars on his shoulder.

When she lowered herself until the pinkest part of her gorgeous body pressed against his throbbing erection, he considered that total permission to indulge. He wrapped his arms around her, pulled her tighter against his chest and sank into her feminine curves.

God, she was soft. He didn't think he'd ever touched a woman so soft before. Didn't know if he could ever touch a woman the same way again without thinking of how soft Emma Hart felt against him.

Like a feline stretching on a sun-warmed rock, she arched against him. Pure lust shot up his thighs, grabbed hold of his insides, and squeezed. He eased his head back just enough to look into her face. The moonlight glistened on her wet lips. Her beautiful blue eyes were heavy but clear. Her slightly uneven breath pressed the hard tips of her breasts into his chest. His erection nudged the entrance to her hot, slick body.

He slid his hands up her sides, cupped the weight of her breasts in his palms while his thumbs slowly brushed her nipples back and forth. The steamy water lapped the small gap between their bodies as the river behind them bubbled over a cascade of rocks on its way to the lake.

"Emma, honey?" Last chance for her to back out. "What do you want me to do here?"

She looked into his eyes, cupped his face in her hands, and pressed her mouth to his in a kiss so hot he almost quit breathing. Her kiss continued across his cheek and down the side of his throat where she sucked his sensitive flesh gently into her mouth. When she came up for air she whispered, "Me, Dean. I want you to do *me*."

"Thank. You. God." Permission granted, he slid his hands down her silky thighs while her mouth continued to do incredible things to his throat. He was inches from paradise. All he had to do was lift her up and onto him. And yet with Emma, he didn't want it to be quick. He didn't want to close his eyes, thrust into her until he came, and then send her on her merry way. He wanted to taste her, wanted her around him, over him. Hell, if he could find a way to have her inside him, he'd put her there too.

He eased her thighs apart and his thumbs found her swollen nub. He circled it and she melted against him. Her mouth broke the suction on his neck and her head dropped back with a long, contented sigh.

Emma shuddered with the unbelievable heat of promise as Dean pressed the long, thick length of his erection against her. She settled down deeper, aching to have him inside her. Before she got too comfortable, he shifted her off his lap and up onto the rock ledge. She shivered when her butt hit the icy rock, but he warmed her when he cupped his hands beneath her bottom and kissed the inside of her thigh. Lightning shot up into her center.

"This is one of those hot and wet things I've dreamed about doing to you." He kissed the inside of her thigh again, then he parted her folds and found her with his tongue.

Oh. Dear. God.

His warm tongue slid across her slick flesh. His moan vibrated against her clit. He knew exactly what he was doing and she was loving every second. He licked her, stroked her, teased her, and sucked her like a ripe, juicy peach. He loved her like there was no such thing as time. When the fireworks began to explode above the frozen lake, he lifted his head. "Can you see the fireworks, honey?"

Her eyes fluttered open. "Not . . . yet."

"Then lay back." He chuckled. "How about now?" He sucked her sensitive, swollen flesh into his mouth and rolled his tongue across the tip.

A roman candle shot off above their heads, and a warm, slow tingle started at her toes and moved up through her body. When the hot orgasm hit the target, she moaned. Loudly. "Oh . . . yes." Her hips lifted from his hands. Her thighs pressed against his cheeks. "Yes. Yes. Yessssss."

Dean let her float down from the cloud for just a moment, then he eased her back down into the water with him. But if he thought Emma was done, he'd be wrong.

Again, she took over, feeding him hot kisses full of passion and desire. He groaned deep in his throat as her hand circled his cock and she slid her palm down to the base and then back up to the engorged head.

"I want you, Dean," she whispered against his mouth. She climbed back onto his lap and straddled his hips. "And I want you right now."

He shuddered beneath her touch as she ran her hands up his chest, positioned herself, and slowly sat. As he slid into the gripping pleasure of her body, the breath squeezed from his lungs. His passion twisted into a steamy, mindless coil. He slid his hands to her waist. She felt so hot, so slick, so . . .

He gripped her hips to keep her in place. No time to run in the house and grab a condom. It wouldn't work in the hot springs anyway.

Between long, wet kisses he asked, "Birth control?"

"On it."

Another kiss. "Clean?"

"Squeaky."

"Me too." Either she was too far gone to care or she believed him, because she lowered herself fully until he was pressed against her cervix. "God, Emma, you feel so damned good."

Hands gripping her waist, he controlled his thrusts by raising and lowering her onto his cock. He pushed into her with long, powerful strokes, then lifted her until just the head stayed put. Each time he sank into her again she'd moan and her inner muscles would pull him in deeper. He drove into her again and again. He lost himself inside her. Became one with her. And when he felt the tightening of her orgasm, it pulled a release from deep within his soul.

He thrust hard and a gush of liquid heat exploded around

him in the most intense pleasure he'd ever known. Fire spread across his skin and his pulse pounded in his blood as he clutched her to his chest. They cried out together as a burst of red and blue exploded across the sky.

They held each other close while their hearts continued to fly. And in that moment Dean thought he just might have died and gone to heaven.

For twenty years he'd played it smart and safe. A guarded heart and reliable condoms.

Emma Hart was his first without either.

CHAPTER NINE

Mornings after always came with regret.

New Year's Day? No different.

Beyond a break in the curtains, sunrise lifted its head above the earth. Emma awoke on cool sheets, wrapped in a pair of strong arms, with her back pressed against a warm chest. Her butt was nestled against a sizeable part of Dean Silverthorne that, judging by the firmness, probably woke way before his eyes even opened.

She flicked her gaze across the shadows to the elegant bedroom decorated with rich furniture in a timeless design. Silk draperies framed a set of French doors, and against the far wall the last burning embers danced up into the chimney of a river-rock fireplace. She glanced at the door, tried to remember where she'd left her clothes, then tried not to groan. After several mind-bending orgasms in the hot springs alone, she hadn't been coherent enough to pull them from the corral fence and bring them into the house. Embarrassment flooded her cheeks when she vaguely recalled walking down the snow-covered path to the house, wearing nothing but the arm of the man who'd given her those multiple orgasms. If she could just sneak—

"Don't even think about it."

Shoot.

Dean turned her on her back, leaned over her, and looked down into her face. "No regrets, Emma."

"Easy for you to say." She looked up into his eyes, trying to read his thoughts. "I'm sure you're used to waking up in strange beds."

"Actually, I've *never* woken up in a strange bed."

"Am I supposed to believe that?"

"What?" His dark brows tipped together in a frown. "Doubt from a woman who trusted me enough last night to have unprotected sex?"

They'd had unprotected sex *once*. The other times he'd been covered.

When she flinched, he drew her deeper into his embrace. "We all have our moments of insanity," she said.

"True." He kissed the side of her neck. "And I'm so glad you decided to have yours with me. But let's move forward, shall we?"

"I'm not sure where to go from here."

"We could grab a bite to eat, then head back into the hot springs with a couple mugs of coffee."

And let him see every single imperfection in stark sunlight? No way. "I might be crazy enough to skinny-dip in the dark, but there's no way you'd get me back out there in broad daylight."

"I promise not to stare."

She raised an eyebrow.

"But I might drool." He chuckled when both of her eyebrows shot upward. "Come on, I'm not that bad of a guy. I'd probably only drool a little. You'd hardly even notice."

"I find that hard to believe," she said, trying to scoot out from beneath him. "Not fishing for compliments here but I'm sure I'm not the type of woman you usually find in your bed."

His serious green gaze stared down at her and searched her face. "The tabloids put it all out there so I won't bother to lie. Yes, I've been with my share of supermodels. And yes, they are very beautiful. But I have never woken in my own bed with my arms wrapped around a single one. You're my first, Emma. In many ways."

Now why did he have to go looking all sincere?

"I don't do this," she protested. "I don't have sex with random men and wake up in their beds."

"I know you don't, honey." His long fingers brushed her hair away from her temple. "And that's exactly why I don't want you to have regrets about last night."

Either he was a very good liar or he was honest as hell. She didn't know him well enough to be able to decide which. He'd always been the handsome and successful hometown hero who lived a charmed life most people couldn't even fathom. And last night, it had only taken a few paper cups of cheap champagne and one sappy idea for her to jump onto his lap. Ugh. Where had been her self-control?

She'd had sex with the man three—no, make that four times last night. And once more very early this morning before the sun even rose over the snow-covered mountain tops.

So what did that say about her? She didn't like *him* but she liked his body?

He leaned down and kissed her forehead.

Okay, so maybe she liked him a little.

Then he gave her that smile. The one she'd seen in a hundred post-game interviews. The one she'd seen grace the covers of magazines. The last place she'd ever expected to see that half good-old-boy, half man-of-the-world expression was in bed next to her on the very first holiday of the year.

Good God, what did that mean for the remaining twelve months?

Several hours later, after soothing Emma's obvious misgivings and making love to her one more time, Dean woke to find the sheets next to him cold and empty. He laid there for a few minutes and waited for her to come back. When she continued to be a no-show, he got out of bed. He shoved his legs into his jeans and went in search of the woman who confused and intrigued him more than a change of signals on game day. He rambled through the big house, checking the kitchen, the bathrooms, the media room. No Emma. He finally looked out back toward the corrals. Her clothes were gone and so was her little Subaru.

Damn.

He thought he'd gained an ounce of trust with her over the past ten hours, but apparently it would take a lot more than holding her in his arms or giving her multiple orgasms. He looked out the window, over the wide expanse of forest and meadow that now belonged to him, and wanted to slap himself in the forehead.

Of course it would take more than that with Emma.

The women he dated were bright and beautiful. But he'd never connected with any of them on an emotional level. Something about Emma rang a different bell.

After a quick shower, he dressed in whatever clothes he could find, grabbed his keys, and was out the door in less time than it took to huddle his team. He backed his mother's bomber out of the garage and sped toward town. With one small detour, he turned up the radio and headed straight for Spotted Fawn Avenue. From the crackling speakers Tom Jones sang a *whoa-ho-ho*, and Dean waited for the inevitable.

"You're whistling."

Ah, and there she was. Dean smiled. No matter how much he thought he had it together, the persistent appearance of his dead mother proved he was never too far from a dance with the dark and crazy side. "Am I?"

"Happy about something?"

"The sun is shining," he said, keeping the car on the road. No need anymore to turn around to check who was in the seat behind him. "It's a beautiful day."

"Sleep well?"

"Didn't sleep much at all."

Icy air swirled through the interior of the car. "Oh, do tell," she said, her voice much closer now. "What had you up all night?"

"How much do you follow me around?"

"Oh, not at all. I'm not allowed to be a Peeping Tom. *Somebody* takes all the fun out of the ability to pop about without getting caught. What do you think all those ghost shows are about?"

He chuckled. "You sound disappointed."

"You bet I am. I didn't know there'd be so many restrictions on the other side. But there are definite rules, and if you break them you have to answer to *him*."

"God?"

"Don't be silly. He's too busy for mischief makers like me."

"So who's *him*? And where do you go when you're not cruising around in the back seat of your piece-of-crap car?"

"I believe answering those questions would break rule number four. And since I'm still doing penance for breaking rule number three, I reserve the right to keep my big yap shut."

Dean laughed. "I miss you, Mom."

A sudden cold settled on his bad shoulder and eased the ache still throbbing from his nighttime activities. Not that he minded those activities.

"And I'm so glad you're home," his mother said. "Otherwise we'd miss the opportunity for these little visits."

"You do realize I'll have to leave soon, though. Right?"

"We'll see. In the meantime, tell me what has you whistling like a meadowlark."

Dean glanced in the rearview mirror. He couldn't see her. Couldn't see her glow in the bright sunlight, but he knew she'd be illuminating pink in about ten seconds. "I bought a house."

"Thought you already had one in Houston."

"I have a high-rise condo in Houston. I bought a *house*. Specifically I bought the Clear River Lodge."

"Oh goodness, that's a big one." The excitement in her voice elevated several levels. "But if I know you like I think I do, you've got some big plan in your head. Am I right?"

He loved the enthusiasm in her voice. She'd always been 100 percent behind him. He hoped she'd be just as on-board now. As he told her of his plans for the charity organization and camp, she remained silent. The longer he took to explain, the quieter she got. He wondered if maybe she wasn't happy about his plans at all. Maybe she didn't think he could pull it off. Or maybe she'd just popped out of there.

"You're the one who taught me the importance of charity, Mom, so I'm naming it the Leticia Silverthorne Sunshine Camp."

Still no response.

"So what do you think?"

A cool tingle materialized on his right cheek and he knew he'd just been granted a kiss.

A sigh whispered through the air.

"I think I have the most wonderful son in the world. And even though you're this big rough-and-tough football player, I'm so glad you still listen to my advice."

"Which was?"

"I told you to remember that life was about more than football. That *you* were about more than football."

"Even when I've got one foot in the grave, football will still be a huge part of my life, Mom. I don't even know if I'll be able to pull this off. It's a full-time commitment, and I'm already committed to a $48 million three-year contract with the Stallions."

"That's absurd."

"With a $10 million signing bonus."

"Whew! Hard to make that kind of cash at the Gas and Grub."

"Pretty much."

"You'll work it out, Son. I've never known you to not get everything you wanted."

He knew she meant well, but that was the biggest pile of crap he'd heard in a long time.

If he could have everything he wanted, his mother would still be alive instead of hanging out in ghost form in an old Buick. He'd never have been drilled into the turf on Thanksgiving Day. And right now he'd be warming up on the field, ready to kick his opponent's ass.

Instead, he was about to bust down the door of the Sugar Shack.

When Dean rolled up in Emma's driveway, he found her car parked by the garage. He grabbed the box on the seat beside him. Several long strides later he rang the doorbell. No answer. He pounded on the door. No answer. Now why did she want to go ignoring him? They'd had a great time last night. Hadn't they?

He pounded harder and shouted, "Emma? I know you're in there. Answer the door."

Irene Evans, the woman who checked groceries at Gridley's Market, which sold not only canned peas but firearms and fishing worms, stepped out of the house next door.

"Dean Silverthorne?" She squinted against the bright sunshine and planted her fists on her well-padded hips. "Is that you?"

"Yes, Mrs. Evans." Guilt rolled through him as though he'd just stolen a pack of Double Bubble.

"Why are you making such a fuss?" she asked.

"Um . . . Emma isn't answering her door and I . . ." He held up the pastry box. *Nice save, Silverthorne.* "I brought her some muffins from the bakery."

"Well, she's in there. Saw her come home just a bit ago. Give her a few danged minutes. No sense pounding on the door like the dogs of hell are after ya. Some of us are hung over from the hoedown at the Grange last night."

"Sorry, Mrs. Evans."

As the neighbor disappeared back into her house, he lifted his knuckles to knock on Emma's door again. The door creaked open. Half-hidden, Emma stood there with a plush pink towel wrapped around her shapely, flushed body and knotted right between her perfect breasts. Her blond hair hung in wet, wavy strands around her shoulders, and she smelled like a strawberry and peach parfait. His mouth watered. His fingers itched to toss aside the pastry box and unwind her from that towel so he could get his hands all over her.

"What are you doing here?" she asked as though she hadn't just been in his bed.

"I came to see why you ran off." He held up the box. "And I brought you muffins."

"The muffins are welcome." Her perfectly arched brows pulled together as she reached for the pastry box. "You, I'm not so sure about."

"Aw, come on."

"Pouting doesn't work well for you," she said, then stepped away from the door. "But you can come in anyway."

He walked through the doorway and was met by the glare

of Oscar, the evil elf cat, sans costume, and a living room now void of Emma's plethora of Christmas decorations. "Wow. You work fast. By Valentine's Day we were all begging my mom to take down the Christmas stuff." He closed the door behind him and watched her walk half-naked toward the kitchen.

"Coffee?"

"Sure." Mesmerized, he watched her towel-clad hips sway with each barefoot step she took.

She turned and caught him looking as she set the pastry box down on the counter. She lifted the lid on Kate's double-chocolate-chip banana muffins and groaned. "Shoot. I was going to start a diet today."

His gaze slid over the length of her body, from her pink painted toenails to the tops of her silky smooth shoulders. Why did women with curves always think they needed to diet? She was perfect. And soft. He didn't think he'd ever touched a woman as soft as Emma. And while she worried about her weight, all he could think about was touching her again.

"Why would you want to do that?" She rolled her eyes as if he'd asked the most ridiculous question. "Come on, you'll break Kate's heart if you don't at least taste one of her best sellers."

"Well, we can't have that, can we?" With one hand she clutched the pink towel tight to her chest. With the other she handed a muffin to him, then she snatched one up for herself. Her teeth sank into the bread and her eyes rolled closed. "Mmmm."

When her perfect lips came together in a smile, heat

flooded his groin and all Dean wanted was to sink into *her* and stay there for a good, long time.

Emma set the half-eaten muffin down on a napkin on the counter and lifted her hand to wipe the crumbs from her mouth.

"I'll take care of that." Dean caught her arm, lifted her fingers to his mouth, and licked the crumbs away. Each stroke of his tongue brought back memories of the night before and the fireworks he'd introduced into their lovemaking.

"Mmmmm. You taste good, honey." He tugged her against his wide chest and his thick arms surrounded her with firm muscles. The scent of soap on his skin and a hint of aftershave sent a tingle right through her middle to all her good parts. Damn him for always smelling so good.

He lowered his head and kissed each corner of her mouth.

She settled her palms on his chest. "I should probably get dressed."

"Now that would be a real shame." His big hands slid down her back, grabbed hold of the bottom of the towel, and yanked it away.

Before she could grab the towel and re-cover herself, it fluttered to the floor.

He grabbed her wrists and pinned them behind her. Her body arched against him and a slow smile spread across his mouth. "That's much better."

He kissed her neck in the sensitive spot beneath her ear. A spray of effervescent bubbles shot up from her core and settled right in the center of her heart. His hot, moist mouth slipped down to the curve of her shoulder and his big hand covered her breast. He rolled her erect nipple back and forth between his thumb and finger. And she was gone, gone, gone.

"Merrrrooowww."

Startled, they both looked up to find Oscar in the doorway, watching them as though they were HD Kitty Porn TV.

"Pervert." Without letting her go, Dean nudged the kitchen door closed with his foot and shut out her snoopy cat.

In that split second, common sense reeled back as bright sunshine flooded through the window. "Dean?" she said as he returned his mouth to that really sensitive spot just below her ear that sent tingles down to her hard nipples.

"Yeah, honey?" he muttered against her throat.

"I . . . uh . . ." *Damn that felt amazing.* "Don't think this is a good idea."

His head tilted slightly as he lifted her hand and held it to his heart. Beneath her fingertips she felt the quick rhythm skipping through his chest. Then he slid her hand lower and cupped her fingers over the bulge behind the zipper of his worn Levi's.

"*This* is what you do to me, Emma. So right now, I'd sincerely appreciate it if you just wouldn't *think*." He gave her a smile ripe with promise. "Okay?"

"O-kay."

Thinking really was overrated anyhow.

His big hands slid down her back to her bare bottom, grabbed hold, and lifted. She felt the flinch in his arm as he settled her on the counter and stepped between her thighs.

"Your shoulder—"

"Is fine." His mouth slid from her throat down to her

breast. He circled the erect nipple with his tongue, sucked it into his mouth, then lifted his head to look up at her. "But if you want, I'll let you kiss it better."

One part of her wished she could take away that pain and agony and disappointment. The other part of her knew that once his pain was gone, he'd be gone too.

She leaned forward and gently pressed her mouth to those places where a scalpel had sliced into his perfect, tan skin. As far as seductions went, she knew she could start at his shoulder. But eventually she'd want to work her way down.

All the way down.

His broad shoulders were smooth. Nice. But there were other parts of him intimately more impressive. She placed her palms on the sides of his face, kissed him on the mouth, then guided those magical lips right back to her breast. "Now where were you?"

He chuckled against her skin but didn't hesitate to do exactly as she directed. Each tug and pull of his mouth caused a responding tug lower. Her thighs squeezed his hips and pulled him closer until she felt his long, hard erection press between her legs.

"One of us is wearing too many clothes." She reached for the buttons on his flannel shirt. Her fingers hurried each one through the buttonhole, then she slipped her hands beneath the soft, warm material to push it away. While it floated to the floor, she tugged the hem of the blue t-shirt from his jeans. He withdrew to help. Still unable to lift his arm over his head, he did a one-sided tug with his left hand and the fabric sailed to the floor.

He reached for her.

"Stop."

Disappointment darkened his eyes. "What's wrong, honey?"

"I just . . . want to look." Her gaze ran over him like he was a playground. From his broad shoulders down the defined planes of his chest to the perfectly spaced muscular ridges of his stomach.

"And touch." Emma ran her hands down the fine light brown hair on his wide chest, hard muscles, and hot skin, then over his shoulders, taking care to lighten her touch at the angry scars dotting his perfection. With her fingers she traced the sexy narrow trail of soft, fine hair that circled his navel and disappeared beneath the waistband of his 501s.

"And taste." She kissed the center of his chest and he groaned in appreciation. Then she flattened her tongue against the bud of his erect nipple and gently sucked it into her mouth.

"I want you so much," he growled.

Emma leaned back to look at him. He was a hot, sexy man. Dangerous. Yet somehow he made her feel safe.

Foolish girl.

He had her sitting butt-naked on top of her kitchen counter in broad daylight. She should be embarrassed. Mortified at her own behavior. His warm hand curled at the base of her neck, and she forgot all about being good.

His mouth captured hers in a sizzling, wet kiss. The tips of her breasts brushed against the fine hair on his chest and created an ache deep inside while his talented hands teased the hot pulsing points of her body. She reached for the button fly on his 501s, pulled the metal buttons from the holes then slid the material down. When he was naked between her thighs, she wrapped her hand around his thick, hard shaft. He dropped his forehead to hers and a shudder rippled down his back as she moved her palm down his hot skin to the plump head, then back up. He pushed himself deeper into her hand and groaned.

A feeling of power came over her. An amazement that she, a schoolteacher from Deer Lick, could make a football giant like Dean Silverthorne practically melt in her hands.

She liked that feeling.

He covered her hand with his and moved her palm up and down his erection.

"I want you, Dean."

"I want you too."

"Condom?"

"Anything for you, honey." He smiled, released her hand, and reached into his wallet. "A little help?"

"Anything for you . . ."

He chuckled as she tore open the gold Magnum packet and rolled the thin latex down his long, hard shaft. When he pushed into her hand again she flooded with heat and dampness. She wrapped her legs around his waist and guided him toward her entrance.

His head lifted and he looked into her eyes. He kissed her, eased himself deep inside, then stilled. He dropped his forehead to hers. "No regrets, Em."

He would leave. That was a given. Still . . . she pulled a deep breath of air into her lungs. "No regrets."

He withdrew slightly, then pushed until he was fully seated. She felt the head of his penis press against her cervix and then he withdrew. The push and pull friction nearly drove her over the edge.

"No regrets," he murmured as his hips pumped faster, as he reached between them and rubbed her sensitive spot with his thumb. She planted her hands on the counter behind her and he gripped her thigh as he moved deeply, possessively inside her.

The back of her head bumped the cabinet. Her hand slipped on the counter and knocked the lid off the cow cookie jar. Each thrust made her crave him more, made her skin hot, made her breasts tingle. He increased the pressure on his thumb and shot her right toward the edge.

She cried out his name. "Don't stop. Please. Do. Not. Stop." He moved, rotated, pressed. *Oh, God.* Fire swept from her heart down her body and she fell into a long, hot, breath-stealing orgasm. Her muscles contracted, grabbed at him, and pulled him in deeper.

He grasped her hips tighter, dropped his head back, and thrust one final time with a deep, throaty groan. When their breathing returned to somewhat normal, he wrapped his arms around her and brought her against his chest. His heart pounded against hers. "Damn, honey," he said between breaths, "you keep that up and you're going to make me fall in love with you."

Emma turned her head, pressed her cheek to his warm chest, and tried not to think about how that made her feel. Or that no matter how she felt she would have to let him go.

"You're killing me, Em."

Dean glanced at the woman next to him dressed in Hello Kitty pajama bottoms and a skimpy bra-less tank top. They were watching his alma mater beat the snot out of Michigan in the Rose Bowl. Or he was trying to watch. The soft and pretty distraction on the sofa beside him was far more stimulating than the one-sided butt-whomping the Trojans were giving to the Wolverines. Over the top of her silky blond hair Emma had stuck a Green Bay Packers ball cap, the team his Stallions were matched against in the divisional playoffs. "You live in the hometown of the Houston Stallions quarterback and you don't own a team cap?"

"I don't like the Stallions."

"And why not?" he asked, biting into a spicy nacho chip.

"Their quarterback is full of himself."

The second bite halted before it even got to his mouth. "Are you serious? The guy has the sixth-highest career passer rating of all time." Speaking of himself in third person was weird.

"Tom Brady has the fifth-highest. And he's better-looking."

"Brady!" He tossed his tortilla chip back onto his plate. "He's a girl."

She laughed. "What do you mean, he's a girl? He's married to a supermodel."

"Have you seen the guy's hair?"

"He says his wife likes it."

"See? Like I said. He's a girl. No man lets a woman pussy him into wearing long hair if he doesn't want to."

"Maybe he loves her and just wants to make her happy."

"If he wasn't such a girl, he'd know how to make her happy." He grinned, enjoying every second of this back-and-forth banter. Most of the women he dated didn't know a pigskin from a pig's ass, let alone a QB's stats. Emma impressed the hell out of him. Not to mention he liked kissing her a whole lot. "How do you know all this stuff anyway?"

A smirk lifted the corners of her mouth. "I live in the hometown of the Houston Stallions quarterback, where everyone talks football stats. I've been collecting data for years, just waiting for the bigheaded butt to fall from the town's enormous pedestal."

"Oh, really?"

She nodded. Dean grabbed the Packers cap off her head and tossed it to the chair, where it landed on her cat, who'd been staring at him like he was a fresh sardine. The cat wiggled from beneath the cap, hissing and spitting like he had been attacked by a cougar. "Your cat hates me."

"I believe that was established the first time you came over."

"Right. I'm still trying to get the cat drool out of my coat sleeve."

She stroked the cat's head and laughed. "Maybe you could try to make friends with him."

"Yeah. That's never going to happen. I've got to practically overdose on antihistamines before I even come over here." Not that he minded. He stretched his arm behind her on the sofa and thought of all the things that made Emma special. "You mentioned your grandmother raised you. I'd like to meet her."

She leaned back and looked at him. "Why?"

"To tell her she did a good job." Emma looked down at her hands. "Uh-oh. Did I say something wrong?"

"I appreciate the gesture but it really wouldn't matter. My Memaw has dementia."

"I'm sorry, honey. How bad?"

A small shrug lifted her shoulders. "Some days she doesn't even recognize me. She puts up a good front. If I give her enough cues she can play along like she knows what I'm talking about. But as soon as I'm done talking she asks who I am. Most of the time now she thinks I'm the sister she lost when they were just teenagers." An almost imperceptible sigh squeezed from her lungs. "She's still here, but most of the time it feels I've already lost her."

Dean tightened his arm around her shoulder and drew her closer. "So it's just you, then? No other family?"

"Nope. Just me."

He let that filter through him, wondering what it would be like not to have Kate or Kelly to talk to, bounce ideas off, or debate with until he was convinced they were both abandoned by aliens. He'd lost his mom and that left a huge hole in his life. With the exception, of course, that she insisted on popping up in the back seat now and again. Thank God he still had his dad. He didn't know what he'd do if he'd lost him too.

Emma had no one.

He looked down into her face, where crinkles of distress spread from the corners of her unique blue eyes. "I'm sorry, honey. I can't pretend to know what that's like, but I imagine it must be very hard."

She nodded. "Especially around the holidays."

"I'd still like to meet your Memaw."

Her gaze lifted to his. "We'll see."

Her response sounded exactly like that of a schoolteacher. "It depends on how good you are."

He laughed as the corners of her luscious mouth curled upward. "Is that so?" Before she could squeak, he had her flat on her back beneath him. "I can be good. Or I can be bad. Really, really bad." He silenced her giggles with a press of his lips to hers. He swept his tongue inside her mouth, where she tasted like spicy cheese sauce. He liked spicy cheese sauce.

"Which do you prefer?" His hand slid up beneath her little tank top and he rolled her puckered nipple between his fingers. His cock hardened. God, he couldn't get enough of her. He loved the way she smelled. The way she smiled. The way she tasted. And the way she made love to him with such unadulterated passion.

He'd had plenty of beautiful women before, but none who'd wrapped themselves around him the way she did. None that had ever snuck into his jaded heart and made him start thinking of things he had no business thinking. None who'd ever made him want to sit on a sofa in her living room while her cat made his nose itch and he only half-assedly watched one of the biggest college games of the year.

Damn, he liked Emma Hart.

Before he got carried away and carted her off to the bedroom, he kissed her forehead and looked down into her eyes. "When do you go back to school?"

"Tomorrow." She looked up at him and a little crease formed between her eyes. "Why?"

"I wanted to know if you'd help me."

"With what?"

"Getting this charity and camp started. I'd like to have it up and running by this summer."

"Summer? That's not that far away."

"That's why I need to get started now. I need to hire the right person to get it going."

"Hire?" She rolled from beneath him and sat up. "So, you're really not asking for help, you're looking for someone to do it for you?" She leaned away. "You had no intention of investing any blood, sweat, or tears into making this camp happen, did you? You just plan to *pay* someone to do it for you."

"You make that sound like a dirty word."

She shrugged.

"I don't have time, Em. I have to get my shoulder back in shape, and that's going to take months of concentration. Besides, I make enough money to hire the best."

Emma stood, folded her arms beneath her breasts, and looked down at him. "I should have known."

"You should have known what?" He patted the sofa beside him. "Come sit back down and let's talk about this."

She shook her head. "I should have known you'd take the easy way out. Men—"

"Stop." He dropped his head back with a groan. "Are we seriously going to have another *men like me* conversation?"

"Keep giving me ammunition and I'll keep firing it back at you." Her jaw tightened as she lifted her chin.

"Come on, honey. Come sit down. I don't want to fight."

A humorless laugh broke from her throat. "You fooled

me, Dean. You had me believing that this camp was a passion for you. But the only passion you really have is for your football career, isn't it?"

"I've fought hard for that career," he said. "I'm not about to just walk away from it. Or apologize."

"No one's asking you to. But if you're going to name a charity after your mother, I'd think you'd at least want to put in the effort to make sure it happened the way you envisioned." Her lips curled in disappointment. "So your mother would be proud of what you'd accomplished instead of just how much money you paid someone else. Where's your pride?"

Damn it. He had pride. And his mother *was* proud of him. She'd told him so. She wouldn't care who put the organization together, as long as it got put together. Would she?

At his silence Emma turned and walked toward the hall. "I need to take a shower. Maybe," she said, biting that perfect bottom lip, "when I come out you could be gone."

"You're going to make me miss the rest of the game?" he said, knowing it was a lame excuse.

"Do you want me to tell you how it ends?" She glanced at the TV and the landslide score in the top corner of the screen, then back at him. "You win."

Like usual.

The words were unspoken but there all the same. Fine. If that's the way she wanted it. He stood, grabbed his jacket from the chair, and brushed the cat hair off the sleeve. The evil elf cat hissed and Dean wanted to thump him between his pointy ears. Instead he reached down, took a risk, and gave him a quick pat on the head as if to prove to Emma he wasn't the bad guy she tried to paint him to be.

He opened the front door and looked back at where she stood in the hall. "I don't want to leave this way."

"All good things must come to an end," she said.

"I have a doctor's appointment this week. I'm going back to Houston."

"Have a nice trip."

His head came up. "That's it? A few hours ago you let me get up close and personal, and now you're kicking my ass out with a *have a nice trip?*"

"What do you want me to say, Dean? You knew this was temporary. I knew too." She gave him a smile so bogus it made his stomach turn. "So, thank you, it's been fun. I hope your shoulder heals and you're able to rocket passes into the end zone very soon. Please lock the door behind you."

CHAPTER TEN

The following afternoon, Emma sat at one of the bistro sets in the Sugar Shack, sipping hot coffee, reviewing her class agenda for the following day, and working on an assignment for her Issues in Special Ed class. Dark clouds hovering in the sky outside the big window were swollen with snow and the gray weather only added to her mood. After two weeks off from school, her kids had been a bit wild and out of control. With little sleep the previous night, her morning had dragged by. By the time the afternoon bell rang, she needed a serious caffeine fix. No one in Deer Lick made better coffee than the Sugar Shack. But it would take more than that to make her forget about the ache floating around in her heart.

Yesterday, Dean had no sooner put his mother's car in reverse and backed out of her driveway before she'd wanted to run after him.

How had she allowed herself to build up such a need for him? Sure, it had been a long time since she'd had sex. And there weren't many men who could make love the way Dean Silverthorne did—not that she'd had many men. But it had been about more than the sex. Lately, she'd discovered him as a man with a heart and soul. Even if he seemed to be a little misguided at times.

She'd known about his life, both professional and personal. His escapades were out there online, in magazines, and on entertainment news shows for everyone to see. And judge. But during the time she'd spent in his arms, he'd seemed differently. Instead of a spoiled superstar, he'd been warm and tender. Caring and wonderful. Somehow she'd lost her edge. She'd allowed him to find a vulnerable space in her heart and he'd crawled inside.

It hurt like hell to know it had all been an act and she'd been right about him in the first place. And in that moment of clarity, she'd realized it was better for her to close the door and let him leave than to hold onto the hope that he'd hang around.

"Look what I brought you."

Emma looked up as Kate slid a plate filled with a mountainous slice of chocolate chip cheesecake in front of her. "Wow. How'd you know I've been dying for a sugar fix?"

"Actually, I just thought you looked like you could use a friend." Kate smiled as she perched herself on the chair across from Emma. "But before you think I'm ready for sainthood, my intentions aren't all that noble. Actually I needed a sugar fix. Dad's gone home and I still have to decorate a sheet cake for Barbara Klautmeir's sixtieth birthday. I thought maybe you could help me."

Known for her way-out and often X-rated cake designs, Emma asked Kate, "What crazy idea have you come up with this time?"

"An old-fashioned record player with a Tom Jones record spinning on top."

"Tom Jones? Why not Frank Sinatra or Elvis?"

Kate shrugged. "Special meaning. You want to help?"

"I have no idea how to decorate a cake. Besides, I have this yummy slice of cheesecake to eat."

Kate handed a spoon to Emma, then whipped out another spoon from her apron pocket. "Correction. You have half of a yummy slice of cheesecake to eat."

The two of them scooped and chatted about everything from the spaghetti dinner Matt had cooked for Kate last night to how their father fared without their mother to what Hollywood celebs wore Spanx. Emma was shocked to learn that even a few high-powered *male* movie stars refused to leave the mansion without them.

Time flew and Emma felt like she'd been let into a very exclusive club. Like she belonged. It was nice, but it also served to remind her how badly she wanted her own family. Her own someone-to-love.

Minutes later, Kate dragged her behind the counter, slipped an apron over her head, and tied it in the back. Then Kate went to the cooler and brought out a large, dirty-iced sheet cake, and spun Emma toward the counter. "You, my intelligent friend, are going to find your creative side."

"I don't think I'll be much help," Emma said. "I can barely show the kids how to finger paint."

"Hey, if Maggie can do it, so can you."

Kate opened the lid of a plastic bucket and withdrew a big glob of hot pink goo, which she then set at the top of a stainless machine and punched a button. The glob on top disappeared and perfect sheets of fondant rolled out the bottom.

"Besides." Kate lifted the fondant away from the machine. "I sense you need to release a little stress."

"Stress? Me?" Emma laughed. "A classroom of five-year-olds has a way of doing that, I suppose."

"And working toward your master's."

"Yeah. That too." Emma watched as Kate carefully laid the big sheet of fondant over the top of the iced cake, then showed Emma how to smooth it with her hands. Next a glob of black fondant ran through the machine while Kate grabbed a round piece of wood off the counter.

"It's easy to complain, but I honestly love every minute of teaching," Emma said. "You know that old quote that kids say the darndest things? This morning Billy Ware asked me if I knew a good place to buy a new a top hat because his was broken. Apparently the one he'd put on his snowman didn't make it magically come alive."

"I can't wait to have a baby," Kate said.

"What?" Emma's hands still on the layer of fondant. "You just got married."

"I didn't say I planned to have one any time soon. We have to get Matt elected sheriff first." Kate grinned. "Plus, I'm having way too much fun practicing right now. What about you?"

"What about me?"

"Do you want children?"

An empty pang rippled through Emma's stomach. "Of course. But I really can't even think about that now. Too much to do."

"And . . ." Kate rolled the black fondant over the circle of wood. "There's the little issue of having a daddy to go along with that picture?"

"Yeah. Kind of hard to conceive alone." She really did need to consider a dating service. There must be a man out there who'd be interested in a kindergarten teacher with no history of arrests, violence, or vices.

"Hmmm." Kate handed Emma the smoothing trowel. "So how was your New Year's?"

"Nothing special." Emma leaned down with the pretense of making sure the fondant was centered properly. "I took down my Christmas decorations, reorganized my cupboards, watched a movie." *Had amazing sex with your brother.* "The usual."

"I thought you had a date with Jesse."

"He canceled at the last minute. His uncle in Missoula had a heart attack."

"That's too bad," Kate said.

"He called today to say his uncle would be fine and he wanted to reschedule our date."

"He is a very nice-looking man." Kate clapped the flour from her hands.

"I suppose."

"So are you going out with him?"

"I told him I would."

"If you ask me, I don't think Jesse Hamilton flips your switch." Kate gave Emma a pair of latex gloves to put on. Then she slapped down another glob of white fondant, and with a toothpick added in a pinch of turquoise coloring. She handed the ball to Emma to knead. "Now, my brother—"

Is a spoiled superstar. "Your brother?" Emma squeezed the ball of fondant with all her might. "What about him?"

Kate shrugged. "I saw the way he looked at you Christmas night at our house."

"He didn't *look* at me in any way. He merely walked into a conversation Jesse and I were having about . . . cat food."

"Hard to imagine Dean being interested in anything that doesn't have to do with good hands and fast passes."

"Exactly."

"Okay then," Kate said. "Let me rephrase that remark. I saw the way *you* were looking at him and I think there might be something there."

"Oh, no." Emma shook her head and smushed the ball of fondant down on the counter. "I guess you missed those frown lines between my eyes. No offense—your brother might be handsome but he can irritate me faster than anyone I've ever known."

"Yeah, that's what I thought about Matt too." Kate sighed. "When I first came back, I had no interest in even talking to that man, let alone falling in love with him. But I fell hard. Like I'd jumped out of a perfectly good airplane without a parachute."

"Well, whether your brother interests me or not—and I lean heavily on the *not*," Emma said, intent on putting a lock on the subject. "He went home to Houston."

"Aha!" Kate pointed her finger. "I knew there was something going on."

"There's nothing going on, Kate."

"Then how did you know he went back to Houston?"

Oops. "Kate. Population: six thousand. *Everybody* knows he went back to Houston. Martha Cooke knows he took one overloaded duffel bag for which he will most likely have to pay the airline an extra fee. Jack Stanton knows he wore his cowboy boots and slipped as he got into your daddy's truck at the G & G. And Mrs. Mayberry, the office lady at the elementary, thinks he walks on water because he stopped by the school on his way out of town to bring her husband Ned the autographed ball cap he promised."

"Oh." Kate's know-it-all grin fell like a bad soufflé. "Well, my brother might be a lot of things, but when he says he's going to do something he generally means it."

Not. Emma could tell Kate her brother was a huge BSer and didn't have the guts of a squirrel, let alone a man who would step outside his comfort zone. Or that Emma doubted he meant *anything* he said.

Then again, her disappointment in him really was all her own fault. She'd known who he was and for some reason she'd put expectations on him. That wasn't his fault. Somewhere down the road she'd be able to look back on the twenty-four-ish or so hours they'd spent together with fondness. Somewhere *way* down the road.

He'd gone home to Houston, where he belonged. With his team, his fans, and his supermodels.

She belonged in Deer Lick.

A thousand miles and a world of differences separated what they wanted. And though she'd never be able to forget the hours she'd spent in his arms, Emma knew she'd go on with her life. She would get her degree and move toward helping special kids with needs. She would find a man to love, a man who would love her, and marry her, and give her a family to love.

That man would never be Dean Silverthorne.

Not even if she wanted it with all her heart.

Dean stripped off his shirt and lay back while warm fingers stroked his skin.

"I'm not getting a response here." The feminine voice was low and calm.

"Sorry, Dr. Henderson."

"I'm not a doctor, Mr. Silverthorne." Her fingers slid over the first of three fresh scars on his shoulder. "I'm a PA." She moved his arm slowly in various directions and said, "I think I'll call the doctor in here to check this."

"I promise I'll be good."

She laughed. "Oh, I doubt that." She left the exam room and moments later, Dr. Kip Powell walked in with his usual stern demeanor.

"How's the shoulder?" The doctor glared at the small computer he held in his hands.

"Stiff."

"Will be for awhile. You haven't been overdoing it, have you?"

Other than lifting Emma up onto the kitchen counter so they could make love? "No."

"Because I know guys like you want to push it to the max, thinking, no pain, no gain. But that won't work with this tear, Dean. You've got to give it time."

"I'm doing what you told me to do. Which is basically diddly-squat."

The doctor set the computer on the counter, then tested Dean's range of motion and his grip. Finally the doctor eased his arm back to his side. "You're right. It is a little stiff." He grabbed the computer again and began to chart notes on Dean's file. When he was done with that, he pulled some papers from a drawer and handed them to Dean. "Here are some ROM exercises. Some scapular squeezes. You can go ahead and start walking, but no treadmill, no running, and no swimming. I'll have the PA go over those exercises with you."

"How about a hot tub?"

"Fine. As long as you don't overdo."

Hmmm. Was having mind-numbing sex with a soft, hot blonde in his own personal hot springs considered overexertion? Nah.

"No raising your arms over your head. At all. Got that?"

"Got it." Dean looked down at the exercise instructions in his hands. "So that's it? No doom and gloom?"

The doctor stopped on his way out the door. "Don't get me wrong, Dean. I'm not being a naysayer. I'm not Dr. Death. What I am is a realist. You had a very severe labral tear over the top of two previous tears. You were working with a weak spot to begin with. I won't stand here and fill you full of promises. I will tell you that I believe in optimism. But I will also tell you that if I were you, I'd start thinking about what I wanted to do with the rest of my life. Beyond football. Because the chances of that shoulder coming back to 100 percent . . . well, they aren't high."

"But there's a chance."

"A slim one. And," the doctor continued, "as fine a quarterback as you are, I cannot and will not lie to your coach. The Stallions main office is very aware of your condition. And the prognosis."

With those words, Dean heard the hiss of air leaking from his balloon of happiness.

Wwhile freezing rain pounded the roof of his Houston high-rise, Dean shoved his key into the lock of his front door and gave it a hard twist. The door down the hall opened and Dean's head came up as Misty Peterson slinked toward him in black leggings and knee-high dominatrix boots.

"I didn't know you were back," she purred through perfectly applied lipstick.

Dean pushed past the funk he'd been in since he'd left the doctor's office and smiled at his neighbor, who also happened to be the knockout blonde host for *Houston Live*. In the past year he'd had the pleasure of *viewing* her once or twice in a very personal format.

"Got back yesterday."

She slung her leather tote over her arm and smiled up at him. "How's the shoulder?"

Again with the depersonalization of his well-being. "Getting better every day."

"Oh, I'm glad to hear that."

One minor detail that bugged him about women like Misty—women who spent most of their time on camera? Their smiles. They never allowed the gesture to fill their entire face. Instead, for fear of creating wrinkles, they kept the action toward the lower part of their face. If they showed more teeth it would be more convincing, right? Funny how a little factor like that had never bothered him before he'd gone back home and found himself face-to-face with a blonde who smiled with everything she had.

Misty glanced at her watch. "I've got an interview right now, but maybe we could get together later?" Her fingers danced up the front of his coat. "Have a bite to eat and . . . catch up?"

Decoded, a *bite to eat* meant the olive in her martini and *catch up* meant she hadn't had the big O in awhile and knew he could deliver the goods. In the past, the underlying promise of a good time with a beautiful woman between some very expensive sheets would grab his attention between his legs. None of that tingly action happened to be going on right now. All he could think was how wrong it felt to have her hand roam his body.

"That would be great," he lied. "But I've already agreed to meet up with the boys tonight before they head out to the playoffs day after tomorrow."

Her manicured hand skated past his open coat and down the front of his polo. "I'm free tomorrow night too."

"Having dinner with Bo Miller and his family." He shrugged. "Sorry."

She gave him an exaggerated pout. "No worries. I'm sure we can fit in a nooner or something. I don't need all of you for very long." Her hand slid from his chest down to the zipper on his khakis. "Just *this* for long enough." She gave him a little pat, then turned on her high heels and strutted down the carpeted hall toward the elevator.

Meaningless sex. A one-nighter, nooner, or whatever time of day you manage to find a willing body.

Emma's words roared back.

His neighbor may not be brainless, but sex with her would definitely be meaningless.

Sex with Emma? Definitely not meaningless.

Unfortunately Emma appeared to be done with him.

Have a nice trip. All good things must come to an end, she'd said.

What if he didn't want them to end?

And why did they have to?

Damn.

He knew she was attracted to him. So why would she push him away when all he'd done was say he planned to hire someone to get the charity going?

Dean exhaled hard, opened his door, and stepped inside his professionally decorated condo. The room had been assembled in magazine-quality perfection. From the expensive art, the leather sofas and chairs, the seventy-three-inch HDTV, and even the rugs which had been recently vacuumed by a maid service that came in once a week. All had been put there by someone who didn't know him and was taken care of by someone he'd never met.

He tossed his keys on the table beside the door and strolled into the party room, where in the center of the pool table the balls were racked and ready for a game. He glanced up at the built-in bookcase, crowded with photos of him in various stages of his career. Photos of him with celebrities and legendary NFL stars. Plaques and trophies and autographed balls were squeezed in the spaces between his number-eleven jersey and a field towel autographed by his football hero, the great Ken Stabler. A legend whose "Holy Roller" play against San Diego in 1978 led to a game-winning touchdown, not to mention a modification to the NFL rulebook.

But where were the family photos?

Dean turned, leaned his butt against the pool table, and glanced across the room. Everything in the condo was pristine and impersonal, yet no amount of temperature manipulation would help stave off the detached formality. He thought of his friend Bo Miller's house and the number of plastic trucks and building blocks you had to kick out of the way just to make a path to the sofa.

Where were the toys?

Where was the sweet chaos of laughter and voices all talking over one another?

In silence he walked to the wall of windows and looked down at the cars far below, to the elegant pool currently closed for the night, and up to the city lights blurred by the freezing rain. He'd paid plenty for those great views. It seemed odd that now he'd traded the meaning of *great views* for ancient pines, craggy mountaintops, and a schoolteacher's killer smile.

He walked into his exercise room and glanced at the recently unused weights and equipment that stood like solid steel reminders of his injury. Then he moved into the bedroom, shrugged off his coat, and tossed it on the navy blue comforter of his California king-sized bed.

Before he moved into the lodge house, he'd been dying to get out of the twin-sized disaster he'd slept in at his parents' house and back home to Houston. But now the bed in front of him looked big and empty and Houston no longer felt like home.

He pulled off the rest of his clothes and went in to shower before he met up with some of the guys at Johnny Ray's for wings, beer, and gridiron gossip. Adjusting the spray on the hydrotherapy nozzle, he stepped inside and let the hot water pulsate over his head and shoulders. As his body warmed, his heartbeat slowed, and an ache twisted in the center of his chest.

Emma.

He missed her.

She'd made it clear that she wanted nothing to do with him.

The challenge now would be to learn to live without her.

Or could he?

Chapter Eleven

The Naughty Irish was wall-to-wall with Stallions fans and even the occasional Packers fan like Emma, waiting for kick-off on the Wild Card Playoffs game. The Stallions' blue and red team colors had become the overall decoration theme. The noise level had risen above thunderous, and anticipation rippled through the crowd.

Though the game would be played on Lambeau Field in snowy Green Bay, Emma had no doubt Dean would have traveled with his team. He'd have wanted to help in any way he could to get them to the championship game. For her own selfish reasons she hoped they wouldn't put his face on camera, but of course they would.

He *was* the team.

So with a sip of her diet soda—it was a school night, after all—Emma resigned herself to be distracted across the room when he appeared.

Padded chairs were scattered around the large round table where she sat next to her date, Jesse, amid Dean's friends and family. As special guests, they'd been given the best seats in the house in front of the Irish's newly purchased large screen HDTV. While their friend Ollie pulled beers on tap and Maggie scooted between tables to deliver their group a tray loaded with Moose Drool, Fat Tire Ale, and other assorted brews, Emma settled in for the celebration.

Double celebration, if the Stallions won.

The ballots had been counted and tonight the town could revel in the landslide election for their new sheriff.

"No umbrella drinks today, kids." Maggie grinned as she leaned over the balding head of Robert Silverthorne to set his Guinness on the table. "But the nacho bar is free. And if you tip your waitress she'll be happy to bring you some of those really yummy mini-tacos she has hidden in the kitchen."

"Aw, Maggie, you're a girl after my own heart," Kate's father said.

Maggie kissed him right on top of his shiny head. "Sorry, handsome. I'm already taken."

"Raise a glass, Deer Lick," Maggie shouted above the clamor of the bar and lifted her shot glass in the air, "to your new sheriff, Matt Ryan."

Glasses clinked. Cheers abounded. And Emma figured from the way Kate looked at her new husband, as soon as they got home he was going to get really, really lucky.

Beside Emma, Jesse sipped from his glass of ale. She watched his throat work as he swallowed. Watched him clean away the foam by sliding his bottom lip over his top. He caught her looking and smiled with his warm, dark eyes. Since they'd arrived he'd been very attentive. He'd opened her door, pulled out her chair, hung up her coat—the typical date stuff. He'd done everything a woman could expect on a date.

"You look good in that Packers cap," Jesse said.

She thought of how much Dean hated her hat. "Obviously I'm not the majority. I feel like I'm in enemy territory."

Jesse gave her a smile. "I think your friends will forgive you."

"They wouldn't if the almighty *Mr. Perfect* was playing." The sound of Dean's nickname coming off her tongue sounded odd. Her heart squeezed and she took a sip of her soda to swallow down the awful burn his name fired up in her stomach. The burn that acknowledged how much she missed seeing him around town. More precisely, how much she missed seeing him an arm's length away with that hungry look in his green eyes.

"I've always been a Packers fan," she told Jesse. "My Memaw was born in Wisconsin. She always rooted for them. Even when they struggled for a lot of years. She was a huge Bart Starr fan."

"Not Favre?"

"Wasn't everyone at some time or other?"

Jesse leaned closer and his arm settled across the back of her chair. "I like you, Emma."

"Oh." She leaned back to look at him. "Well, I like you too. Wow. Those are some numbers for Aaron Rodgers, huh?"

The commentator's pre-game banter was filled with ego-boosting stats and the obligatory warm-up interviews with the coaches spewing all the PC stuff about how the other team was so good at this or that, and how they were a challenging opponent. As the TV cut away to a soda commercial, Emma entertained herself with the sporadic conversations that popped up throughout the bar. Then as the pre-game show came back on, Emma looked up to find exactly what she'd been dreading.

In what appeared to be a locker room interview, a female reporter stuck a microphone in Dean's face and asked him the question that had plagued him since the Thanksgiving Day sack.

"How's the shoulder?"

Dean in street clothes and a team jacket flashed his famous smile. "Doing great."

"What do you think the Stallions' chances are against the Packers?"

"Rodgers is a red-hot quarterback right now. His pass completions are over 70 percent. That's going to be a challenge for Jacoby during the game. Their defense is going to target him. But he's a strong kid with a good head on his shoulders. I think he's going to surprise everyone. And I know the team is 100 percent behind him."

The interviewer flashed her perfect teeth. "How does it feel to be on the sidelines instead of on the field?"

Emma cringed. What a bitch to ask such a question. How did she think he felt? Football was the most important thing in his life. Emma hoped he'd shut the nasty interviewer up with one of his quick comebacks.

Dean shrugged his broad shoulders and tilted his head. "It doesn't matter where I stand. I support my team. And I know Jacoby will be a great captain."

Emma melted.

Dean had been given every opportunity to piss and moan. Instead he'd stood there like a true gentleman and thrown all his support into the kid who'd replaced him in the career he loved more than life.

The rest of the interview was a buzz in Emma's ears. She watched his smile and felt the power as strongly as when he used that beautiful mouth to kiss her. She looked at the warmth in his eyes and thought of the way they'd glimmer when he tried to coerce her into taking off her clothes. He made gestures with his big hands and she remembered how they touched her with such gentleness and care.

The kickoff went with a long boot for a twenty-four-yard Stallions return, but Emma barely noticed. On the second play of the game Dean's replacement got sacked for a loss of ten yards.

"Not a good way to start the game," Jesse said. "Care for some nachos?"

Unfortunately the cheesy snack made her think of New Year's Day and Dean. "No, thank you."

"Okay. I'll be right back."

Emma watched Jesse walk toward the nacho bar. His broad shoulders had no problem getting him through the crowd. He was tall, and lean, and handsome. And there wasn't a chance in hell she'd ever be able to not compare him to Dean Silverthorne.

In all fairness, Emma knew tonight would be their last date. Her thoughts were on someone else. And until she managed to eliminate those warm and tingly reflections, she had no business leading Jesse on.

Her gaze slid back to the screen just as the Stallions' new quarterback released a long spiral pass into the hands of the wide receiver. The bar crowd jumped to their feet and roared as the Stallions' receiver broke two tackles, raced down the field, and carried the ball into the end zone.

While the enthusiastic Stallions fans celebrated, Emma lifted her soda and took a sip.

"*Great* way to start the game."

Emma turned her head toward the voice. Which did not belong to Jesse.

Beside her sat the man who should have been freezing his incredibly tight butt off on the sidelines in snowy Green Bay. "What are you doing here?"

"Watching the game."

"Why aren't you *at* the game?"

"Aren't you happy to see me?" Dean snagged a nacho from Kate's plate and it went *crunch* in his mouth.

"Sure." The tingles tumbling through her stomach said *hell, yes.* "But—"

"Pre-recorded interview."

"Ah. So, again, why aren't you at the game?"

"They uninvited me." He drank from the beer in his hand.

"Why?"

"Didn't want the extra pressure of me being on the sidelines. They didn't want Jacoby to be distracted."

By the frown creasing his forehead, Emma could tell that bothered him. And *that* bothered her. "But didn't they think you could help? I mean . . . he just got sacked."

"He's got coaches." His eyes darkened as took another drink of beer, then sucked a drop from his top lip. "Besides, he doesn't want my advice. Told me so himself."

"Is he crazy?"

Dean looked at her and smiled. "He's young and eager. That's all."

Translation: the kid is young and cocky and doesn't think he needs anyone's advice. Stupid kid.

"How did you get in here without anyone seeing you?" she asked.

"They saw me." At that moment Maggie set another bottle of beer down on the table in front of him. "See. One of the perks of being a player. Free beer."

"Like you can't afford to buy your own?"

"Of course I can. But why would I want to take away the opportunity to make someone feel good about buying me one? It's an age-old guy thing, Em. Just go with it. If the Stallions win, I'll pay the bar tab for everybody."

"And if they lose?"

"They won't." He balanced the chair back on the rear two legs just as Jesse walked up with a full plate of nachos.

Emma looked between the two men, recognizing the moment when the testosterone flared and competition began.

"Silverthorne."

Dean grinned. "Hamilton."

Jesse nodded. "You're in my seat."

"Am I?" The chair landed back on all four legs and Dean stood. "Sorry about that."

"I'm sure someone can find you another chair," Jesse said.

"No need." Dean stepped back and waved his hand gallantly at the chair. "Have a seat."

Jesse set his plate down on the table in front of Emma, settled into his chair, and picked up his glass of beer. "I brought enough nachos to share."

"Oh, I'm not—"

"Hey, Emma? Can I talk to you a minute?"

Emma looked up to find Dean practically leaning over her shoulder.

"I'm . . . watching the game."

"I know." Dean tried to look as apologetic as possible. Too bad the deepening of the dimple in his chin gave him away. He knew exactly what he was up to. "But I'd really like to talk to you."

"Can't it wait until the game is over? Don't you want to watch your team play?"

"Of course." He glanced up at the screen as Jacoby got sacked again and hit the ground hard. "Ooooh. That one's gonna hurt." He looked back at Emma. "This won't take long. I promise."

"She asked you to wait until the game was over." Jesse tried to sound cool but didn't quite accomplish the feat.

"Understood," Dean said to Jesse. Then he slid his gaze back to Emma. "This is about the project I told you about a few weeks ago. What do you say, Em? Can you give me just a couple of minutes?"

Her heart turned over. If he meant the charity, then yes, she was interested. "Oh. You mean *that* project?"

He nodded.

"I'll be right back, Jesse." Emma got to her feet and slid her arms into the coat Dean held out for her. Whether a glutton for punishment or plain curious, she'd soon find out. She placed her hand on Jesse's shoulder. "This really might be important."

"Sure." He gave her a hesitant smile, then slid a glare to Dean. "I'll wait for you here."

Dean took her hand off Jesse's shoulder and practically dragged her through the bar and out the door. He didn't stop dragging her until they crossed the street and came to a huge black SUV parked in front of the Yee-Ha Trading Post.

Before she could blink, he had her back up against the car door, his hands cupping her face, and his mouth on hers. He tasted like passion and promise, with a healthy dose of hunger.

God, he tasted good.

Before she gave into the tingling sensation sweeping across her breasts and pulled him closer, she pressed her hands against his flannel-covered chest. It was freezing outside. Snow drifted down in big fat flakes. Yet from beneath his shirt, his hard, defined muscles warmed her palms. His heart pounded beneath her fingers. And she came dangerously close to throwing common sense out the window. Again.

He lifted his head. But he did not move.

"What are you doing?"

His hands lowered to her shoulders. "I'm kissing you, honey."

"Well, don't."

A corner of his mouth curled upward. "But I like kissing you."

"You said you wanted to talk to me." She sighed. "So talk."

He glanced down the street where parked cars filled every empty space and a few stragglers hurried toward the bar. "How about we go somewhere a little more private?"

"I'm on a date, Dean."

His smile flattened. "Sorry." Then he pulled the Packers cap from her head and looked down into her face. "You were right," he said.

"About?"

"The camp. How it needs to come together. When I was in Houston last week I visited a friend's house. Do you remember the teammate I told you about whose son has autism?"

She nodded.

"While I had dinner with Bo and his family, I had the opportunity to watch the interaction between him and his son." He took her hands in his and intertwined their fingers. "Watching them together . . . able to laugh together, but without the ability to reciprocate the affection. Em, I swear I could feel the desperation of how badly my friend wants to help his little boy. It broke my heart."

He gripped her hands, which helped to steady her.

"I went home and got on the internet. I started compiling research on therapy for kids like Brenden. The more I looked, the more fascinating it became." The enthusiasm in his voice was tangible. "Do you know that one of every 110 children will register somewhere on the autism spectrum?"

"Yes, I do know. I learned that in one of my classes."

"Those are awful statistics."

"I agree. But what does this have to do with me, Dean?"

He looked away. His wide shoulders lifted on a big intake of air. Then he looked back at her with serious eyes. "You were right, Em. If I want to make a difference I have to get my hands dirty."

"So you're saying . . ."

"I have almost seven months before I need to be in training camp. There's no reason I can't rehab here and get the organization started."

Emma melted like butter on a summer sidewalk. She squeezed his hands. "That's great, Dean. I'm really happy to hear that. You should be very proud of yourself."

"That's the funny thing. For the first time in my life, I'm not doing something for me. And it feels pretty damned good."

The happy gleam in his eye reached out and grabbed hold of her heart.

"It would be nice to know you're behind me."

Her throat felt so tight she could barely speak. "I support you 100 percent."

"That's what I hoped you'd say." He wrapped his arms around her and tucked her head beneath his chin.

The scent of his soap clung to his warm skin and she stayed in his arms for several greedy breaths. It took everything she had to step from his embrace when all she wanted to do was stay right there in the sanctuary of his arms, snuggled up against his strong, compassionate heart. But being in his arms was too risky. He was still a temporary fixture. Once his shoulder mended, once his organization got off the ground, he would leave.

"I'm very happy for you. But . . ."

His dark brows lifted. "But?"

"I really need to get back inside." She turned.

"Em." He caught her hand, smoothed his thumb across her fingers. "Please, don't go. Can we go somewhere? Talk about the details?"

She couldn't look at him. If she did, she'd run the risk of leaping into his arms and hanging on for dear life while he revved up his engine to leave her behind like roadkill. "This is *your* project, Dean. It doesn't involve me."

"Sure it does."

"No." She shook her head. "Nothing you do involves me."

"You're wrong. Look at all the time and energy you're investing to learn more about these issues. To get a specialized degree so you can work toward helping these kids. Don't you think this might be a perfect opportunity for you too?"

"It might be. But I just can't." She looked up and for the first time realized that Dean Silverthorne might be able to take a thousand-pound hit on the field, but he was not unbreakable. "Look, I think it's wonderful that you plan to stay here and take on this challenge. And I know you'll be successful. But nothing has changed since New Year's Day."

"A lot has changed."

"Not for me. I have plans, Dean." The urge to flee reached up and strangled her. And in her anxious state the words rushed out much harsher than she intended. "And you're not in them."

Well, hell, that didn't go the way he'd planned.

Dean watched Emma retreat across the deserted road and back into the bar. Arms folded, he stood beside the SUV he'd bought in Bozeman and debated whether to follow her back into the bar or head home.

He'd hoped she might be a little happy to see him. Excited he'd made the decision to organize the camp on his own instead of hiring others to do the majority of the work. He'd still have to hire those more knowledgeable in specific areas, but none of that seemed to make a difference.

He'd never had a woman walk away from him.

Hell, he'd never had a woman tell him no for anything.

Emma Hart was his first in many ways. In a weird way he completely respected that. He didn't like it. But he respected it.

That didn't stop him from wanting her, however. From the moment he'd walked into that bar and seen her sitting there in her ridiculous Packers cap to the moment he touched her, he'd wanted her. Right then. Didn't matter how. Didn't matter where. What surprised him most was that he didn't just want to have sex with her. There'd been no doubt about that.

But he wanted more.

He wanted *her*.

As the bar door slowly closed behind her and the sound of jeers and boos from inside the place faded, Dean unfolded his arms and started walking.

No matter how difficult or awkward it might be, he would go back into that bar and sit down with his friends and family. He'd ignore Emma's stubbornness and Jesse Hamilton's glares, and he'd watch his boys kick Green Bay's cheese-head asses.

Come tomorrow, he'd find a new tactic to entice Emma onto his own team.

The Stallions' chances for the Big Show went cleats-up in the third quarter.

While Dean had nursed a bitter ale and his wounded pride, his team had allowed two turnovers to the Packers that turned disastrous. One had been taken in for a touchdown, the other had ended up a field goal that perfectly split the uprights.

Guilt hung like a chain around his neck. Sure, he hadn't been the one throwing the ball that night. But he'd let his team down as sure as if he'd thrown that intercepted pass. Jacoby had gone into the game overconfident, and when the going got tough, the backup QB had quit on the team.

Even with his shoulder out of the socket and pain ripping through his body, Dean had needed to be dragged off the field and into the locker room. Or at least that's the way he saw it. And maybe a few other vocal online critics saw it that way as well.

He had always fought against failure. He'd never given up. The desire to succeed pushed him. Drove him. But even as he watched his team lose their chance at the Super Bowl, his hammering need to triumph hadn't completely kept his mind occupied.

As expected, Emma had ignored him the rest of that night and to make matters worse, he'd had to suffer through watching Hamilton flirt with her. Emma appeared to have gotten sucked right into the farm supply owner's "Look at what a good, upstanding guy I am" routine.

When the game had ended with a series of groans and complaints from the inebriated spectators at the Naughty

Irish, Jesse had accompanied Emma out the door. *He'd* taken her home while Dean had gone home to an empty house. With thoughts of Emma traipsing through his head, Dean had been unable to sleep. To keep those thoughts of her at bay, he'd stayed up all night researching the internet for more information on how to create a non-profit organization.

Days later he sat in the downstairs office of the lodge house, turned on the laptop he'd brought from Houston, and checked emails. One from his agent asked the progress of his recovery. Dean hit the delete key. Two more were from his coach, asking the progress of his recovery. Delete. Delete. None of the emails were personalized. There had been no "Hey, what's up, butthead?" and Dean began to realize that they valued his arm more than him.

Outside the big picture window in his office, snow drifted down and steam rose from the hot springs. He should just take a bottle of Jack down there and have a good sip and soak. But whiskey at ten in the morning had never been his breakfast of champions. Besides, every time he looked at that damn hot springs, he thought of Emma naked and wet and so hot for him she nearly melted the granite surrounding the pool.

He thought of the way the moonlight had peeked through the clouds to come out and dance in her hair. The way the fireworks over the lake had glittered in her eyes. The way she grabbed his hair between her fingers and cried out his name while she came against his tongue. He couldn't ever remember celebrating New Year's in such a dynamic way.

The following day changed things for him. In his mind he could see them cuddled up and laughing together. Something he never did with the women he usually dated. He'd never been a cuddler. Hell, just using the word threatened the retraction of his "man" card.

He shook his head. Emma was a strong woman who knew what she wanted.

Unfortunately, she didn't want *him*.

He stood and with the backs of his knees he shoved the desk chair away. He went into the kitchen for another cup of coffee. He'd just dropped in two cubes of sugar when the doorbell rang. His bare feet squeaked against the hardwood floor as he went to the huge double doors and opened one. His sister Kelly stood on the veranda. Snow dusted her blond hair. Her nose was pink and she clasped the front of her soft pink parka together.

"Let me in, I'm freezing out here." She pushed past him and strode into the living room. Snow clung to the soles of her boots and left a trail of melted droplets across the floor.

"Nice to see you, little sister. How was your flight?"

"Typical. Why is it these airlines can never seem to get out of the gate on time?"

"They try."

"Yeah. Tell that to the screaming kid who sat behind me all the way from Chicago to LA kicking the back of my seat. And please remind me of that the next time you need a favor."

"I really do appreciate it, Kel."

"I know. Actually, I had a moment to stop in at the Shack on the way here."

"How's it going?"

"Busy." She tugged off her coat, tossed it on the back of the leather sofa, and went to stand by the fire in the enormous stone fireplace. "Kate's up to her elbows in Valentine's Day specialty cake orders. Dad's off helping Edna Price install a new water heater. And I'm here to help you."

He lifted the cup to his mouth and sipped the tepid coffee. "When do you head back to Chicago?"

"Tomorrow. So let's get this summer camp deal off the ground. There's a ton of paperwork to file."

"That's why I called you back. Cup of Joe?"

"Please. Fake sugar. Got cream?"

"Milk."

"That'll do." She followed him into the kitchen where the bank of windows overlooked the snow-covered meadow. "I still can't believe you bought this place. You must have paid a fortune."

"Nope." He picked up the glass carafe and poured the coffee into a mug. "It had been on the market for so long the owners were eager to make a deal. When I told them what I wanted to do with the property I must have touched something in their hearts because I only paid half of what it's worth."

Kelly's green eyes widened. "Seriously?"

"Seriously." He handed her the coffee. "Want a tour?"

"Duh. I've driven by this place a million times and have never set foot on the property before."

Dean led the way up the stairs. "Not even to sneak in a soak in the hot springs?"

Kelly gasped. "It has a hot springs?"

Dean stopped so fast she ran into his backside. "Man, you really are Sister Serious, aren't you?"

"I'm *what*?"

"Didn't you ever put down the books and break out of the scholar dungeon for a little fun when you were a kid?"

Her small nose wrinkled. "Apparently not."

"Then I say put them down right now and learn to cut loose a little."

"Yeah. See, that's not a good idea." She sighed. "When I *cut loose* I have a tendency to lose all control."

They reached the top of the stairs. "Hmmm. Kate's wedding reception?"

"Don't remind me."

"Hangover?"

"You don't want to know."

"Would I have to kill someone?"

"Yeah. Me."

"Not a certain deputy with a wild reputation?"

Kelly's head jerked up. "Why would you say that?"

"Personal knowledge of going in for the easy score."

"I am *not* an easy score."

Dean laughed. "Everybody's easy when they're drunk off their ass. Come on, wipe off that prosecutor's glare. A tour of this place might take awhile."

True to his word, it took Dean almost half an hour to show his sister the five-bedroom, four-bath house plus adjacent acreage and outbuildings. She'd appropriately oohed and ahhed over his plans to turn the guest cabins into bunkhouses for the kids and counselors, and grinned at his dream of adding horses and smaller animals for sensitivity therapy. She made him promise to hold a big BBQ as soon as the weather warmed up and the snow melted.

They strolled back into the house and Dean poured her another cup of coffee before he guided her toward his office.

"Don't take this as an insult," she said, admiring the rough timber grandfather clock in the hall. "But I can't believe you came up with this idea all on your own."

"I do have a business degree."

"Oh yeah. I forgot about that."

"And I might have had a little help," he admitted.

"From who?"

A certain ghost mama. He shook his head and grinned. "If things go forward, as I expect they will, you'll find out at the appropriate time."

"Wow. That's cryptic."

"You have no idea." He chuckled. "Guess we better get down to business." When they reached his office he opened his laptop. She sat across from him, studied him like he was a two-legged spider. "Got something else on your mind?"

"Ugh. Am I that transparent? Or are you really that good at reading me?"

"I read signs for a living. I watch the eyes of my opponents to see what their next move is going to be. You're not transparent, but you're pretty damned close."

"And yet, I chose to be an officer of the court."

"Spill, Kel."

"What's up with you and Emma Hart?"

Unfortunately nothing. "Why?"

"For starters, everyone saw how you acted the other night at the Irish. Your team was playing and yet you couldn't keep your eyes off her."

"And you know this because you have a magic mirror in your Chicago apartment?"

"I know this because—"

"Baby sister ratted me out."

"Yeah. Kinda."

"Well, Kate must have been seeing things," he said, "because if she failed to mention it, Emma was on a date."

"With Jesse Hamilton. I know. Look, Jesse is a stand-up guy. He's one of the nicest, most responsible *younger* men in this town."

"And what am I, the big bad wolf?"

"I don't think of you like that and you know it. Kate does, though. She thinks you suck at relationships."

"I do not."

"Seriously?" She gave a tilt of her head and her ponytail flopped to one side. "When was the last time you had a relationship with someone that lasted more than two weeks?"

"They all last more than two weeks."

"I meant to say two months."

"Okay. You got me." Dean took a slug of coffee, winced at the burn on his tongue, and set his mug down on a stone coaster. "The only long-term relationship I've ever had is with a football."

"Exactly." His sister brushed her blond hair behind her shoulders. "Which is what has Kate's apron in a knot. Emma Hart is looking for love, Dean. A real one-on-one connection that will lead to a forever relationship. She wants children. She wants her own happily-ever-after."

"Did she send you here to tell me that?"

"Emma? Are you kidding? She's a very private person.

Kate knows more about her than I do and that isn't much."

Hell, *he* probably knew more about Emma than both his sisters put together. But they didn't need to know that. What Emma had told him would remain private unless she decided otherwise.

"And this has *what* to do with me?"

Kelly leaned forward and placed her hand on his arm. "You're a good guy, Dean, but Emma's not your type. Like I said, *everyone* saw the way you watched her the other night at the bar. She needs a man who will be there for her. And as much as I love you and I think the world of you—"

"I get it. I'm not a keeper."

Jesus. Who did they think he was, Hannibal Lecter?

"No worries, Kel. You and Kate can sheath your Power Ranger swords. Your sacred little schoolteacher is safe from the big bad quarterback."

For now.

T he car keys twirled in Dean's hand as he punched the garage door opener and headed toward the less-than-economical SUV he'd bought when he'd come back into town. But as he opened the driver's door, he glanced at the rusted heap of crap parked next to the SUV. He hadn't had a conversation with his mother since he'd come back from Houston. Maybe he'd take the Buick and see if she had time to pop in for a chat.

Several miles down the road Tom Jones began to moan through the radio.

"Oh, goody! You're back!"

Dean smiled, pulled to the side of the road, and turned in

his seat. She hadn't changed. Same red flannel over her overalls. Same gray bun on top of her head. Same bright golden glow hovering all over the place. "Hi, Mom. Fancy seeing you here."

"Well, you wouldn't have if you'd driven that big old gas guzzler. What's up with that?"

"I thought it would come in handy with transporting people around."

"For the charity?"

"Yep."

She clasped a transparent hand to her chest. "Oh, Son, I just can't tell you how wonderful this is going to be. I know you'll be so involved you won't even miss football."

"Of course I'm not going to miss football. I'll be headed out to training camp in July."

"Yes. Of course." She glanced away. "That's what I meant."

He lifted a brow. "Is it?"

"Is it what?"

"Stop dodging the question." He leaned closer. "You can't see into the future, can you?"

"Pffft. No. Of course not. That would be ridiculous."

"And me sitting in your car talking to you after you've been dead for five months isn't?"

"Well, there is that. So what's the plan? Tell me all the details."

"You are so transparent."

"Well, of course I am, silly boy. I'm dead."

Dean laughed, turned in his seat, and leaned against the door. For the next ten minutes he ran his whole game plan by his mother the same way he had when he'd been in high school and college. If anyone had driven by, they would have called the men in little white jackets to take him away. As it was, their in-depth conversation hadn't been disturbed. The strange reality that he happened to be having this exchange with someone who no longer existed did not slip past him.

"Does dad know you still hang around?" Dean asked when they'd wrapped up.

"Well, not like you and Kate. I've got to catch him when he's sleeping. He doesn't believe in ghosts and things that go bump in the night."

"Mom? *I* don't believe in that stuff either."

"But you're more open-minded. Someone," she pointed her finger skyward, "who shall remain nameless says that within every mind there is the possibility to see what does not always seem believable. Which is why children are so open to the possibilities. No one has told them what they can or cannot see. Their imaginations are works of art. But when you get older, the heart gets jaded and you rely too much on the evidence instead of the possibility of the miracle."

"Wow. That's pretty deep."

"Yeah." She laughed. "Weird, huh."

He nodded. "Pretty damn weird."

"Just saying, it doesn't hurt to keep an open mind and open heart at the same time. You just never know what might be right around the corner." She leaned forward and patted his shoulder. "Who knows, you could even fall in love."

"That wouldn't be a miracle, Mom. *That* would be a disaster."

Fire crackled and popped in the woodstove as Emma sat on her floor and prepared the week's lessons. Between her notations, she'd put down her pen and dangle a catnip mouse in front of Oscar's twitching whiskers. Instead of his usual pounce and attack, he barely touched it with his pink nose. He looked up at Emma with his one blue eye and one green eye as if to say he wasn't in the mood for felt mouse-chasing or for getting catnip-tipsy.

"What's the matter, boy?" She lifted his chubby body into her arms and stroked him between his pointy ears. "Did you eat something that upset your tummy?"

Oscar turned on his motor and head-butted her chin. His way of saying *I love you*. She held her old friend in her lap. His warm body curled up on her legs and his purr got louder while she stroked his silky fur.

She and Oscar went way back to a time when she'd learned about life the hard way. She'd been eighteen and so far off the radar with the cool kids she didn't even register. Then she'd met the college buddy Dean had brought home for the summer. Nick Harris had been cute and muscular and for some reason he'd singled her out and invited her to the bonfire party. Up to that point the closest she'd ever gotten to one of the infamous bonfire parties was when her Memaw had driven past it on their way to a friend's house to play Yahtzee.

To Emma the invitation had been huge. A sign of acceptance into the cool kid club. She'd gone there with good intentions. She'd left there without her pride or her virginity.

On the way home from that bonfire party she'd discovered Oscar. A tiny kitten who'd been abandoned by a dumpster at the school yard where she'd hidden until she could gather herself together. She'd known she couldn't go home until she made that happen. Causing any distress for her Memaw had been out of the question. She'd cuddled that kitten against her chest all the way home and they'd become one.

At night, Oscar slept beneath the covers between her ankles. She'd always been careful not to move suddenly so as not to injure him. But Oscar hadn't minded the occasional bonk on the head. When he grew from a kitten to a cat, he'd seemed to sense her moods. On those nights when loneliness crept up, she'd lie on her side so the tears would slide down her face and onto her pillow. Oscar would settle himself against her body with his head on her shoulder. He'd look up at her with his mismatched eyes as if he wished he could take away her pain.

She stroked his soft fur and leaned down to kiss his head right between his pointy ears. "I love you, Oscar. Even if everybody else thinks you're evil and grumpy. They just don't know you like I do."

"Merrrrooowww."

Emma laughed. Her cat never just said a plain meow. He always had an extra little *grrrr* to add.

The knock on the door surprised her. Who would come by this late? She lifted Oscar from her lap and gently set him on the floor. Tail swishing, he followed her as she reached for the deadbolt and swung open the door.

Dean stood on the other side of the threshold in the dark gray Kodiak parka that made the green in his eyes almost glow.

His gaze lowered down her legs then climbed back up to her face. "You're really into cartoons, aren't you?"

She glanced down at her Minnie Mouse pajama bottoms. "They make me smile."

His gaze lowered again to her tank top and the hard peaks poking against the thin fabric. A corner of his mouth lifted. "Me too."

"Merrrrooowww."

Dean looked down where Oscar rubbed against her leg. "Hello to you too, evil cat."

"He's not evil. He just has discriminating taste."

"He hates me," Dean said.

"Like I said."

Dean laughed.

"Why are you here?" Emma asked. "It's nine o'clock at night. Shouldn't you be out carousing at the bowling alley or something?"

"Good one, teacher. Aren't you going to invite me in?"

"Probably not."

"It's cold out here."

"Then maybe you should get back in your—" She glanced out the door to see his mother's rusted bomber parked in her driveway. "Where's that monster of an SUV you bought?"

He shrugged. "Long story. Can I *please* come in?"

When his gaze slipped down the front of her tank top again, she folded her arms. No need to give the man a free show. "Fine." She stepped aside and he walked in. Oscar arched his back and hissed.

"See," Dean said. "He hates me."

"He just doesn't understand the fine art of playing with an egg-shaped ball for a living. He prefers yarn."

Dean's head whipped up and a huge grin curved his sensuous lips. "See what happens when I leave you alone for a few days? You become a total smartass."

She shrugged. "I could be worse things."

"I'd pay money to see that."

She sighed. Looked away. Anywhere other than at him and those gorgeous eyes, that slightly dimpled chin, and those big shoulders and broad chest. He overwhelmed the place with his over-the-top masculinity. And he made her want to peel off his clothes, push him down to the floor, and have her way with him. "And why was it that you wanted to come in?"

"I told you the other night that I wanted to talk to you about the charity. You didn't give me the chance."

"*You* started off the conversation by kissing me against my will."

"*You* didn't seem to mind it so much at the time."

"*You* weren't paying attention."

"On the contrary." Another smile deepened the dimple in his chin. "I was paying very close attention."

"Does everything you say have to be filled with sexual innuendoes?"

"Why, Emma, I was referring to the Packers hat you were wearing. Which is why I yanked it off your head. If you ask me, you caused my team to lose."

"I had nothing to do with that. Maybe you should talk to that over-inflated-ego-driven backup QB."

He liked the way she thought. Giving the second-stringer a piece of his mind was exactly what he had planned. "I'll do that, just as soon as I get to training camp."

He tossed his coat on the chair and pointed a finger at Oscar. "No drooling on the sleeve this time, cat." Then he sat down on her sofa, leaned back, and folded his hands behind his head like he owned the place. "So how was your date?"

She sat on the far end of the sofa and tucked Oscar up onto her lap for protection. "I'm not discussing my social life with you, Dean."

"Why not?"

"Because it's none of your business."

"Of course it is. I care about all of the Letty Silverthorne Sunshine Camp's board of directors."

"The what?"

He reached out and took her hand. For a few silent moments he inspected her fingers as if searching for the secret of life. Then he looked up at her and all the tease had disappeared from his eyes. "That's what I wanted to talk to you about the other night, Em. I'm putting together the organization's board of directors and I'd like you to be a member."

"Me?" She pointed to herself and Oscar jumped from her lap. "Why?"

"Because this organization is important. And because I want to know it will always be given the amount of respect and consideration it deserves. I want every action to be reviewed by the people I trust the most. My dad, my sisters . . . and you."

Emma couldn't have been more surprised. Or more honored. "But, you've only known me for a short time."

"Honey . . ." He gave her hand a little squeeze. "I know you better than most people. I know you like to be kissed right here." He gently touched the curve of her neck. "I know you have a tiny little mole at the top of your right thigh. I know—"

"Okay!" She moved away from him and those talented hands, even though she wanted to feel them roam all over her body again. "I get it. You *think* you know me."

"Regardless of what people choose to think of me, Emma, I'm a pretty good judge of character. There isn't a doubt in my mind that you're the right person to sit beside my father and sisters on the decision-making for this organization."

"That's quite a leap of faith."

"Someone once told me you've got to keep an open mind."

"Smart person."

"Yeah. She was. Just like you."

Emma thought about his proposition while he sat next to her and tempted her with his amazing scent and blatant masculinity. While he teased her with that smile that said he could do all those wonderful things she'd dreamed about since she'd last been in his bed.

She bit her lower lip. Concentration was really, really hard when you had that much of a sensory overload.

"Tell you what," he said in a smooth, low tone. "You sign on for the inaugural year and after that, if you're dissatisfied, you walk away."

The word *dissatisfied* and anything to do with Dean Silverthorne did not belong in the same thought.

"Okay."

His dark brows lifted. "Okay?"

"I'll do it on two conditions."

"Which are?"

"No touching." Her index finger popped up. "No kissing." Her middle finger joined the pop-up party.

He chuckled. "I don't know where your head is at, Emma, but I came over here to strictly talk business. You've made it clear you're dating Jesse and I have to respect that."

"You do?"

"I swear I will keep my hands to myself. If there's going to be any hanky-panky, you'll have to be the one to initiate it." He stood and extended his hand. "Deal?"

She nodded and placed her hand in his. He used that leverage to pull her into his arms for a hug.

Great. Two minutes into the deal and he'd already broken her first rule.

Chapter Twelve

While heavy snow fell from the late-afternoon sky, Dean stood inside one of the guest cabins with Amylynn Swain, a transplant from the great state of Alabama. She was also the decorator he'd hired to add a few of his own personal touches to the lodge house and to completely overhaul the guest cabins. Her southern-accent-flavored comments made him wonder how much all this would cost him.

Amylynn was a pro and she didn't come cheap.

With hair the color of maple honey and deep brown eyes, she was also beautiful. But any stirrings in his system were surprisingly only those for the transformation of the seldom used guest cabins into giant playhouses for kids like Brenden Jones.

"So, were y'all thinking of keeping at least one of the cabins available for non-camp guests? The two-bedroom we just left has the potential to be perfect for high-profile visitors."

"I don't plan to have many personal guests. The ones who do visit I thought could just stay in the main house."

"If you don't mind me throwin' a little suggestion your

way . . . Deer Lick is the perfect place for summertime fundraisers. You have fishing and hiking, mountain-biking, and even the golf course available for a celebrity tournament. All right at your fingertips. The Cottage Motel isn't much to look at or stay in, so you might want to consider having the capability of converting your cabins into private getaways for your rich and famous friends. All you have to do is keep the furnishings in storage until you need them. Everything could be transformed in less than two days."

Dean smiled. "That's a great idea."

"Why, thank you." She flashed him a big toothy grin and gave a little jerk of her head. He'd recognize that pep squad gesture anywhere. If he guessed right, his decorator had once been a cheerleader for the Crimson Tide.

"Now." She rubbed her manicured hands together. "Shall we head on up to the big house? I've been dying to see it."

"After you." Dean swung his arm toward the door.

After slogging back through the snow, they entered the house from the French doors off the back deck that led into the English country kitchen.

"Oh, my. A double oven. An island with both a chopping block and marble area for baking tasks." Amylynn batted her lashes. "Every woman's dream."

What? They didn't dream about *doing it* on top of all that marble? "I'm pretty good with a grill, but that's about it." He gave her the same nickel tour he'd given Kelly, then led her upstairs to the master bedroom. "This is the room I'm interested in changing," he said.

"It's huge." Amylynn crossed the room toward the river rock fireplace in the center of the far wall. She smoothed her hand across the pine mantle, then she strolled to the double set of French doors and looked out over the snow-covered deck and the lake beyond. "And it's not being used to its fullest extent."

"Right. I was thinking of furniture a little less cheesy," he said, referring to the pine-log bed and dressers, "The style works okay with the house, but it's definitely not me. And I want the biggest bed available."

Amylynn lifted a nicely arched brow as if she wondered what he had planned. She sat on the mattress with a little bounce on the moose-and-bear-motif quilt. "No wonder. This is only a queen size. You're definitely more in the . . ." Her gaze scanned him from head to toe. "King-sized category." Then she lay back, spreading her arms out like a snow angel. "But it is comfortable."

She lifted her head. "Does this level of *bounce* work for you?"

"I'm sorry, am I interrupting something?"

Dean turned at the sound of Emma's voice. She stood in the doorway, one hand on the frame, the other raised to the blue knit scarf draped around her neck.

"I knocked but no one answered," she said with a rushed apology.

Censure darkened her eyes. *Go ahead, honey, think the worst of me.* "Come on in, Emma. Amylynn and I were just talking business."

He could almost hear Emma's lips form the words, *I'll bet.*

She took two hesitant steps into the room. Her eyes darted from him to the bed where the decorator had risen from the mattress and now stood with her professional edge back in place.

"I got your message to meet you here," Emma said.

He went to her, placed his hand on the small of her back, and guided her toward Amylynn.

"Emma, this is Amylynn Swain from Big Mountain Decorating. I've hired her to refurbish the guest cabins and the master bedroom."

Emma walked forward. The two women shook hands and exchanged awkward pleasantries. Then Emma turned to him and stuck her hands in the pockets of her cream-colored coat. "Why did you want me to meet you here?"

He stepped behind her, eased the coat from her shoulders, and tossed it on his bed. Great excuse to lure her up here later. Just in case she changed her mind about the *no touching* or *no kissing* stuff.

"How about we all go down to the kitchen and have some coffee while Amylynn fills you in on the details."

"Why does she need to fill *me* in on any details?" Emma asked him as he escorted her down the staircase.

"Because you're on the board of directors, honey. I need your approval."

"What about your dad and sisters?"

He guided everyone into the kitchen. "They'll get a vote later."

While they all sat at the huge kitchen table, sipping coffee and exchanging ideas, Dean watched enthusiasm light up Emma's face. Before he knew it, she had made suggestions of adding more yet still cutting costs. When she learned of the celebrity golf tournament fundraiser, she jumped into the brainstorming with ideas of a barn dance, a fishing tournament, and even a sleigh ride / dinner package fundraiser for the winter months. No doubt about it, Emma was a natural-born doer.

By the time he'd walked Amylynn to the door, Emma had even chipped in her two cents' worth with ideas to make his bedroom *super yummy*. Her words, not his. He did recognize, however, that pleasing a woman in the bedroom wasn't all about giving her a trip to heaven between the sheets.

When he came back into the kitchen, he found Emma had kept busy by rinsing the coffee cups and placing them in the dishwasher. The high ceiling in the room dwarfed her, but she looked perfectly at-home in front of the huge window that overlooked the cluster of pines following the banks of the river. She'd look perfect in any room of this house, he decided. And it did not go unnoticed that when she was here, the place felt a whole lot less empty.

It was then that Dean remembered something his mother had said years ago.

It takes more than furniture and knickknacks to make a house a home.

He thought of his stylish-yet-impersonal condo in Houston. Comparing it to the home in which he now stood, he realized his mother was a very, very wise woman.

"Let me help you with that."

Emma lifted her head as Dean's long strides brought him to her side. He took the dishtowel from her hands and shut the dishwasher door.

"How was school today?"

Emma felt her eyebrows shoot upward. "You're asking me about school?"

He shrugged. "If I came by your house after I'd gotten out of practice, wouldn't you ask me how it went?"

"Yes."

"Then there you go. Just making conversation."

Nothing about Dean was *just* this or *just* that. She'd known him long enough to recognize that every move he made was as calculated as if he were on the ten-yard line computing the play it would take to get the ball into the end zone.

The voice mail he'd left her had sounded urgent. Otherwise she may very well have blown it off.

She looked up to find him watching her. Like he hadn't eaten all day. And she was a Happy Meal. As his intense gaze perused her up and down, pausing at all the interesting places, Emma realized no man had ever looked at her like she was lunch. Or dinner. Or, heaven forbid, a midnight snack.

Dean looked ravenous.

She didn't want that to feel good.

She didn't want the slow heat rising up into her chest to confirm that she had fallen for a man who was wrong for her in every way that mattered. There were no brakes on that bullet train.

"Hungry?" he asked.

"As a matter of fact, before I got your message I'd planned to go to dinner."

"With?"

She didn't respond, allowing her silence to make him wonder.

His dark gaze wandered over her face. "And I ruined your evening?"

"Why don't you look sorry?"

He shrugged. "I hate to eat alone. I have some steaks in the refrigerator." He moved closer. Backed her up against the counter and reached behind her head to pull down two wineglasses from the cabinet.

She started to duck out of his way but then his other arm came up to remove a bottle of wine from the built-in wine rack. In a matter of milliseconds she'd become caught between his hot body and the counter. Everything started to tingle from her toes up.

"Potatoes. Some salad." One corner of his mouth curled upward. "Have I whetted your appetite?"

Like he'd been dipped in chocolate fondue.

"You are coming very close to breaking the *no touching* rule, Mr. Silverthorne."

His half-smile amplified as he lowered his arms and moved away to hunt for a corkscrew. "Lucky for us, the previous owners left behind a nice collection of wine." He held up a bottle of Chateau Montelena Cabernet.

She didn't know the difference between Two-Buck Chuck and Dom Perignon, but she was willing to learn. "I shouldn't have any wine. I have school tomorrow."

He twisted the corkscrew down into the bottle. "One glass won't hurt."

Said the spider to the fly. "School aside, I'm pretty sure it's not a good idea for me to sit here and drink with you."

"Why?" He pressed the wings of the opener down and the cork slid out of the bottle with a soft *pop*. "Do I scare you?"

Yes. "No."

"Then what's the big deal, honey?" Without looking at her, he poured a splash of the dark red liquid into each of the glasses. "I ruined your dinner plans. The least I can do is try to make it up to you."

He handed her a glass with a nod. "Make sure that tastes okay."

She lifted the glass to her nose. The perfume wafted up from the bowl and reminded her of New Year's Eve, when he'd drunk cheap champagne from her paper cup and then kissed her. The slightly bitter wine had sweetened on his tongue. A hot shiver sizzled from between her legs up to her heart when she thought of all the creative things he'd done with his tongue that night and the way he'd made her feel wanted. Desired. Craved.

She took a sip and let the rich, exotic flavors of violets, cherries, and cocoa roll across her tongue. "Mmmm. Very good."

Relaxed, he leaned back against the counter, one hand slipped into his pants pocket, the other held the crystal goblet. He watched her over the rim of the glass. Emma watched his throat work as he swallowed. She pictured that long, tall, muscular body naked. She thought of how his warm flesh tasted salty and sweet beneath her tongue. The urge to strip off his clothes and lick the smooth wine off all that delicious skin knocked her in her boots. She had to remember that she'd put herself on a *No Dean* diet.

"You're right. It is good." He took her glass and filled it. "I'm usually not a fan of wine."

"Because you're more of a beer-and-pretzels kind of guy?"

He opened the refrigerator door, reached inside, and withdrew two plastic storage bags of marinated steaks.

"Because wine goes straight to my head. Beer? No problem. Wine and tequila? I'm a total lightweight."

"So I guess I won't be asking you for a ride home."

A grin spread across his perfect mouth. "I'll give you a ride anytime you need one." He plopped the bags of steak on the counter. While she digested the undertones behind his comment, he went back to the fridge and brought out a bag of mixed salad greens and yet another bag of what looked like seasoned, diced red potatoes.

"Judging by the amount of food you have there, I'll guess you're a big eater."

An obvious smirk on his face confirmed he wasn't thinking about steak. *Hoo boy.* She'd have to find a way to ignore all the crazy rip-his-clothes-off images in her head. She couldn't keep doing this to herself. But it was difficult, because hidden behind that sexy facade was a man with depth. Oh, one might have to dig through the BS to find him, but he was there— brimming with gentleness, and sincerity, and complex layers. Even as much as he was all that, he was also not a man who could give of himself for more than a little while. And for a woman looking for forever? Not a good match.

She should just go home and make herself a nice tuna sandwich before she ended up doing something foolish. Yes. That's what she would do. Decision made, her body betrayed her by opening cupboards in search of a salad bowl.

Glutton for punishment? Yep.

"How can I help?" she asked.

"You want to finish the salad?"

"Sure." She grabbed an anemic tomato from the bowl on the counter and a knife from the drawer to start slicing. Dean switched on an under-counter radio and Keith Urban's voice filled the kitchen with a sweet song that seemed to mimic the love story of his own life. Her knife thunked down into the well-used chopping block. Deep in concentration of the lyrics, she didn't notice that Dean had put down his bags of steaks until he came up behind her. His big hand covered hers as he eased the knife from her grip.

"I found a better way to do that," he said, his words a warm breath against her ear.

Emma closed her eyes. The heat of his chest warmed her back and it took everything she had not to melt against him. As the knife glided through the barely red tomato, Emma wondered if he truly was interested in showing her his culinary skills or something more. Would it be breaking the rules if she asked him to please kiss her on that really sensitive spot just below her ear? Or to move just a smidge closer so she could feel *all* of him pressed against her?

Her heart kicked into hyperspace. How about if she just turned around and took full advantage of the close proximity of their bodies? Dean had already proven he knew how to heat up a kitchen.

And when had she become such a slutty thinker? Still, maybe this whole *no touching, no kissing* thing was a bit ridiculous. "Dean, I—"

The doorbell chimed with a happy tune.

"It's about time." He laid the knife down on the chopping block and pointed to the vegetable in her hand as he disappeared through the door. "Keep going. I'll be right back."

Moments later Emma heard the buzz of voices coming toward the kitchen. She turned just as Dean's family walked in chattering like magpies in the spring.

Ah, saved by the bell.

Literally.

Hours later, Dean sat at the head of the long kitchen table and smiled as enthusiastic conversation surrounded him and he reveled in the first unofficial gathering of his board of directors—minus Kelly, who'd once again gone back to Chicago. As a group they'd barbecued steaks and roasted potatoes and traded the events of their days just as any family might.

Whether Emma realized it or not, she'd taken up the role as hostess. She refilled wine glasses, made coffee, and helped clear the table when dinner was done.

They'd moved on to dessert and now she sat to his right, her cheeks rosy from the wine and, he hoped, the excitement of the journey on which they were all about to embark. She fit right in with the rest of the gang. He liked that about her. He liked seeing her beside him. He liked that he didn't exactly know what to do with her, or where her thoughts meandered. He liked the element of mystery that either she was going to throw her arms around his neck and kiss him with that incredible mouth or kick his sorry ass out the door.

Seeing her seated next to him in his new home—planning a future that would help a lot of kids and the parents who loved them—made him feel really good.

Sure, he could have outright asked her to come to a dinner

meeting. But what would have been the fun in that? Before they'd gotten down to the business at hand, he'd needed to find some way to try to change her mind about her *hands-off* rule. And he wasn't beyond using every trick in the book to make her think it was all her idea when she cried "uncle." When it came to Emma, he didn't like hands-off. He wanted his hands all over her soft, sweet, hot body. And then some.

Kate took a bite of the warm apple cobbler she'd brought to the table. "So what do you call this touchy-feely thing, again?"

He looked at Emma. *Infatuation? Enchantment? Lust?* With a blink he turned his attention to Kate. "Equine-assisted therapy. It's a fairly new method, but the experts I've spoken to say it seems to have excellent results."

"When do you think you'll be able to bring actual livestock here to the lodge?" Matt leaned back in his chair, stretched his arm out, and absently caressed Kate's shoulder. The glow of the chandelier reflected off his shiny new sheriff badge.

"Soon. Several local ranchers have given me a line on a couple geldings that are known for their extreme gentleness. That's going to be key in whatever animals are brought here. They've got to be used to loud, abrupt noises, and lots of little kids running around. A spooked horse can be a big danger and that's the last thing I want."

"Seriously. That's over a ton of scary muscle and energy," Kate said. "Which reminds me, I read an article not too long ago where a rodeo queen decided she'd been bucked off during too many grand entries. So she sacked out her horse by tying Mylar balloons to a corral fence and playing AC/DC full blast."

"Well, that's certainly a colorful method," Emma said.

"Pretty clever too," Kate agreed. "She said after awhile he'd trot in tune with *Dirty Deeds Done Dirt Cheap*."

When the laughter quieted, Dean noticed the smile had slipped from his father's face. He reached over and patted his dad on the back. "You okay?"

His father nodded. "I wish your mother could be here to see you." He looked around the table then clasped his hand over the top of Dean's. "All of you. And what you're accomplishing. She'd be so proud."

"She's not far, Dad." Dean caught Kate's eye and she gave him a collaborative wink. "Trust me on that."

Hugs were passed around as Dean said goodbye to his dad, Kate, and Matt. He'd just closed the door behind them when Emma came down the stairs, slipping her arms into the sleeves of her coat.

"You're leaving too? I thought maybe you'd be interested in an après-meeting soak."

She settled her knitted scarf around her neck and looked up. "I don't have my bathing suit."

He grasped the ends of the scarf and used it to tug her closer. "You didn't have it on New Year's either."

"Not so fast." She planted her hands against his chest. "I told you—"

"Yeah, I know. You're dating Jesse. You've got plans and they don't include me." He smoothed his palms down the tails of her scarf. "So what are these plans, honey? Marriage? Babies? Happily-ever-after?"

"Yes." She stepped back and her scarf fell from his hands. "All of the above. Is that such a surprise?"

"And you plan on marrying Jesse Hamilton?"

"He hasn't asked."

Shit. She didn't say no. "If he did, would you say yes?"

"I've only been dating him for a few weeks."

"That doesn't answer the question, Emma."

She buttoned up her coat and put her hand on the doorknob. "I'm sorry, Dean, but I really don't think my life and what I do or don't do with it is any of your business."

He'd take that as a yes.

A flare of good old-fashioned rivalry streaked right up his spine, grabbed him by the throat, and gave him a good shake. Before she could turn to walk away he cupped his hands over her shoulders and drew her against him. Without a word of protest from her sweet mouth, he lowered his head and kissed her.

As if it were routine she raised to her toes. Her hands threaded through his hair and she settled against him. A perfect fit. Passion kicked in and it was all Dean could do not to tear that wool coat from her body and mark her as his own.

The racing of his heart told him she was right where she belonged. His arms tightened around her. But just as he began to think he'd won her over, she broke from his embrace. Her lips were flushed. Moist. Nothing mattered more than kissing her again. He reached for her but she dodged him, pulled open the door, and stepped out onto the veranda.

"That kiss didn't feel like you're convinced Jesse is the right guy for you, Emma."

"And *you* are?"

Not sure of that himself, he shrugged.

She gave a humorless laugh. "You are a lot of things, Dean. Handsome. Gifted. And you are probably the sexiest, most charming man I've ever met."

All good. Right? "Why do I hear a *but* coming?"

"*But* you are not now, nor will you ever be the kind of man to settle down with one woman. Or change a baby's diapers. Or, God forbid, hold that woman's hand when she grows old and her face wrinkles and her boobs droop."

He'd never thought of life in quite that way before. To his credit, he'd helped his mother change plenty of diapers when Kate had been a baby. And to him, holding a woman's hand throughout life sounded like a pretty damn good deal. Even if her boobs did droop. "You want to know what I think?"

"No."

"I think you're a coward."

"*Me?*" She pointed to the buttons on her coat.

"Yeah. You. I think you're too chicken to admit that there might be something more between us than a one-night stand."

She looked over her shoulder toward her little Subaru, looked for an escape. Then those blue eyes shot back at him. "I am *not* a coward. I just don't like you."

"You like me."

She shook her head. Her chest and the buttons on her coat lifted on a vast intake of air. "The night of Kate's reception, I asked if you remembered me. You said no."

"A lot of time has passed since I was a kid, Em."

"True. But the funny thing is I remembered *you*, Dean."

By the edge to her words she had not just paid him a compliment.

"Look," she said, "when I was eighteen I couldn't buy my way into the cool kids' club. And in those days I really, really wanted to belong. Then I graduated. And summer began. And I found myself just biding my time until I could leave behind Deer Lick and its gossipy girls and boys who only liked girls who said yes."

"And you did."

"Yes. But before I did, someone came into town. Someone new. Someone who paid attention to me. Someone I liked. A lot." Her head tilted and the porch light slanted across her cheek. "Nick Harris. Remember him?"

"The guy I played ball in college with?"

She nodded. "One night there was going to be a bonfire party out at the back forty acres of Old Man Carter's place."

"There were a lot of bonfires out there in those days," he said. "Everybody who was anybody went."

"Exactly. But I was a *nobody*. And I'd never gone before. And when Nick invited me to go, my eighteen-year-old curiosity got the best of me. So I broke all the rules. I waited until my Memaw went to bed. I put on my cutest cutoffs, a tank top, and tennis shoes and I snuck out of the house. I walked all the way there to see what the cool kids did on hot summer nights."

"And?"

"When I got there the keg was almost empty."

"I do remember a lot of alcohol got consumed at those parties."

"I'd never drunk before. Pretty pathetic, right? Never been to the bonfire. Never tasted anything stronger than lemonade."

"You were a good girl. Completely understandable."

"I wasn't a *good girl*." Her face crumpled and she looked down at her feet. His heart stalled. "Do you know who my mother is?"

"Should I?"

"I'm sure you've heard of her." Her chin came up. "Everyone in Deer Lick has. Suzanne Hart?"

Where the hell was she going with this and why did it matter so much? "Suzanne Hart is your mother?"

"Surprise."

"What about your daddy?"

"If you know my mother is Suzanne Hart, then you know my father could be any man in this town or any other town for miles around. According to gossip I learned over the years, my mother prided herself on being the only paid whore in the entire county."

"I'm sorry, Emma, I didn't know." The story unfolding was unexpected, but it didn't change who Emma had become or the way he thought of her. Still, he had a feeling this was important for her to say. So he shoved his hands in his pockets and waited. "Tell me the rest."

"Nick offered me a drink. I took it." She dropped her gaze and shook her head. "I think I took several. The next thing I knew Nick was kissing me. And touching me. I didn't want him to stop. I figured I was eighteen and that was what everyone did at that age." A heavy sigh pushed from her lungs. "One thing led to another and by the time it was over, I'd given a guy I didn't even know my virginity."

"I'm sorry."

She shrugged. "After I got myself together I came back

to the bonfire. You and Nick were talking, and laughing, and then I felt everyone staring at me, talking behind their hands. About me. The outsider who didn't belong. I needed to get out of there. I asked Nick to give me a ride home but he said you wouldn't loan him your car. So I walked."

"And then what?"

"Oh, you know. The usual. Nick avoided me. The gossips had a free-for-all. Summer came to an end. I missed my period and I panicked. I didn't know what to do. I knew you and he were getting ready to go back to USC. I was a stupid, naive eighteen-year-old and I felt like I needed to tell him. One day I saw you and him go inside the Gas and Grub. I waited until you both came outside. While you flirted with Fawn Derick I told him I might be pregnant."

"Em, I—"

"At first he laughed and asked why I thought it would be his." Her hands worried the strings that hung from the ends of her scarf. "But drunk or not, he knew I'd been a virgin. Then he told me he planned to take the advice of his love-'em-and-leave-'em good-time buddy Dean Silverthorne. Apparently you'd already warned him off the local girls who might be marriage-minded. You'd told him to focus on his football career and not any backwoods slut who might try to trap him."

"I would never say that." Anger curled his fingers into fists. "You know my mom and dad would never raise a son who'd say something like that."

"Doesn't matter. He ran and I got lucky." A chill settled into her voice that reached out and burned his heart. "Unlike my mother, I never had to bring an unwanted child into this world."

"Were you pregnant?"

She nodded so slightly he almost missed it.

"I lost it," she whispered.

"Did anyone else know?"

She shook her head.

"Em. I'm so sorry. He reached out for her but she backed away until her backside bumped the veranda rail. Her message was loud and clear and he had no choice but to drop his hands. "Why didn't you go to someone who could have helped you?"

"I was eighteen, Dean. I just wanted it all to go away. I didn't want to be an outsider anymore. I didn't want people to think of me like they thought of my mother. I wanted them to like me."

"They like you, Em. *I* like you."

She stared at him for a moment. Then blinked her eyes once. Twice. "I know you do. But that's just not enough." She clutched her coat beneath her heart in one small hand. "And I think it's best if you find someone else to be on your board of directors." She turned and hurried down the steps to her car.

"Emma." He followed her. "Don't go."

When she reached the Forester she opened the door, turned, and looked up at him with more courage than any man he'd ever met on the field. "You're the first person I've ever told about this. It feels really good to get it off my chest. For years I blamed myself. Whether I was a tease or just a stupid girl flattered that a handsome college football player seemed attracted to her, it doesn't matter anymore. But in that lesson I did learn something important about myself. I may not be much, but I don't ever want to be forgettable."

She slid into her car and shut the door.

"Don't lump me in with someone like that, Em. Please." Before he could blink her engine turned over and her headlights burned up the row of pines that bordered the long path to the road until her taillights disappeared.

Despair gnawed at his gut and clawed at his heart. For the first time since he'd received word that his mother had died, Dean felt truly helpless. He couldn't change the past. And without Emma, the future looked empty.

Chapter Thirteen

The classroom was filled with color, and laughter, and gusts of activity that encouraged hand-clapping and hoorays. But the class Emma stood in was not her own. As a part of her master's program she'd been invited to spend a day at the Missoula Academy for Developmental Needs.

There were ten children in the class. Each had his or her own teacher. The children appeared focused and happy. Best of all, they were learning and communicating.

"We're building intensive interaction into our programs," Donna Lee, the guidance counselor, told Emma. "We've found that body language and touch are really helpful in teaching the children to cope better in the real world."

Emma's heart raced as if she'd had too much caffeine. "It's fascinating. Wonderful."

"Would you like to join in?" The gray-haired woman looked as if she could be a Florida retiree, soaking up the sunshine. Instead she'd chosen to continue to work. And her love for her work was apparent in the huge smile on her face.

"I'd love to," Emma responded, although she did feel a bit nervous.

"Good." Mrs. Lee took her by the hand. "Then let's start here with lead and follow."

Donna led her to a corner filled with colorful pillows. "Amy will show you how it's done. I can't guarantee you won't get addicted. So don't blame me if you don't want to leave at the end of the day."

Emma laughed. "I'm just going to be happy to take one thing back to help the little boy in my own class."

"Oh, you'll take more than one thing. Guaranteed."

For the next two hours Emma engaged in chair games and methods of repetition, learning the importance of touch and patience. And by the time she sat on the floor across from a little girl named Heather, Emma had learned the importance of sign language for communication. Within minutes of sitting down on an orange and yellow butterfly pillow, she and little Heather were laughing. Emma learned that equally as important as sign language, sounds and facial expressions were key. The more these children could communicate, the less frustration they would face.

At the end of the day, Emma waved goodbye and walked toward her car with a smile on her face. Tomorrow when she returned to her own class, she was going to ignore the school superintendent who had told her to put Brenden Jones at the back of the class. She would put the boy at the front where she could incorporate all the lessons she'd learned. Her solitary goal by the time the bell rang would be to see Brenden laugh and to tell her goodbye in sign.

She turned and took another look at the school, and an exhilarating sense of accomplishment danced before her eyes.

This was what she was meant to do. To help children with needs.

And in that thought she realized that though they were miles apart on many other things, on this issue, she and Dean were very much alike.

At half past four a few days later, Dean stood beside his sister in the Sugar Shack, scooping measured amounts of cherry-chocolate cupcake batter into bake cups. His father had taken a coffee break at one of the bistro sets with a few of his hunting buddies. And from the radio perched on a shelf above the mixer, Dierks Bentley sang a song asking if he was the only one. That'd be a big *hell no*, cowboy.

"Thanks for the offer to help me get these Valentine's orders filled." Kate squeezed pink icing down into a pastry bag. "Chelsea, my usual helper, has a report due in Honors Civics tomorrow."

"No problem. I didn't have anything else going on."

"Really?" She looked up from the small heart she had piped onto the bright red icing of a chocolate caramel cupcake. "With all that shoulder rehabbing, and charity planning, and organizing stuff you have to do?"

Out of mere frustration he'd overdone it with his workout. Tomorrow he'd pay. Today he was paying for something else. "The plans have stalled."

"Why?"

"Because . . . we lost a board member."

Kate's hand dropped to the counter with a clunk. "What the hell did you do now?"

"I don't want to talk about it."

"Of course you don't. You're a man. Men don't talk. They grunt and groan and piss and moan, but God forbid they tell you what they're really thinking."

"Trouble in newlywed paradise?"

"No. I'm talking about *you*, you big dork." She pushed her hand against his chest, leaving a flour print on his green apron. "You've been moping around all day and just *now* you're telling me that everything for Mom's organization has come to a halt because we lost a member? Since everyone else is related, the only member we could have lost is Emma. So what did you do to piss her off?"

"You don't have a very high opinion of me, do you, Kate?" He set down the scoop, and batter oozed over the sides onto the counter. "I'm your big brother. You're supposed to think of me fondly. Don't you know I've got people all over the place who admire the hell out of me?"

She ignored his sarcasm. "Yeah, well they don't know you snore like a freight train and that you picked your nose when you were a kid."

He shook his head. Leave it to Kate to cut right to the heart of things and knock his sometimes over-inflated ego down to the size of a sunflower seed.

"So what did you do?" she asked again.

"Nothing."

Kate threw the pastry tube down on the counter. "All

right. That's it. I'm calling her." She grabbed her cell from the pocket of her apron.

The bell over the door jingled. He looked up and placed his hand over Kate's. "No need," he said, as Emma walked into the bakery, her arms loaded down with books and a laptop. His father got up to greet her and she gave his dad an easy smile that pumped blood faster through Dean's heart.

He watched as she set her books down, slid her coat down her arms, then scooted up onto a bistro chair.

"Oh goody." Kate dropped her cell back into the pocket of her apron. "Now I can ask her in person."

Dean gave his sister his bullshit glare, the one he used on the field when he tried to mess with someone's concentration. "Let it go, Kate. Believe me, the last name on earth she wants to hear is mine."

"Then maybe you should go hide in the storeroom until she leaves. Take the cowardly route."

"I'm not hiding."

"But the thought crossed your mind."

"No." Yes.

"What is the big deal, Dean?"

"She hates me."

"'Hate' is a strong word. Maybe she just thinks you're pond scum."

"Nope." He shoved the tools he'd been working with off the counter and into the stainless sink.

"Sounds serious." Kate tossed a glance at Emma, who hadn't noticed them yet. Then his sister dug her icing-coated fingers into his sleeve, dragged him into the office, and shut the door. She folded her arms. "So what's going on between the two of you?"

"Like you don't know? You're her friend. I'm sure she's already told you everything."

"Apparently you don't know Emma as well as you think you do. She doesn't talk much about her personal life."

"She doesn't talk much or at all?"

"Much. We talk about general girl stuff. But believe me, your name has not come up in conversation once. And if I wasn't your sister and didn't see the way you two look at each other, I'd be clueless as to what's got your tighty-whiteys in a twist."

"Do you know who her mother is?"

"Everyone knows who her mother is, Dean. And nobody cares. Emma is a nice person. She's a good friend. And she's done a lot for the kids in this community. How could you not love her?"

He wasn't sure he didn't.

Last night after she'd left, his instinct had been to go after her, wrap her in his arms, and kiss away her doubt. He always got his way and he'd initially thought he could sway her into his way of thinking. But Emma was too smart to be sweet-talked into something she didn't believe or didn't want to do.

"If she doesn't talk about her personal life much then I'm not going to betray her privacy and talk about anything between me and her," he said to Kate.

"Sure." Kate smacked him in the arm. "Be respectful for the first time in your life." Then Kate gasped and backed up a step. "Oh my God, you're in love with her."

"Come on, you know me better than that. I don't do love." So what was that crazy thing going on in his chest?

"Yeah, yeah. That's what I thought and look what happened to me. *Pffft*. Crazy in love. Go figure."

"This has nothing to do with love, Kate. Something happened. A . . . misunderstanding. That's all."

Kate folded her arms across her flour-splattered apron and stared up at him for a good long, uncomfortable, mom-like moment. Then she raised her hands and shook her head. "I don't want to know. The least you can do is apologize." She opened the office door, went to the display case, slid a slice of mocha cheesecake onto a plate, and handed it to him with a cup of coffee.

"Here." She handed him the food. "This is her absolute favorite. She can hardly hate you if you show up with a peace offering."

He doubted even a truckload of cheesecake would get him back in her good graces. But he took the order anyway.

Emma looked up as he approached her table.

"Hi." Holy crap. He felt like a middle-schooler with a crush.

"Hi."

"I brought you your favorite." He set the dish and cup down and slid a fork and napkin beside the plate.

"Thanks."

Even in a simple pair of jeans and a pullover, she looked so amazing his eyes stung. When a *thanks* was all she offered, he sat down in the chair across from her. He didn't care that his sister stood behind the counter glaring at him like he was plotting to blow up the Sugar Shack. Or that his father and his hunting entourage were two tables away chatting about the ten-point buck they'd get next season.

He needed to make things right with Emma.

"So is this how it's going to be between us now, Em? Brief pleasantries as if we're strangers?" God, he hoped not.

"You won't be here long." She pushed aside her classroom planner and lifted the coffee cup to her beautiful mouth. Her soft lips pursed over the rim as she took a sip before she returned the cup to the table. "So I'd say that should work for the duration."

"I don't want it to be this way, honey. I'm sorry. For whatever it is you think I did or said or didn't do, I'm truly sorry."

One slight shoulder lifted beneath the soft pink sweater. "I appreciate that."

"But?"

"It doesn't matter anymore." She leaned back and twisted the napkin in her hands. "I've forgiven myself for being so foolish back then. And I've forgiven myself for repeating my mistakes."

"You mean for being with me?"

"Yes."

That single word shoved a fist inside his chest, grabbed his heart, and yanked.

"I'm moving forward, Dean. I'm done with looking into my past and beating myself up over something that happened a lifetime ago." She crumpled the napkin into a ball.

He placed his hand over the top of hers. Her fingers were cool beneath his touch. "Then why won't you forgive me?"

"There's nothing to forgive. Besides, I'm just too busy to dwell on the negative." She slipped her hand from beneath his. "I'm moving into a new chapter of my life. Yesterday I drove to Missoula and spent the entire afternoon at the Academy for Developmental Needs. I had the most unbelievable day. I learned at least three new methods of teaching, and half a dozen games that instill communication. I even learned some sign language."

"That's great." The excitement dancing in her amazing eyes made him smile.

"The first thing I did when I got to school today was to move Brenden's table up to the front of the class." She folded her hands together and leaned forward. "I need him to be closer so I can give him more attention and teach him what I learned. So far, so good. By the end of the day he signed good-bye to me." She leaned back in the chair and her hand went to her chest. "It made me cry."

He wished he could reach across the table and hug her. "Like I said the day I brought the cupcakes to your class, you're in the right place at the right time."

"I am. I'm in no-big-deal Deer Lick, Montana. And I'm responsible for helping a little boy learn to cope with a great big world. He needs me." She leaned forward again, reached across the table, and squeezed his hand. The warmth of her fingers flowed straight to his heart. "You, on the other hand, will head back to your team and you'll forget about me before your boots even hit Texas soil."

"I'd never forget about you, Emma."

"But you *will* leave."

He glanced out the window to the piles of snow lining both sides of the street, to the gray sky. He couldn't lie. He wouldn't lie. Not to her. And not to himself. Because as important as her teaching was to her, his career was just as important to him. "Yes. I will leave."

"And that's exactly what you should do." She gave his hand a dismissive pat. "You have a spectacular life and you should be excited to get back to it as soon as possible."

He turned his head to look at her again. When she gave him the smile she'd given him the first time he'd made love to her, the fist surrounding his heart constricted.

If he should be excited to get back to his life, why did he feel so fucking sad?

As Valentine's Days went, this one wasn't so bad. It wouldn't go down in the history books as the greatest ever, but it didn't suck.

Jesse had asked her out, but Emma knew it wouldn't be fair to lead him on, so she'd been honest and declined. She decided if she wouldn't have a date for the evening, then she would at least give the parents in her community a chance to share the love by arranging a party for her students at the Grange. Her kids had made construction-paper hearts in class and they'd decorated the white cinder block walls. They'd had red punch and heart-shaped cookies. They'd danced and played games. And every time her mind wandered in the direction of a certain quarterback, she'd find another method of entertainment. Karaoke had become the hit of the night. Even after several chipmunk-sounding renditions of Justin Bieber's *Baby*. By the time their parents had come to pick them up, Emma was exhausted. Happy, but definitely stick-a-fork-in-her done.

When she went into her house and locked the door, she leaned back against it with a sigh. Her kids had made the dreaded Valentine's Day bearable. She was a busy woman with goals stacked one on top of another, but that didn't mean she wanted to spend every Valentine's Day alone.

"Merrrrooowww."

Emma looked down as Oscar began his figure-eight rub around her ankles. "Hello, man of my life." She reached down, picked up his chubby body, and snuggled him close.

Oscar turned on his motor and rubbed the top of his head beneath her chin. "Looks like you're the only guy I can rely on these days." She gave him a little squeeze, then transferred him to the sofa as she reached behind to unzip her sweater. Her boot heels tap-tapped across the hardwood floor as she walked into her bedroom to pull on the cartoon pajamas Dean always joked about. She washed her face, smoothed her hair back into a ponytail, and went back into the living room to watch the remainder of *Runaway Bride*.

She settled onto the sofa with her fuzzy monkey slippers propped up on the antique trunk she used as a coffee table and pulled Oscar onto her lap to stroke his soft fur. "Hard to be a runaway bride if no one will even ask you to marry them."

Oscar licked her fingers with his rough tongue.

"Are you trying to comfort me? Or just looking for leftover cookie crumbs?"

He looked up at her with his mismatched eyes. "Merrrooowww."

She laughed. "That's what I thought." Then she gathered him up and kissed the top of his head. "I know I can always count on you. I love you, old friend."

As Julia Roberts lifted the hem of her wedding dress, crawled out the window, and jumped into a FedEx truck, Oscar's purr vibrated against Emma's chest. "Silly woman. Who would run from Richard Gere? Hmmm? Sure, he's no Dean Silverthorne, but still." She nuzzled her chin on top of the cat's head. "Maybe it will always just be you and me, old boy. That wouldn't be so bad, would it?"

He was a damn stalker. No doubt about it.

And pathetic, too.

Dean sat outside Emma's little bungalow in his mother's heap of a car with the engine running, trying to decide whether to knock on her door or go home where he belonged. But the constant reminders on TV of Valentine's Day diamonds and chocolates and lingerie had been driving him crazy. Not that he minded spending a hokey holiday alone. He'd done so dozens of times. And he'd never given a rat's behind. Half the time he was on the road when one of the greeting card industry's top money-makers would come along, and he'd be glad he didn't have to worry about sending candy and flowers to anyone except his mother and sisters.

He glanced at the seat next to him and the beribboned pastry box that held six perfect red velvet cupcakes topped with a decadent cream cheese frosting. He doubted he'd get brownie points for having made them himself. But just in case there were favors of gratitude being handed out, he'd added red fondant hearts topped with sugar sprinkles. When trying to get back in a lady's good graces, his father always said, go for over-the-top.

He needed all the help he could get.

Emma had come to mean something to him. He hadn't

wanted or expected it, but she'd crawled inside him when he hadn't been looking. He didn't know what, if anything, he could offer her. And if he were thinking of her needs instead of his own, he'd leave her alone. He just wasn't that unselfish.

He glanced at the small house and from behind the closed curtain he could see the flicker of the television. Hopefully she was alone. If not, he'd find out what Jesse Hamilton was really made of.

A cool breeze swirled through the interior of the car and Tom Jones came on the radio to tell him it wasn't unusual.

Right.

"Mmmmm. What's in the box?"

Dean smiled. "Your favorite."

"Oh, I love red velvet. It's what your daddy used to make for me when he needed to apologize."

"Yeah, well, I'm hoping that will work for me too."

"You think cupcakes are enough?"

Dean shook his head. "I doubt it. She's been pretty clear about what she wants. And I don't know if I can give it to her."

"Then why are you sitting outside her house with a box of apology?"

Dean turned in his seat. His mother's glow was tinged with a shade of blue tonight. "Because I'm not a hundred percent sure?"

"Are you asking me?" His mother gave a low chuckle. "Or telling me?"

He leaned back against the door and slid his arm along the back of the seat, made a fist, and tapped the duck tape covering a wide slit in the artificial leather. "Do you remember when I played Pop Warner and I was just a scrawny little geek who didn't know the difference between a Hail Mary and a Statue of Liberty play? But oh, how I loved to throw that football?"

"You were a *cute* scrawny little geek. And I remember that you loved being the quarterback because you didn't like ending up on the bottom of the dog-pile."

"I still don't." He lowered his head and chuckled. "But I remember what you always use to tell me."

"Oh, Lord, Son. I had a million things I used to tell you. Mostly a bunch of BS just to keep you out of trouble."

"Maybe. But you were consistent on this one. You used to say that if I wanted something bad enough, I had to be ready to work hard for it because it wouldn't just fall in my lap."

"And I was right." She gave a little jerk of her head that wiggled her gray bun. "You put everything you had into an already God-given talent and look where it got you."

"That might be the problem. I'm not used to being told I can't have something without it becoming a huge challenge."

"And you're afraid that because Emma told you no, you see her as just a mission you need to overcome to prove her wrong?"

"Something like that."

"What if she's more?"

"How do I know?"

"You won't unless you give it your best effort, will you?"

"I think she's pretty done with me."

"I . . ." His mother paused, looked heavenward, then back at him. "Oh . . . Son, I think you'll be surprised at how receptive she'll be. In fact, if I were you, I'd quit all this hemming and hawing and get in there in a hurry."

"That sounds ominous."

"Right *now*, Dean," she said and disappeared, taking her blue-tinted glow with her.

Yes, ma'am. Dean grabbed the pastry box, stepped out into the icy air, and knocked on Emma's door. He waited several heartbeats, raised his hand to knock again, and the door opened.

Emma stood there in her usual cartoon PJs. Her face red and blotchy. Her eyes swollen. She trembled and a huge sob wracked her chest.

Dean looked down.

In her arms she cradled her very limp and very lifeless cat.

CHAPTER FOURTEEN

Dean had been hit by thousands of pounds of flesh. He'd been pile-driven into the ground. And he'd sat silent as a doctor told him his injury could be a career-ender. But he'd never felt as helpless as he did at that moment.

Emma's face crumpled. Her beautiful mouth wobbled. "He licked my hand," she whispered between sobs. "Closed his eyes and just . . . quit purring."

"I'm so sorry, honey." Dean stepped through the doorway, set the pastry box on the table by the door, and drew her into his arms. The weight of her dead cat pushed against his abdomen while he tucked Emma's head beneath his chin. She sobbed into his shirt with her broken heart and he rocked her until her tears subsided to sniffs and dribbles. Then he kissed her on her forehead and took the burden of her heartache from her arms. "Let me hold him for you, honey."

The cat was heavy and limp, and as much as Dean hated cats, this one in particular, he wished the furry beast would just open his mismatched eyes, put on his evil cat scowl, and meow, "Just kidding," for Emma's sake.

Dean moved to the sofa and sat down, gingerly holding her beloved pet as she sat down beside him and stroked the cat's smooth white fur with her trembling fingers.

"I don't know what I'm going to do without him, Dean."

"I know, honey. You loved him. He knew you loved him."

She nodded and her barely controlled tears broke free. "He and I have been together for so long." She sniffed. "I found him that night, you know. After the bonfire. I realized I couldn't let my Memaw know what had happened. I didn't want to worry her or upset her."

"But you needed her, Em."

Her long, delicate fingers continued to stroke the cat's fur. "I couldn't think straight. So I went to the school. That's when I found Oscar. He was hiding behind a trash dumpster. When I tried to lure him out, he hissed and spat at me like some big ferocious lion. But he was just a little kitten with a big attitude." Her lips tilted into an unsteady smile. "So I named him Oscar the Grouch and I tucked him inside my shirt and held him close to my heart all the way home. We've been together ever since."

She leaned down and kissed the cat between his ears.

Something inside Dean broke. He realized that when Emma loved, she loved with her whole heart and soul. And any man she loved had better be damned deserving.

He looked down at the motionless cat in his arms. "What do you want to do with him, honey?"

"It's late." She glanced across the room at the white iron clock on the wall. Her chin quivered. "I guess I'll have to wait until morning to take him into the vet to have him . . . cremated. I guess I can just . . . wrap him in a blanket until then."

She stood on shaky legs and Dean reached out and took her by the hand. "I have a better idea. Go get his favorite blanket."

Without hesitation she disappeared into her bedroom. When she returned she handed him an old fuzzy blue blanket with shredded edges. "I used to fold this up so he could sit on the windowsill and watch the birds fly by."

Dean spread the blanket out on the sofa and gently laid the cat on top. "Those are all the great things you're going to remember about him."

"I know." Emma dropped to her knees and curled her fingers in his fur. "I'm so sorry, Oscar. I didn't know you were sick."

"He was just old, honey." Dean reached down, brought her to her feet, and wrapped her in his arms. "He knows you wouldn't ignore him. You took great care of him."

"When he licked my hand," she said, her watery gaze seeking solace, "he was really saying goodbye. Wasn't he?"

Dean's heart gave a hard twist. "I'm sure in his own cat way he was letting you know how much he loved you."

She nodded against his shirt and he felt the warm wet from her tears. He stroked her soft hair and wished there was something he could do to bring the cat back. "I think Oscar deserves a really nice place to rest."

"Where?"

"If you can hold him close to your heart for one more ride, I have a place in mind I'm sure Oscar will love."

It had taken a ride on a snowmobile up Deer Lick Trail to the widest pine tree Dean could find in the moonlight. At the top of a rise he'd found a soft spot beneath the umbrella of a huge pine and a bed of needles. There he dug a hole for Emma's beloved cat. Emma had given her pet a last kiss on his head, then together they'd wrapped him tight in his favorite blanket and buried him. They'd covered his grave with a pile of rocks to protect him and so Emma could always find her way back to visit.

Together they stood beneath the pine. Dean wrapped her shivering body in his arms and he held her close. "He'll like it here. He can watch the birds fly all over the place. Maybe even chase a few."

She nodded against his chest. "Thank you."

"You're welcome."

When she looked up at him beneath the glow of the moon, he could almost read her mind.

"Why don't you stay with me tonight, Em? You don't need to go home to that empty house." He tucked a lock of her silky hair behind her ear. "You can have my bed. I'll sleep down the hall."

Silently she nodded. He helped her back through the snow to the snowmobile, where she climbed on the back. He'd barely gotten the engine started before he felt her lean into him and wrap her arms around him. Her body trembled all the way back to his house.

They parked the snowmobile in the garage and he led her upstairs. He removed her coat and boots, pulled back the covers, and tucked her into his bed. While he stacked some logs in the fireplace and struck the match he could feel her quiet gaze on him.

"Dean?"

He turned. Beneath the comforter she looked so small and sad his heart broke.

"I don't want to be alone tonight," she whispered and reached out her hand.

"Then I wouldn't dream of leaving you alone, honey." He pulled off his boots, stripped down to his boxer-briefs and T-shirt, took her hand in his, and crawled in beside her. He wrapped an arm around her waist and drew her back against his chest. Her breath caught on a silent sob. Dean stroked her hair until finally the tension left her body and he knew she'd fallen asleep.

In his arms she felt warm and wonderful, and he hoped that somehow he'd given her a little peace of mind in taking care of her beloved pet in a dignified manner. But the way she'd turned into his arms at the grave and sobbed against his chest might haunt him forever. All he could think at that moment was how she must have cried the night she'd mistakenly given herself to a selfish boy who didn't value her. She'd been so young and innocent. And so all alone. Yet her only thought at the time had been to protect her aging grandmother and a small helpless kitten.

Close to midnight he pressed his lips against her soft hair and didn't find it at all unusual that the pillow was wet with tears.

Hers.

And his.

Morning light filtered through the bedroom drapes when Emma woke surrounded by Dean's warmth and comfort. Judging by the stiffness in her right side, she guessed they hadn't moved all night.

Before she'd met Dean she'd never woken in a man's bed. He was the last man she'd ever have imagined waking next to. This morning, even with the sad ache weighing heavy in her heart, she was glad to be there. Glad to know when she'd opened the door with her dead cat in her arms, Dean had cared enough not to run. Even though she'd previously pushed him away. She'd be forever grateful that he'd helped her when she'd been sad and didn't know what to do. Dean Silverthorne had offered a safe haven from her sorrow.

Behind her he came awake slowly, his breathing less languid, his heartbeat picking up its pace. Instead of stretching and slipping away, he held her close, leaned over, and kissed her cheek.

"You awake?" His voice was rough with sleep.

She nodded.

"You okay?"

"I'm sad."

"I know, honey." His fingers stroked her hair. "What can I do to help?"

She sighed. He'd given her so much last night. She missed her cat, but she knew she had to move forward without him. "Do you have eggs?"

"Yes." He smiled against her shoulder. "And I can make a mean Denver Omelet."

She rolled to her back and looked up into his green eyes.

"Do I look like total crap?" she asked, knowing her eyes were swollen and red.

Slowly he shook his head, his gaze dropped to her lips, then back up to her eyes. "You look beautiful to me."

"My no-makeup, bed-head, slept-in-my-clothes appearance doesn't gross you out?"

He chuckled. "It'll take a hell of a lot more than that to make me squeamish."

"Then I'll take you up on that omelet."

"Perfect." He leaned down and pressed a gentle kiss to her forehead. Something moved and shifted like a swarm of butterflies in her chest.

Without warning or pageantry, Emma fell heart over heels in love.

A week later Emma stood in front of her class and tried to convince the group of five-year-olds to settle down. At the same time she also tried to convince her heart not to put any more thought into Dean's constant yet very unusual and distant attention.

He'd taken her home the morning after Oscar died and told her to call him if she needed him for anything. She'd been tempted to pick up the phone several times to tell him *exactly* what she needed. Each night he'd call before she'd gone to bed to check and see that she was okay.

On Wednesday night he'd asked her to dinner and convinced her to stay on the board of directors. The late-night cookie-baking session at the Sugar Shack was strictly for discussing a fundraiser idea he's come up with. The invitation for lunch at the lodge house? Merely a means to review the renderings the designer had come up with for the guest cabins.

Dean Silverthorne, player both on and off the football field, had not given one single indication that he was interested in her in any way other than as a friend and a member of the organization he'd created.

He'd kept his hands *and* lips to himself, and he'd not uttered one suggestive word. In the past week, she'd learned that for such a solid man he had soft spots all over the place. Especially if it had anything to do with family or the children he intended to help. He'd been relentless in his pursuit of information and guidance in both the planning and design of the new organization.

The sweat effort he'd put into regaining the strength in his shoulder? Amazing. On several occasions he'd asked her over to help with some paperwork while he worked out his shoulder. On those same occasions she'd found herself using any lame excuse she could to enter his exercise room. Any excuse to see his big rugged shirtless body and defined abs in a pair of workout pants that hung low on lean hips over muscular thighs. She could spend all day watching his muscles bulge and contract as he lifted the free weights. When he'd finish his workout, he'd wrap a towel around his neck and shoot water from a plastic bottle into his mouth. If she was lucky some of that water would drip from his bottom lip and slide down the smooth contours of his chest and hard stomach. Her mouth would water and her hands would tingle as she'd look at that perfect physique and remember how it had felt against her, pressed into her, bringing her more pleasure than she'd ever thought possible.

He'd spend hours working all those muscles, relentlessly advancing his workout though he'd yet to throw a pass.

Especially not at her.

So when the door to her classroom opened and he stood there in his Kodiak parka with a big grin, she had to wonder why.

"Can I help you, Mr. Silverthorne?" she asked, keeping it light and professional.

He gave her a nod, then slid his gaze out over the classroom of kids who wondered why he hadn't come bearing cupcakes like last time.

"Who's up for a field trip?" he asked.

All little hands raised, except Brenden Jones. So intent on his sketch of a field of flowers was Brenden that he didn't acknowledge anyone new had even entered the room. Dean strolled to the table where Emma's blossoming student sat bent over his work. Dean tapped on the table and Brenden's head came up.

"How about you, Brenden? Would you like to go on a field trip?" Brenden gave an enthusiastic nod and Dean's grin grew even wider. "Great, then everybody grab your coats and let's go."

Twenty-four chairs scooted against the tile floor and made a huge racket as the kids jumped up and scrambled for the alphabet coat rack on the wall.

"Whoa," Emma said. "You can't just take a group of kids out of school, Dean. You have to let the office know. Permission slips have to go home for their parents to sign and—"

Dean lifted his hand. "Already taken care of. All papers have been signed and Mrs. Mayberry has already filed them. The bus is outside."

"Why didn't you discuss this with me ahead of time?"

"It was a surprise."

Emma tilted her head as pure excitement danced in his eyes. "What have you got up your sleeve?"

"It's not what I have up my sleeve." He grabbed her coat off the hook and settled it over her shoulders with a gentle squeeze. "It's what I have in my barn."

A rocky bus ride and several renditions of *John Jacob Jingleheimer Schmidt* later, the Deer Lick kindergarten class clamored out of the big yellow bus door and dashed toward the big red barn behind the Clear River Lodge.

"Slow down, you guys," Emma called as Dean helped her down the steps.

"Let 'em go, Em. They're excited."

"I have to admit, I am too."

"Good." One corner of his beautiful mouth curled upward. "I like it when you get excited."

Her head whipped around to find that familiar flirtatious gleam in his eyes. She smiled. Ah. He was back. She'd missed flirty Dean. Not that she didn't admire his serious side. But oddly enough, she missed his bigger-than-life personality.

Once he saw she was stable on her feet and wouldn't slip on the icy drive, he rushed ahead of her to open the big double doors. With a *whoosh*, the interior of the barn was revealed along with the sounds of goats and cows and chickens and horses—and even a llama Dean introduced as Hal.

The kids scrambled, some holding Dean's hands as they made their way inside where the scent of hay tickled Emma's nose. The superstar quarterback led them toward a big man at the opposite end of the barn. Emma recognized him as Buck Doody, a sweet-souled farmer who last year had lost a large portion of his land to the bank and his wheat crop to a fungal disease. Buck had seven children, all under the age of twelve, and a wife who spent most of her time canning vegetables and chasing kids. The Doody family had fallen on hard times, and by the smile on Buck's face, Emma knew that Dean had just relieved some of the man's financial pressure.

"How many of you kids have animals like these at home?" Dean asked his eager audience. A few hands shot into the air.

"We got goats but they're mean," said Emily Anderson.

"We got chickens," said Tristan Roberts.

"Ah," Dean grinned, "But can you catch your chickens?"

"If we chase 'em till they get tired."

"Then I think these chickens might be better. Go ahead and see if you can catch one."

Tristan looked up at Dean to see if there was some kind of trick, but Dean just stepped back while the boy finally walked over to where several hens pecked at the ground. As soon as Tristan got close a fat Rhode Island Red spread her wings and squatted until Tristan picked her up. The boy's small hand smoothed over her shiny feathers. "She's nice."

"All these animals have been hand-raised. None of them are mean; they want you to pet them." That's all it took for the kids to scramble in twenty different directions. Whether they lived on a farm or in a subdivision, they all were eager to get up close and personal with their farm friends.

"There's one just for you, Brenden," Dean said to the boy who'd stood still while the others had run off.

Her most challenging and inspirational student looked

up, but he did not make eye contact. Dean waved him toward a stall near the back of the barn. "His name is Blue," Dean said, and gave the gray gelding a pat on the rump. "And he's looking for a special little boy like you to help brush his coat. See how fuzzy he is?"

Brenden nodded.

"All that hair keeps him warm in the winter."

Brenden took a small step back. Dean hunkered down and held out a soft bristled brush. "He looks big, but he won't hurt you. I promise. Want to give it a try?"

Emma watched as Dean took Brenden's hand and placed the brush in his palm. Then Dean lifted the boy and guided his hand to the horse, showing him how to stroke the brush across the animal's long back.

Emma's heart did a funny side-step. Dean looked completely comfortable in the midst of children. He had no problem communicating with them. He didn't talk down to them or discount them if they asked a silly question. She sincerely hoped that someday he would settle down and have children of his own. He'd make an excellent father.

After several strokes of the brush, Brenden let out an excited grunt and buried his short little fingers in the horse's thick hair. He wiggled them, forked them through, then gently floated them down the back. Beneath his soft touch the horse's flesh rippled. Brenden looked at Dean and smiled.

With a grin that matched her young student's, Dean glanced at her over the boy's head. "It doesn't get much better than this, Em." Then he leaned toward her and kissed her on the cheek.

That's all it took before she was looking for a hankie.

CHAPTER FIFTEEN

Night fell without a breeze. Pale moonlight stroked the pine tops and cast deep shadows across the forest floor while the snow-covered meadow basked in a wintry glow.

Dean eased down into the hot springs with a sigh and made a mental note. He needed a camera. Or a poetry book. Or both. Montana encompassed some of the prettiest land in the nation. And he'd bought himself a piece of the glory. He glanced toward the darkened house where he'd left on a small light in the kitchen so he wouldn't stub his toe in the dark. Again. Lesson learned.

His body ached from the solid workout he'd had just an hour ago. While he'd stood in the shower with the spray massage on his shoulder he realized he should have been out soaking up nature. Anyone could stand in a shower. It was Friday night and he had the opportunity to sit in his very own hot springs.

God, it was good to have money.

Not that he necessarily needed more. His newest contract

was generous and he'd never been greedy. His paycheck and smart financial management had given him the opportunity of a lifetime—to buy a piece of heaven and help out a bunch of kids in need at the same time. This afternoon with Emma's class had been amazing.

Life was good.

For the most part.

He lifted the bottle of Sam Adams to his mouth, took a drink, and thought of Brenden's wide smile that afternoon as he'd sunk his little fingers into the horse's thick winter coat. Dean grinned all over again. That Emma had been there to share the moment had made it even better.

His heart gave an extra thump and his stomach fluttered. Not from hunger. He always got that flutter when he thought of Emma. He missed her. Which is why he'd gone to some really lame lengths to have her around as much as possible. At night when she went home to her own little house, he missed seeing her smile. Hearing her laugh. He missed touching her, and holding her, and making love to her.

He had tried so hard to be a good guy, to respect her wishes not to get involved with him. But Emma had that killer smile that just knocked him out. She had that soft, feminine body that made his hands tingle. Her sweet scent always made him think of wildflowers and sunshine. And she had the biggest, warmest heart.

Shit.

He dropped his head back to the rock ledge and stared up through the canopy of pine as moonlight broke through the branches. When he was with her, he didn't want to be anywhere else. The thought of getting on a plane and leaving her behind while he went back to his life in Texas soured in his stomach.

Maybe he could ask her to come along.

And what?

Move in with him?

Be his Tuesday, Wednesday, Thursday girlfriend while he went out the rest of the week, flew in chartered jets, hung out with the team? While supermodels flirted with him and A-list actresses asked him to escort them to movie premieres? That was the life he'd created.

Emma would never leave Deer Lick. She loved the place. She loved the people who lived there and they loved her. The kids in her class depended on her. She thrived on small-town life. Hell, she'd come right out and told him she wanted a husband and children and the whole happily-ever-after.

And what the hell did *he* want? A few more years of sweat and blood and glory and a big fucking paycheck? Yeah, *that* would be fun to cuddle up next to in the middle of the night.

The sound of a car engine vibrated the air. Studded tires crunched on packed snow and brought his head up. Headlights swept the meadow then shut off and all went back to moonlight. A car door opened and closed. Dean groaned.

He should get out and go see who'd decided to drop by unannounced. Most likely Kate, armed with another lecture on life's little secrets outside the NFL and inside the state of matrimony. Or maybe his father had come by for a beer and a thought-provoking chat.

A moment later he glimpsed a shadow coming toward the hot springs. As the shape came into the meadow and moonlight reflected off silky blond hair, a smile broke across his mouth. He slunk deeper into the water, back beneath the cover of the pines.

A beautiful trespasser.

She came to the edge of the hot springs and he watched in silence as she kicked off her shoes and unzipped her coat. Her old parka slid down her arms with a whoosh and hit the ground. Underneath, Emma was completely naked. Her exquisite thighs and flawless breasts were an erotic outline beneath the illuminating touch of nature's spotlight.

If Dean hadn't been smiling before, he was now.

As if standing naked in the cold didn't bother her a bit, she stretched upward, lifted her hair, and secured it on the top of her head. The rush of cold air pebbled her nipples and Dean fisted his hands to keep from reaching out for her. No need to ruin the show.

She had the most amazing curves.

Seriously amazing.

With sleek moves she stepped down into the water and made her way toward the center of the pool. With each step, more and more of her beautiful body disappeared beneath the steaming water.

It was his good fortune that his water nymph wasn't quite ready to completely disappear beneath the bubbly. She scooped up a handful of water and dribbled it over her peaked nipples.

"Mmmmmm." She moaned and leaned her head back while her hands did a leisurely slide down her wet breasts and stomach until they disappeared beneath the water. Dean happily imagined where they went.

Oh, baby.

He pressed his palm against his erection for a momentary relief of the ache. His testicles tightened and he bit back a groan as she rolled her head and gave another low moan deep in her throat.

He should let her know he was there.

He really should.

It was the gentlemanly thing to do.

Too bad at the moment he didn't have a noble bone in his body.

One of Emma's hands eased out of the water and skated up her flat stomach to caress her breast while the other hand remained hidden beneath the steamy bubbles.

He was one lucky sonofabitch.

Who'd have ever thought his proper little schoolteacher could put on a show so sexy he was about to burst without any kind of manual stimulation?

Her head dropped back again as her fingers played across her nipples. When her head came back up she looked right into the shadows. Right to where he'd sat dead still, afraid to move and ruin the entertainment.

"This feels so . . . good," she murmured. "But it would feel even better if you touched me. Dean."

Surprise. "You knew I was here?" His words were tight and rough in empathy for the intense ache in his groin.

She nodded.

"Was that all for me?"

Again, she nodded.

"You are fucking amazing." He pushed through the water and grabbed her around the waist with both hands. He brought her hard against his body and kissed her. Once.

Twice. When his tongue swept into her mouth she kissed him back with unleashed passion and enthusiasm. She tasted sweet in his mouth. Hot and eager. Her arms wrapped around his neck and those wet hard nipples lifted against his chest. The warmth of her body against his twisted his belly with pleasure.

She drew her head back and looked up at him through eyes glittered with lust. "Just for the record." Her low and tantalizing tone hummed through his body. "*This* is hanky-panky and *I'm* initiating it."

"Thank God you came to your senses." His hands stilled on the small of her back. "What about Jesse?"

"Jesse who?"

"That's what I'm talking about." He slid his hands down to her nicely rounded ass and pushed his erection against her pelvis.

"Come on superstar." She stroked her fingertip across his bottom lip. "You can do better than that."

He laughed. "Is that a dare?"

One slim, sexy, naked shoulder shrugged. "Take it any way you want it."

"In that case, I'm happy to oblige." He lifted her. "Wrap your legs around me."

He plunged inside her. He wasn't gentle. He didn't think that's what she wanted. She wanted to know he desired her. Needed her. And as an honest man, he had no trouble admitting he needed her more than he needed to breathe.

He rocked his hips forward and her breath caught in her chest. "You okay, honey?"

She smiled against his mouth. "I'm perfect."

Yeah. She really was.

She was also so incredibly hot and slippery inside it took all the power he had not to come the moment he entered her. Even as his desire tried to deter him, he knew he wanted to make it last, to give her what she wanted.

He'd been on an involuntary hunger strike and he planned to have Emma until he'd had his fill.

And that just might take a lifetime.

Bubbling water sloshed up between their heated bodies as Emma clung to Dean's neck. The plump head of his penis stroked her inside, against that special place that made her want to scream out his name. Or curse. Or growl like a damned tiger.

He lifted her up and down over him like she weighed nothing. As if he'd never slammed his shoulder into a hard-packed football field. And with every stroke she wanted more. She loved the feel of him inside her. The heat of his chest warmed her breasts. The thick length of him pushed as deep inside as he could go. Lightheaded, she moaned, thrust her fingers into his hair and pulled his head down to feed him long, hot, wet kisses.

"I need to go deeper, honey."

Deeper?

Impossible.

"I want to touch your soul." He stepped backward and lowered them to the rock seat. Hot water lapped between their bodies as he put her in total control. His hands slid up her thighs to her waist. "I'm all yours, Em. Do with me what you want."

All hers?

She liked the sound of that. She kissed his smiling mouth then leaned down and slicked her tongue across his hard, flat nipple. His breath hissed from his lungs as she slowly raised her hips then lowered herself until the head of his cock bumped her cervix.

Ah, *deeper.*

Her muscles clenched around him, drew him in, then slid back up, creating that undeniable friction that pushed them both toward release. His hands gripped her waist, helped her rise and come down harder. Faster. She leaned her forehead against his as they found the perfect rhythm. With each thrust she whispered against his mouth. "Don't stop. Don't stop."

His hand moved upward to her breast. "Come on me, honey." He pulled her aching nipple between his fingers and lightly pinched. "I want to feel you come." He pinched again and thrust so far up inside her she gasped. Again and again he thrust until the first hot waves of her orgasm rolled up like a tidal wave. Each surge more and more intense until her skin lit on fire. Her toes curled. She hit the flashpoint, arched against him, and dropped her head back with a silent scream.

"That's it, honey." He thrust harder and her orgasm gripped him tight. With one last powerful thrust he groaned her name and every muscle in his body turned as hard as rock.

Her contractions milked him and she wrapped her arms around him while he buried his face in her neck.

"God, I love you, Em."

Emma's heart almost stopped beating. It felt as if he'd taken a bat to her chest and she gasped for air.

She knew the words had escaped out of passion.

She wished they'd been from his heart.

At midnight Dean decided a snack was in order. With his fingers intertwined with Emma's, he decided she'd taste better than anything he had in the refrigerator.

He moved over the top of her and nudged her knees apart. Heat met moist heat while he kissed the side of her neck. "Do you know that right after we met I thought you were the proverbial crazy bridesmaid?"

She gave a low, sexy laugh. "Do you know that right after we met . . ." She tilted her head to give him better access and sighed with pleasure. " . . . I thought you were an overrated Casanova?"

"Mmmm." He slicked his tongue down the long, smooth column of her neck. "Good thing we didn't go off first impressions."

Her soft hands glided down his back to grip his buttocks. "Very good thing."

He nibbled at her ear. "I like that we can talk like this."

"A little less talk and a lot more action would be even better." She wrapped her leg around his waist, drew his mouth down to hers and fed him a wet and wild kiss.

"All in good time, honey. I'm just snacking right now." He eased his body down and captured her budded nipple in his mouth. "We'll get to the full meal soon."

Dean knew he could wordplay all night long, but he'd never get enough of the woman in his arms. He didn't know what to do about that. It was easier to play and laugh with her than to deal with real emotions. They confused the hell out of him. He was barely in control of his little corner of the universe.

She untangled their fingers, reached down between them, and cupped her hand around his balls. "Please?" she whispered.

Confused?

Who was he kidding?

She had him right where he never thought he'd be.

Falling for her and falling hard.

She gently squeezed him.

"You sure do know how to get a guy's attention."

"Like I said." She gave him a smile, kissed him, and lightly bit his bottom lip. "Please?"

"Who am I to deny a beautiful woman?" He slid into her hot, wet core with a slow, deep thrust and received a sexy moan for his efforts.

As long as he danced on the edge of insanity, he intended to enjoy the hell out of it. Because as an honest man he knew that in Emma's tender embrace and hot hands was exactly where he wanted to be.

"I want you still here in the morning when I wake up." He dropped his forehead to hers. "No running this time."

"Okay." Her fingers dug into his butt, urging him down.

"That's what you said last time." He moved inside her.

"Then—" She gasped and moaned a needy sound. "I promise."

"So I don't have to tie you up?"

She gave his butt another squeeze and that killer smile turned him inside out. "Only if you want to."

"Maybe next time." He ran a hand down her thigh to the back of her knee and lifted. He rotated his hips, pushed inside her full tilt, and gave her what she'd begged for. He gave it to her hot and he gave it to her hard. And when he felt the first wave of pleasure ripple through her body, he let go and loved her for all he was worth.

On the current market, that was still pretty damned good.

On Saturday morning the Sugar Shack had opened for business and bustled with folks who needed a sugary fix. Once the shop cleared out, Dean opened the door and walked in with Emma's hand in his. His father looked up from bagging brownies for Edna Price and gave him a nod. Then his father's gaze slipped down to his and Emma's intertwined hands. His father smiled.

Edna turned to see what brought about his father's expression. When she saw their hands together, she clasped her old red coat above her heart and nodded.

As Dean and Emma stood side by side, hand in hand, looking up at the menu, Kate pushed a baker's-dozen mixed donuts across the counter to Willa Franklin, the second biggest gossip in town. Kate tilted her head at the two of them. When realization dawned, she shrieked like she'd been poked with a stick. She rushed around the counter at full force and launched herself into their arms.

"I knew it!"

Dean looked at Emma, realized he probably had a big goofy grin on his face, and he didn't care. He felt goofy. And happy.

"Oh, you guys, you are so freaking cute together."

Somewhere in the months Kate had been married, her snooty Hollywood-speak had converted to happy, sappy talk. She hugged Emma but Dean didn't let go. Not when Emma's hand trembled and her eyes darkened with hesitation.

Then his baby sister looked up at him and doubled up her fist the same way she had when she'd been nothing but a little squirt who barely reached his waist with her red head.

"I swear, Dean, if you screw this up, I will take you out like a rabid dog."

He dropped a kiss on Kate's forehead. "Before you do me in and before I've done anything wrong . . ." He turned to Emma. "I haven't done anything wrong yet, have I?" She shook her head. "Good." He turned back to Kate. "How about some of your apple and sunflower-seed muffins and a side of the raspberry-coconut?"

A perceptive grin flashed across Kate's face. "Worked up an appetite, huh? Well, I've got just the thing." She hooked her arm through Emma's and carted his girl off behind the counter.

Dean had no choice but to let go of Emma's hand.

His girl.

He rubbed his palm and didn't like the way it suddenly felt cold and empty. He needed to put a football in it. Soon. That way he'd have two of his favorite things to hold onto. He lifted his head and watched Emma move with familiarity behind the bakery counter where Kate had put her to work choosing and boxing up their breakfast.

Family meant everything to him. Even more now that he'd lost his mother. Well, he'd sort of lost her.

The day he'd ended up in surgery after his hit on the field, his father had taken the first flight out of Montana. He'd been there beside the hospital bed when Dean had woken, groggy from the anesthesia and pain meds. His father had held his hand and forced hope into his heart when Dean had had very little. For several days after the surgery, his father had slept in his spare room and waited on Dean with as much care as his mother would have, had she been around. His sisters called nightly, asking what they could do to help. They'd all been there for him when he'd needed them most.

His gaze tracked Emma as she closed the lid on a pristine white pastry box, then licked a drop of sugary topping from her index finger. Everything inside him turned to mush.

Family.

That's what Emma had become to him.

He liked waking up with her in his arms. He liked falling asleep with her cuddled against him. And this morning he would thoroughly enjoy sitting across from her while they snacked on muffins, and hopefully afterward, each other.

He planned to take her back to the lodge house and build an inferno in the outdoor fireplace. On this amazing sunny morning where the snow glittered like diamonds and the scent of pine wafted across the deep blue sky, it seemed a perfect day to eat out on the back deck.

A perfect day for a proposition.

CHAPTER SIXTEEN

Surrounded by forest and a blue sky, Emma tilted her head back and let the winter sun touch her face. Dean had built a roaring fire in the outdoor fireplace, yet the air remained cool and crisp. When she'd shivered, he'd brought out a thick wool blanket and covered her legs. Cozy and warm, she smiled.

"What's that for?" Dean leaned over and kissed her mouth.

"What?"

"The smile."

"The sun feels good."

"*You* feel good." He took her hand, brought it to his lips, and kissed it. "Mmmmm. Taste good too."

Her heart gave a little flutter while he rubbed her cold fingers between his palms and glanced out over the frozen lake. Emma wished she had a camera because she'd never seen quite such a peaceful expression on his face before. No twists of pain tightened his beautiful mouth. No furrows of worry creased his brow. "I don't have a penny for your thoughts but I'd be willing to take it out in trade," she said.

He turned his head and those green eyes of his literally glittered in the sunlight. "Can I choose what I get?"

"I'm not taking my clothes off out here." She shivered. "It's too cold."

"Come here." He opened his arms. "I'll keep you warm."

She pulled the blanket off and climbed onto his lap. He covered them both and she laid her head against his non-injured shoulder.

"You don't have to be so careful, Em. I'm not made of glass."

"I know. But you've worked so hard to get your shoulder back in shape, I'd hate to damage that."

"Honey, it was fine when I lifted you up on your kitchen counter and had my way with you. It was fine when I lifted you up in the hot springs so you could wrap your legs around my waist and I could have my way with you. So your head on my shoulder is easy. And very nice."

"You just like having your way with me."

A huge grin curled his sexy mouth before the corners slipped downward.

"What is it?" she asked, suddenly alarmed.

"You mentioned me working hard on my shoulder. It just made me think about all the stuff I need to get done before I go meet up with the doctor again."

"Is that when you'll find out how well the surgery worked?"

He nodded and tucked her into him a little closer. "But I don't need him to tell me. I can feel the strength coming back more and more each day. Another couple of months and no one will even remember that I tore the hell out of it."

She patted his chest. "You're a fighter, Dean."

"I've got no choice. Football is all I know. It's been who I am since I learned to strap on a helmet. I refuse to believe I can't get it back. That I can't have it all."

Thoughts of him having it all led to thoughts of her losing it all.

Soon the gentle, charming man she'd learned to love would get on a plane that would take him away from her. Out of her life. Back to the celebrity world in which he belonged. And which she had no part of. She curled her fingers into his shirt and sighed.

"When I go back to Texas," he said, gliding his palm slowly up and down her arm, "I want you to come with me."

Her head came up. "What?"

"I've been thinking about it, Em." His hand cupped her face. "Thinking about *us*. I think we're good together."

So did she, but . . .

"I want to be with you." He looked deep into her eyes. "I want to know when I come home that you'll be there, waiting for me."

His words drew the air from her lungs. Could this be . . . ? "Exactly what are you saying, Dean?"

"I think . . . we should live together."

"Live together?" She leaned back.

"Yeah. You know, as in, you move your clothes into my closet and take over so I have to use the closet down the hall."

"I can't go to Houston and move in with you."

A crease slashed across his forehead. "Why not?"

Why not, indeed? This was what she'd wanted, right?

Commitment? Then why wasn't she jumping up and down? "Because I have a class full of kids who depend on me. I'm not about to walk out on them."

"You wouldn't have to. You could stay until summer break and then move."

"I'm in the process of obtaining my master's."

"The University of Houston would love to have you."

"I'm just starting to apply the knowledge I gained at the Missoula Academy to help Brenden."

"In a few months Brenden will be going into the first grade."

"I can still help him."

"But think of how many kids you'll be able to help once you get that degree. And you could get it faster if you went to school full-time."

True. "I can't afford that kind of education right now."

"I can."

"Are you offering to pay my tuition?"

"Absolutely. And you wouldn't have to worry about paying me back like you would a student loan."

"That's really generous of you."

"So you'll do it?"

"Ummm, let me think about that." She tapped her chin several times. "Yeah, that would still be a no. I don't want you or anyone else paying for my education, Dean. I'm old-school. I believe you gain more if you have to work hard at something. Besides, I'm not leaving Deer Lick."

"We could live here for the months I'm off football. You could substitute-teach."

"Still a no."

"Why?"

"Because what would the town think? What would my students think? What kind of example would I set?"

"You can't base your life on what everyone thinks, honey. They'll be happy for you. For us. You saw the look on Dad and Kate's faces. They were ecstatic we were together."

"Not everyone is so understanding."

"You don't think they'll compare you to your mother, do you?"

"No." But she did. She thought about what her students' parents would think. What her next-door neighbor would think. Yes, since Oscar died she'd been beyond lonely. She hated going home to an empty house. But to leap to such an extreme when all she really needed to do was bring home a new cat? She didn't even know if she was ready for a new cat. She wanted her old cat back. And she didn't want life to be so complicated that she had to tell the man she loved no.

She understood what a huge step this was for him even to consider. Unfortunately, as earth-shattering as it may seem to him, for her, it wasn't enough. She was old-fashioned. She didn't want to *move in* until he got tired of her and moved on. She wanted a lifetime commitment.

"Aren't relationships about compromise?" he asked.

"I haven't changed my mind about what I want."

"You mean marriage, kids, the whole pretty-picture-tied-up-in-a-bow thing?"

Her chest compressed. "Yes. That whole tied-up-in-a-bow thing."

"Come on, honey," he coaxed, kissed her neck. "Living with me wouldn't be so bad. I promise I'd pick up my dirty socks and I wouldn't leave dishes in the sink."

"Ah, if it were only as simple as dirty socks and dishes."

"It can be."

"What would I do for the seven-plus months you'd be gone? Take up knitting?" The tension between them had escalated, so Emma went for a laugh. "I know. Don't they have a big rodeo there? I could take up bull riding."

He gave her an edgy chuckle instead of a full-blown belly laugh. "I'd be home."

"Not every night."

"Almost every night." He kissed the side of her neck again and warmth rushed right down to her heart. "At least think about it for more than two seconds."

Emma thought of being able to sleep next to him every night, wake up next to him every morning, and make love with him whenever she wanted. She thought of sitting across from him at the dinner table to discuss their day. In her mind it unveiled like an episode of *Ozzie and Harriet*. In reality it would be more like *Desperate Housewives*, the non-married version.

"Come on, honey." The big hand that earned him millions of dollars slid to the back of her neck and drew her mouth down to his. "Just think about it."

A reality check assured Emma that Dean Silverthorne did not make long-term commitments. Just thinking about it could amount to emotional devastation.

But that didn't stop her foolish heart from wanting to say yes.

For two weeks Emma and Dean played house and nobody caught wind of their game. Not Kate or their father. Not the educators in the school district. Not even Emma's nosy neighbor.

Emma kept her car in the garage and each night after the sun went down she left the loneliness of her empty house and snuck out her back door to meet Dean down at the end of her dark street. In the mornings she'd return to her little cottage before the neighborhood woke up. At first Dean had thought her idea ridiculous, but then he got into the whole secrecy, and the game-playing worked its way into their lovemaking. He didn't mind that at all. For a time they'd laughed at their undercover capers, especially the night she'd met him wearing only her coat and boots.

Two weeks had turned into three, and Emma now found herself staring at the bright pink toothbrush Dean had bought her that was sitting in the cup next to his. She'd closed the shower door where her bottles of shampoo and conditioner sat perched next to his on the built-in tile ledge. Downstairs he waited for her with a fire roaring in the fireplace and a glass of delicious cabernet.

She'd grown used to cuddling with him at night, working together with him in the kitchen to make grilled chicken and vegetables. Or the lemon cheesecake that never made it to the oven because they'd ended up licking the batter off each other.

Her loneliness had disappeared, and the man she was used to seeing on magazine covers and big-screen TVs became more important to her than breath. She used the fluffy towel to dry off, then she slipped into the long, red spaghetti-strap nightgown he'd bought for her on his last trip into Bozeman.

He'd asked her to think about moving with him to Texas. She'd thought about it. At the end of the day, she knew she wouldn't. Not that she didn't care about him. But she didn't belong in Texas. She'd never fit in with his friends, his coaches, and the team. She couldn't live a life wondering when he would tire of her, and she'd see him on entertainment news with his arms around a cheerleader, or an actress, or a supermodel.

And she wouldn't give up on her goals and ambitions to become a door mat.

After months of being with her day after day, he'd discover that she was just Emma. A small-town girl who was happy to be just that. She'd never fit in with the cool kids and Dean Silverthorne was their leader.

Every breath she took reminded her that their time together would soon draw to a close. Dean would return to Texas sooner rather than later and he'd be going there alone. She'd return to her too-quiet house. Try to pick up the pieces. And move on.

For children who couldn't yet tell time, Emma's students somehow managed to figure out the afternoon bell was about to ring. Their little butts squirmed in their seats as, in unison, they stared up at the clock. The bell about to chime would signal more than just the end of a Thursday afternoon—the bell would signal the countdown to just one more week of school before spring break.

While warmer climates boasted swimsuits and water fun, Deer Lick had a different set of spring break traditions. Like shoveling soggy snow so the daffodils could pop their yellow heads up through the earth. Or poking holes in the thinning ice to cast a line in the lake. Avid skiers could still hit the slopes and thrill-seekers would now be able to attempt to rock climb on some of the most beautiful cliffs in the west.

For Emma, the bell about to chime meant something very different.

When the loud buzz broke through the silence of her classroom, her students leaped from their seats and rushed out the door. In two seconds Emma found herself alone amongst walls covered in primary-colored, finger-painted works of art. She laughed and spoke aloud. "Was it something I said?"

"If you were talking dirty, I completely missed it."

Emma spun to find Dean with one broad shoulder planted into the door frame, his arms crossed, and a smile on his face.

"I believe I covered talking dirty last night." She straightened the papers on her desk to hide her blush. She'd never done most of the things Dean had talked her into during sex play. The first time she'd been shocked. The next time she'd become an avid participant.

Dean pushed away from the door and strolled toward her. She loved to watch him move. For a man of his size and muscle, he moved with elegance and grace. When she'd mentioned that to him, he'd made her promise never to say things like that about him to anyone else. At least not in front of the guys who could pound him like sand into the turf. And had.

He wrapped her in his arms, nuzzled her neck, and said in

a heavy Texas twang, "Mmmm, I do love the way you smell, Miz Hart."

She did her best to dodge him and was thoroughly unsuccessful. "You can't do that here. Someone could walk by and look in."

His hands began to roam down her backside and she realized, too late, she'd just thrown down the gauntlet.

"Well, I'm sure they'd understand that I'm about to board a plane and I have to make every moment I have with you count."

All day she'd tried to forget that he was leaving and she wouldn't see him until who knew when.

If ever.

If the doctors cleared him to work out with the team, as Dean expected them to, he'd stay in Texas for good. Or at least until his schedule allowed him to come up for air. He'd handed over some of the duties for the organization to his trusted board members. The rest, he said, he would handle via phone or email.

She looked up into green eyes full of mischief.

Make every moment count.

Without a word she wrapped her arms around his neck and kissed him. His strong arms brought her tight against his chest and he kissed her back.

"Ahem."

Emma broke from Dean's embrace to find the school principal inside the door of the room. His enormous belly pushed against a mustard yellow button down shirt and drooped over a pair of red pants.

"Mr. Prince. I—"

"Hello, Dean." Hand extended, Walter Prince walked past Emma as though she didn't exist. He shook Dean's hand with a big, meaty paw. "Well, now, I haven't seen you around since you came back."

Dean's wide shoulders lifted in a shrug. "I've had a pretty busy schedule putting together a charity to honor my mother."

"Yes, Brenden Jones's mother mentioned that. Very admirable."

"She was a good woman," Dean said.

"Indeed she was." Principal Prince glanced over his shoulder at Emma.

"I'm sorry, Mr. Prince," Emma glance up at Dean. "We . . . uh . . ."

"Yes. I've heard."

"You heard?" Distress rippled up Emma's back. "From who?"

"Now, Miss Hart, you know how this town operates."

"I thought we'd been rather discreet. How many people know?"

"Might be easier to count who doesn't know," the principal muttered.

Emma pictured in her mind all the fingers wagging in her direction and groaned.

Dean laughed. "See, honey, I told you no one would care."

"Wouldn't go so far as to say that." Principal Prince scratched the tuft of mouse fur on top of his head.

"Maybe so," Dean said in her defense. "But we're both single and it's really no one's business."

"Well, you know how it is. Folks get curious."

Emma looked up at Dean with a solid "I told you so" fire in her eyes.

"They're wondering . . ." The principal's discomfort was palpable, but Emma could see his curiosity had a stronghold. "If—"

"If I plan to make an honest woman of her anytime soon?" Dean interjected. "Or if I'm just playing the field?"

The muscles in Dean's jaw were clenched and Emma knew he was about to give the big buttinsky educator a piece of his mind. Dean would defend her. Of course he would. Her heart warmed at the thought.

"I'll admit, sir," Dean's previously clenched jaw slid into his good-old-boy wink-wink-nudge-nudge grin. "I do get paid a lot of money to play."

The blood in Emma's veins froze. Her jaw dropped. And her heart stuttered.

He hadn't even made it back onto Texas soil yet, but playboy Dean was already open for business.

"Come on, honey. You know I was kidding. That man had no business insinuating anything. I was just trying to deflect."

Emma tightened her grip on the wheel of Dean's monster SUV and gritted her teeth. "It didn't sound like you were kidding. Principal Prince didn't think you were kidding. And I certainly didn't think you were kidding." She glanced over at him, then shot her eyes back to the road. "That's three strikes."

A dark brow lifted. "And I'm out?"

"So go the major league baseball rules."

"But I'm a football player."

"Among other things."

He gave a great sigh like he'd just lifted the weight of the world. "Pull over."

"Why?"

"Because I don't want things to end this way."

"*End?*" Her stomach clenched. A few days ago he'd asked her to live with him. Now he was saying goodbye? Literally?

She glanced across the cab of the SUV. Creases marred his perfect forehead.

"Poor choice of words," he said. "Please. Pull over."

"Fine." She flipped on the blinker and eased to the side of the highway. He was about to get on a plane and fly out of her life. Was it temporary? Or permanent? She had to face the truth. No matter how much it might hurt. She forced her eyes back to his. "You're not usually one who has trouble with words, Dean."

"I am when they count. In case you haven't noticed, I say some really dorky things when I'm around you." He tucked a lock of her hair behind her ear. "I care about you, Em."

"I care about you too." She clasped a hand to the front of her coat while the grilled cheese sandwich in her stomach curdled. She had to say it. Get it over with. Know the truth. "In fact, I've completely fallen in love with you."

No emotion registered on his face. Several silent heartbeats passed. And Emma realized she'd been foolish to think he would respond otherwise. While she'd told him she loved him, he sat there looking at her like she'd eaten a worm.

"Guess you're used to hearing that a lot." Still no reaction. Great. Before she shriveled into a blubbering idiot, she reached for the ignition. "Sorry. I didn't mean for it to happen. It just did."

He stopped her from turning the key by bringing her hand up to his mouth and pressing his lips to the backs of her fingers.

Her gaze traveled up his arm, to his oh-so-handsome face.

"You're the first," he said, eyes dark and serious. "And the only in many ways."

"What?"

"You're the first and only woman I've ever made love to without protection. You're the first and only woman who's ever told me she was in love with me. And you're the first and only woman I've ever opened myself up to." He framed her face with his hands and drew her toward him. "When I say I care about you, Em, it's more than that. You mean a lot to me. More than I ever thought possible."

He lowered his head and his mouth covered hers in an almost reverent kiss which ended much too soon. He tilted his head back and looked her straight in the eye. "Do you understand what I'm saying?"

She nodded. In that kiss she found more meaning than a wordy declaration could ever express.

"I'm glad," he said, then gathered her in his arms. They sat in that SUV, hugging each other until a car speeding by laid on the horn. They eased apart with a laugh.

"Guess we'd better get you to the airport."

"Yeah." He leaned back in the seat. "Want me to drive?"

She shook her head. "I'm okay."

"Good." He smiled. "Then I can sit here and look at you the rest of the way."

When he leaned across the seat and kissed her again, happiness settled into a nice little place in the corner of her heart where she could keep it safe.

The rest of the drive they talked about the camp organizer prospects Dean had interviewed and the projects he or she would need to complete to have the camp ready to open by the beginning of summer. Too soon Emma pulled into the parking lot of the Missoula Airport and parked in a spot near the terminal. After a bit of shuffling, they both got out of the SUV.

Dean grabbed his bag from the backseat, dropped it to the ground, and pulled her into the warmth of his arms. "I'm going to miss you, Em."

"I'll miss you too." She would not cry. She would not . . . *Damn it.*

He kissed her mouth. Kissed her tears. "Don't cry, honey."

She nodded against his shirt, then with a sniff let him go.

He picked up his duffle, slung the strap over his good shoulder, and gave her one more quick kiss. "I'll call you as soon as we land."

"Okay." *Love you.*

With a wave he walked through the big glass doors and disappeared.

CHAPTER SEVENTEEN

Springtime in Houston delivered vibrant shades of green and carpets of dazzling flowers in a rainbow of color. Much different than the day before, when he had traded the snow flurries in Deer Lick for Texas t-shirt weather. Dean wasn't sure which he preferred. Colder weather did have its advantages. Cuddling with his favorite blonde sat high on his list.

Alone in his enormous kitchen he pushed the "liquefy" button on his blender and watched the yogurt, fruit, and powder swirl in the glass container. Time to get back to his daily routine of protein shakes and grueling workouts. It wouldn't be long before he'd be out on the field again and trying to avoid having his shoulder driven into the turf by three-hundred-pound tackles. He needed to be at 110 percent. No more scarfing on Kate's cheesecake cupcakes. No more late-night snacking after a vigorous round of making love with Emma. His chest squeezed just thinking of her.

She was in love with him.

Even now her words stumbled around in his heart. At first he hadn't known how to take her declaration. For a moment those words had blindsided him. He hadn't known what to say or how to react. But the last thing he'd ever wanted to do was to hurt her. So he'd been honest. Sitting in that car, looking at her beautiful face, he'd let her know he cared for her. But he'd stayed far away from the word love.

He didn't do love.

He didn't do marriage.

He didn't do forever.

He enjoyed touching her, laughing with her, being with her. And when he wasn't with her he missed her. He felt genuine affection.

But love?

He loved his family. Loved his team. But being *in* love? He didn't know what that meant.

Before he'd walked into the airport he'd taken her into his arms and she'd melted into him like a chocolate kiss left in the sun. Then he'd given her a quick wave and stepped through the glass doors of the terminal. Inside he'd checked his bag, gone through security, and stopped at a restaurant for a to-go snack for the long flight home.

Every step he'd taken he'd felt like he'd forgotten something. Like he'd forgotten to pack his shaver, or his toothbrush, or one of those essential items you couldn't get through the day without. When he'd settled into his first-class seat and buckled the belt around his waist, the sensation had intensified.

By the time the plane had lifted from the runway, he knew by the intense grip on his heart he hadn't forgotten some*thing*. He'd forgotten some*one*.

He'd looked out the plane window, searching for the parking lot, his SUV, and the beautiful woman with the amazing heart, but saw nothing. As the city lights dimmed to darkness, he wondered if the huge ache rolling through his chest might very well be love after all.

A week later on a sunny Friday morning, Dean trailed behind the medical assistant into his surgeon's office. The week before, he'd gone through a series of MRIs and x-rays, much as he had the night he'd been drilled into the field. Today he'd find out his long-term prognosis. He'd woken feeling optimistic, much as he did on game days. That optimism had never let him down before. It wouldn't now. As soon as he got the good news, he'd call Emma and make arrangements for her to fly to Houston for spring break. They'd figure out things from there. All he knew was he wanted to be with her. *Needed* to be with her.

He settled into the leather chair, grabbed a *Men's Health* magazine off the table, and waited for the doctor to arrive. He fanned through the pages, not really interested in the manliest restaurants list, and he was too late to learn from the NFL Pro's *How to Prevent Injuries* article. He closed the magazine and tossed it back onto the table, just as Dr. Powell walked in studying the chart in his hand.

"How's the shoulder?" the doc asked.

Again with the depersonalization. "*I'm* great."

Powell lifted his gaze over his gold-rimmed glasses and looked at Dean as though he'd said something odd.

"On a scale of one to ten, ten being the worst, how's your pain level?"

"Depends. I usually run around a three or four consistently. Are those the test results?" Dean asked, anxious to get the good news so he could get on with his life.

"Most of them. We're still waiting on the blood screen, but I think we have enough information here to get a clear outlook."

Dean settled deeper into the chair. "Which is?"

"Not good."

Those two words hit him like a lead mallet. "Excuse me?"

"The cartilage just hasn't healed the way we'd hoped. Thus the reason for the lingering pain." The doctor stuck an MRI image up on the light box, grabbed a pen off the desk, and motioned for Dean to join him.

Dazed, Dean stood in front of the image and looked at all the dark and light areas the doctor quickly pointed to. They made no sense to him.

"There doesn't appear to be enough blood flow to generate the healing. See these lighter places here?" He pointed to some areas above the bone. "It wouldn't take much for these to tear again. They're just weak."

Weak.

Bam! Dean hadn't seen that one coming.

"So how long is it going to take to completely heal?"

The doctor looked him straight in the eye. "Six months. A year. Maybe never."

Fuck.

Dean returned to his chair, dropped down, and put his head in his hands.

"It's a wait-and-see situation, Dean." The doctor slid into the chair behind his desk. "I'm sorry I can't make promises on when or if. I can't even tell you that this won't require another surgery, because it might. My professional opinion is that unless something drastic changes in the next couple of weeks, you'll be out for the season." The doctor lowered his gaze like he just realized how harsh his words sounded but knew he had to say them anyway. "I tried to prepare you."

"Yeah." Dean looked up. "I know you did." The world spun like he'd drunk a bottle of Jack without the benefit of a mixer.

Out for the season.

When the room slowed to a manageable twirl, he asked, "Does the coach know?"

Dr. Powell tossed his pen back onto the desk. "I always update the patient before the report goes to headquarters."

"I appreciate that."

"You're a hell of a quarterback. I wish I had better news."

"Yeah, me too." Scrambled images ran through his head. "Can I ask a favor?"

"Sure."

"Give me twenty-four hours before you release the report?"

The doctor studied his face like he understood what Dean was feeling. But that was impossible.

"No one but you and I need to know before Monday," Dr. Powell said. "If you choose to talk to the Stallions' front office before then, so be it. Now let's go over the next course of physical therapy."

For the next ten minutes the doctor ran through timelines and exercises, but Dean barely heard through the buzz in his ears. His heart rate had doubled in speed and seemed like it was trying to push through his chest. Inside he felt hollow. Lost. Ashamed.

Weak.

When finally he left the office, he calmly walked to his Mercedes, opened the door, and slid inside. He yanked the seatbelt over his hips, dropped his head back, and released the roar that had been brewing inside him.

Slowly his heart came back to normal and the buzz in his ears lessened. He grabbed his Oakleys off the dashboard and slipped them in place over his eyes, twisted the key in the ignition, and roared out into heavy traffic.

For the first time in his life he'd been hit with a professional penalty bigger than he could handle.

On Saturday afternoon, Emma finished up her housecleaning and jumped in her car to run errands. A week had passed since she'd taken Dean to the airport. He'd called her when he'd arrived and he'd called her in the middle of the night. She'd never had phone sex before but after several days she'd become quite good. At least that's what he told her. Sounding positive and upbeat, he'd called her yesterday morning before his doctor's appointment.

Then nothing.

More than twenty-four hours had passed.

Had he been abducted by aliens? Had he been in a car accident and was now lying dead on some back country road? Had he been given a green light and jumped back into his full work schedule? If so, was he really too exhausted or too busy to call? As her pessimistic imagination ran wild, worry dug razor-sharp nails into her heart.

With her car loaded down with bags from the grocery

store, she decided to stop by the Sugar Shack, give herself a break, and treat herself to one of the white-chocolate tarts Kate had concocted last week.

As she went through the shop door, the little bell rang over her head. As usual the place was packed. While Emma waited her turn near the door, Kate looked up from boxing up an order and waved her back. One of the perks of being friends with the shop owners was you got to go behind the counter, select, and package your own treats.

"Hi." Kate gave her a one-sided flour-dusted hug as Emma came around the counter.

"Wow. Busy today."

"I know." Kate shoved a loaf of honey wheat bread into a white bag and added a dozen sourdough dinner rolls. "Which is totally great because I've got my eye on a new fryer and it's going to set us back a little. I'm going to break into a new direction."

"Uh-oh."

"Nothing R-rated this time. Just cake pops. People like fried things on a stick. I'm going to rise above and invent something totally fresh and addictive."

Emma laughed. "You are a baking goddess, Kate."

"Either that or I've completely gone over to the dark side. What's on your list today?"

"Mmmm." Emma peered into the display case. "I thought I'd try one of those new white-chocolate tarts."

"Great. And you'll be happy to know I topped them this morning with fresh strawberry glacé. Go ahead and help yourself."

"Thanks." Emma leaned down, slipped her hand into the

glass case, and plucked out one of the desserts wrapped in a frilly tulip shaped baking cup. It looked so delicious she was tempted to stuff the treat in her mouth right then and there.

Kate handed the loaf of bread over the counter to Linda Daylon, the clerk down at the courthouse. "So what did you think of my brother's news?"

Emma straightened.

"Crap." Kate's eyes narrowed. "Didn't he call you?"

A chill shot up Emma's spine. "The last I talked to him was yesterday morning before he went to the doctor. When did he call?"

Kate glanced up at the clock. "He called Dad around eleven."

Four hours ago.

"I can't believe he wouldn't call you. You know how important you are to him."

Obviously not.

"Check your cell," Kate said. "Maybe you didn't hear it ring."

Emma pulled her phone from her purse but there were no voice mails, no text messages, no emails. She looked up at Kate. "What did he say?"

"I can't believe he didn't call you."

"What did he say, Kate?"

Her shoulders lifted beneath her pink apron. "Game over."

"What does that mean?"

"The doctor wouldn't clear him to play. They released him from the team."

Nausea rolled in Emma's stomach. If his shoulder was

still too damaged to play, if he'd lost his job, how could he have *not* called her? She set the once-tempting dessert down on the counter. "Can I pick this up later? I . . . ummm . . ." Her gaze darted toward the bakery door and the new customers who had just walked in. "I have to go."

On her way out the door Edna Price barged in. "Emma. What are you doing here? I thought you would have flown to Houston to be with Dean."

Emma took a step back. "What do you mean?"

"Well, he's going through a traumatic time, dear. Surely you sensed his distress when he called you after he found out his career was over."

She would have if he'd actually called.

And how the hell did Edna Price know?

"It was good to see you, Mrs. Price." She pushed open the bakery door and strode to her car.

Why hadn't he called her?

Screw it. She wasn't going to wait for him to call. She grabbed her cell from her purse and tagged his number in her contact list. Her call went straight to voice mail and her heart hit the basement. Two blocks down the road, her hands were shaking on the wheel while her gas gauge bounced on empty. Unable to ignore the real world, she pulled into the G & G to fill up.

A cool breeze blew through the pump islands while she unscrewed the gas cap and stuck in the nozzle. A bell jingled and Emma looked up as Ollie Barnett came out the glass door.

"Hey, Em, what are you still doing here?"

Still? *Oh, no.* "Filling up my gas tank."

"Heading out to the airport?" he asked, as he opened the door to his battered F–150.

"Why would I do that, Ollie?"

He leaned into his truck and twisted the key in the ignition. "Figured you'd be heading out to pick up Dean. Sure is a shame."

She inhaled a huge lungful of air. "What's a shame?"

Ollie turned his head and looked at her really hard for a second. "You don't know?"

"Apparently not." She fought back tears and shrugged. "But it appears you do, so why don't you fill me in?"

He straightened. "You do know that Dean's career is over. Right?"

"Oh, that." Unable to expound further, she turned to watch the small fortune add up on the gas pump. Two dollars poorer she said, "How did you find out?"

"Mags called me about an hour and a half ago," he said quietly. "She saw it on ESPN."

"So the whole world knows about it?"

Ollie shrugged. "The PGA Masters is on so I guess plenty of people were watching when they announced it."

"Oh."

"He did call you, didn't he?" Ollie's expression softened.

The gas pump clicked off and Emma yanked the nozzle from her car. "Sure."

"Yeah, I figured you'd be the first one he'd want to talk to."

Or at least somewhere down the line after he called his family. But nooo. "Hey, I've got to grab . . . a bag of ice." She plastered on a smile and tried to sound as composed as possible, even though her throat was as dry as Death Valley. "Give Mags and the boys my love."

She pushed through the convenience store door and strode to the back cooler to grab a bag of ice for which she had no need. On her way to the register she ran into man-eater Gretchen Wilkes who had oddly paired her bright red cowboy boots and jeans mini-skirt with a Stallions jersey bearing the number eleven.

"Emma." She grabbed Emma's shoulders and drew her in for an air kiss. "You must be on your way to get Dean. I saw the news about an hour or so ago and I just had to put on this jersey in mourning."

"He's not dead, Gretchen." Although he might be if she got her hands on him.

"Well, bless his heart, I'm sure he wishes he was." Gretchen tsked and shook her head, which caused her wild red curls to fly. "That man is going to need some cheering up for sure." She patted Emma's cheek. "Now, if you're not up to the job, you just have him call me."

With the bag of ice melting in her hands, Emma watched as Gretchen turned on the pointed toe of her boot and flounced up to the front counter. When she got there she leaned over the counter and whispered something in the clerk's ear. The both turned their heads and looked at Emma with a mix of pity and laughter in their eyes.

Emma sucked in a deep breath, made her way up to the counter, and paid for her ice. Somehow she found her way across the parking lot to her car. Somehow she managed to open the door, throw the bag of ice in the back, and strap herself in. Somehow she found the nerve to turn on the car radio to the local sports station.

At the top of the hour, the news reporter confirmed what apparently everyone else on the planet *except her* had known. Dean Silverthorne had been dismissed from the Houston Stallions due to a career-ending shoulder injury.

She looked down at her watch. Four o'clock. He'd been told his shoulder had not healed and he'd been let go from the career he loved a full day ago.

And he'd not called her once.

In a moment of crisis when he should have looked to her for support, he'd gone to everyone else. Before he'd left Deer Lick he'd made her feel like she really meant something to him. That she was important. She loved him with her whole heart, with every fiber, muscle, and bone in her body. She was meant to love him. She'd thought there was a chance they could really be together.

Instead, the one thing she'd feared the most had happened.

She'd been forgotten.

Chapter Eighteen

On Saturday morning Dean had boarded a plane that was promptly delayed due to a thunderstorm. While he waited for clearance he picked up his phone and opened his contacts list. His finger hovered above Emma's number for the gazillionth time since yesterday afternoon. Without hitting "send call" he shoved his phone back into his pocket.

What could he say to her when he felt like half the man he'd been just a day ago? How could he face her when he could barely face himself? He was in the prime of his life and everything he'd worked for had been cut down. Everything he'd known about himself was wrong. He was devastated. Ashamed. Fearful.

Who was he now that he was no longer *Dean Silverthorne, Starting Quarterback for the Houston Stallions*? No longer *Mr. Perfect*?

On the layover in Denver he'd barely managed the call to his dad. He'd only succeeded at that because he couldn't bear the thought of his dad worrying about him.

So why hadn't he been able to call Emma for the same reasons?

His stomach revolted. He lifted his fingers and pressed them against the interchange of shredded muscles and tendons.

He was afraid.

Today he was a different man.

Weak.

What if he wasn't enough for her?

He glanced across the terminal at a young couple cooing to a tiny baby wrapped in blue blankets. A sigh backed up in his chest. He felt lonely without Emma. Incomplete. It wasn't that he needed her to make his life better. It was that his life was shit without her. With her, he was a better person. She didn't make him that way; she made him want to be that way. He wanted her to be proud of him. To look up to him. But he had a long way to go before that would ever happen.

At the moment he had no life and no career. But he did have a dream. Kindergarten teacher Emma Hart had shown him that life could be simple and fulfilling. That happiness could come in the form of a hug or a touch, a random act of kindness, a selfless deed of giving.

She'd shown him that a future without her was unacceptable.

And unimaginable.

Dean stepped outside of the Missoula Airport terminal and searched for his ride home. Across the street in the front row of the short-term parking lot sat his mother's beast of a Buick. Apparently Kate had arranged the transportation. Anyone else would have sent his SUV. Only his baby sister knew that with his mother's car he wouldn't have that long drive alone.

He glanced up at the snow-capped mountain range as he opened the car door and slid inside, reached beneath the floor mat, and grabbed hold of the keys. He buckled the seatbelt, twisted the key in the ignition, and the engine turned over with a cough. Moments later he was rolling down the highway, rehearsing in his mind what he would say when he knocked on Emma's door. He ran through every scenario as if it was the final play of the Super Bowl and he needed that W behind his name.

In reality Emma was no game. She was the prize.

Twenty miles from home, Dean turned the radio knob when the only song that would play from the crackling speakers was *It's Not Unusual.*

Wait for it . . .

A deep red, pulsating glow that felt like the inside of his head invaded the interior of the Buick.

"You're down fourteen-ten. Midfield. Twenty seconds remain in the game. What's your strategy?"

Dean shook his head at the reminder of how during his career his mother would challenge him to step up his game. To be a better player.

She wasn't doing that now.

Now she challenged him to be a better man.

"No choice but a *Hail Mary,*" he said, pulling the Buick to the side of the road. He thrust the gearshift into park and turned in his seat. He gave her a brief smile.

"And what if you underestimate the pass?"

He swiped his hand over his face. "I lose it all."

His mother leaned forward and settled her icy hand on

his arm, reminding him that miracles were possible. She'd left them months ago, yet here she still was . . . his biggest fan. His best friend.

"You've never given up before." The tone in her voice sounded tight. Disappointed. "Why now?"

"From the moment I first set foot on the field at USC, everyone had expectations, including me. I wanted to be that shining star for everyone. I wanted to be up on that pedestal. When I first put on the Stallions uniform, that expectation grew and I lost myself." He pressed his hand to the ache in his chest. "I forgot the one thing you always taught me . . . to be the best I can be at whatever I do. Even if it's mowing lawns or shoveling horse manure."

"Have you remembered now?"

"Yes."

"I told you that football was what you did. Not who you are. You are so much more."

"It's hard to keep that in mind when you're in the midst of the game and your back is against the goal posts."

"But you remember now."

He nodded. "It's funny but I feel like a new game is just beginning."

"It is, Son. It is." She gave him a brief smile that flashed in her green eyes. "You were always a good boy and you've grown into a fine man."

"I owe it all to you, Mom."

"I know."

He looked up. Their eyes met. And they both laughed.

"Was that a memorable enough *moment* for you?" she asked, mirth still playing at the corners of her mouth.

"Definitely. I shall cherish it in my heart for eternity," he over-embellished.

"Good. Now get this beast moving toward home. You've got some living to do."

"Roger that."

"And, Son?"

He glanced over his shoulder to where her hand had settled. When anyone in their right mind would be completely freaked out, he felt only comfort.

"I really am sorry about your shoulder."

"Actually, Mom, I think that shove into the turf might have been the best thing that could have ever happened to me. It's opened my eyes. I wasn't looking for it, but somehow I found what you and Dad shared. Not everyone is lucky enough to find that other person who makes them whole."

"Now you're talking." She leaned back and her glow turned brilliant gold. "Let's get a move on."

As he pulled back onto the highway, his mother began to reminisce back to when he was just a boy with big dreams and strong hands. To the times he used those hands to protect his sisters. To the times he used them to work side by side with his family after school. To the times he'd fold them together and use them to pray. He'd put those hands together on the flight from Texas to Missoula when he'd thought of Emma and all the feelings he'd foolishly tried to push away. Those emotions were strong and powerful. Protective and hopeful.

He loved her.

He was *in* love with her.

Who knew that deep inside he was a man who wanted the whole ring, marriage, and kids happily-ever-after?

CHAPTER NINETEEN

The wind blew cold against Dean's back and he shivered as he sat on the steps of Emma's front porch. He'd left his heavy coat at the lodge house but he hadn't wanted to waste the time to go get it. All he wanted was to get to Emma.

But she wasn't home.

He could drive all over town to try to find her, but then he'd take the chance of missing her and further delay their reunion. He imagined she'd be a little upset that he hadn't called yesterday. Which meant that when he told her what had happened, he'd have to be more open and honest with her than he'd ever been. He'd need to open a vein and let it all spill out.

No more holding back.

He picked up a pebble from the porch and tossed it onto the drive. He'd been sitting there for well over an hour when finally he spotted her little Subaru coming up the street. She pulled into the driveway and stopped when she saw him sitting there.

Yep. She was mad.

After a lengthy hesitation she finally pulled the rest of the way into the driveway and parked. He stood and went to her side of the car. With her hair up in a loose ponytail and wearing his favorite pink sweater, she looked so beautiful she stole his breath. Instead of opening the door and stepping into his arms like he'd hoped, she remained behind the wheel and took several deep breaths before she finally reached for the handle.

Dean's heart thumped hard and his throat went dry.

As soon as she was clear of the car, he captured her in his arms, lifted her to her toes, and held her tight. He ignored the stiffness in her body and the fact that her arms hung limp at her sides. "I'm so glad to see you, honey."

She eased from his arms and stepped back. "I assume you had a nice flight."

Those flat, emotionless words sent a chill up his spine and he knew. This was about more than just him not calling when he said he would. "You already know, don't you?"

She opened the back door to her car without looking at him. "Everyone knows, Dean."

"Everyone?"

"Yes. *Everyone.*"

"How is that possible? The only person I called was my dad and I asked him not to tell anyone until I came home. I wanted to tell you myself."

"Too late." She hefted a bag of groceries into her arms.

He took them from her, followed her into the house, and set the bag down on her kitchen counter. "Who else knows, Em?"

"Edna Price." She yanked a loaf of Wonder bread from

the bag and stuffed it into the bright red bread box on the counter. "Maggie and Ollie. Even Gretchen Wilkes. Who, by the way, offered herself if you need consoling."

"Damn that Kate."

"Don't blame your sister. If it wasn't for her I'd still be wondering if you were dead or alive. Besides, she didn't have to spread the news."

He leaned against her counter. "Then who did?"

"Blame ESPN and anyone watching the Masters. It appears everyone knew . . ." She grabbed the bag and started pulling out cans of corn. "Except me."

"Shit." He ran his fingers through his hair. "There's a reason I didn't call."

"I'm sure there is." She turned and shoved the cans into a cupboard. Her small shoulders lifted in a shrug. "It just doesn't matter anymore."

"Sure it does." God, the disparagement in her eyes made him want to crumble.

She dropped her head with a sigh, then turned toward him and folded her arms. "Look, I'm really sorry about your shoulder. And I'm truly sorry about you losing your career. I understand you must be devastated."

"I felt dead."

"I can only imagine." She blinked once. Twice. Then she glanced away. "I would have been there for you, but . . . obviously you didn't want that."

"I couldn't face you, Em," he stated honestly.

"Why? Because I'm so big and scary?"

"No. Because *this* was big. Because all my life I've been great with a football and not much else. Because for the first time I had no control over my life. Because I'd lost everything."

Her chin came up. "You hadn't lost me."

He shook his head, knowing what he wanted to say but unable to find the right words. For the past sixteen years he'd barked out orders, plays, and demands. He was proving now to be far less articulate when it came to matters of the heart. "Emma, I'm really sorry I didn't call."

"Don't you get it, Dean? This is about so much more than the fact that you didn't call. This is about more than me being publicly humiliated. Again. This is about *you* not trusting *me*. This is about you not wanting me to be a part of your pain or your happiness or whatever emotion you're dealing with at the moment. This is about you shutting me out. This is about you . . . forgetting me."

He reached out for her but she took a step back. "You were never forgotten, honey. I started to call you at least a million times. I just . . . couldn't do it. Can we sit down and talk about this?"

"*Now* you want to talk?"

"*Now* I'm *ready* to talk. There's a difference."

"Well, maybe *now* I'm not ready to listen. Call me selfish. I'm sorry you're going through a tough time and that truly breaks my heart." She shook her head and gave a little laugh that sounded anything but funny. "I knew when I fell in love with you that it was the dumbest thing I'd ever done. I tried to convince myself that I could be happy with what little you chose to give me." Beneath her sweater her shoulders squared. "But I can't. And I won't. You've proven that you aren't willing to share the important moments in your life. I wish you would. But I just can't base a relationship on fantasy."

Her words struck home and he rubbed the expanding ache around his heart. She was right. In the past he hadn't opened himself up. Everything had been a game. Until now.

"I'm sorry, honey. I truly am." He wrapped his arms around her. "And I promise I'll make it up to you. We're good together. You know we are."

Tears flooded her eyes as she untangled herself from his embrace. "It's too late," she whispered.

Her voice was so calm, so detached, so utterly reasonable it sent a chill through him. Her chin lifted as she went to the front door, opened it, and waited for him to leave. He didn't know what to do to make her understand. He didn't know what he planned to do with his future. He only knew what he'd done with his past. When faced with keeping his team in limbo or walking away so they could move forward, he'd walked away. But he wouldn't walk away from her too. Because whether he sat behind a desk at a nine-to-five or baked cupcakes for the rest of his life, he wanted her there beside him.

His chest felt so tight he could barely breathe. "I love you, Em."

"No. You don't." Her trembling bottom lip conflicted with the finality of her words. "If you did, I would have been the first person you'd have wanted or needed to talk to when your world came crashing down. I wouldn't have been an afterthought."

"That's not the way it is, Emma."

"That's the way I see it."

"You love me, Emma."

"Maybe so." Her eyes met his and held steady. "But I'll endure it. I've survived worse."

Desperation sliced through him as he reluctantly walked out onto the front porch. "I don't want this to end, honey."

"I'm sorry, Dean. I really am." She shut the door. Quietly. Calmly.

After a day of deep thought, life management, and little sleep, Dean sat at a bistro set in the Sugar Shack nursing a strong cup of coffee. He'd showered and shaved and paced every square foot of the lodge house until dawn broke in a spray of gold across the sky.

During the miles he clocked on his hardwood floor, he'd deconstructed, reconstructed, and finally figured things out. For years he could have recited any page of the Stallions playbook at any time. But beyond those pages, he'd never given much thought.

Then he met Emma and she'd sparked something inside him. She'd given him the courage to start the charity. She'd made him want more than life between the goal posts. She'd made him want a life with her. To hold her in his arms every day. To give her children they could raise together. To grow old beside her.

Damn it. *He* wanted the fairy tale.

He'd had a great ride with his career. Now it was time to work on the rest of his life. To show Emma he was a worthy teammate.

Kate walked toward him with a fried egg sandwich on a fresh croissant. She set the plate down in front of him, then whacked him across the back of his head with the palm of her hand.

"Ow."

"I can't believe you are so stupid. Did Mom chew your ass out?" Kate scoffed. "I'll bet she did. Your head is probably still reeling from it."

"No, Mom did not chew my ass out."

"What?" His baby sister dropped to the chair beside him. "That is so not fair. That woman dogged me for months, butting her transparent nose in wherever she could."

"Maybe she thought you needed more help than me."

"Me?" Kate pointed to the Sugar Shack logo in the center of her apron. "Emma's still talking to me. *You*, not so much."

No one had to hit him over the head with a bat to know that. The empty ache in his chest was all the proof he needed. He picked up the croissant and took a bite. Then with his mouth full he looked up. "You didn't lace this with arsenic, did you?"

"Damn." Kate snapped her fingers. "I knew I forgot something."

He took another bite while his sister stared at him. "What?"

A know-it-all smirk lifted her mouth. "Didn't I tell you?"

"Didn't you tell me what?"

"I warned you that someday you would fall in love. And when that happened, nothing else in this world would be more important to you than every breath she took." She gave a cocky wag of her head, folded her arms across her pink apron, and leaned back. "Was I right?"

"Yeah." He shook his head. "And I don't even mind."

"So now what are you going to do about it?"

The bell over the door jingled and Edna Price hobbled in on her moosehead cane and headed right toward them. Kate got up and gave her a hug and then they both stood there glaring down at him.

"You better not be wallowing in self-pity, young man." Mrs. Price growled.

Dean swallowed the bite of croissant. "No, ma'am."

"Well, good." She pulled out a chair and sat down. "At least we're not going to have to hog-tie you."

"Hog-tie me?" Dean looked up at Kate whose grin had evil written all over it.

At that moment his father joined them at the table. The door bell jingled again and in walked Matt, James Harley, and Ollie and Maggie Barnett. His father locked the Sugar Shack door behind them, and they all gathered around him like a pack of hungry wolves.

"What's going on?" he asked.

"You ever see *Intervention*?" Kate asked.

"No."

"It's a show where friends and families gather to intercept a drug addict to help them kick the habit."

"And that has what to do with me?" He set down his croissant. "I'm not an addict."

"That's a matter of opinion, dear," Edna Price said, giving him a quick pat on his arm. "This here is what we like to call a *fool's intervention*. We're here to save you from your ridiculous self and help you put your love life back together."

If he could put his love life back together.

He'd never been one to take a knee. Never give up. Never

surrender. Even if it took forever, he had to find a way to convince Emma he loved her and that he was the right man for her.

He looked up at the concerned faces surrounding him. He may not have it all figured out yet, but it looked like they might have some suggestions. And as much as this was really none of their business, he knew they were there because they cared about him. And Emma. His heart melted. Just a little.

Besides, this could be pretty damned entertaining.

With the sun shining at her back, Emma sat in a semi-circle of wide eyes and open ears. She held up the Dr. Seuss book so her class could see the silly pictures in *Green Eggs and Ham*, one of her favorite books to read. It was easy to get lost in the rhythm of the words, the silliness.

She wished it were as easy to get lost in her own life.

When Dean had shown up on her front step, she'd half-expected him. He'd looked drawn and tired, and a part of her wanted to gather him in her arms and give him comfort the way he'd given her comfort when Oscar died. But everything with Dean had been an emotional roller coaster and she just didn't have the energy for an endless ride. She didn't think he knew who he really was or what he really wanted. Everything had come so easy for him. He'd been handsome and charming. He'd been great at athletics from the moment he'd picked up a football and he'd been handed a skyrocketing career. He'd had gorgeous women throwing themselves at his feet with more waiting in the wings.

He'd never learned to want for anything and it wasn't up to her to teach him.

She had a lot going on in her life. And though there may be that one big gaping hole in her heart, she would do her best to focus on her career, and her kids, and her community. Someday, hopefully, all the rest would fall into place.

As she closed Dr. Seuss, the recess bell rang and class jumped up to grab their coats and dart outside. Emma rose from the pint-sized chair she'd been sitting on and stretched.

"Hey, Em."

Emma's gaze darted to the door. "Hey, Kate. What are you doing here?"

Kate strolled into the room and leaned against the desk while Emma returned *Green Eggs and Ham* to the bookshelf. "I wanted to come tell you there's a board of directors meeting this Saturday."

"Why didn't you just call me?"

When Emma approached her desk, Kate hugged her. "Because I didn't want to give you the opportunity to hang up on me."

The genuineness in the gesture made Emma melt. "I would never hang up on you."

"Even if I told you that my jerky brother will be there?"

Emma's heart flipped a one-eighty. "I really don't want to talk about him, let alone have to see him."

"I know. And I completely understand. But we really need you to be there, Em. We're voting on a few important items and they can't get passed unless you vote too."

"Kate, I really don't think it's a good idea for me to be involved anymore."

"I know being in the same room with him and not killing him will be impossible. Falling in love sucks, doesn't it?"

"I didn't mean to fall in love with him." A huge sigh pushed from Emma's lungs. "I knew better. But he's so . . ."

"Dean," Kate said.

"Exactly."

"Boy, do I know how that feels." Kate sighed too. "Matt put me through hell before I finally realized we were meant for each other. When I came back to Deer Lick, there was a whole ocean under the bridge between Matt and me. It took us awhile to figure things out. We had our good moments and we had plenty of bad before we came to the conclusion that we just really loved each other so much we couldn't stand to be without the other. Life isn't always simple. One minute you're staring at a building and the next your dead mother is popping into the backseat of her Buick so she can meddle in your love life."

"What?"

One of Kate's eyebrows lifted. "I'll have to explain that one later."

"Will I need to be drunk at the time to understand?" Emma asked.

Kate laughed. "Probably. All I know is that sometimes things aren't always as they seem. And neither are people."

The end-of-recess bell clanged through the room.

While Emma pondered Kate's cryptic message, her friend grabbed her up in another hug, then headed for the door. "Promise me you'll be at the lodge house at noon on Saturday?"

Resigned to facing Dean one last time, Emma nodded. "I'll be there." *With my resignation from the board.*

CHAPTER TWENTY

Saturday turned out to be the best day of the year so far. Weather-wise, anyway. Emma woke to sunshine beaming through her kitchen window, and she had the sudden urge to stick her fingers in the warm earth to plant something and watch it grow. Instead she climbed in her little Subaru to go face the dragon. How in the world would she contain herself in a room of only three people plus *him*? What about Kelly? How were they going to vote without her?

Emma knew this would be her final task as a board member for the Leticia Silverthorne Sunshine Camp. That reality made her sad. She'd liked being a part of the organization. She'd found herself getting wrapped up in the excitement of the planning stages and she'd been excited to see it come to fruition.

She'd never forget the day Dean had pulled his surprise field trip for her class. Or the look on his face when he'd opened the barn doors to let the kids in to see the animals. Or the attention he'd paid to Brenden Jones, a boy who needed all the special consideration he could find.

Emma's heart squeezed. Had she only created a fantasy of Dean? Had she been like everyone else in Deer Lick and put him up on a pedestal where he had no choice but to fall?

She slowed her Forester to make the turn into the long driveway of the lodge house. As soon as she'd made the turn she had to pull to the left of the drive to avoid the line of cars parked as far as she could see.

What was going on?

At the end of the drive she squeezed her car into a space between a blue Explorer and a white Chevy Silverado. Grabbing the sealed envelope off the passenger seat, she walked up the steps to the veranda surrounding the house and heard the sounds of music and laughter. She knocked on the door, which swung open almost immediately.

Dean stood in the opening. His face lit up at the sight of her and her heart clenched in her chest. He looked much more put together than the night he'd appeared on her doorstep seeking the forgiveness he'd never been granted. He was clean-shaven. His hair had been styled instead of receiving his usual finger-combed treatment. His black button-down shirt was crisp, and the crease in his khakis knife-sharp. He looked like a businessman and not the sometimes-ruffled athlete most saw on the football field.

But then his career, much like their brief affair, was over, wasn't it?

"Em. I'm so glad you came."

With her heart thudding in her throat, she knew the only

response she could give without giving away her emotions was a simple nod.

He stepped back and waved his arm. "Come on in. We were all waiting for you to arrive."

At once the house full of friends and neighbors turned and smiled. Waved and called her name. Robert Silverthorne stood there, as did Kate and Matt, James Harley, and even Maggie and Ollie and their three rambunctious boys. Emma warmed from their welcome.

Dean settled his hand on the small of her back like it belonged there and guided her toward the crowd. The touch of his hand sent a shiver up her spine. And all she could think of was the way he'd held her in his arms. The way he'd said her name when he'd made love to her. And the way he'd smiled at her when he thought she wasn't looking.

Panic settled in her chest and sent a "*run*" signal to her feet. Apparently Dean sensed her reluctance to go any further because he tightened his hold at her waist.

"Now that Emma's here for the ribbon-cutting ceremony, how about we all go outside?" Dean said, and everyone quieted their conversations.

Ribbon cutting?

"The guest and bunkhouses are all open to view, as is the counselor's cabin and the barn. Kate and my dad have a great set-up of desserts and Edna Price was kind enough to bring some of her apple cider. And don't worry, it's not spiked." He tossed a look to Mrs. Price, who gave him an odd curling of her lips in response. "I hope."

Chattering, the group filed out of the room toward the French doors that led to the back patio. Emma stepped forward to join them, but Dean caught her hand. Once the room had cleared, Dean turned her to face him.

"I want to thank you for coming today, Em." His big hand circled her forearm.

"I'm not feeling very friendly toward you at the moment. So please . . ." She glanced down.

Slowly he pulled his hand back and stuck it into the pocket of his khakis. "I know this must be difficult for you."

"You have no idea." She ignored the trembling that began in her heart and made its way down to her fingers as she handed him the envelope. "*This* is the only reason I came."

He studied the envelope and made the correct assumption of what was inside. Then he turned those green eyes on her. "I can't accept this."

She took a step back. "You have no choice."

"Please, Em." His jaw clenched. "Please just come outside and be a part of this ribbon cutting. Beyond anything else, my mom would want you to be here. If after that, you still want to resign, I promise I'll accept it without any hassles."

"Your promises aren't worth much, I'm afraid."

A wistful smile lifted the corners of his beautiful mouth. "That's the past."

She gave a humorless laugh. "You expect me to believe that you've turned over this new leaf in, what, six days?"

"It's not a new leaf, Emma. It's who I am. But I guess you'll have to judge that for yourself." He pushed the envelope back at her. "Hold onto to this and see me after the dedication if you still want to resign."

Walking away from Emma at that moment was even harder than handing in his own resignation to the Stallions' coach and owner. He knew what the news said, that he'd been dropped from the team roster. The details didn't matter. He'd walked away because it was what had been best for the team. He respected the fans, the owner, the coaches, and especially the players, who deserved a captain who could take them to the Super Bowl.

He was not that man.

He had more important things on his agenda. The only team member he wanted and needed was right now standing inside his house, holding a piece of paper that would forever cut ties with him.

No way in hell could he let that happen.

Emma Hart meant more to him than a game and a ring. Unless that ring happened to be around her finger after she'd said I do. To him.

On his way to the front of the crowd, Edna Price clamped an arthritic hand over his mending shoulder. Her weathered face smiled. "You've got a chance to make this right, young man. We've given you the ball. Now you have to throw it into the end zone."

Dean looked up into the old woman's steady gaze. He patted the hand she'd settled on his shoulder. "I plan to give it everything I've got, ma'am."

He made his way to where his and Brenden Jones's families stood in front of the old barn. Where a giant red ribbon had been stretched between two tall pines. Dean watched his brother-in-law kiss his sister on the cheek and settle his hand at the small of her back in a gesture of protection and familiarity. Dean's chest constricted.

That's what he wanted.

The right to love and touch Emma whenever he wanted.

Just because he could.

And more importantly, to have that level of trust and intimacy reciprocated.

He ruffled Brenden Jones's spiky hair, then turned toward the community that had supported him throughout his career and who had let him know when his behavior didn't meet their standards. Though he'd once mocked Emma for the way she worried about what her neighbors would think about their relationship, he found himself caring deeply about what the people in this town thought.

Deer Lick, Montana, may be as far removed from the bright lights, big city as a place could get, but for Dean, it was exactly where he wanted to be.

Movement caught his eye and he watched Emma walk out onto the back deck. In her baby-blue sweater and white hoodie, she glanced over the crowd and the dozens of balloons that floated in the sunshine. Her eyes widened as she glanced around the property. In the past week the entire place had been cleaned up and redesigned to suit the many campers Dean hoped would come to stay. He'd hired all the locals he could, plus a few extra, to make today happen. Not only to move forward with his life and the organization, but because if there had been a chance that Emma would forgive him, he needed it to happen now and not later.

"My family and I would like to thank you all for coming today. But before we dedicate this camp, I personally want to thank you all for the support you've given us to make this dream a reality. My mother," he said, clearing the clog of emotion stuck in his throat, "would be very happy to see you all here and to know that this place will help a lot of kids like Brenden Jones in the future." He glanced across the crowd to Emma. Though she squinted against the bright sunlight, he could feel the intensity of her blue eyes all the way into his soul. Their gazes locked as he spoke.

"It's hard to believe that just a week ago my world came crashing down. I'll be honest. I didn't know what to do. I'd played football for as long as I can remember and I thought that's all there was. When they told me I may never throw a football again I was devastated. Lost. Embarrassed. I haven't always been the best in showing my appreciation for all the love and support you've shown me. And I know I let some very important people down."

Emma's expression didn't change. Her hands remained clutched around the deck rail.

"I will do better in the future," he said, purposely omitting the word *promise*. Knowing that for the most important member of his audience, that term held little meaning when it came from him.

"I'm proud to be a member of this community. This is home. And I plan to stay." Dean forced himself to break eye contact with Emma when all he wanted to do was hold her until she forgave him. He glanced at his family beside him and smiled when his father's arm slid around his shoulders. Someone handed him a giant pair of scissors. "So it's with pride and honor that we welcome you to the Letty Silverthorne Sunshine Camp."

The crowd applauded as the scissors sliced through the ribbon. Kate moved closer, took his hand, and gave it a squeeze of encouragement. He glanced up to the deck to find Emma again, but she was gone.

Once the attendees of the ribbon-cutting ceremony were happily chowing down on Kate's newest pastry creations and visiting the new animals in the barn, Dean slipped into the house expecting to find the dreaded envelope sitting on his kitchen counter and the love of his life gone for good. But when he walked through the French doors, there she stood, looking out the windows at the water sparkling on the lake. The envelope clasped in her hand.

He came up behind her and placed his hands on her shoulders. "Em? You okay?"

She gave him a nod that was barely visible. "It really is a spectacular view."

"It's more spectacular when you're here to share it with me." He turned her to face him and wasn't surprised to find tears wetting her long, dark lashes.

Her bottom lip quivered. "I really don't want to like you."

"I know, honey. But before you go getting all wrapped up in that ugly stuff, I just want to say one thing. And I want you to know I mean it from right here." He placed her palm against his heart. Then he cupped her face in his hands and looked deeply into her eyes. "I love you, Em. I'm *in* love with you. I have been for a while."

She glanced away. "No, you're not."

"Yeah. I am." He tucked his fingers beneath her chin and

brought her gaze back around. "I just wasn't sure what it was, because . . . I've never been in love before. When I went back to Houston I felt lost without you. You're the best part of my life, honey. Even before the doctor told me the chances of my shoulder ever being a hundred percent again were slim, I knew what I wanted to do. What I needed to do. That's what made it easy."

"What was easy?"

"To resign."

"You quit?"

He nodded.

"The news said—"

"Doesn't matter what they say anymore."

"But why did you walk away when there's a chance your shoulder will heal?"

"My football career was a really great ride and I'm not going to lie and say I won't miss it." Beneath his hands the tension in her body slowly unwound. He took a chance and slid his arms around her waist. When she didn't push him away he felt the weight lift from his shoulders. He could make this right. He had to make this right. She felt so good in his arms again. "But it needs to be a great ride for every man on that team. They matter to me. The organization and the fans matter to me. I didn't want to leave them in limbo, wondering who their captain was, who they should show their loyalty to. For the sake of everyone the best thing to do was to walk away."

"I don't know what to say."

"Then just listen. At some point," he said, "a man needs to realize where he wants to be for the rest of his life. I want to be with *you*, Emma."

He tucked her into him just a little closer. "At Kate's wedding you said something to me that really stuck. You said it again the other night."

She shook her head and her silky blond hair resettled over her slim shoulders. "I said a lot of things."

"You told me you were completely forgettable."

She shrugged. "And?"

"You were so wrong, honey. From the moment we met I've thought about nothing *but* you."

Moisture seeped into her eyes and brightened their depths. "Then why didn't you call when the doctor gave you the news? I was worried about you."

"I know. And I apologize. Believe me, I'll never let that happen again. But, Em, that news hit me hard. I'm a thirty-four-year-old man. I'm in my prime. Football is all I've ever known. When someone tells you you've just lost your livelihood, it's like they're saying you're no longer man enough. I didn't know how to face you. I didn't know what you'd think of me. And I wouldn't have been able to stand it if all I saw was pity in your eyes."

"I apologize too. Because even though I didn't really understand, one thing was clear. I've always thought you were about more than football, Dean."

Relief flooded his bloodstream and he smiled. "Someone else once told me that too." He cupped his hands around her arms and lowered his forehead to hers. "Since I was seven years old I've strapped on a suit of armor to get done what needed to be done. I just didn't know how to react without the armor."

"What makes you think you'll be able to do without it now?"

"Because *this* is who I am. Not the guy who's been playing a part for the media all these years. I'm not Good Time Charlie. I'm just Dean Silverthorne, the man who loves you. I need you to believe that."

"I want to, but—"

"Just give me a chance, honey. I promise I won't let you down ever again. I want us to build a life together. Once we have the camp going, I want to build a school for developmentally disabled kids where you can help kids in our community and the surrounding areas."

"You're unemployed. How can you afford that?"

"I have a job. Here. But I've also been offered a color commentator position with ESPN. I won't be gone as often as I would have been as a player, so you wouldn't have the burden of responsibility all on your shoulders." His palms slid down her arms and he took her hands in his. "Can I show you something?"

"What?"

"Just come upstairs with me." He tugged.

"I'm fine right here." She tugged back.

"I'm not taking you upstairs for *that*. I really want to show you something."

She released a sigh. "Fine."

He took the resignation envelope from her hand. "Can we leave this here?"

"I haven't made up my mind about that yet."

"I know." He set the envelope on the kitchen counter. "It will be right here if you still want to give it to me."

He took her soft hand in his again and led her up the

stairs. When they reached his bedroom doors he told her, "Close your eyes."

"Why?"

"So suspicious." He chuckled. "Close your eyes, honey. Please."

She shook her head but complied.

He opened the door and led her inside. "Keep them closed and stay right here."

"I don't trust you."

"I hope to change that." He went to the walk-in closet and retrieved his surprise. When he came toward her, he couldn't keep the smile from his face. "Okay, now open your eyes."

Her long-lashed eyelids fluttered open and then widened at the tiny fluff of fur he held up in front of her.

"A kitten!" She took the little grey fur ball into her hands and he could feel the chill melt from her heart. "Oh, he's adorable."

"He's yours."

"Are you serious?"

Dean nodded and grinned at the way she held the tiny cat up and nuzzled his nose with her own. He knew how much she missed Oscar and he was so happy to see the joy on her face. "If you look at the ribbon around his neck, I believe he has a present for you."

"For me?"

"Yeah, honey. Only for you."

Her brows came together as she cradled the kitten against her chest—lucky cat—and untied the blue ribbon at the top of his neck.

A substantial—but not ridiculously large—Tiffany engagement ring fell into her palm.

She looked up at him, her mouth forming a perfect O that he wanted to kiss very much. Instead he took her hand in his and lowered himself to one knee.

"I love you, Emma Hart. The only other women I've ever said that to are my mother and my sisters." He kissed her fingers. "You're the most *unforgettable* woman I'll ever know. I don't deserve you. I know that. Honey, you were right about the whole marriage, babies, and happily-ever-after. I want to marry you and love you and have enough kids to start our own football team. I want it all. With you. Please say you still love me."

Her fingers tightened around his hand and he laid them against his heart. "Please say you'll marry me."

"Oh, Dean." She crumpled to her knees and took his face in her hands. Tears filled her blue eyes and spilled over her long, dark lashes. "Yes, I do love you. And yes, I will marry you." And then she gave him that smile that always gave him a kick in the heart. "*If* you promise to include a few cheerleaders on that team."

"I'll give you anything you want as long as you promise to love me forever."

She leaned her forehead against his. "I'll love you forever and then some."

Complete and utter joy rushed through his veins like it did when he ran out onto the field to the roar of the crowd. Only this was even better.

For the last and most important game in his life, Dean stepped back into the pocket, slid the ring on Emma's finger, and the Hail Mary spiraled into the end zone.

He leaned back on his heels and laughed like a fool.

The love of his life laughed along. "What's so funny?"

He pulled her to her feet, planted a big kiss on her soft mouth, and thrust a victorious punch into the air.

"*Touchdown!*"

A t three a.m. Dean held the kitten against his chest and tip-toed down the stairs so as not to wake Emma. He'd kept her busy in bed for the rest of the afternoon and evening. This was the first time she'd actually been able to sleep.

His bare feet squeaked across the hardwood floors and into the kitchen. From the counter he picked up Emma's resignation and ripped it in two, flipped the lid on the trash can, and dumped the envelope inside. Then he opened the door into the garage. Side by side sat the SUV he'd bought and his mother's piece-of-crap Buick. He walked past the new vehicle, lifted the door handle of the rusted heap, and slipped inside. The kitten curled beneath his chin. The fur tickled and he laughed.

"Such a happy sound."

Dean looked up. Instead of her usual place in the back-seat, his mother had taken the shotgun position.

"You're allergic to cats." Her green eyes twinkled.

"Yeah. I know." He stroked the kitten's soft fur and the little body rumbled with a deep purr. "My eyes and nose are itching like crazy. Don't care, either."

"Wow. You must really be in love."

"That would be an understatement, Mom."

"Not a disaster?"

He laughed. "Did I actually say that?"

"Oh yeah. Among other absurd things." She laid her hand on his arm. "Took you long enough to realize she was the one."

"Hard-headed."

"Yeah. Probably why your shoulder got busted up and not your brain. Although there were moments I wondered." She shot him a grin. "You going to be okay with never playing football again?"

His shoulders lifted. "I'm not going to say I won't miss it. But honestly, I've got so much dancing around inside me right now . . . it just feels too good to care about a game. Besides, if I'm ever lucky enough to have a son . . ."

"Oh, I like the way you think."

"Me too. I may never throw another touchdown pass, but all I really want is to be able to hug my wife and pick up my kids. You know?"

She nodded. "Best feeling in the world. Have you and Emma set a date?"

"Ummmm." He thought of Emma sprawled out in the big bed upstairs. "We've been . . . a little busy."

"TMI, young man."

He laughed again and it felt great. "As soon as we figure it out I'll let you know." He glanced up and found his mom studying him with a smile that lifted her almost-invisible dimples. "Hey, will I still be able to see you, now that your mission impossible is accomplished?"

"Oh, you know me." She chuckled. "I'm like Tom Cruise. I'll come back for another sequel. Two down. One to go." She leaned forward and kissed his cheek. "I'm happy for you, Son. And so proud. Love you."

"Love you, Mom." He blinked and she was gone.

He snuck back inside the house, grabbed a drink of water, then he and the kitten headed back upstairs. After he tossed another log in the fireplace, he slipped between the sheets. The mischievous gray fur ball took this as a cue to play *attack the feet* whenever Dean made the slightest move.

Emma slid over and pressed her warm naked body against his. "Where'd you go?"

He leaned over and kissed her soft, sexy mouth. "Just had a little business to take care of."

"Mmmm." She gave a sleepy sigh, then snuggled deeper into his arms.

Without warning, the kitten pounced between them. Dean lifted the wiggling attacker to minimize the damage. "Hey, honey?"

"Yeah?"

"Can I name the cat?"

She tucked her hand beneath her cheek on the pillow and looked up at him. "I don't think *Mr. Perfect* fits him."

"I've got a better name." Dean laughed and kissed her nose. "One that fits exactly how I feel."

She gave him his favorite smile. "What's that?"

"Lucky."

Return to the Sugar Shack in Spring 2012 . . .

Letty Silverthorne has her work cut out for her
when her middle child, Kelly, returns home to
Deer Lick reeling from a major courtroom loss
and needing to shake the "Sister Serious" moniker
she's been carrying since childhood. With the
help of her dead mother and a former bad boy in
uniform, anything is possible at the Sugar Shack.

Avon Impulse

If you loved *Any Given Christmas* and want to
see where it all began . . . turn the page for a
peek at *Second Chance at the Sugar Shack*!

Available wherever eBooks are sold

CHAPTER ONE

Kate Silver had five minutes. Tops.

Five minutes before her fashion schizophrenic client had a meltdown.

Five minutes before her career rocketed into the bargain basement of media hell.

Behind the gates of one of the trendiest homes in the Hollywood Hills, Kate dropped to her hands and knees in a crowded bedroom *In Style* magazine had deemed "Wacky Tacky." Amid the dust bunnies and cat hair clinging for life to a faux zebra rug, she crawled toward her most current disaster—repairing the Swarovski crystals ripped from the leather pants being worn by pop music's newly crowned princess.

Gone was the hey-day of Britney, Christina, and Shakira.

Long live *Inara*.

Why women in pop music never had a last name was a bizarre phenomenon Kate didn't have time to ponder. At the end of the day, the women she claimed as clients didn't need a last name to be at the top of her V.I.P. list. They didn't need one when they thanked her—their stylist—from the red carpet. And they certainly didn't need one when they signed all those lovely zeros on her paychecks.

Right now she sat in chaos central, earning every penny. Awards season had arrived and her adrenaline had kicked into overdrive alongside the triple-shot latte she'd sucked down for lunch. Over the years she'd become numb to the mayhem. Even so, she did enjoy the new talent—of playing Henry Higgins to the Eliza Doolittles and Huck Finns of Tinsel Town. Nothing compared to the rush she got from seeing her babies step onto a stage and sparkle. The entire process made her feel proud and accomplished.

It made her feel necessary.

Surrounded by the gifted artists who lifted their fairy dusted makeup brushes and hair extensions, Kate brushed a clump of floating cat hair from her nose. Why the star getting all the attention had yet to hire a housekeeper was anyone's guess. Regardless, Kate intended to keep the current catastrophe from turning into the Nightmare on Mulholland Drive.

Adrenaline slammed into her chest and squeezed the air from her lungs.

This was her job. She'd banked all her worth into what she did and she was damn good at it. No matter how crazy it made her. No matter how much it took over her life.

After her triumph on the Oscars red carpet three years ago, she'd become the stylist the biggest names in Hollywood demanded. Finally. She'd become an overnight sensation that had only taken her seven long years to achieve. And though there were times she wanted to stuff a feather boa down some snippy starlet's windpipe, she now had to fight to maintain her success. Other stylists, waiting for their star to shine, would die for what she had. On days like today, she would willingly hand it over.

In the distance the doorbell chimed and Kate's five minutes shrank to nada. The stretch limo had arrived to deliver Inara to the Nokia Theatre for the televised music awards. With no time to spare, Kate plunged the needle through the leather and back up again. Her fingers moved so fast blisters formed beneath the pressure.

Peggy Miller, Inara's agent, paced the floor and sidestepped the snow-white animal shelter refugee plopped in the middle of a leopard rug. Clearly the cat wasn't intimidated by the agent's nicotine-polluted voice.

"Can't you hurry that up, Kate?" Peggy tapped the Cartier on her wrist with a dragon nail. "Inara's arrival has to be timed perfectly. Not enough to dawdle in the interviews and just enough to make the media clamor for more. Sorry, darling," she said to Inara, "chatting with the media is just not your strong point."

Inara made a hand gesture that was far from the bubble gum persona everyone in the industry tried to portray with the new star. Which, in Kate's estimation, was like fitting a square peg into a round hole.

"Kate?" Peggy again. "Hurry!"

"I'm working on it," Kate mumbled around the straight pins clenched between her teeth. Just her luck their wayward client had tried to modify the design with a fingernail file and pair of tweezers an hour before showtime.

"Why do I have to wear this . . . thing." Inara tugged the

embossed leather tunic away from her recently enhanced bustline. "It's hideous."

The needle jabbed Kate's thumb. She flinched and bit back the slur that threatened to shoot from her mouth. "Impossible," she said. "It's Armani." And to acquire it she'd broken two fingernails wrestling another stylist to the showroom floor. She'd be damned if she'd let the singer out the door without wearing it now.

"Inara, please hold still," the makeup artist pleaded while she attempted to dust bronzer on her moving target.

"More teasing in back?" the hair stylist asked.

Kate flicked a gaze up to Inara's blond hair extensions. "No. We want her to look sultry. Not like a streetwalker."

"My hair color is all wrong," Inara announced. "I want it more like yours, Kate. Kind of a ritzy porn queen auburn." She ran her manicured fingers through the top of Kate's hair, lifting a few strands. "And I love these honey-colored streaks."

"Thanks," Kate muttered without looking up. "I think." Her hair color had been compared to many things. A ritzy porn queen had never been one of them.

"Hmmm. I will admit, these pants seriously make my ass rock," Inara said, changing gears with a glance over her shoulder to the cheval mirror. "But this vest . . . I don't know. I really think I should wear my red sequin tube top instead."

Kate yanked the pins from her between her teeth. "You can *not* wear a *Blue Light Special* with Armani. It's a sin against God." Kate blinked hard to ward off the migraine that poked between her eyes. "Besides, the last time you made a last-minute fashion change you nearly killed my career."

"I didn't mean to. It's just . . . God, Kate, you are so freaking strict with this fashion crap. It's like having my mother threaten to lower the hem on my school uniform."

"You pay me to threaten you. Remember?"

"I pay you plenty."

"Then trust me plenty." Kate wished the star would do exactly that. "Once those lights hit these crystals, all the attention will be on you. You're up for the new artist award. You should shine. You don't want to end up a fashion tragedy like the time Sharon Stone wore a Gap turtleneck to the Oscars, do you?"

"No."

"Good. Because that pretty much ended her career."

Inara's heavily made-up eyes widened. "A shirt did that?"

"Easier to blame it on a bad garment choice than bad acting."

"Oh."

"Kate? Do you want the hazelnut lipstick?" the makeup artist asked. "Or the caramel gloss?"

Kate glanced between the tubes. "Neither. Use the Peach Shimmer. It will play up her eyes. And make sure she takes it with her. She'll need to reapply just before they announce her category and the cameras go for the close-up."

"Kate!" Peggy again. "You have got to hustle. The traffic on Sunset will be a nightmare."

Kate wished for superpowers, wished for her fingers to work faster, wished she could get the job done and Inara in the limo. She needed Inara to look breathtaking when she stepped onto that red carpet. She needed a night full of praise for the star, the outfit, *and* the stylist.

Scratch that. It was not just a need, it was absolutely critical.

Inara's past two public appearances had been disasters. One had been Kate's own oversight—the canary and fuchsia Betsey Johnson had looked horrible under the camera lights. She should have known that before sending her client out for the fashion wolves to devour. The second calamity hadn't been her fault, but had still reflected on her. That time had been cause and effect of a pop royalty temper tantrum and Inara's fondness for discount store castoffs. It may have once worked for Madonna, but those days were locked in the fashion vault. For a reason.

Kate couldn't afford to be careless again. And she couldn't trust the bubble gum diva to ignore the thrift store temptations schlepping through her blood. Not that there was anything wrong with that for ordinary people. Inara did not fall into the *ordinary* category.

Not anymore.

Not if Kate could help it.

As soon as she tied off the last stitch, she planned to escort her newest client right into the backseat of the limo with a warning to the driver to steer clear of all second-hand clothing establishments along the way.

"This totally blows." Inara slid the shears from the table and aimed them at the modest neckline. "It's just not sexy enough."

"Stop that!" Kate's heart stopped. She grabbed the scissors and tucked them beneath her knee. "Tonight is not about selling sex. Leave that for your music videos. Tonight is about presentation. Wowing the critics. Tomorrow you want to end up on the best-dressed list. Not the *What the hell was she thinking?* list."

Inara sighed. "Whatever."

"And don't pout," Kate warned. *Or be so ungrateful.* "It will mess up your lip liner."

"How's this look?" the makeup artist asked, lifting the bronzer away from one last dusting of Inara's forehead.

Kate glanced up mid-stitch. "Perfect. Now, everybody back away and let me get this last crystal on."

"Kate!"

"I know, Peggy. I know!"

Kate grasped the leather pant leg to keep Inara from checking out the junk in her trunk again via the full-length mirror. She shifted on her knees. A collection of cat hair followed.

Once she had Inara en route, Kate planned to rush home and watch the red carpet arrivals on TV. Alone. Collapsed on her sofa with a bag of microwave popcorn and a bottle of Moët. If the night went well, the celebration cork would fly. If not, well, tomorrow morning she'd have to place a *Stylist for Hire—Cheap* ad in *Variety*.

Kate pushed the needle through the leather, ignoring the hurried, sloppy stitches. If her mother could see her now, she'd cringe at the uneven, wobbly lengths. Then she'd deliver a pithy lecture on why a career in Hollywood was not right for Kate. Neither the Girl Scout sewing badge she'd earned as a kid nor the fashion award she'd recently won would ever be enough to stop her mother from slicing and dicing her dreams.

Her chest tightened.

God, how long had it been since she'd even talked to her mother? Easter? The obligatory Mother's Day call?

In her mother's eyes, Kate would never win the daughter-of-the-year award. She'd quit trying when she hit the age of thirteen—the year she'd traded in her 4-H handbook for a *Vogue* magazine.

Her mother had never forgiven her.

For two long years after high school graduation, there had been a lull in Kate's life while she waited anxiously for acceptance and a full scholarship to the design school in Los Angeles. Two years of her mother nagging at her to get a traditional college degree. Two years of working alongside her parents in their family bakery, decorating cakes with the same boring buttercream roses, pounding out the same tasteless loaves of bread. Not that she minded the work. It gave her a creative outlet. If only her mother had let her shake things up a little with an occasional fondant design or something that tossed a challenge her way.

Then the letter of acceptance arrived.

Kate had been ecstatic to show it to her parents. She knew her mother wouldn't be happy or supportive. But she'd never expected her mother to tell her that the best thing Kate could do would be to tear up the scholarship and stop wasting time. The argument that ensued had led to tears and hateful words. That night Kate made a decision that would forever change her life.

It had been ten years since she'd left her mother's unwelcome advice and small-town life in the dust. Without a word to anyone she'd taken a bus ride and disappeared. Her anger had faded over the years, but she'd never mended the damage done by her leaving. And she'd never been able to bring herself to come home. She'd met up with her parents during those years, but it had always been on neutral ground. Never in her mother's backyard. Despite her mother's reservations, Kate had grown up and become successful.

She slipped the needle through the back of the bead cap and through the leather again. As much as she tried to ignore it, the pain caused by her mother's disapproval still hurt.

Amid the boom-boom-boom of Snoop Dog on the stereo and Peggy's non-stop bitching, Kate's cell phone rang.

"Do *not* answer that," Peggy warned.

"It might be important. I sent Josh to Malibu." Dressing country music's top male vocalist was an easy gig for her assistant. He'd survived three awards seasons by her side. He could walk the tightrope with the best of them. But as Kate well knew, trouble could brew and usually did.

Ignoring the agent's evil glare, Kate scooted toward her purse, grabbed her phone and shoved it between her ear and shoulder. Her fingers continued to stitch.

"Josh, what's up?"

"Katie?"

Whoa. Her heart did a funny flip that stole her breath. *Definitely not Josh.*

"Dad. Uh . . . hi. I . . . haven't talked to you in, uh . . ." *Forever.* "What's up?"

"Sweetheart, I . . . I don't know how to say this."

The hitch in his tone was peculiar. The sewing needle between her fingers froze midair. "Dad? Are you okay?"

"I'm . . . afraid not, honey." He released a breathy sigh. "I know it's asking a lot but . . . I wondered . . . could you come home?"

Her heart thudded to a halt. "What's wrong?"

"Katie, this morning . . . your mother died."

Chapter Two

A hundred miles of heifers, hay fields, and rolling hills zipped past while Kate stared out the passenger window of her mother's ancient Buick. The flight from L.A. hadn't been long, but from the moment she'd received her father's call the day before, the tension hadn't uncurled from her body. The hour and a half drive from the *local* airport hadn't helped.

With her sister, Kelly, behind the wheel, they eked out the final miles toward home. Or what had been her home a lifetime ago.

They traveled past the big backhoe where the Dudley Brothers Excavation sign proclaimed: We dig our job! Around the curve came the Beaver Family Dairy Farm where a familiar stench wafted through the air vents. As they cruised by, a big Holstein near the fence lifted its tail.

"Eeew." Kelly wrinkled her nose. "Gross."

Kate dropped her head back to the duct-taped seat and closed her eyes. "I'll never look at guacamole the same again."

"Yeah. Quite a welcome home." Her sister peered at her

through a pair of last season Coach sunglasses. With her ivory blond hair caught up in a haphazard ponytail, she looked more like a frivolous teen than a fierce prosecutor. "It's funny. You move away from the Wild Wild West, buy your beef in Styrofoam packages, and forget where that hamburger comes from."

"Kel, nobody eats Holsteins. They're milk cows."

"I know. I'm just saying."

Whatever she was saying, she wasn't actually saying. It wasn't the first time Kate had to guess what was going on in her big sister's beautiful head. Being a prosecutor had taught Kelly to be tight-lipped and guarded. Though they were only two years apart in age, a world of difference existed in their personalities and style. Kelly had always been on the quiet side. She'd always had her nose stuck in a book, was always the type to smooth her hand over a wrinkled cushion just to make it right. Always the type to get straight A's and still worry she hadn't studied enough.

Kate took a deep breath and let it out slowly.

It was hard to compete with perfection like that.

"I still can't believe it's been ten years since you've been home," Kelly said.

Kate frowned as they passed the McGruber farm where someone had planted yellow mums in an old toilet placed on the front lawn. "And now I get the pleasure of remembering why I left in the first place."

"I don't know." Kelly leaned forward and peered through the pitted windshield. "It's really spectacular in an unrefined kind of way. The fall colors are on parade and snow is frosting the mountain peaks. Chicago might be beautiful, but it doesn't compare to this." Lines of concern scrunched between Kelly's eyes ruined the perfection of her face. "I know how hard this is for you, Kate. But I'm glad you came."

The muscles between Kate's shoulders tightened. Right now, she didn't want to think about what might be difficult for her. Others were far more important. "I'm here for Dad," she said.

"You know, I was thinking the other day . . . we all haven't been together since we met up at the Super Bowl last year." Kelly shook her head and smiled. "God. No matter that our brother was playing, I thought you and Mom were going to root for opposing teams just so you'd have one more thing to disagree about."

"I did not purposely spill my beer on her."

Kelly laughed. "Yes, you did."

The memory came back in full color and Kate wanted to laugh too.

"That's why Dad will be really glad to see you, Kate. You've always made him smile. You know you were always his favorite."

At least she'd been *somebody's* favorite. "I've missed him." Kate fidgeted with the string attached to her hoodie. "I didn't mean to . . ."

"I know." Kelly wrapped her fingers around the steering wheel. "He knew too."

The reminder of her actions stuck in Kate's throat. If she could do it all over, she'd handle it much differently. At the time she'd been only twenty, anxious to live her dreams and get away from the mother who disapproved of everything she did.

The interior of the car fell silent, except for the wind squealing through the disintegrating window seals and the low rumble of the gas-guzzling engine. Kate knew she and her sister were delaying the obvious discussion. There was no easy way to go about it. The subject of their mother was like walking on cracked ice. No matter how lightly you tiptoed, you were bound to plunge into turbulent waters. Their mother had given birth to three children who had all moved away to different parts of the country. Each one had a completely different view of her parental skills.

Her death would bring them all together.

"After all the times we offered to buy her a new car I can't believe Mom still drove this old boat," Kate said.

"I can't believe it made it to the airport and back." Kelly tucked a stray blond lock behind her ear and let out a sigh. "Mom was funny about stuff, you know. She was the biggest 'if it ain't broke don't fix it' person I ever knew."

Was.

Knew.

As in past tense.

Kate glanced out the passenger window.

Her mother was gone.

No more worrying about what to send for Mother's Day or Christmas or her birthday. No more chatter about the temperamental oven in their family bakery, or the dysfunctional quartet that made up the Founder's Day parade committee, or the latest gnome she'd discovered to stick in her vegetable garden.

No more . . . anything.

Almost a year had passed since she'd been with her

mother. But even that hadn't been the longest she'd gone without seeing her. Kate had spent tons of time with Dean and Kelly. She'd snuck in a fishing trip or two with her dad. But an entire five years had gone by before Kate had finally agreed to meet up with her mother in Chicago to celebrate Kelly's promotion with the prosecutor's office. The reunion had been awkward. And as much as Kate had wanted to hear "I'm sorry" come from her mother's lips, she'd gone back to Los Angeles disappointed.

Over the years Kate had meant to come home. She'd meant to apologize. She'd meant to do a whole lot of stuff that just didn't matter anymore. Good intentions weren't going to change a thing. A knife of pain stabbed between her eyes. The time for could have, should have, would have, was history. Making amends was a two-way street and her mother hadn't made an effort either.

She shifted to a more comfortable position and her gaze landed on the cluttered chaos in the backseat—an array of pastry cookbooks, a box of quilting fabric, and a knitting tote where super-sized needles poked from the top of a ball of red yarn. Vanilla—her mother's occupational perfume—lingered throughout the car.

Kate inhaled. The scent settled into her soul and jarred loose a long-lost memory. "Do you remember the time we all got chicken pox?" she asked.

"Oh, my God, yes." Kelly smiled. "We were playing tag. Mom broke up the game and stuck us all in one bedroom."

"I'd broken out with blisters first," Kate remembered, scratching her arm at the reminder. "Mom said if one of us got the pox, we'd all get the pox. And we might as well get it done and over with all at once."

"So *you* were the culprit," Kelly said.

"I don't even know where I got them." Kate shook her head. "All I know is I was miserable. The fever and itching were bad enough. But then you and Dean tortured me to see how far you could push before I cried."

"If I remember, it didn't take long."

"And if I remember," Kate said, "it didn't take long before you were both whining like babies."

"Karma," Kelly admitted. "And just when we were at our worst, Mom came in and placed a warm sugar cookie in each of our hands."

Kate nodded, remembering how the scent of vanilla lingered long after her mother had left the room. "Yeah."

The car rambled past Balloons and Blooms, the florist shop Darla Davenport had set up in her century-old barn.

"Dad ordered white roses for her casket." Kelly's voice wobbled. "He was concerned they wouldn't be trucked in on time and, of course, the price. I told him not to worry—that we kids would take care of the cost. I told him to order any damn thing he wanted."

Kate leaned forward and peered through her sister's sunglasses. "Are you okay?"

"Are you?" Kelly asked.

Instead of answering, Kate twisted off the cap of her Starbuck's Frappuccino and slugged down the remains. The drink gave her time to compose herself, if that were even possible. She thought of her dad. Simple. Hard-working. He'd taught her how to tie the fly that had helped her land the derby-winning trout the year she turned eleven. He couldn't have been more different from her mother if he'd tried. And he hadn't deserved to be abandoned by his youngest child.

"How's Dad doing?" Kate asked, as the iced drink settled in her stomach next to the wad of guilt.

"He's devastated." Kelly flipped on the fan. Her abrupt action seemed less about recirculating the air and more about releasing a little distress. "How would you be if the love of your life died in your arms while you were tying on her apron?"

"I can't answer that," Kate said, trying not to think about the panic that must have torn through him.

"Yeah." Kelly sighed. "Me either."

Kate tried to swallow but her throat muscles wouldn't work. She turned in her seat and looked at her sister. "What's he going to do now, Kel? Who will take care of him? He's never been alone. Ever," she said, her voice an octave higher than normal. "Who's going to help him at the Shack? Cook for him? Who's he going to talk to at night?"

"I don't know. But we definitely have to do something." Kelly nodded as though a lightbulb in her head suddenly hit a thousand watts. "Maybe Dean will have some ideas."

"Dean?" Kate leaned back in her seat. "Our brother? The king of non-relationship relationships?"

"Not that either of us has any room to talk."

"Seriously." Kate looked out the window, twisting the rings on her fingers. The urge to cry for her father welled in her throat. Her parents had been a great example of true love. They cared for each other, had each other's backs, thought of each other first. Even with her problematic relationship with her mother, Kate couldn't deny that the woman had been an extraordinary wife to the man who worshipped her. The chances of finding a love like the one her parents had shared were one in a million. Kate figured that left her odds stretching out to about one in a hundred gazillion.

"What's wrong with us, Kel?" she asked. "We were raised by parents the entire town puts on a pedestal, yet we all left them behind for something *bigger and better*. Not a single one of us has gotten married or even come close. As far as I know, Dean has no permanent designs on his current bimbo of the moment. You spend all your nights with a stack of law books. I spend too much time flying coast-to-coast to even meet up with someone for a dinner that doesn't scream fast food."

"Oh, poor you. New York to L.A. First Class. Champagne. And all those gorgeous movie stars and rock stars you're surrounded by. You're breaking my heart."

Kate snorted. "Yeah, I live such a glamorous life."

A perfectly arched brow lifted on Kelly's perfect face. "You don't?"

While Kate enjoyed what she did for a living, every day her career hung by a sequin while the next up-and-coming celebrity stylist waited impatiently in the wings for her to fall from Hollywood's fickle graces. She'd chosen a career that tossed her in the spotlight, but she had no one to share it with. And often that spotlight felt icy cold. "Yeah, sure. I just get too busy sometimes, you know?"

"Unfortunately, I do." Kelly gripped the wheel tighter. "You know . . . you could have stuck around and married Matt Ryan."

"Geez." Kate's heart did a tilt-a-whirl spin. "I haven't heard that name in forever."

"When you left, you broke his heart."

"How do you know?"

"Mom said."

"Hey, I gave him my virginity. I call that a fair trade."

"Seriously?" Kelly's brows lifted in surprise. "I had no idea."

"It wasn't something I felt like advertising at the time."

"He was pretty cute from what I remember."

"Don't go there, Kel. There's an ocean under that bridge. So mind your own business."

Matt Ryan. Wow. Talk about yanking up old memories. Not unpleasant ones either. From what Kate remembered, Matt had been very good at a lot of things. Mostly ones that involved hands and lips. But Matt had been that boy from the proverbial wrong side of the tracks and she'd had bigger plans for her life.

Her mother had only mentioned him once or twice after Kate had skipped town. Supposedly he'd eagerly moved on to all the other girls wrangling for his attention. Good for him. He'd probably gotten some poor girl pregnant and moved next door to his mother. No doubt he'd been saddled with screaming kids and a complaining wife. Kate imagined he'd still be working for his Uncle Bob fixing broken axles and leaky transmissions. Probably even had a beer gut by now. Maybe even balding. Poor guy.

Kelly guided their mother's boat around the last curve in the road that would lead them home. Quaking aspens glittered gold in the sunlight and tall pines dotted the landscape.

Craftsman style log homes circled the area like ornaments on a Christmas wreath.

"Mom was proud of you, you know," Kelly blurted.

"What?" Kate's heart constricted. She didn't need for her sister to lie about their mother's mind-set. Kate knew the truth. She'd accepted it long ago. "No way. Mom did everything she could to pull the idea of being a celebrity stylist right out of my stubborn head."

"You're such a dork." Kelly shifted in her seat and gripped the steering wheel with both hands. "Of course she was proud. She was forever showing off the magazine articles you were in. She even kept a scrapbook."

"She did not."

"She totally did."

"Go figure. The night before I boarded that bus for L.A., she swore I'd never make a living hemming skirts and teasing hair."

"No, what she said was, making a living hemming skirts and teasing hair wasn't for you," Kelly said.

"That's not the way I remember it."

"Of course not. You were so deeply immersed in parental rebellion she could have said the sky was blue and you'd have argued that it was aqua."

"We did argue a lot."

Kelly shook her head. "Yeah, kind of like you were both cut from the same scrap of denim. I think that's what ticked you off the most and you just didn't want to admit it."

No way. "That I was like Mom?"

"You could have been identical twins. Same red hair. Same hot temper."

"I never thought I was anything like her. I still don't."

"How's that river of denial working for you?"

"How's that rewriting history working for *you?*"

Kelly tightened her fingers on the steering wheel. "Someday you'll get it, little sister. And when you do, you're going to be shocked that you didn't see it earlier."

The remnants of the old argument curdled in Kate's stomach. "She didn't believe in me, Kel."

"Then she was wrong."

For some reason the acknowledgment from her big sister didn't make it any better.

"She was also wrong about you and your financial worth," Kelly added. "You make three times as much as I do."

"But not as much as Dean."

"God doesn't make as much as Dean," Kelly said.

Their big brother had always been destined for greatness. If you didn't believe it, all you had to do was ask him. Being an NFL star quarterback did have its perks. Modesty wasn't one of them.

"Almost there," Kelly announced.

The green highway sign revealed only two more miles to go. Kate gripped the door handle to steady the nervous tension tap-dancing on her sanity.

Ahead, she noticed the swirling lights atop a sheriff's SUV parked on the shoulder of the highway. The vehicle stopped in front of the cop had to be the biggest monster truck Kate had ever seen. In L.A., which oozed with hybrids and luxury cruisers, one could only view a farmboy-vehicle-hopped-up-on-steroids in box office bombs like the *Dukes of Hazzard*.

The swirling lights dredged up a not-so-fond memory of Sheriff Washburn, who most likely sat behind the wheel of that Chevy Tahoe writing up the fattest citation he could invent. A decade ago, the man and his Santa belly had come hunting for her. When she hadn't shown up at home at o'dark thirty like her mother had expected, the SOS call had gone out. Up on Lookout Point the sheriff had almost discovered her and Matt sans clothes, bathed in moonlight and lust.

As it was, Matt had been quick to act and she'd managed to sneak back through her bedroom window before she ruined her shaky reputation for all time. Turned out it wouldn't have mattered. A few days later she boarded a bus leaving that boy and the town gossips behind to commiserate with her mother about what an ungrateful child she'd been.

As they approached the patrol vehicle, a deputy stepped out and, hand on gun, strolled toward the monster truck.

Mirrored shades. Midnight hair. Wide shoulders. Trim waist. Long, long legs. And . . . Oh. My. God. Not even the regulation pair of khaki uniform pants could hide his very fine behind. Nope. Definitely *not* Sheriff Washburn.

A double take was definitely in order.

"Wow," Kate said.

"They didn't make 'em like that when we lived here," Kelly noted.

"Seriously." Kate shifted back around in her seat. And frowned. What the hell was wrong with her? Her mother had been dead for two days and *she* was checking out guys?

"Well, ready or not, here we are."

At her sister's announcement Kate looked up at the overhead sign crossing the two-lane road.

Welcome to Deer Lick, Montana. Population 6,000.

For Kate it might as well have read *Welcome to Hell.*

Late the following afternoon, Kate stood amid the mourners gathered at the gravesite for Leticia Jane Silverthorne's burial. Most were dressed in a variety of appropriate blacks and dark blues. The exception being Ms. Virginia Peat, who'd decided the bright hues of the local Red Hat Society were more appropriate for a deceased woman with a green thumb and a knack for planting mischief wherever she went.

No doubt her mother had a talent for inserting just the right amount of monkey business into things to keep the town blabbing for days, even weeks, if the gossips were hungry enough. Better for business, she'd say. The buzz would catch on and the biddies of Deer Lick would flock to the Sugar Shack for tea and a sweet treat just to grab another tasty morsel of the brewing scandal.

Today, the Sugar Shack was closed. Her mother's cakes and pies remained unbaked. And the lively gossip had turned to sorrowful memories.

Beneath a withering maple, Kate escaped outside the circle of friends and neighbors who continued to hug and offer condolences to her father and siblings. Their almost overwhelming compassion notched up her guilt meter and served as a reminder of the small-town life she'd left behind. Which was not to say those in Hollywood were cold and unfeeling, she'd just never had any of them bring her hot chicken soup.

Plans had been made for a potluck gathering at the local Grange—a building that sported Jack Wagoner's award-winning moose antlers and held all the community events—including wedding receptions and the Oktober Beer and Brat Fest. The cinder block structure had never been much to look at but obviously it remained the epicenter of the important events in beautiful downtown Deer Lick.

A variety of funeral casseroles and home-baked treats would be lined up on the same long tables used for arm wrestling competitions and the floral arranging contest held during the county fair. As far as Kate could see, not much had changed since she'd left. And she could pretty much guarantee that before the end of the night, some elder of the community would break out the bottle of huckleberry wine and make a toast to the finest pastry chef this side of the Rockies.

Then the stories would start to fly and her mother's name would be mentioned over and over along with the down and dirty details of some of her more outrageous escapades. Tears and laughter would mingle. Hankies would come out of back pockets to dab weeping eyes.

The truth hit Kate in the chest, tore at her lungs. The good people of Deer Lick had stood by her mother all these years while Kate had stood off in the distance.

She brushed a speck of graveside dust from the pencil skirt she'd picked up in Calvin Klein's warehouse last month. A breeze had cooled the late afternoon air and the thin material she wore could not compete. She pushed her sunglasses into place, did her best not to shiver, and tried to blend in with the surroundings. But the cost alone of her Louboutin peep toes separated her from the simple folk who dwelled in this town.

Maybe she should have toned it down some. She could imagine her mother shaking her head and asking who Kate thought she'd impress.

"Well, well, lookie who showed up after all."

Kate glanced over her shoulder and into the faded hazel eyes of Edna Price, an ancient woman who'd always reeked of moth balls and Listerine. The woman who'd been on the Founder's Day Parade committee alongside her mother for as long as Kate could remember.

"Didn't think you'd have the gumption," Edna said.

Gumption? Who used that word anymore?

Edna poked at Kate's ankles with a moose-head walking stick. "Didn't think you'd have the nerve," Edna enunciated as though Kate were either deaf or mentally challenged.

"Why would I need *nerve* to show up at my own mother's funeral?" *Oh, dumb question, Kate. Sure as spit the old biddy would tell her ten ways to Sunday why.*

The old woman leaned closer. Yep, still smelled like moth balls and Listerine.

"You left your dear sweet mama high and dry, what, twenty years ago?"

Ten.

"It's your fault she's where she is."

"*My* fault?" The accusation snagged a corner of Kate's heart and pulled hard. "What do you mean?"

"Like you don't know."

She had no clue. But that didn't stop her mother's oldest friend from piling up the charges.

"Broke her heart is what you did. You couldn't get up the nerve to come back when she was breathin'. Oh, no. You had to wait until—"

Kate's patience snapped. "Mrs. Price . . . you can blame or chastise me all you want. But not today. Today, I am allowed to grieve like anyone else who's lost a parent. Got it?"

"Oh, I got it." Her pruney lips curled into a snarl. "But I also got opinions and I aim to speak them."

"Not today you won't." Kate lifted her sunglasses to the top of her head and gave Mrs. Price her best glare. "Today you will respect my father, my brother, and my sister. Or I will haul you out of this cemetery by your fake pearl necklace. Do I make myself clear?"

The old woman snorted then swiveled on her orthopedic shoes and hobbled away. Kate didn't mind taking a little heat. She was, at least, guilty of running and never looking back. But today belonged to her family and she'd be goddamned if she'd let anybody drag her past into the present and make things worse.

Great. And now she'd cursed on sacred ground.

Maybe just thinking the word didn't count. She already had enough strikes against her.

It's your fault. . .

Exactly what had Edna meant? How could her mother's death be any fault of hers when she'd been hundreds of miles away?

Kate glanced across the carpet of grass toward the flower-strewn mound of dirt. Beneath the choking scent of carnations and roses, beneath the rich dark soil, lay her mother.

Too late for good-byes.

Too late for apologies.

Things just couldn't get worse.

Unable to bear the sight of her mother's grave, Kate turned her head. She startled at the sudden appearance of the man in the khaki-colored deputy uniform who stood before her. She looked up—way up—beyond the midnight hair and into the ice blue eyes of Matt Ryan.

The boy she'd left behind.

Candis Terry was born and raised near the sunny beaches of Southern California and now makes her home on an Idaho farm. She's experienced life in such diverse ways as working in a Hollywood recording studio to scooping up road apples left by her daughter's rodeo queening horse to working as a graphic designer. Only one thing has remained constant: Candis' passion for writing stories about relationships, the push and pull in the search for love, and the security one finds in their own happily ever after. Though her stories are set in small towns, Candis' wish is to give each of her characters a great big memorable love story rich with quirky characters, tons of fun, and a happy ending. For more, please visit www.candisterry.com.

Be Impulsive!

Look for Other
Avon Impulse Authors

www.AvonImpulse.com